THE MUSES

VENGEANCE OF TIME

THE MUSES

VENGEANCE OF TIME

N. L. McEvoy

Cover Illustrated by Tammy Pryce
Interior Illustrated by Laura Liu

ISBN-13: 9780990893301
ISBN-10: 0990893308
Library of Congress Control Number: 2016905791
N. L. McEvoy, Orlando, Fl

The Muses: Vengeance of Time

Privately Published by N. L. McEvoy
Printed and Bound in the United States of America

Other Books by N. L. McEvoy:

The Muses: Escaping Montague Manor

For **Sara**, *The Muses'* moral compass and a shining example of what a muse should be.

And for Karyn, an amazing combination of cheer squad and timekeeper, and who ensured that I actually completed the book.

Without these dear friends, *The Muses* would still be languishing in my desk drawer keeping the dust bunnies company.

I will forever be in their debt.

NLM

AUTHOR'S NOTE

Dear Reader:

If you hold this book in your hands, then you have most likely already met Sarah and Nickolas and are ready to find out what new adventures have befallen them. You probably already know that when they left Montague Manor, there were still many things unresolved, and although their cousin Simon had been released and the Muses of Music and War restored to their normal forms, that could hardly be the end of the story.

I have planned, as long as the Muses don't desert me, to write seven books about Sarah and Nickolas. Each book will allow us to get to know two of the muses better. The first book focused on Audiva and Ardus, the leaders of the Muses of Music and War. In fact the original title of book one was *The Muses of Music and War: Ardus and Audiva*—but that was determined to be too much of a mouthful, and it got changed to *The Muses: Escaping Montague Manor*. In this book, Ardus and Audiva are far too busy trying to get caught up with a hundred years of changes to help Sarah and Nickolas, so they send Brigitta and Bard to do so.

Fiery Brigitta and devoted Bard are an interesting couple, and Sarah and Nickolas find that they have great need of Brigitta's brains and Bard's strength before the story is done. All of the old characters find their way into these pages: Fulvio, the head chef; Mr. Benjamin, the almost scientist; Great-Aunt Vivian; and Dr. James are all here again, as is little Sparks.

There are new characters whom I am anxious for you to meet: Zac, the kitchen drudge; his mother, Carole; Louis, who is Great-Aunt Vivian's secretary; Dr. Lucy, who is helping Sarah and Nickolas's parents recover; and my favorite new character is Alec Anderson, whom we only caught a glimpse of in book one, but we get to know him better now.

I do hope that you enjoy the book, for there are more puzzles to ponder, adventures to discover, magic to explore, and things to learn about the world of the muses. As always, I would love to hear your thoughts and comments about the books. Just e-mail me at nlmcevoy@gmail.com.

But enough talk. You really should be turning the page and discovering how Sarah and Nickolas have been faring, and I really should get back to writing book three. Charles is in a bit of trouble, so I had best go help him. Off you go, and don't forget to bring your keys…

Sincerely,
N. L. McEvoy

CONTENTS

Audiva & Ardus

Christina & Charles

Deidre & David

Brigitta & Bard

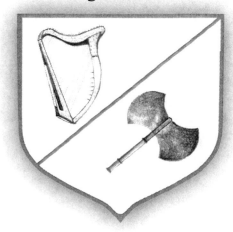

Ella & Edmund

Ferdinand & Francesca

Georgiana & Galahad

Muses of Music and War

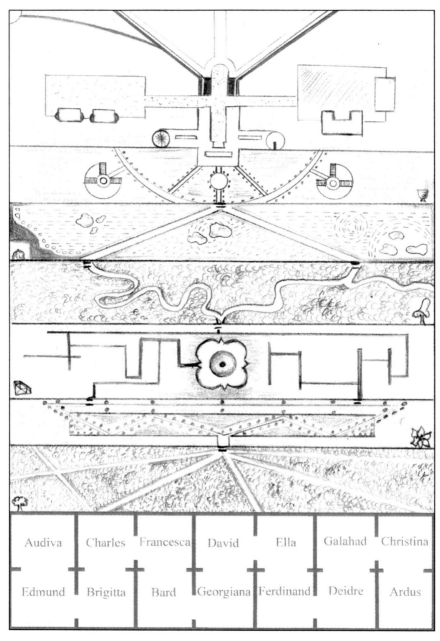

Map of Montague Manor

PROLOGUE

※ 띠 ※

In which Professor Montague visits the university library

Chicago University, Chicago, Illinois; June 9, 1947: Dr. Christopher Montague

Professor Montague closed his battered old suitcase with shaking hands. "I think that is everything, Sparks," he said to the tiny black puppy that sat on his pillow. "Are you up for another journey?"

Sparks cocked her head as if she understood and yapped happily, wagging her tiny stump of a tail. Professor Montague patted her head gently and scooped her up into his hand, placing her in the large pocket of his tweed jacket. "Just one more thing to do, and then we will be on our way," he told the puppy. He picked up his cane from where it rested on the bed and hobbled slowly toward the door.

Next to the entryway was a small table where the professor usually left his keys and umbrella, but today there was a medium-size cardboard packing box, which he picked up and balanced on his hip as he opened the door and exited into the hallway. Taking his keys from his pocket, he carefully locked the door and checked the latch. Once satisfied that the door was secure, he pocketed his keys and made his slow way toward the entrance of the teachers' lodging hall.

It took Professor Montague quite some time to make his way from his remote apartment to the main quad of the campus, but he never lacked for company along the way. First, Professor McBride accompanied him, cheerfully discussing her daughter who had been accepted into the physics program at Boston University. "Of course I would have preferred if she had decided to major in philosophy like me, but we can't have everything." Professor McBride sighed, although she looked far more pleased with her daughter's appointment than her words let on. "I am heading up to the cafeteria for some tea. Would you like to join me, Professor Montague?"

"Not today, Professor McBride. Unfortunately, I have a train to catch this evening, and I have lots of errands to run before I have to go. Thank you for the company, and take care of yourself." Kindly Professor Montague parted ways with tiny Professor McBride and continued slowly up the hill toward the quad.

It was a beautiful summer day, and students had completed their final examinations the week before, so the campus was nearly deserted. The few students who remained were lounging on the quad grass, reading or talking with their friends. One of the students was throwing a ball for his large chocolate Labrador. The dog recognized the professor at once and brought him the rather soggy tennis ball, dropping it at his feet. "Hello, Cocoa," the professor said, patting the happy dog on her blocky head and stroking her seal-soft ears.

"Sorry, Professor, Cocoa isn't bothering you is she?" Cocoa's anxious owner ran up and took hold of the dog's collar. "She tends to get overexcited and jump on people. I wouldn't want her to knock you over, sir!"

"No worries, Tom, she and I are old friends. She's a very smart girl and knows not to jump on ancient, rickety men like me." The professor laughed and scratched Cocoa one last time. "I shall miss her. Throw her a ball or two for me every now and then, won't you, Tom?"

"Of course, Professor. Can I help you get somewhere with that?" Tom indicated the box under the professor's arm.

"I am heading to the library. If you are heading that way too, I would greatly welcome your help." The professor handed the box over, and companionably they continued down the path with Cocoa trotting between them.

"What are you doing this summer, Professor? I didn't see your name on any of the research boards."

"I am not going to be doing any research this summer, Tom. I have decided to take a vacation. I haven't had one of those in decades."

"Where are you going? Anywhere fun?" Tom paused to let Professor Montague catch his breath, and Cocoa sat obediently beside them.

"First I'm going to Michigan to check on a friend of mine, and after that I'm not sure. I am taking it one step at a time; a lot depends on how I am feeling." Professor Montague leaned heavily on his cane and patted one of his pockets absently as if looking for lost keys. "Shall we continue on?"

At the bottom of the stairs, Tom called to one of his friends who was sitting on a bench nearby. "Hey, Howard, can you take this box up the stairs for the professor? I would do it, but last time the head librarian caught me with Cocoa in the library she threatened to kick me out of the university."

"No problem. I was just thinking about heading in myself. Elizabeth is working the front desk, and I promised I would stop by and give her a kiss. Come on, Professor, you can be my excuse for going in there for the fourteenth time today." Howard cheerfully tucked the box under his arm, and with his free hand, he helped guide the professor up the steep marble stairs.

They paused often on the way up to allow Professor Montague to catch his breath while Howard tried to hide his concern for his favorite chemistry professor. It was because of Professor Montague's freshman introductory chemistry course that Howard had switched majors from mathematics to chemical engineering, and he was proudly telling the professor about the internship he would be starting the following week, thanking him profusely for the kind letter of recommendation the professor had written for him. "They will probably have me counting lightbulbs all summer, but it is one foot in the door, and they are a great company. I would give anything to work for them after graduation next year."

"I am positive that you will. Just be the best lightbulb counter they have ever seen this summer, and they will hire you for sure once you have your degree." The professor smiled up at Howard. It was funny how all the students seemed to tower over him now. There was a time when Professor Montague was considered tall, but age had stooped his frame, stealing inches from his former height. "I think I am ready to take the last few stairs. Shall we go?"

Howard helped the professor up the last six steps and into the cool, dark library. The head librarian rushed from behind her counter to greet the professor and took the box from Howard, dismissing him with a quiet sniff.

"Professor Montague, what a pleasure to see you today. What can I help you with?" she whispered.

Professor Montague smiled to himself; he had never heard Mildred speak above a whisper in the four years he had been at the university. "I am going to the records room, Mildred. I wanted to put that box in the archives for the summer if that is acceptable. I am heading on vacation and don't want these papers just lying around in my room."

"I quite understand, Professor, right this way."

Mildred helped the professor into the small records room that branched off the main entrance. "Eleanor will be very happy to help you. Take care of yourself, Professor." Mildred set the box on the counter and nodded to the back office where an elderly librarian was emerging. Without even talking to Eleanor, Mildred left and quickly returned to her post guarding the doors to the library.

"Good afternoon, Professor. How are you today?" Eleanor asked. She was a sweet, short, slightly plump woman with soft wrinkled hands and a warm smile.

"Eleanor, it is always a pleasure." Professor Montague squeezed both her hands in his, and his blue eyes twinkled with merriment. "I was hoping you would be a dear and guard a little box of mine."

"Of course, Professor, let me get you the form." Eleanor bustled back to the office and out of sight. Professor Montague could hear her rustling about, opening and closing cabinet doors as she searched for just the right form out of the thousands she maintained. Eleanor did love her paperwork.

As he waited, Professor Montague noticed a tiny shoe, a hand, and half of an eye peering out from around the office doorjamb. His eyes twinkled more merrily as he recognized Eleanor's granddaughter, and the moustache above his gray beard twitched a little as he gently called out, "You surely aren't afraid of me, now are you, Miss Anne?"

The little head shook, and a plethora of blond curls bobbed as the little girl ran out to greet him. Soon the professor found himself smothered in wiggling lace and ribbons.

"Oh, Professor Montague! It has been ages since you last came! I have missed you so. I have lost a tooth and got a new dolly, and I have even learned to read since I last saw you! Why have you been away so long?"

"Little Miss Anne, have I been away as long as that? I surely did not mean to. Now where is this missing tooth?" Anne obliged him and showed him the gap in her teeth, which he admired at length. "Very well done, Miss Anne. You are becoming quite grown-up, I must say. Is there anything else that I have missed in the past few weeks?"

"Past few weeks?" Anne said indignantly. "It has been months and months! But I forgive you. I always do, as you are by far my favorite professor, unlike Professor James. He scares me."

"Professor James? I am not sure I know him." Professor Montague looked slightly alarmed, but Anne did not notice.

"Yes, he came in a week or so ago right after term ended asking about you, but none of us liked him, so we told him we didn't know of any Professor Montague from Australia. Mrs. Mildred sent him to the dean by the long way and then sent one of the boys right quick to warn him he was coming. The boy came back and told Mrs. Mildred that the dean wouldn't rat on you either. Something about a promise he had made you when you came. I saw Professor James leaving campus when Grammie took me home. He looked really angry and was muttering something about knowing you were somewhere in America. But I say good riddance. If someone that nasty was looking for me, I would hope that my friends would tell him that I never existed, too."

"I owe you a deep debt of gratitude, Miss Anne. If Professor James is as unpleasant as you say, it seems you saved me from a very ugly meeting." Professor Montague bowed to the little girl, which made her giggle.

"You are so old-fashioned, Professor Montague." She laughed, quickly forgetting about Professor James and all unpleasantness. "Would you like to take tea with Grammie and me? My mother packed me a cookie, and I would share it with you." She pulled a paper bag from the pocket of her pinafore and produced from its depths a large chocolate chip cookie.

"How could I possibly refuse tea with you and a homemade chocolate chip cookie? Of course I will if your grammie says that I may. Could you please get the time for me off the clock? I am afraid my eyes are a bit tired today."

Anne skipped over to the mantle clock and carefully read the time. "It is nearly three o'clock, Professor. Please say you have time."

"Yes, my train doesn't leave until six, so I do have time for tea. Now ask your grammie, politely."

Eleanor had just emerged from the office clutching a stack of yellow papers in her hand.

"Grammie, Grammie, can Professor Montague join us for tea? Please?"

Eleanor gave the little girl a quick hug with her free arm. "Of course, child. Start setting up the tea things and put the kettle on while Professor Montague fills out this form for me." Anne ran off into the office to turn on the hot plate and reemerged with table linens in her chubby arms.

While Anne set the table in the corner of the records room, Eleanor placed sheets of carbon paper between several copies of the form and put the whole stack in front of Professor Montague. She handed him a pen and cheerfully reminded him, "Press hard so that it goes through all the copies. I need them all clear and legible if I am going to keep this place organized." Eleanor bustled off to help Anne set up the tea while the professor filled out the form. Once complete, he looked up to find a pretty table set and the two ladies cheerfully waiting for him. Anne had even found a small handful of dandelions out in the courtyard and placed them in a spare milk jug as a centerpiece.

"What a lovely tea. Thank you, ladies," Professor Montague said as he sat down in the seat next to Anne and quietly waited while Eleanor poured out. Anne reached her hand in her pocket once again and pulled out her mother's cookie. She carefully broke it into two pieces and placed the larger half on the professor's plate.

"My mother always told me that if you like someone you should share your dessert with them, and if you really like someone you should let them have the larger half, but only if they are really special," she said matter-of-factly and sat back down at her seat. The tea was lovely, and Anne and her grandmother kept the conversation rolling, so the touched professor didn't have to say too much. They were nearly finished when another professor entered the records room and required Eleanor's attention.

Anne and Professor Montague finished their tea, and then the elderly professor helped the young girl clear the table and shake out the linens, returning all of the items to their places in the office. Eleanor was still busy caring for the other professor who needed to get some old documents out of the records room, so Anne escorted Professor Montague to the door.

"Before I go," he said kindly, "would you like a peppermint?"

Anne smiled. Professor Montague always gave her peppermints when he visited the records room. At her assent he reached his hand into first one and then another of the many pockets of his jacket and trousers before finally pulling out a round metal object. But it wasn't the usual peppermint tin that Anne was expecting. It was a gold pocket watch.

Professor Montague stared at it sadly for a moment and then turned to Anne with the watch on his outstretched shaking palm. "I forgot to put this in the box. Would you be a dear and do it for me, little one?"

"Of course, Professor," Anne said, taking the watch in her dimpled hand. "But won't you need it on your vacation?"

"Oh, sweet little one," he said, placing his hand on her curls, "where I am going, you don't need to know the time." And with that he gave her little cheek a kiss and watched as she skipped across the room to the box and popped the watch inside.

By the time Anne had closed the lid and turned back toward the professor, he was gone.

CHAPTER 1

THE COPPER POT

In which Fulvio cleans up the kitchens

Fulvio was completely dumbfounded by what had just taken place in his normally well-ordered and calm kitchens. If he hadn't seen it with his own eyes, he would not have believed it himself.

And yet, here he was, standing in his striped pajamas, pink fluffy bathrobe, and bunny slippers, surrounded by twelve dead and one living Faerie. A whole horde of strangely dressed adults wearing what looked suspiciously like a combination of bedsheets and Roman armor had just left with Mistress Sarah, leaving him with instructions to watch the one remaining guard.

Watch him do what, exactly, and for how long, had not been specified.

Fulvio had not even known that the guards weren't really guards—until, of course, the first one had been killed at the end of the tall blond man's sword. For then, the six-foot guard had turned from a man into a rather squat, conical, potato-looking thing, which the pretty woman standing next to Mistress Sarah had called a Faerie.

Not that Fulvio hadn't been rather busy himself, fighting alongside the strangers with nothing more threatening than his rolling pin. The fight had been over rather quickly, with Mistress Sarah's friends perfectly unscathed and the guards completely decimated. Fulvio was rather proud that he too had dispatched a guard or two and had also emerged from the fight with nothing worse than a bruise and a distinct feeling that the situation was well outside his job description.

But staring at the door where Mistress Sarah and her companions had disappeared did nothing to solve Fulvio's problems, so the head chef shook his head to clear it and began to assess his situation.

The kitchen staff would be arriving in a few short hours to start the morning's tasks, so Fulvio had very little time to fix the mess he found himself in. The first thing he had to take care of was the one living Faerie/guard who was currently trussed up and attached to the table leg. Fortunately, he was completely knocked out, and, being in his Faerie form, was only two feet tall and weighed a fraction of what he would have had he been in his guard form. So Fulvio tucked him under his arm and carted him off to the disused pot room, depositing him in a rather large copper soup pot and closing and locking the door behind him.

The next thing Fulvio needed to do was to dispose of the remains of the twelve dead Faeries. For that he would need the large wheelbarrow behind the greenhouses and every bit of time he had left to bury the small creatures in the woods.

The sun was well above the horizon when Fulvio returned the wheelbarrow and shovel. His bunny slippers were covered in mud, and his bathrobe and pajamas were spattered and torn. He wearily entered the stairway passage to the kitchens, longing for his bed but knowing he had no time for sleep.

A shape loomed ahead of him, and it took Fulvio a moment to realize that it was Zac, the lumbering kitchen drudge. Fulvio adored Zac. He was sweet and kind and hardworking. Zac's mother, Carole, one of Fulvio's sous chefs, had always worked very hard to make sure that simple-minded Zac had a place at the manor. Zac was wearing a pristine, freshly laundered and starched uniform. By midday it would be rumpled and stained past recognition, but Carole would launder and press it again in time for the next morning.

Fulvio placed his hand on Zac's shoulder and gave the boy a fatherly squeeze as he passed him, unaware that he was leaving a dirt-covered handprint on the tidy white uniform. "Good morning, Zac," he called.

"Good morning, Chef," Zac answered. He paused, shocked to see his idol looking so disheveled. "Chef, are you OK?" Zac asked.

"Oh yes, of course I am," Fulvio replied, pasting a pale version of his usually warm smile on his face. "I am just a little tired this morning; I was up very late last night."

"OK," Zac replied and then moved into his usual routine, which was much easier for him to understand than why the normally impeccable and unflappable head chef looked so disheveled and disoriented. "I am on dish duty today, Chef," he said, puffing up with pride.

"Glad to hear it. Knowing you're in charge of the plates, I won't have to worry that they will cause us any trouble whatsoever," Fulvio said, sounding a bit more like himself.

The two men arrived at the kitchen doors, and Fulvio had not stepped even one foot through them when several members of the kitchen staff accosted him, led by Zac's efficient mother, Carole.

"You must follow me at once, Chef Fulvio," Carole said in an urgent whisper. "Lady Vivian is in the kitchens looking for you. She is in high dudgeon, and she cannot see you looking like this." As she spoke, Carole and the other kitchen staff hustled Fulvio into his office, just to the left of the kitchen doors.

Fulvio wondered if this day could get any worse. Lady Vivian was the owner of the manor and essentially Fulvio's boss, although he had been hired by her father, Dr. Montague, years and years ago. Whereas Fulvio had loved working for Dr. Montague, doing so for his daughter had been nothing but a trial. She was cold, strong-willed, brilliant, quick-tempered, imperious, and, if Fulvio was being honest, somewhat evil. She even had replaced most of his favorite parts of his job, the actual cooking, tasting, and creating of dishes, with her scientific versions of his food made from four solutions she had developed in her lab. Granted, the imitation food tasted the same as his own creations, but it just wasn't the same as handcrafting meals from scratch. If he hadn't loved the manor so very much and the people who worked for him, Fulvio would have left long ago.

Once the door to his office was firmly shut and one of the larger sous chefs positioned outside as a guard, Carole and two of the kitchen maids started removing Fulvio's torn robe and dirty slippers. "Zac, give me your uniform jacket," Carole ordered, "and your shoes. They will be a bit too big, but that can't be helped."

Zac struggled with the buttons on his white kitchen coat until Carole turned from Fulvio and helped him out. The coat was quite a bit too large for the head chef, but Carole quickly turned up the sleeves and tucked the back until it was a passable fit. While Carole was fussing over the jacket, the other two maids had put Zac's overly large shoes on Fulvio and tied the laces extra tight in hopes that they would stay on his feet.

Carole snatched Fulvio's dress toque off the shelf and placed it on his tousled head. She threw a fresh tea towel over his shoulder—effectively covering the muddy handprint and Zac's embroidered name—and pushed him out into the kitchens, telling Zac to stay put until Lady Vivian had left.

Fulvio looked around at the mayhem his normally well-ordered kitchens had become. Lady Vivian, her auburn hair piled high on her head in a precarious updo with her steely blue eyes flashing and still dressed in her evening clothes from the night before, barked orders left and right while the kitchen staff bounced around like pinballs trying to carry them out. Her eye fell on Fulvio, although in her harried state, Fulvio was pretty sure she didn't really see him. "Fulvio, at last. Where have you been? It doesn't matter. I need all of the vials of essence, right now."

"Yes, ma'am," Fulvio replied. "Carole, please get me a tray." As soon as Carole had returned with a silver tray, Lady Vivian snatched it from her hands.

"I can see that I need to do this myself as all of you do not understand how urgent this is," Vivian shouted, whirling toward the stairs to the food stations. Fulvio followed her down the steps. Surprisingly, there were very few of the stations occupied with Lady Vivian's footmen. Usually by this time every station would be busy preparing breakfast for the staff who worked and lived in Vivian's manor. But today only two of the twenty stations were manned.

Vivian approached the first empty station. An alcove to one side held the four vials of solution that were used to replicate the food. Three of the vials were large. One contained a bluish liquid and had a mushroom on its cap. The second contained a thick brown liquid and had a tree finial. The third contained a sparkly, rainbow-colored liquid and had a faceted gem for a stopper. Vivian reached for a tiny vial nearly hidden behind the other three. The vial contained a small amount of milky pearlescent liquid and had a crystal hand finial. She placed this vial on her tray and quickly moved to the next station. She rapidly collected the hand-topped vials and approached the first footman.

"Give me that," Vivian ordered the footman, pointing to the vial in front of him. The footman carefully placed his hand-topped vial on the tray with the rest, giving Vivian a respectful bow. She did not even acknowledge him; instead, she picked up her tray and moved to the final station.

This footman's back was turned toward Vivian, and he seemed absorbed in filling a breakfast order. He had already placed drops from each of the three large vials on the plate and goblet in front of him and was just reaching to add the final drops from the tiny vial when Vivian snatched it from his hand. Startled, the footman jumped and the vial flew out of their hands and smashed on the stone floor.

Vivian was momentarily frozen in place, and then rage effused her face. Grabbing the plate off the tray in front of the footman, she dove to where the tiny vial had shattered, hoping to scoop up as much of the liquid and glass shards as she could. She shouted a stream of angry vitriol at the footman as she bent to capture the spilled liquid. However, almost the instant the vial had smashed on the slate floor, the porous stones had absorbed all of the essence. Even the glass shards melted into the stone and disappeared without a trace. Lady Vivian had worked herself up to such a state that she desperately scraped at the floor for several moments, even though there was no hope of recovering any of the solution. Fulvio carefully removed the plate from Vivian's shaking hands and placed it gently on the tray with the other vials.

He was not surprised that the vial of solution had disappeared into the stonework, for it had always been one of the properties of the manor that dropped items disappeared and messes cleaned themselves up. Often the items reappeared, neatly cleaned and put away on their shelves, unless, of course, they were broken beyond repair. New staff were always startled by this, but after it became a frequent occurrence no one questioned it. Besides, right now Fulvio did not have time to ponder over the manor's idiosyncrasies, for Lady Vivian was still in quite a state.

"Come, my lady," he said gently, raising her to her feet. "Where do you want me to take these vials? Shall we take them to the lab?"

Realizing that every eye in the kitchens was upon her, Vivian straightened her shoulders and pushed a wayward lock of hair behind her ear. "Upstairs, to my office, Fulvio," she ordered, kicking the train of her gown behind her as she turned toward the kitchen entrance.

Fulvio gently picked up the tray and followed Lady Vivian, being extra careful not to trip on his overly large shoes.

⚜

After delivering Lady Vivian's tray, returning to the kitchens, showering, and dressing in his own clothing, Fulvio sat in his office, his head in his hands. He was beyond exhausted and had no idea what he should do next. Leaving his staff in the clutches of Lady Vivian without his protection was completely out of the question, but the idea of staying had never seemed more oppressive.

He had just reached the conclusion that the only answer was to soldier on as always, when a soft knock came on his door. After straightening his jacket and running his hands quickly to smooth his hair, Fulvio called, "Come in!"

Carole entered and gave him a slight bow. "Chef Fulvio, do you have a moment?" she asked.

"Of course I do, Carole. But first I need to thank you for your quick thinking this morning. I owe you far more than you will ever know for your assistance." Fulvio rose and shook her hand warmly. "And make sure you thank young Zac for his part. It could not have been done without him."

Carole smiled. "He will like that. It is so rare that someone praises him for quick-wittedness. But right now we seem to have a bigger problem. Well, actually, two bigger problems." She paused and sadly shook her head. "How on earth can the footmen make food without the fourth vial? We have orders backing up and no way of fulfilling them. Add to that that only two of the twenty footmen who normally man the food stations have shown up for work today, and we are very behind."

Fulvio reached above his head and pulled down a dusty old binder, bursting with yellowing scraps of paper. "Before you came to the manor, Carole, we made food without the fourth vial. I think I have the recipes here," he said as he flipped the pages. "Ah, yes, here they are. Could you have the staff copy them and give them to the footmen?" He removed the pages and handed them over. "As to why only a few footmen have arrived for work, leave that to me—I will find out. And your second question?"

Carole looked quizzical. "There seems to be some sort of banging sound coming from the storage closet. As it is locked, may I have the key to investigate?"

Fulvio turned pale and then took a deep breath. "Don't worry about the storage closet, Carole. I will take care of that too." Fulvio rose to grab the storage room key off the peg where it hung, wondering what in heaven he was going to do about it.

CHAPTER 2

SARAH'S HALF BIRTHDAY

In which Sarah and Simon compare heights

Sarah awoke to sunlight pouring through her window and the smell of waffles cooking in the kitchen. What a relief it was to be back in her own pretty teal-blue room and her own bed with her own soft sheets. It had been a little over a week since she had returned from her adventures in Australia at her Great-Aunt Vivian's manor. If it hadn't been for the eleven new horses in the paddock and her cousin Simon in the bedroom down the hall next to her brother Nickolas's, Sarah would have dismissed it all as a horrible nightmare. One not worth giving a passing thought to when there were so many more exciting things to do at home.

Sarah threw back the covers and jumped out of her bed. "No time to be lazy today, Sparks," she told the tiny black puppy curled up on her pillow. "Today is June twenty-sixth; it's my half birthday!"

Sparks opened one sleepy eye and yawned, finding a more comfortable position on the pillow as if Sarah's ten-and-a-half birthday wasn't all that exciting, at least not exciting enough to get up extra early for.

Sarah quickly got dressed in her favorite blue jeans and T-shirt, pulled on her riding boots, and headed downstairs to the kitchen.

Grandma Vera greeted her, standing at the stove cooking bacon and tending the waffle irons. Sarah grabbed her apron from the wall and took over the waffle fork.

"Good morning, Sarah. Happy half birthday!" Grandma Vera smiled. "What are your plans for today?"

"I think I'll eat myself silly on these wonderful waffles." Sarah grinned, pulling the first ones off the griddle and putting them on the warming plate. "Then I'll go and check on Blaze and see how she's adjusting." Blaze was the six-month-old foal Sarah had brought back from Great-Aunt Vivian's with the other horses. She was black with a white star on her forehead and was easily Sarah's favorite.

Blaze's mother, Moonstone, like all the other horses from the manor, was a Windsor Grey, and Sarah could just see the two of them in the pasture out of the kitchen window. Sarah had been surprised that the ten adult horses—like her grandmother's puppy, Sparks—were invisible to all but a handful of people at the ranch, but little Blaze, for some reason, could be seen by everyone. Since the best thing to do about Sparks was not to worry too much about what made the puppy odd, Sarah decided to do the same about the horses.

"There are some apples in the bin you can take to Blaze if you would like," Grandma Vera was saying, interrupting Sarah's musings. Grandma Vera was one of the people who could actually see all of the horses, and she had never mentioned that their invisibility was anything out of the ordinary. "I was thinking about visiting your parents this afternoon. Would you like to come with me?"

Sarah's parents were still in the critical ward at Denver General. Her mother was in a coma from the car accident more than a month ago, but her father had recently opened his eyes and was more and more alert every day.

"Of course I want to come! Have you heard anything new about Dad?" Sarah poured more batter into the waffle iron, all thoughts of the Windsor Greys forgotten.

"Nothing more since yesterday. At this point, no news is good news. They would only call in the middle of the night if something bad happened," Grandma Vera said reassuringly. "Perhaps after we see your parents we could go out to eat in Denver for your half birthday."

"Oh, could we go to the Moroccan place where you sit on the floor and eat with your hands?" Sarah begged.

"Yes, of course." Grandma Vera smiled and gave Sarah a hug. "Can you watch the bacon? I'll go take care of the arrangements now."

A second after Grandma Vera had disappeared into their mother's den to log in to her computer to make the reservation, a tousle-haired Nickolas entered the kitchen. He snagged a waffle off the warming plate and sat down on one of the stools, munching happily.

"Morning, Sarah," her older brother said around a mouthful of waffle. "Did I just hear we're going out for dinner tonight?"

"Yes, it's the twenty-sixth, so we're going to celebrate!"

"Why are we celebrating?" an equally tousled Simon asked from the kitchen door. He was wearing a pair of Nickolas's old pajamas, which were much too big for him. Although their tiny cousin had put on weight since Nickolas and Sarah had rescued him from Great-Aunt Vivian's scary experiments, he was still very thin and peaked.

Resolutely, Sarah put two waffles and some bacon on a plate and placed it on the breakfast bar in front of Simon. "We're celebrating my half birthday! It's kind of a funny tradition that my mom and dad dreamed up when we were little. We don't get presents or cake, but we do get to do whatever we want to that day and a special dinner out. I think it's because my birthday is December twenty-sixth, and they wanted a day when we weren't overdone from the holidays to celebrate. They didn't think it was fair. Of course Nickolas got a half birthday too, but he's already had his in March. When is your birthday? We can add it to the list!"

Simon screwed up his pointed face as if he was thinking very hard. "You know, I really don't remember." he said, and then his face crumpled. "I don't even remember ever having a birthday. It is just too long ago." Simon, who looked like any other six-year-old, was actually more than fifty years old. He had been imprisoned and tortured by Great-Aunt Vivian for years until Nickolas and Sarah rescued him and brought him home to their ranch in Silver Springs, Colorado.

Because of the food Great-Aunt Vivian had developed through her experiments, everyone at her manor didn't age. Even Sarah and Nickolas, who had only been there for two weeks, noticed the effects of the antiaging food, so it was with great relief that Sarah had cut her nails the week before.

Thinking of not growing reminded Sarah of something. "Oh, and we also mark our height on the wall next to the pantry on our half birthdays. I'll go get the ruler and pencil. Nickolas, you're in charge of the stove. Don't burn the bacon, and don't eat it all. I want some too!"

Sarah returned with the measuring tools and asked Nickolas and Simon to help her. Nickolas balanced the ruler on Sarah's head and marked the wall with the pencil, adding her name and date to the mark. "You grew about an inch since last time," he announced, pointing at the wall.

"Can I see how tall I am?" Simon asked quietly, looking rather sadly at the two rows of marks that showed Sarah and Nickolas's progress since they were old enough to stand to be measured.

"Of course you can!" Sarah exclaimed. "You can put your marks right over here, next to mine."

In a moment, Sarah had Simon standing against the wall, and Nickolas measured and marked his height. "Forty-three and a half inches," Nickolas read off the tape and marked Simon's name next to it. "You're taller than Sarah was at your age and just a little bit shorter than I was."

"So I am going to be taller than Sarah?" Simon said, a huge smile on his face.

"Not necessarily," Sarah retorted, "and not for a long time." Sarah was not overly happy to think that the two boys would someday be bigger than her. Having one freakishly tall older brother was enough, thank you very much.

"I wish we knew when your birthday was." Nickolas frowned at the row of dates on his marks. "Wait a minute, we do know your birthday! It was on your chart. On the first page right after your blood type." Nickolas's brow creased in concentration, like he was trying to see something written in very tiny print. "It's...it's...Got it! August 19, 1956."

"Are you sure?" Simon asked, looking shocked but pleased.

"Oh yeah." Sarah nodded. "If Nickolas says that he read something somewhere, you can pretty much bet on it. He remembers everything he reads—and probably the page number and the publisher's address as well."

"Really? Wow! So my half birthday would be..."

"February nineteenth," Sarah furnished. "But we can start with today and then measure you again in two months on your birthday. I can't wait to see you grow. Then we'll really know that you've been rescued and all is back to normal."

"How old should I put next to your name, Simon? Six and five-sixths or fifty-four and five-sixths?" Nickolas asked, still holding his pencil to the wall.

"I think six and five-sixths. People will ask fewer questions," Sarah replied, and Simon nodded.

"Perfect," Nickolas agreed, writing Simon's age next to his height.

⚜

Sarah thoroughly enjoyed her half birthday. After breakfast, she and the boys went down to the stables and saddled up their horses. Although Sarah loved the Windsor Greys, it had been a relief to get back into her western saddle on her beloved mare, Chestnut, and travel the well-known trails near her home. She was pretty sure that Nickolas was happy to be back on his favorite paint, Splotchy, as well, and he was definitely happy not to be horse jumping anymore.

Sarah and Nickolas had been teaching Simon how to ride on one of the ponies, and since the summer camps that were held on their ranch were in full swing, the three of them joined the campers on their morning trek into the mountains. While they were saddling their horses, one of the camp counselors approached Sarah. "Do you have a minute, Sarah?" she asked, patting Chestnut's neck.

"Of course, Beth." Sarah looked a bit surprised as she looked up from tightening her horse's girth. Beth had been a counselor at the camps for a long time and rarely if ever had a problem.

"It's about Simon," Beth said, lowering her voice and glancing quickly over to where the smaller children were saddling their

14

squat little mounts with help from the junior counselors. "I caught him whipping his pony yesterday with his crop. He seemed quite angry. I told him not to do it and he stopped, but I wanted someone to know. Normally I would tell your parents, but I didn't want to worry your grandma. Six-year-olds aren't usually that angry, and it didn't make any sense. He had a wonderful ride in the mountains, and all the other kids have been very welcoming."

"Hmm," Sarah said, pulling her brows together. "That's odd. Did he tell you what was bothering him?" Sarah knew that Beth was a favorite with the littler campers and that she usually could get them to tell her everything.

"No, he doesn't seem to like me much." Beth looked confused. "And he talks so funny sometimes, like he's a hundred years old not just a little kid. He said something like 'My business with this pony is none of your concern, madam.' If I hadn't been so upset about his treatment of Flopsy, I would have laughed. Do all kids talk like him in Australia?"

"He's the only other kid we met in Australia, so maybe they do, but I kind of doubt it. Simon is unique!" Sarah said, hoping Beth wouldn't ask too many more questions. She would have to have a word with Simon about fitting in a little better. "I think he's just struggling with all the changes of moving and leaving his old home and everything. I wouldn't read too much into it. I'll talk to him."

Beth nodded. "Thanks, Sarah. He seems to listen to you. But if it doesn't get better, I'll have let your grandma know. I just don't want to add anything to her list of worries. Speaking of which, how are your mom and dad doing?"

Sarah was grateful for the change in subject. "I'll let you know—we're visiting them this afternoon." Shortly after that, Beth moved back to her class of young campers, and Sarah swung up into Chestnut's saddle and came alongside Nickolas, who was mounted on Splotchy.

"We're going to have to be careful with Simon," she said in an undertone so only her brother could hear.

"Why, is he sick?" Nickolas asked, looking sharply at Simon across the paddock.

"No, he's just having some trouble acting six and half. I think six-year-olds are a little different than they were fifty years ago, and the counselors are noticing."

"I still think we should tell Grandma Vera everything about Simon," Nickolas said, a serious note entering his voice that wasn't usually there. "I think he needs some help, like from doctors. And I don't think we are exactly qualified for the job."

"He asked that we not tell anyone," Sarah said just as seriously. "And I think it's important that he be able to trust us. He hasn't had anyone he can trust for a very long time."

"Isn't that the truth," Nickolas said with a sigh. "And he needs doctors poking and prodding him like a polar bear needs sunscreen."

In spite of the serious conversation, Sarah giggled. "Like a polar bear needs sunscreen? Seriously, Nickolas, where do you come up with these things?"

The two children vowed to talk to Simon, but they both felt that he just needed to have some more time to recover from everything that had happened at Great-Aunt Vivian's. "And like Beth said, if he doesn't, we can always talk to Grandma Vera about it then," Sarah said as they maneuvered their horses into line with the other advanced riders for their ride in the mountains.

They returned to the ranch three hours later and stabled their horses. Grandma Vera had lunch ready, and once they were cleaned up and fed, they all piled into the van and headed into Denver toward the hospital.

They were pleasantly surprised to find Mr. McGuire was sitting up in a wheelchair in his room while an orderly was making his bed.

"Happy half birthday, Sarah," he said, a huge smile on his bandaged face. "Are you having a good day?"

Sarah carefully hugged him. "Seeing you up and about is the best half birthday present I have ever had. How are you feeling, Dad?"

"All right, better every day. Grandma Vera was telling me about your adventures a bit last night. She said that she would bring young Simon to meet me today. And this must be him." Sarah's father held out his hand to Simon, who was shyly standing behind Nickolas.

"H-h-hello, s-sir," Simon stuttered, shaking Mr. McGuire's hand. "I-it is good t-to see you d-doing be-tter."

"It's good to see you too, Simon. Grandma Vera tells me that you will be joining the McGuire clan. I cannot tell you how pleased we are to have you with us. I never met your parents, but if they are related to my mother, then they must have been wonderful people."

That might have been true, based on what Sarah knew of Simon's parents, though it didn't seem to hold where Grandma Vera's sister, Great-Aunt Vivian, was concerned, but she didn't want to say so.

"Dad, what should Simon call you? He has been calling Grandma Vera 'Grandma,' but she really is like his second cousin," Sarah asked.

Nickolas interrupted: "Actually, I looked it up when we got home. Simon is Grandma Vera's first cousin once removed, and he is your second cousin, Dad. He is Sarah and my second cousin once removed. There isn't a title for that, like uncle or nephew."

Mr. McGuire looked confused for a second but then shook his head as if to clear it. "Thank you, Nickolas. As an only child of two only children, I never really got to know all of that. Well, at least I always thought Grandma Vera was an only child. We didn't find out about Aunt Vivian until after you two were born." He cracked a rueful smile and turned to Simon, adding, "Simon, you can call me anything you like, as long as it's something nice: 'Mr. McGuire,' 'Uncle John,' 'sir,' 'Your Royal Majesty,' 'Hey, tall guy with the horses'; whatever you feel like."

Simon looked a little less shy. "I will think on it, sir, th-thank you."

A young intern entered at that moment, carrying a clipboard. "Mr. McGuire, I hate to interrupt, but I need to get your vitals. It's OK for the children to stay, if you don't mind. It's just temperature, blood pressure, and oxygen levels."

"Of course they can stay. Simon, tell me what you've been doing since you got to the ranch." Mr. McGuire held out his arm to the intern without turning his attention from Simon.

"N-not much." Simon sat down at Mr. McGuire's feet. "I-I have been eating a lot; Grandma Vera is a very good cook. And I have been spending a lot of time playing with Sarah, Nickolas, and Sparks."

Mr. McGuire looked questioningly at Grandma Vera. As far as he knew, Grandma Vera, Grandpa Patrick, Sarah, Nickolas, and he were the only ones who could see Sparks. His wife had never been able to and had thought that her in-laws were pulling her leg for years about the invisible puppy. Until the day that baby Nickolas, who at the time was only fifteen months old, started playing and laughing with the imaginary dog when Grandma Vera and Grandpa Patrick had visited. "Mama, Mama, puppy," he had squealed, toddling up to her with his arms outstretched like he was bringing her a toy, but there was nothing in his cupped hands. After that, Amelia McGuire had taken it on faith that the puppy actually existed.

"He can see Sparks?" Mr. McGuire asked, looking meaningfully at the intern and giving Grandma Vera a warning look not to say too much. But Nickolas either didn't see the warning look or chose to ignore it.

"Yes, he can, and so can everyone at Great-Aunt Vivian's!" Nickolas exclaimed. "They thought she had been there before. The chef and the butler knew her!"

"Really? How extraordinary." His father looked thoughtful. "Sounds like I have a lot of catching up to do." Mr. McGuire turned and faced the intern. "So how much longer do I get to stay here as a guest of Denver General?"

"Well, you are much improved over a week ago. But we still need to run more tests to make sure there are no lasting effects to your brain, and we need to get you walking again. Some of that we can do outpatient, though, so give us a few more days, and we will talk about an exit plan." The intern smiled. "But if these vitals are anything to judge by, we might even get you home by the end of the week."

Sarah clapped her hands, and Nickolas smiled broadly. It was the best news they had received in a very long time.

⁂

Grandma Vera didn't let them stay long with their father. It was obvious that the visit had tired him, but knowing that he might be home soon made the parting seem much more temporary.

When they piled into the van to head to the restaurant, Grandma Vera returned to the subject of Sparks.

"You said that other people at Vivian's could see Sparks? The only other person I ever met who could see him was your grandfather Patrick, and when John could see him I just assumed that it was because he was family. That explains why Simon can see him, but not the chef and the butler. Are they distantly related, too?"

"I don't think so, Grandma," Sarah replied. "Nearly everyone could see Sparks at Great-Aunt Vivian's, and they told us that she was over seventy years old!"

"That could be." Grandma Vera did not seem surprised. "I've had her since I was four or five years old, so that makes her over sixty at least. Yet, I am very intrigued that others can see her. For years, until I met Patrick, I thought I was the only one. Perhaps I should take her out more. Maybe more normal people can see her than I thought."

"Well, everyone at Great-Aunt Vivian's is a little odd, so I'm not sure 'normal' describes them. Maybe sometime we could have Fulvio visit us. He could see Sparks, and I wouldn't mind seeing him again!" Sarah chimed in.

"I don't want to see anyone from Cousin Vivian's again," Simon whispered to Nickolas.

"Me neither," Nickolas agreed.

By that time, they had arrived at the restaurant, and the topic had turned to food. They each ordered a different dish and passed them around the table, eating with their hands. Simon had never had Moroccan food, and he enjoyed it thoroughly, having seconds and thirds of everything at the table. Afterward, they rolled out of the restaurant and into the van.

"I am so full," Sarah complained, rubbing her distended stomach.

"Me too," Simon agreed. "I don't think I should have had those last two briouats. But they were so good I couldn't refuse!"

"I'm still hungry," Nickolas added. "Grandma, do we have anything to eat at the ranch?"

They all laughed. "You're impossible, Nickolas," Sarah gasped out once she could talk again, "absolutely impossible!"

⧊⧊⧊

Sarah was tucked happily into bed with Sparks on her pillow and her reading light illuminating the page of her book. The whole house was quiet; even the horses were all settled in the barn for the night. Sarah was just about to turn off the lamp when an ear-splitting scream came from the boys' rooms. Sarah grabbed her bathrobe and, shoving her arms into it as she went, ran down the corridor toward the sound.

When she arrived, Simon's door was thrown open, and Nickolas and Grandma Vera were sitting on either side of his bed. The little boy was screaming in pain, thrashing about, tangled in his covers. His skin was gray, and his blond hair was plastered to his sweat-sheened face.

Grandma Vera talked in a soothing voice, trying to get the panicked boy to calm down and tell her what was wrong, but all he could manage to gasp out between anguished sobs was that he hurt, everywhere, and to beg Grandma Vera to make it stop.

CHAPTER 3

What the Intern Heard

†⧓†

In which we watch as the experts disagree over Simon's diagnosis

"We need to get that drip in now," a tall, rotund doctor was barking at the intern who was struggling to get a line into Simon's vein.

"Let's move him off the stretcher. On three…One, two, *three!*" the head EMT instructed his two assistants, lifting Simon from the stretcher onto the hospital bed.

Soon there were so many doctors, nurses, and other hospital personnel surrounding Simon that Sarah could no longer see anything of the small, pale boy except one tiny bare foot poking out from under the blanket the EMT had thrown over his legs. She and Nickolas stood unobserved just outside the curtains that separated Simon's bed from the others in the emergency ward.

The hospital staff worked feverishly over Simon to get him to stop thrashing in pain. Finally, whatever solution was dripping into his hand seemed to take effect, and he went still. His breathing was shallow, and his skin was still shiny and gray.

Now that he was calm, the doctors started taking blood, temperature, pressure, and checking his symptoms. It was about this time that the intern noticed the two children peeking around the curtain.

"Hello there, is this your brother?" she asked kindly, removing her face mask and smoothing her curly brown hair back from her forehead.

"He's our second cousin," Nickolas informed her. "Once removed. Is he going to be all right?"

"We can't tell yet," the intern replied. "But some of the best doctors in the world work here. I'm sure they'll figure out what's wrong with your cousin very soon. Why don't you come with me to the waiting room? There are lots of books and things to do there, and I promise I'll update you whenever something comes up."

"You pinky swear?" Sarah asked skeptically, not moving from her spot.

"I pinky swear," the intern said with a laugh, extending her pinky for Sarah to shake. "I'm Dr. Lucy Reynolds. And you are?"

"Sarah McGuire," Sarah said, linking pinkies with Dr. Lucy. "And this is my brother, Nickolas."

Dr. Lucy held out her little finger to Nickolas too, who rather sheepishly hooked pinkies as well. "Very well, Sarah and Nickolas, who else is with you here at the hospital?"

"Grandma Vera is over there at the nurses' station." Sarah indicated with her head as they walked with the intern toward the waiting area.

"And our parents are upstairs in the recovery unit," Nickolas added.

"John and Amelia McGuire are your parents?" Dr. Lucy asked, astonished. At Nickolas's nod she continued. "They're my patients too; in fact, I think I met you yesterday. I was taking your dad's vitals while you were visiting him. Wow, your cousin got sick quickly. He was fine yesterday afternoon. What did he have for dinner?"

"We all went out to a Moroccan restaurant last night," Sarah replied, and then she looked thoughtful. "But we shared each dish, so wouldn't we be sick too if that was the cause?"

"Hmm, possibly. Has your cousin complained of any pains lately?"

"No, we just got home from visiting our great-aunt in Australia last week. That's where we met Simon, and he came back with us. He actually has been looking healthier here in Colorado than he did in Australia," Sarah answered.

"Yeah, he wasn't eating much when we met him. But we started making sure he got three meals a day. Sarah was pretty confident that he just needed good food and rest to recover. It looked like she was right. Well, until last night." Dr. Lucy looked a bit confused at Nickolas's words.

"He wasn't well when you met him in Australia?" she asked.

"It's a long story," Sarah said, looking meaningfully at Nickolas and hoping he would keep quiet. "I think he had been sickly for a long time at Great-Aunt Vivian's. But like Nickolas said, once we started making sure he was eating properly, he seemed to get better. You probably need to talk to Grandma Vera; she knows more about Simon's medical history than we do."

Nickolas looked open-mouthed at Sarah. What was she getting at? They knew far more about Simon than Grandma Vera did because Simon had asked them not to tell anyone about what went on at the manor. Then it dawned on him: Simon didn't want them to tell, so this was Sarah's way of keeping that promise.

But then Nickolas started thinking that perhaps they should tell the intern everything. Wasn't Dr. Lucy trying to help Simon?

And wasn't there a high probability that having his essence sucked out of him for fifty years would cause some medical problems? Yeah, and the pretty young intern would believe two kids when they told her that their six-year-old cousin Simon was really over fifty years old. Nickolas started to see Sarah's point, and he closed his mouth with a snap.

"Well, then I had best go ask your grandma. But if I have any more questions, can I come ask you two?" the intern asked, turning to leave.

"Of course you can," Sarah said with a smile. And with that and a wave, Dr. Lucy headed over toward the nurses' station.

❧❧

Nickolas was getting bored. He had been pacing the same line on the gray carpet in the waiting area for hours. The line went all the way around the room, and at last count, he had done the circuit forty-seven times. Sarah was reading a mangled paperback she had found in the toy bin, and Grandma Vera was chatting with another lady whose husband had come into the emergency room with chest pains about an hour before.

Worse than being bored, Nickolas was hungry. They had come to the hospital in the middle of the night, and now the sun was well up into the sky. Grandma Vera had given them money for the vending machines in the corner of the room, but somehow chips and candy didn't seem to fill Nickolas's stomach for very long.

The pretty intern had come out several times to give them updates on Simon. She said he was resting, but all of his tests had come back negative, and the doctors were stumped as to what was causing his pain. About two hours ago, Grandma Vera had signed some documents that gave the doctors authority to scan Simon's insides, and since then they had heard nothing.

"Grandma?" Nickolas asked for the tenth time that hour. "Can we get something to eat? I mean, really get something to eat, like a hamburger, not just chips."

"Soon, Nickolas," was the reply, the same reply he had gotten the other nine times. "I don't want to leave Simon alone while they still don't know what's wrong. We'll get food just as soon as they say we can leave the waiting area. I wish you and Sarah were just a hair older, and then I could send you down to the cafeteria on your own."

Sarah put down her book. "We could go, Grandma. I won't let Nickolas get lost, and he's tall enough to pass for fourteen, so no one would ask us."

"I know, Sarah. But right now I am just about as worried as I can be, and adding worry about you two running around in a huge hospital alone? My nerves are just not ready for that. Next time the doctors come out I will ask. OK?"

"OK," Nickolas said, trying not to grumble.

Just then, Dr. Lucy returned. "Please come with me," she said to the three of them. "The doctors would like to talk with you." She led them back through the double doors and down several white corridors to a small conference room. There were three doctors waiting for them at the table and five empty chairs.

"Mrs. McGuire, please sit," the eldest and thinnest of the three doctors said. Grandma Vera, the children, and Dr. Lucy all found seats. Sarah noticed that Dr. Lucy sat on their side of the table next to her and not the other side with the doctors.

"Let me get right down to it," the thin doctor continued. "Simon is definitely in a great deal of pain, exhibiting every pain indicator in the book, but from the test results it looks like nothing is wrong. The only thing we see is evidence of growing pains. Simon appears to be in the middle of a rapid growth spurt. Certainly not uncommon for his age, but they shouldn't be this strong. We are at a loss. With your permission, we would like to keep him overnight for observation."

"Of course," Grandma Vera agreed.

"Let me show you some of the results." And with that the doctor moved over to a computer screen in the wall and began to pull up Simon's X-rays, scans, and test results, using a lot of long words and hand gestures to convey their meaning to Grandma Vera.

Nickolas was fascinated, drinking in every word and committing each image to memory. People who didn't know Nickolas very well might have dismissed his intent staring at the screen as being bored; he was anything but. Nickolas had what could best be described as a photographic memory, and Sarah was confident that he could tell her every detail down to the scan numbers on the bottom of each page if she asked him later.

"That's odd," Nickolas muttered as he looked at yet another screenshot.

"What's odd?" Sarah asked him quietly.

"We measured Simon yesterday, right?" Nickolas didn't wait for Sarah's nod. "He was forty-three and a half inches. The chart says that he is forty-five inches today. You don't think he could grow an inch and a half in a day, do you?"

Sarah looked at the chart and saw that he was right. "We probably just measured badly. It isn't as if the put-a-ruler-on-your-head method is all that perfect."

"Yeah," Nickolas agreed, still looking thoughtful. "But if it's true..."

He paused, thinking deeply. Sarah sighed, exasperated. Sometimes Nickolas could be so infuriating. His mad scientist, absentminded professor persona had its good points, but seriously, carrying on a conversation with him was challenging at best. "If it's true...?" Sarah prodded after several minutes and a few eye-rolls.

"If it's true, then that might explain the pain. Your bones stretching one and a half inches in twenty-four hours would have to hurt. I remember that month I grew an inch. It felt like I was being racked."

"Ew, that's gross, Nickolas," Sarah admonished. Then after a moment's thought she added, "But why would he be growing that fast? I know he has a lot of catching up to do, but doesn't he have time?"

"One thing I noticed when we came home from Great-Aunt Vivian's was that overnight my fingernails grew like crazy. They went from not needing to be cut at all to an eighth of an inch in no time. Now don't look at me like that, Sarah! I know I don't usually notice my nails growing, but in this case I was really interested to see what would happen. They had stopped growing at the manor completely, so I wanted to see if they would catch up growing or just start growing again at their normal rate. And after that first spurt they grew like normal again. Do you think the same thing is happening to Simon?"

"It couldn't be. We've been here for over a week, and you said that your nails grew in a day. Why has Simon been fine and now all of a sudden started growing? And why only an inch and a half? Doesn't he have feet of growth to make up? Besides, his nails look fine." Sarah scoffed.

"Don't attack me." Nickolas shrugged. "I have no idea how this works. And of course Simon's nails look fine. Haven't you noticed he's always biting them? Besides, I was just throwing out a hypothesis. You have any better ideas?"

"None that make any sense. I hope it's just something quick and that Simon is fine soon. The last thing he needs after what he's been through is to be locked up here hooked up to machines like a lab rat like he was at Great-Aunt Vivian's."

"Isn't that the truth," Nickolas agreed, falling silent and turning to the display screen once more.

Unnoticed by either of the children, Dr. Lucy took out a small pad of paper from her lab coat pocket and made some quick notations.

⚊⚊

Sarah sat on her bed later that night, unable to sleep. She had been up for nearly forty hours and her body was very tired, but she just couldn't turn off her brain.

Sparks seemed to have a similar problem. The little dog would settle on Sarah's pillow, then roll over and try a different position, and then get up and turn around a few times and lie down again. Finally, she jumped down off the bed and paced the room, every bit as agitated as Sarah.

Sarah tried getting comfortable once more and stared at the ceiling, thinking over the day. After the meeting with the doctors, they had gone down to the cafeteria and finally gotten Nickolas some breakfast, which, to everyone's relief, at least stopped him from asking when he was going to get some food every three minutes.

They had gone to visit their parents next. Mr. McGuire was awake again and seemed much stronger than the day before. He had even been able to take a few steps with the aid of a walker. His doctors had nothing but good news to report and told Grandma Vera to be ready to take him home by Thursday, or Friday at the latest.

Their mother was also recovering, albeit at a much slower rate. The doctors said that tests they had run the previous day had indicated that her coma was getting lighter, and that they wouldn't be surprised if she woke up within the next few weeks.

The good news about her parents and the bad news about Simon had Sarah feeling jumbled up inside. It was nearly dark by the time they had visited Simon again and made the long trip home.

All of the horses had been tucked in for the night, so Sarah just had time to go and see little Blaze and her mother in the pasture for a quick hello before being called into the house by Grandma Vera for dinner, baths, and bed.

Only *bed* didn't equal *sleep* for some reason.

Sarah was thinking about turning on her lamp and reading another chapter of her book when Sparks gave a muted woof from beneath Sarah's bed.

Intrigued, Sarah slipped from under the covers and knelt by the headboard, looking for Sparks. All she saw in the gloom were several dust bunnies and the satchel in which she had brought the horses home from Great-Aunt Vivian's manor. The plain leather cross-body had belonged to one of the Muses of Music, and Georgiana had given it to Sarah for safekeeping.

The satchel wiggled a bit, and Sparks poked her tiny head out the opening and woofed again. Sarah pulled the satchel, with Sparks inside, out from under the bed, setting it on top of the comforter and opening the flap. Sparks dove back into the depths for a moment and then returned to look at Sarah as if asking her to follow. "I can't fit in there," Sarah said, laughing at the little dog, but she opened the satchel as wide as she could and peered inside.

Sparks was in the very bottom, worrying one of the satchel's seams in her mouth. She shook and pulled on the seam, but nothing happened. Looking imploringly up at Sarah, Sparks woofed a third time, sat down, and put a paw on the seam. Sarah understood Sparks enough to know that she wanted her to do something with the satchel, but just what was beyond her. So she put her hand on the seam and worried it the way Sparks had. Much to her surprise, the seam moved and then split in her hand, the bottom of the bag pulling away from the sides.

Then Sarah saw that it really wasn't the bottom of the bag, but a panel of fabric covering a false bottom. For there, beneath the scrap of fabric, was hidden a small wooden box covered in intricate inlays.

Sarah carefully pulled the box out and examined it. All six sides were covered in pretty geometric patterns formed by inlays of seven different colors of wood. There were no openings in the box and no lid—no apparent entry points at all. If it hadn't been so heavy, Sarah would have thought that it was just a decorated block of wood. But it was heavy, very heavy. Just what was it doing hidden in the bottom of Georgiana's satchel?

Sparks was no help, for once she had gotten Sarah to discover the satchel's false bottom, she had promptly curled up on one of the pillows and was peacefully (and loudly) snoring. Sarah was rather impressed that such a loud and unladylike noise could come from the little dog. Shrugging, Sarah turned the box over in her hands for several minutes, looking for a way to open it with no success. So she placed it on the bookshelf far above her bed and snuggled down next to Sparks, soon adding her own snores to the mix.

CHAPTER 4

CHARLES'S APARTMENT

In which we find out where he gets his tools

Charles discreetly exited the Tube station at Saint John's Wood, London. He had not managed to return to his old flat since escaping Montague Manor with his brothers. Ardus, his eldest brother, had him hopping from one end of the globe to the other on various reconnaissance missions without even giving Charles a chance to change out his pockets, something he had longed to do for nearly a hundred years.

He had finally finished everything on Ardus's urgent to-do list, and he had snuck away before the head of the Muses of War could think of something else that needed Charles's skills.

At first, Charles had been worried that his old apartment might have been destroyed, for Saint John's Wood looked nothing like it had a hundred years ago. New concrete buildings had replaced many of the old brick mansions, and the ones that remained had been broken up into hundreds of tiny apartments. But luckily for Charles, when he walked along the canal toward his old home, he found that the house he was searching for still stood, and it appeared to be unchanged.

Charles slipped on his glasses, waving a pestering fly away from his face as he observed the house from the back gate. A tiny human-shaped maroon glow emanated from one of the first-floor rooms, and a brighter Kelly-green one was bustling around the ground-floor kitchen. The upper levels of the mansion, however, were quiet and glow free, so Charles knew they were uninhabited. He pocketed his glasses and moved to the back corner of the house.

He climbed up the side of the mansion quietly and carefully, using the mortar lines in the brick as toe and finger holds until he reached the slate roof. To his consternation, he once again had to swat at the fly that seemed intent on following him. Studiously ignoring the buzzing insect, Charles ducked low so he would not be observed from the houses across the canal. He moved to the first dormer window of the attic. He reached into his pockets and carefully extracted a tiny crowbar and forced the window open. He was pleased to note that the stiff window gave every indication that it had not been opened since he had last been in London. He was less pleased when the fly promptly flew through the newly opened window into the attic, but, with a furtive look over his shoulder to make sure he had not been discovered, he slipped through the opening, shutting the window behind him.

The diminutive muse straightened and turned from the window, his eyes adjusting to the attic's gloom. A quick look at the various discarded trunks and broken furniture, as well as the thick covering of dust undisturbed on the floor, gave further evidence that he would find his lair as he had left it. Charles moved from trunk to trunk, making sure not to touch the floor and leave footprints. He arrived at a large wooden wardrobe and, using his lock picks, opened the intricate brass lock he had installed over a century before.

The wardrobe door creaked open, and Charles cringed, reaching into another pocket and withdrawing a small vial of lubricant for the hinges. Once he was confident that they were silenced, he slipped into the wardrobe and shut the door firmly, but not before the fly buzzed through as well. The wardrobe was empty, with the exception of Charles and the bug, and not very deep. Charles pulled out a tiny bright-blue square of glass from another pocket in the sleeve of his tunic and placed it against the inside rear wall of the wardrobe. With a snick, the entire back section slid to the side, revealing the hidden room behind.

The room, like its owner, was small and unassuming. The four paneled walls were bare, and the room contained no furniture. In fact, at first appearance, it contained nothing at all. But then Charles placed the blue glass square in a niche next to the doorway, and the panel slid closed. Charles noticed with some satisfaction that his tiny follower remained trapped in the wardrobe. Once the panel had clicked into place, the rest of the room began to transform.

Large portions of the walls dropped down, revealing cupboards and glass panels. Some slid into hidden recesses and disappeared, while others attached themselves and formed worktables. A wheeled stool shot out of one recess and came to a halt just under the main workstation. Lights flickered across the glass panels, and various machines whined to life.

Charles grinned and pulled the stool out. He laced his fingers and cracked his knuckles in anticipation. A keyboard materialized on the desk in front of him, and a quiet voice emanated from the screen on the wall: "Welcome back, Charles. How may I assist you today?"

⊰⊱

Charles looked at the hologram in front of him with a satisfied smirk. It was an exact replica of the *Musca domestica* that had followed him into the attic, right down to the buzzing of its wings and the way it rubbed its front legs together. But this *Musca domestica* was no ordinary housefly—no, it only looked like a housefly. This *Musca domestica*, inspired by its living cousin in the wardrobe, was Charles's latest spying invention.

In his travels over the past week for Ardus, Charles had seen the advances in surveillance that had occurred over the past hundred years. He found that he had to be much more careful than he used to be to avoid being seen—not only by people, but also by security cameras, motion detectors, and the like. Not that he hadn't been able to foil them, just the last time he had gone on reconnaissance for Ardus before his capture, things like that had not existed. Their introduction into society, however, had made Charles long for time in his laboratory even more. The tools that he had filled his pockets with all those years ago before becoming a statue in Vivian Montague's garden just weren't equipped to handle some of the things he faced in the world he now inhabited.

Thinking about it made Charles push back from his worktable and approach one of the other walls. This wall had exposed hundreds of tiny drawers when the room had transformed, and each was neatly labeled with spiky characters that would appear to be gibberish if the home's other occupants had tried to read them. But they obviously made sense to Charles, for he began quickly opening them and depositing things and just as quickly closing them again.

He worked systematically, starting with the three pockets on the outside of his left arm, and then moving to the four pockets on the underside. He moved on to the pockets hidden in his collar and then the body of his shirt. By the time he had reached his right boot, Charles felt significantly lighter—and definitely less armed than he had been ten minutes prior. He then moved farther down the wall and opened a tall, thin panel, revealing his closet.

It was apparent from the items hanging on the rail that Charles's favorite color was black, for every shirt, trouser, jacket, boot, and shoe was in that shade. He pulled out new clothing, comparing two identical shirts for a moment before selecting the one on the left. "More small pockets," he muttered, returning the right one to the rail. He quickly changed, trading his skintight pirate's trousers for black jeans and his soft thigh-high boots for shorter, sturdier ones that fit under his pant legs. The shirt was less billowing than the one he had previously worn, and once he had tied his chestnut hair back into a ponytail and trimmed his goatee, he looked like a very tiny recording studio executive, and definitely not like the muse Sarah and Nickolas had freed in Great-Aunt Vivian's garden.

Charles returned to his workbench and tapped a quick command into the keyboard. A machine resembling a miniature 3-D printer slid onto the workbench from a hidden cubby. The light on the flat table of the machine flickered to life, giving off a blue glow and a faint hum.

Charles typed in a few more commands, and suddenly the screen in front of him glowed with line after line of angry red script in the same spiky font as his drawers. Cursing softly under his breath, Charles removed an access panel on the side of the machine. There were a series of tiny glass tubes, most of them completely empty and backlit with a red light. Only a few of the tubes were filled with various substances and were backlit blue.

Charles opened several of the tiniest of drawers in front of him and extracted various vacuum-sealed packages. Checking the labels, he tore some open, revealing tiny replacement tubes. Using a set of tweezers, Charles carefully replaced the tubes one by one, and the backlit lights turned slowly from red to blue as he went. Finally he came to the last tube, which was even smaller than the rest. He opened a tiny cupboard door in the wall, revealing a set of nine infinitesimal wooden drawers. He looked inside the central drawer and carefully pulled out the one package it contained. With a deep sigh, Charles opened the package and replaced the last tube, putting the cover back on the machine and sweeping all of the rubbish into a recycling chute in the corner of the desk.

The red lines on his screen had turned blue as he worked and then disappeared with a faint *pop*. He closed the panel, and a green line appeared along with a dialog button, which Charles jabbed with his finger. The machine gave a quick *zap*, and then, hovering over the glowing blue top of the device, was the *Musca domestica*, completely re-created down to the last hair on the last of its six legs.

Charles smiled to himself, removed the fly from the machine, and carefully placed it on a tiny pillar on his desktop, depressing a button that slid the replication device back into its cubby in the wall. Deep inside the machine, the blue light behind that last tiny tube turned to red.

✦

Charles worked late into the night programming his housefly. First, he selected a tiny pale-blue tanzanite no larger than a dewdrop from a drawer that held several of the gems in various sizes.

He placed the stone on another pillar, and punching a few more commands into the screen, he selected programming attributes that he wanted his *Musca domestica* to have. He selected the programs necessary for the insect to fly at his command in all directions. He added acceleration and deceleration, as well as the ability to record sounds and video and transmit them to the operator. Finally, he added a homing device so it could fly directly back to him once its reconnaissance was over. Having selected the attributes he wanted, Charles pressed the play button, and the sound of Christina's dulcian filled the workroom. She had recorded the program blocks for him years ago, for she was far better at programming than he was, and at the sound of the music, the tanzanite began to glow and pulse in time to the tune. When the music finished, the tanzanite faded again, and Charles, using a pair of very fine tweezers to handle the still-hot piece of tanzanite, plucked it from the pedestal and installed it in the back of the *Musca domestica*, right in between its wings, soldering it in place with a jeweler's soldering iron.

Charles retrieved his glasses from their drawer once the fly had received its programming, and peering through them, he made minute adjustments to the *Musca domestica*, observing the slight changes in the tiny fly's aura. As he worked, the aura slowly shifted from deep purple to a pale blue before he was satisfied that the fly was complete, and then he turned his attention to creating a case to house it. He took even more time devising a portable control device, so he could carry the fly in his pocket and use it remotely.

He was just putting the finishing touches on the controller design when a square popped up on his screen showing a picture of a very stern 1850s schoolmaster pointing his finger accusingly out of his picture frame at Charles and buzzing loudly. The sound was not so very different from that made by his *Musca domestica*, so it took Charles a moment to notice and tap the schoolmaster's finger with his own.

The schoolmaster transformed into a holographic projection of Ardus, the leader of the Muses of War. "Charles, I need you to take on another mission," Ardus said without preamble, striding determinedly across Charles's desk.

"I am very well, Ardus, thank you for asking. And how are you?" Charles bowed slightly to the projection with his fist to his chest.

The rendering of Charles's tall blond brother looked annoyed, and he perfunctorily returned Charles's salute. "I am very well. Charles, I need you to pay attention. Edmond has pinpointed James's location, and I want you and Bard to tail him for me."

Charles immediately turned serious and put down the tin he had been tinkering with. "Where is James? Wait a minute. Did you just say you wanted Bard to accompany me on this mission? Bard...big, lumbering, tripping over his own feet. You want *that* Bard on this covert mission?"

"Yes, that Bard." Ardus sighed exasperatedly. "Do you have any other brothers named Bard?"

"Well, no, one really is enough. But why Bard?"

"Because he and Brigitta are the ones assigned to this mission, not you. I just want you along to help him out a little, and everyone needs backup when dealing with James, even Bard. Besides, perhaps you could take this as an opportunity to teach him some of your skills. And he can teach you some of his along the way." Hologram Ardus looked sternly up at his little brother, and his manner clearly stated that he wasn't in the mood for an argument on the subject.

Charles could have argued all day, but he knew he wasn't going to win when Ardus was in head muse mode, so he shrugged and changed tactics. "Where is James, and what do you need me to do?"

"James appears to be heading to Beijing. I am sending you the coordinates now." Ardus's hologram typed in the air, and a line of blue script immediately rolled along the bottom of Charles's screen. "It appears that James is visiting a group of scientists on his way back from Oslo. Edmund has a few things he needs to finish up in Norway for me, so he cannot follow James himself. Besides, espionage is your expertise and not Edmund's."

"Not Bard's either," Charles muttered under his breath. But to Ardus he said, "On it. I will gather a few things and be on my way within the half hour."

"Good, I will send Bard to meet you at the coordinates. Ardus out." And with that the hologram of Ardus dissipated, leaving the desk clear of everything but the design plans for the *Musca domestica*'s controller.

Charles finished up his work quickly and tapped the print button. He returned to the wall of drawers and selected items to fill his many pockets while the replication device slid out of its slot and began printing the controller. Once both the printing and the pocket filling were accomplished, he returned to his workbench and fitted the tiny controller into the tin and placed the *Musca domestica* on top, closing the lid with a snap.

He pulled a small, decorative wooden box from its spot on the shelf and placed it on the worktable. He caught sight of his hands and cursed under his breath in some language that fortunately could not be translated into English, for Audiva, head of the Muses of Music, would definitely not have approved. He jabbed a few frustrated keystrokes into his keyboard, and a pretty elfin hologram stepped onto his desk.

Christina had been sweeping the floor of the tiny cottage she shared with Charles, and she still held the broom in one hand. She smiled warmly at her husband, and her gray eyes twinkled. Charles was pleased to notice that around her tiny wrist was wrapped the iridescent green bracelet that he had made for her so many years ago. He had wondered why she wasn't wearing it the day they were turned into statues, for if she had, she might not have been so easily captured. But there was time enough to ask her later, now he had more pressing issues.

"Darling, if you have a moment," he said, "could you help me out? I seem to need some assistance traveling to Beijing."

CHAPTER 5

FULVIO GETS COOKING

In which the manor's occupants get to eat real food

Fulvio looked down the long kitchen trestle table from where he sat at the head. Normally, the table was used by the many chefs and staff to prepare the meals for those who dwelled upstairs, but three times a day, the kitchen staff used it as their own dining table, and boisterous laughter would fill the kitchens as they swapped stories and filled their stomachs with their own wonderful cooking.

But now those boisterous meals had taken a definite change for the worse. Since Lady Vivian had removed the fourth vial from the kitchen stations, the food had become abysmal. Those who had lived at the manor as long as Fulvio could remember how the synthetic food had tasted before Lady Vivian had introduced the fourth ingredient, and time had done nothing to improve how truly awful it was. Fulvio looked down the table and saw that even Zac, who was more gormless than gourmand when it came to food, was pushing his stew around his plate with very few forkfuls reaching his lips.

This just would not do.

"Carole," Fulvio said to the plump, motherly sous chef who always sat on his right, "would you like to accompany me to the laboratories this afternoon?"

Carole was a bit startled, as they hadn't visited the lab since the explosion the week before. With the labs in ruins, the scientists were no longer working at the manor, so there was no reason for the kitchen staff to troop to the laboratory kitchens to prepare the noon meal. Lady Vivian did not share her lab-created food with the scientists, so the chefs and sous chefs would create meals for them the old-fashioned way and serve it in the cozy cafeteria. The noon meal at the labs and Lady Vivian's frequent parties were really the only times that the kitchen staff truly had enough to do and were encouraged to use their culinary skills. Since the implementation of the scientific food at the manor years before, the staff had dwindled, and now, with the destruction of the labs and abandonment of the manor, there wasn't even enough work to keep the small staff that remained busy.

"Of course, Fulvio." Carole rose, picking up her barely touched plate to take to the sinks. "I will grab my wrap, and we can go immediately."

⇥⇤

Fulvio met Carole on the steps to the greenhouses a few minutes later. She had covered her white uniform with a brightly colored floral shawl and changed her soft-soled shoes for sturdy boots. Carole was nothing if not practical, and Fulvio smiled at her.

Carole had not been born at the manor as he had been, but rather, Fulvio had hired Carole and her son, Zac, in the 1960s, long after the scientific food had been fully implemented. Fulvio had not needed new staff at the time, but one of the scientists from that era had pulled Fulvio aside and told him that his widowed sister needed a position that would take her and her sick son. Fulvio hadn't hesitated for a moment and hired them on the spot. He smuggled them into the kitchens with Lady Vivian none the wiser. And by the time that Lady Vivian noticed the new staff members, they had already been there so long, and they were so integral to the kitchens, that she had no choice but to keep them on.

"What are we going to do at the lab?" Carole asked, falling into step with Fulvio on the path to the greenhouses.

"We are going to see what, if anything, is left of the kitchens there. Did you see how the staff just pushed around their food today without eating?" Fulvio asked, and when Carole nodded he continued. "Well, that just won't do. I don't think Lady Vivian will be giving us any more of the fourth ingredient. We will just have to find another way to solve the problem. I was thinking, since everyone is rather bored anyway, that we would start cooking our meals the same way we cooked for the scientists. I have plenty of vegetables and fruits in the greenhouses, but we will need more ingredients than that. If the lab kitchens are intact, I will have all the things we need there. What do you think?"

"I think that is a wonderful idea, Chef Fulvio. We should stop by the greenhouses and gather some baskets to carry home our finds."

The two put her words into action and soon were trudging through the woods, laden with empty wicker baskets. The path that wound toward the labs was well worn. Only the servants had ever used this path, so Fulvio was pretty sure that they wouldn't run into anyone, nor would they be overheard.

"What has the staff been telling you about the explosion in the labs?" Fulvio asked, knowing that the staff often confided their troubles in the motherly Carole.

"Not much, really. They've been concerned about the lack of work, of course—wondering if Lady Vivian is going to lay us off now that there's so little cooking to do. They have noticed that the footmen and guards all seem to be missing from the grounds, with the exception of the two who show up in the kitchens to make the meals. There are lots of whispers that Lady Vivian sacked them all after the explosion. The general consensus is that she blames them for the destruction and in a fit of anger kicked them all out."

Fulvio had his suspicions that there was more to the story than that, as he had seen the battle with the guards in his kitchens, and he figured that the other guards and footmen from around the manor were more likely dead at the hands of Mistress Sarah's strange warriors than being merely sacked by Lady Vivian. Furthermore, Fulvio was not sure that the defection of the guards was a bad thing for him and his staff, as he could remember a time when the identical guards and footmen had not been in the manor, for they had come right before the fourth ingredient had been introduced and had been brought by Lady Vivian's associate, Dr. James.

Suddenly, the guards had been everywhere, questioning Fulvio's every move and reporting it all to Lady Vivian. Fulvio, of course, had just taken this as a sign that he needed to resort to the covert tactics of his youth, returning to the hidden passageways of the manor, where the guards and footmen never seemed to be. But he kept his observations to himself and returned his attention to Carole.

"Peggy, the serving maid who delivers trays to M. Craubateau and Mr. Fairchild, stopped me the other day. It seems that the head butler has left the manor," Carole was saying.

"The head butler? Whatever for?"

"She didn't know, but she did overhear Lady Vivian talking about it, and she was quite upset. Oh, and Mr. Benjamin is also missing."

Fulvio was more concerned about this disappearance, as he really liked the portly, balding scientist who was Lady Vivian's right-hand man. He was always kind to Fulvio, and he seemed to have a mellowing influence on Lady Vivian. Mr. Benjamin was always talking about ways to help mankind with their scientific discoveries, and he seemed to genuinely care about the staff and those around him. That, and he was madly in love with Lady Vivian. Well, everyone has their faults.

"Did Peggy know why Mr. Benjamin was missing?" Fulvio had stopped to look at Carole.

"No, she only mentioned that Lady Vivian seemed particularly angry about him, much more so than she was about the butler. The butler situation just seemed to annoy her, but she was positively spitting about Mr. Benjamin, saying that he had betrayed her." Fulvio nodded, looking quizzical, and they began walking again. "Oh, and Peggy also told me something that was rather worrying. She saw Louis in the greenhouses gathering apples one day. When she asked him why, he told her that it was for some prisoners Lady Vivian kept in the dungeons and that if she asked too many questions she would be next! Does the manor really have dungeons, Fulvio?"

"Actually"—Fulvio looked thoughtful—"yes, the manor does have dungeons, but they have never been used as far as I know. Australia was a very different place when the manor was built, but even so, I think they were more the architect's idea of what a manor house should be rather than intended for real use. I used to explore them when I was little, and I never saw any signs that people had actually been chained up there. And Lord Myers, who owned the manor at the time, had them boarded up when he caught us boys playing in them one too many times."

"Should we go down there and check sometime?" Carole asked. "I would hate to think that Lady Vivian had anyone locked up. Perhaps we could help them."

Fulvio stopped short again. "Carole, what makes you think that Lady Vivian would do such a thing?" Even Fulvio, who had seen Lady Vivian's temper more times than he could count, could not fathom that she would actually lock anyone up. The butler, perhaps, but not Lady Vivian.

Carole just laughed her throaty chuckle. "Fulvio, just because you keep her as far away from the kitchen staff as possible doesn't mean that we don't know what she is really like. We do appreciate all that you do for us, but we aren't stupid. Of course Lady Vivian is capable of heinous things, especially if she thought it would gain her favor with that Dr. James person."

Fulvio paused for a moment. "Perhaps you are right. And though I highly doubt that we will find anyone, I think we should visit the dungeons, if only to relive my childhood explorations." And then he brightened as they came into a clearing in the trees and saw the familiar wooden door to the laboratory kitchens. "But here we are. Let's see what we can find in here first."

The door opened easily, and Fulvio found that the lab kitchens were almost exactly in the same condition as he had left them the week before. A few items had fallen off the shelves in the blast, but beyond that, there was little or no damage to this wing of the cavern. A quick look outside the dining room door, however, showed that a cave-in had occurred in the corridor leading to the labs, and that the cafeteria was completely blocked off.

Returning to the kitchen storeroom revealed that all of the supplies were as he had left them the day of the explosion. Some of the more perishable items had gone bad, but the sugar, the flour, the eggs, the butter, and all the other staples were in perfect condition. Soon, Carole and Fulvio had loaded their baskets and started lugging them back along the path to the main kitchens.

The walk back consisted of no more depressing matters, for they were too busy planning what wonderful food they would be making for dinner.

⊰目ᴇ⊱

The evening meal was a huge success. Carole had made home-made bread, and Fulvio had set the rest of the staff to making a flavorful vegetable stew while he made his famous chocolate chip cookies. Cheerful conversation and raucous laughter filled the kitchens once more as the staff dug into their soup bowls and sopped every last bit of the gravy up with thick slices of bread. There was an instantaneous change in the kitchens, as the staff was busy once more and the promise of good meals cheered everyone's mood.

Carole quickly organized the staff to have all of the stores from the laboratory kitchen transferred to the main manor, and then she created a rotation for making meals from scratch again.

Before long, the upstairs staff started joining them for meals at the long trestle table. Fulvio noted how depleted their numbers were without the footmen and guards. The parlor maids and under butlers looked overworked and weary, complaining that without the footmen, they had triple the work, and no time to get all the tasks done.

Lady Vivian, it seemed, was quite upset, and she was taking out her frustrations on the hired help. Poor little Ester, one of the head parlor maids, had come down to breakfast with an angry red mark on her face where Lady Vivian had slapped her. Fulvio had fetched a cool cloth for her cheek and comforted her as best he could, but since she reported to the now missing head butler, and not to Fulvio, there was little more than sympathy and first aid that he could provide her.

So even though his own staff seemed to be getting better, things in the manor were apparently not, and kindly Fulvio felt the weight of it most heavily. With a sigh, he picked up a large plate of food and headed toward the storage closet where his prisoner still lay. Of all the things that weighed on him, this, perhaps, weighed the heaviest, for Fulvio didn't have the heart to be a jailer, and if he hadn't feared that the prisoner would cause trouble for the staff and bring the wrath of Lady Vivian into his kitchens, he would have released him long ago.

"Here you are," Fulvio said as brightly as he could as he delivered the mountain of food to the guard.

The guard, who had returned to his human form as soon as he had come to, tiredly sat on an overturned copper pot and pulled the plate onto his knees. He poked at the scalloped potatoes half-heartedly. "Where is the regular food?" he asked.

"Regular food?" Fulvio was confused for a moment; he too was feeling so tired lately. "This is regular food." And then it dawned on him. "Oh, you mean the scientific food. Well, no one is eating it now that we are making the meals, so the two footmen who were preparing it stopped coming to the kitchens. I haven't seen them in a couple of days."

"But I cannot live on this," the guard said, pushing the plate onto the floor with a crash and throwing his fork at Fulvio.

Fulvio dodged the weak throw and looked carefully at the guard. He was much thinner than he had been a week ago, and he seemed to be having trouble holding his human form. Even now his complexion was more reminiscent of the brown, lumpy skin he wore as a Faerie, and his features were more bulbous and alien. "Are you all right?" he asked cautiously.

"No," the guard said with a sigh. "I am definitely not all right. Without the regular food, I will die."

"Is it really as dire as all that?" Fulvio tried to joke, but at the guard's sad nod, he turned serious. "Would it help if I brought you the solutions from the food stations? My staff and I don't know how to make the synthetic food, as that has never been part of our job descriptions, but if you know how, I would be happy to bring you the ingredients."

The guard brightened immediately, so Fulvio slipped out of the storeroom and returned with a tray and three vials of solution. "Lady Vivian has confiscated all of the fourth vials, so this will have to do," he said, putting the tray down in front of the guard.

Eagerly the guard grabbed the first vial and, throwing the tree-topped stopper aside, drank the thick brown liquid down in two gulps. He reached for the second vial, which he dispatched as quickly as the first. He was just grabbing the third when Fulvio stayed his hand.

"Should you be drinking that straight like that?" he asked, concerned. "The chemicals are quite concentrated. It only takes a drop to make a meal of that stuff, you know."

But the guard ignored him and finished off the sparkly gem solution in one huge gulp, wiping the back of his uniform sleeve across his mouth with satisfaction. "It feels, *hic*, so good, *hic*, to drink that, *hic*, properly," he said, slurring his words as he fell off the copper pot and landed solidly on the floor, the empty vials rolling across the room.

"I will see what I can do to make sure that you get plenty of 'regular' food," Fulvio promised doubtfully, thinking of the limited number of vials left in the food stations. But the guard did not hear what he said, for he had fallen asleep, with one arm thrown lovingly around the nearest copper pot.

Fulvio squared his shoulders, shifted the plate of chocolate chip cookies he carried to his left hand, and raised his right to knock on Lady Vivian's study door. Her personal secretary, Louis, appeared a moment later. Louis was short and thin. Fulvio was not sure of his age, as he had that slightly balding, greasy-haired look of someone who could have been in his late twenties or decades older. Louis had been working at the manor since before Fulvio's mother had died, and Fulvio always tried to keep as much distance between himself and the odiferous man as possible.

"Chef Fulvio, what a pleasant surprise." Louis eyed the cookies greedily. "How can I help you?"

"I am looking for Lady Vivian." Fulvio's mouth was dry. "I wanted to discuss the weekly order with her."

"Hmm." Louis brought his brows together and continued a touch insincerely. "I am afraid that Lady Vivian is very busy at the moment. Come in and let's look at her calendar and see where she can squeeze you in." He motioned for Fulvio to follow him into the anteroom where Louis had his office.

Fulvio placed the cookies in front of him and perched on one of the uncomfortable embroidered chairs that were pulled up to the desk. Whether it was intentional or not, the guest chairs in Louis's office were several inches too low, so Fulvio felt like a small child sent to the principal's office every time he met with the personal secretary.

Snagging a cookie, Louis flipped through the gold embossed leather datebook where he kept Lady Vivian's calendar. "Let's see, she can see you a week from Thursday at two o'clock. Does that work for you?" Louis looked up and ate another cookie.

"Isn't there anything sooner?" Fulvio asked, thinking of his dwindling stores.

"No, Lady Vivian is very busy at the moment rebuilding the lab and working on several new projects." Louis flipped through the calendar, reading off entries. "She is meeting with the contractors today to discuss cleanup and repairs to the lab's infrastructure. Tomorrow she is meeting with the bank to discuss funding. Thursday she is meeting with the architects on the new design. She has blocked out two days for that." He ate another cookie. "This weekend she is off the grounds at a science convention in Adelaide. Then next week she is meeting with the Department of Health and Human Services to discuss her expansion plan. She is also meeting with the zoning committee to figure out if the manor can be used as a school. Wednesday next she is working with a supply company who specializes in lab equipment, as she has lots of things she needs to replace. Which means the next available day to discuss things with you would be next Thursday. Sorry, Fulvio, I just can't get you in earlier." Louis finished off the last cookie on the plate.

Thinking fast and eyeing the chocolate chip that caught in the corner of Louis's mouth, Fulvio said, "I see. Well, we will just have to make do until then. Sadly, we are out of chocolate. Guess there will be no more cookies or brownies until next Thursday." Sighing heavily, Fulvio regained his feet and gathered the empty plate.

Louis cleared his throat as Fulvio turned to go. "Wait a minute, Fulvio. I think I just found an opening in Lady Vivian's schedule. Could you come back in an hour? She won't have long, mind you, but a few seconds should be all you need."

"Of course I can," Fulvio replied, hiding his smile. "I will see you in an hour then."

Once he left Louis's office, Fulvio immediately lost his subservient manner and allowed himself a broad grin. He was certain that he would have no trouble getting supplies in the future.

CHAPTER 6

CHARLES'S RING

In which the children call for help

The next morning, Nickolas rose early and headed out to the stables to think. He always did his best thinking in the workroom he had set up in one of the empty stalls, and he certainly had a lot to think about today.

Nickolas was pretty sure that he knew what was causing Simon's problems. Simon was aging again, and by the looks of it, he was aging rapidly. When he reached his workroom, Nickolas clambered up on the bench he had made out of an old discarded stall door and two sawhorses. He and his father had erected shelves along one wall and put pegboard on the other to house his tools. Nickolas was not the neatest of creatures when it came to his bedroom, and he certainly never managed to get his dirty socks anywhere near his laundry basket, but important things, like his tools, were neatly hung on hooks on the pegboard. Every tool had its place, and he could see in an instant if anything was missing. All of his tools were there with the exception of his mini screwdrivers, which, for all Nickolas knew, were still in his backpack in his rooms in Australia at Montague Manor.

But it wasn't his mini screwdrivers that Nickolas was looking for; it was a shoebox he had placed on the top shelf just a week before. He located it and pulled it down. Sitting on his work-bench stool, he carefully opened the lid. Inside he had placed the contents of his pockets after his return from Australia, and sure enough, everything was still there as he had left it.

There were several stubs of candles and a box of matches (how he had gotten the matches on the plane was a mystery, but Nickolas seemed to have a knack for bringing things on planes that should have been confiscated at security), his green army man, some wadded pieces of paper scribbled on with half-developed experiments, a small rubber ball, a paper bag of chocolate chip cookies, a dragon finial from the lamp in his Australian sitting room, and a tiny glass vial half full of the red mushroom acid he had distilled at the manor.

Nickolas looked the lot over and opened the bag of chocolate chip cookies. There were only two left, and they looked exactly as they had when he had ordered them from the food cabinet in Australia over a week ago. Nickolas's inner scientist was intrigued. Why hadn't they gone moldy? Did old chocolate chip cookies normally go moldy like old bread? He had never known a choco-late chip cookie to last long enough to find out. Usually, he ate them before they could even cool completely from the oven.

Nickolas decided to take a closer look; he retrieved his micro-scope from its shelf and a slide and slide cover from their drawer. Unlike his oft-denied requests for a Bunsen burner, his mother had gladly purchased him a microscope several years before and even had splurged to get him a good one. He placed a few cookie crumbs on the slide and carefully covered them with the tiny square of glass. Nickolas then slipped the sample under the micro-scope's lens and placed his eye to the scope.

He adjusted the focus and let out a low whistle of surprise, for the cells that appeared looked nothing like the plant and animal cells he had observed before. The first difference was that they were all uniform. Being that a chocolate chip cookie had different substances in it (chocolate bits, cookie bits, sugar bits, etc.), he was shocked. Secondly, the cells were all perfect, florescent-purple, eight-sided figures that resembled old fashioned bowties. They were so uniform and perfect, in fact, they looked like brickwork or one of the old family quilts his mother had stored in her hope chest. But the thing that had Nickolas reaching for his science journal to scribble notes was that all of the cells were moving, like they were somehow alive, or at least animated, swimming together in a circular formation.

Nickolas wrote down everything he observed in his journal, absently munching away on the last two cookies as he did.

⊰⊑⊒⊱

Sarah was looking everywhere for Nickolas. He wasn't in his room reading, nor in the kitchen having a midmorning snack. He wasn't in the living room playing a computer game either, and when she saw Splotchy in the pasture alone she knew he wasn't out riding. All of the campers were in the tack room being taught how to care for their horses' equipment, but Nickolas was not among them. That meant there really was only one other place to look, and soon Sarah found herself outside of his workroom door. With a sigh, she steeled herself for the inevitable lecture she was about to endure on whatever Nickolas was discovering behind it.

She pushed the door open, and sure enough, there was Nickolas hunched over his microscope and scribbling notes in his science journal.

"Hey, Nickolas," Sarah shouted, louder than she would normally in an effort to penetrate Nickolas's laser concentration on whatever he was working. To her surprise, he turned immediately.

57

"Sarah, check this out!" he said excitedly, motioning her to replace him at the microscope's eyepiece.

Sarah sighed in resignation and put her eye to the scope as directed. She adjusted the focus and looked at the swirling purple bowtie things for a moment before asking, "So what exactly am I looking at? Singing dinosaur pulmonary systems?"

"No, don't be silly, where would I get that?" Nickolas retorted. "It is the chocolate chip cookies I brought back from Great-Aunt Vivian's."

"Ew, we ate that? Yuck!"

"Actually, they were quite tasty, even after a week and a half. But they do look strange at the cellular level. I looked at Grandma Vera's cookies before, and they looked nothing like that. Any idea what makes them move?"

Sarah frowned at him. He thought she would know? Wasn't he supposed to be the stark raving scientist of the pair? "No idea, but I'm glad to not be eating them anymore."

Sarah started poking in the shoebox on Nickolas's desk and held up the small vial. "Did you look at the mushroom acid under the scope? The mushrooms were one of the ingredients Great-Aunt Vivian used to make the food, so maybe there's a clue in here."

Nickolas grinned and took the vial from her. He picked the slide out from under the scope and removed the cover. He swept the crumbs from the slide and onto the floor, carefully putting a drop of the acid in their place.

Once he had clipped the slide under the scope and readjusted the focus, he peered through the eyepiece. Again he saw the bow-ties, but these were not neatly in formation as the cookie crumbs had been. These were swimming independently in solution. Nor were they bright purple, but a pretty red, reminiscent of the mushrooms he had distilled the acid from. It was like looking in an aquarium; some of the bowties swam together in groups, and some swam alone. The bowties would even switch directions in groups like a school of fish.

Nickolas relinquished the scope so Sarah could have a look and scribbled his findings in his journal right under his cookie observations.

Sarah increased the magnification and attempted to get one of the tiny creatures in view. It took her a while to locate one, and then she jumped back in surprise. "Nickolas, they have eyes!" she exclaimed.

Sure enough, when Nickolas looked at the higher magnification, he saw that they did indeed have eyes, six of them in fact, and hundreds of tiny legs along their edges that propelled them forward.

"That is so cool," Nickolas whispered, scribbling frantically away in his journal.

⚜

"Sarah! Nickolas!" Grandma Vera called. "It's time to go to the hospital!"

"Coming!" came the faint reply from the back of the stables, and shortly both of her grandchildren appeared, racing toward her. Nickolas had his science journal clutched to his chest, and Sarah carried an old battered shoebox.

"Are you ready to go?" Grandma Vera asked them when they careened to a halt in front of her.

"Yes!" they chorused and followed her out of the stables to the waiting van.

They said little on the way to the hospital. Nickolas was doodling in his notebook, and Sarah was trying to find a radio station she liked.

"I got a phone call from the intern at the hospital, Dr. Lucy. You remember her, right?" Grandma Vera asked.

Nickolas's head came up from his page. "Of course we remember her."

"Did she have any new news on Simon or Mom and Dad?" Sarah asked.

"Not directly—she was actually asking about you two. She was wondering if you would be willing to meet with her while I talked with the other doctors about Simon. I thought that was rather odd. What does she want with you, I wonder? You two aren't ill, are you?" Grandma Vera inspected Sarah worriedly.

"No," Sarah answered quickly. "Did she say anything more?"

"No, she didn't, but she did ask that I send you to room 558 when we arrived and to let the nurses know that you were there. Are you two OK with that?"

Sarah and Nickolas exchanged concerned glances in the rearview mirror. "Sure," Sarah said. What on earth did Dr. Lucy want with them?

⊣⊨

When they arrived at the hospital, Sarah and Nickolas proceeded to room 558. It was a normal conference room with table, chairs, and a projection screen. They barely had time to sit down when Dr. Lucy arrived.

"Hi, Nickolas and Sarah! I hope your grandmother wasn't too upset about my request to see you two alone, but I need to get some more information about Simon, and I thought you would be more comfortable talking to me without her around." Dr. Lucy set down a stack of folders on the table and took the seat next to Sarah. "I overheard you two yesterday at the meeting about

Simon's growth, so I ran a few tests. I was hoping you could help me out with some of my results."

Dr. Lucy plugged a flash drive into the projector, and immediately a slide covered with numbers appeared on the screen. "This is Simon's blood work. We noticed yesterday that his white blood cell count was slightly elevated, but we thought it was just because he was fighting off some sort of illness. It wasn't so high that we felt he had a major infection, but I put those white blood cells under the scope, and this is what I found." Dr. Lucy advanced the slide.

The screen now showed a microscopic view of Simon's blood. Nickolas recognized the disk-shaped red blood cells and the ball-shaped white blood cells. But that was not all that the sample contained, for there were hundreds of the purple bowtie-shaped creatures that he had seen in his microscope at home.

"Oh no!" Sarah cried. "They're in his blood!"

"You know what these are?" Dr. Lucy asked, incredulous.

"Well, not really," Nickolas admitted. "We just know where they came from."

Since Nickolas didn't add anything more, Sarah jumped in. "They come from the food we ate at our Great-Aunt Vivian's in Australia. Our blood may have some in it too, but probably not as much as Simon. He lived there most of his life, while we were only there for a few weeks."

Dr. Lucy interrupted. "How do you know this was in the food?"

"Nickolas brought home some cookies and was looking at them under the microscope this morning. They looked just like the purple things in Simon's blood, only they were all hooked together and moving."

Nickolas slid his notebook over to Dr. Lucy open to the page of his notes.

Dr. Lucy pored over the page. She must have been used to reading really bad handwriting, because she was able to decipher Nickolas's scrawl. "Wow, this is really interesting. When I looked at the blood, the purple cells weren't moving as rapidly as you describe here, but they were moving. Hmm." Dr. Lucy turned the page and read on. "What are these red ones?"

"Oh, I got those from the mushrooms," Nickolas explained.

"Mushrooms?" Dr. Lucy looked very confused.

"Let me start at the beginning," Sarah said. "Great-Aunt Vivian is a scientist, and she makes all the food at her manor from some chemicals she creates in her lab. There are four main ingredients she uses. One is from some mushrooms that grow on her estate. Mr. Benjamin, one of Great-Aunt Vivian's friends, gave Nickolas an experiment to conduct on the mushrooms, and he brought back the resulting acid solution when we left Australia. We looked at that under the microscope today too, and it looked more like the blood, where the bowties weren't attached, but swimming freely. But they are red, not purple."

"You said something yesterday about Simon growing fast, and my tests back that up," Dr. Lucy said. "He *is* growing very, very rapidly. He grew nearly another inch last night. I've never seen anyone grow this quickly. Do you think those strange cells in his bloodstream are responsible for the growth?"

"Well," Sarah said tentatively. "People at Great-Aunt Vivian's don't age. It's something that she's been working on. She doesn't want to get old, so she has created this food that keeps you from getting older. We were only there for two weeks, and we noticed that we weren't aging or growing. It was really creepy. When we got home, Nickolas noticed that the things that had stopped growing, like our fingernails, suddenly started growing again really fast, and then they settled down to normal. Simon had been there longer than us, so he has more catching up to do than we did."

Dr. Lucy looked very intrigued. "She has found the fountain of youth!" she said, sounding awestruck. After a long pause she added, "How long was Simon there, Sarah?"

"Nearly fifty years, we think."

Dr. Lucy looked up sharply. "Fifty years? Oh my…"

⊰⊱

Dr. Lucy was so willing to believe all the fantastic things they told her that Nickolas was sorely tempted to embroider the story with fire-breathing dragons and constricting serpents, but a stern look from Sarah kept him to only the facts.

Dr. Lucy, with their permission, conducted some experiments of her own, placing the mushroom acid under her own powerful microscope. (Nickolas was rather jealous.) When she saw the red cells for herself, she asked if she could prick the children's fingers and collect a drop of blood from each. She placed the droplets under the scope and saw a tiny number of purple cells hiding in their blood. Nickolas had more than Sarah; in fact, Dr. Lucy had to really hunt to find even one in the drop of Sarah's blood, and the single bowtie she did find wasn't moving at all. Nickolas had several really lively ones in his sample and one or two of the ones that weren't moving. He cleared up the mystery of why his were so active by confessing that he had eaten the two cookies that morning.

"Nickolas, seriously?" Sarah was aghast.

"I was hungry, and they were there, and well, I ate them for two weeks without any horrific effects, so what's two more cookies compared to that?"

Dr. Lucy shared the rest of her test results with them. The purple creatures were found in every cell sample taken from Simon—in his skin, in his hair, in his organs, everywhere, even in his tears.

"But they seem to be dying, and since he isn't eating more of them, they don't seem to be stopping his growth anymore," Dr. Lucy mused. "But why is he growing so fast? I wish I had more of that food and its building blocks to test. You don't happen to have any more of those cookies, do you Nickolas?"

Nickolas looked at the toes of his shoes. "No, I ate them all."

"All of them? You couldn't have left a few crumbs?" Sarah admonished.

"What? I was hungry!"

Sarah was about ready to say more, when Dr. Lucy interrupted their fight. "Never mind. At least we know more about what is going on than we did yesterday. Do you think you could call your great-aunt and have her overnight me some samples?"

"Um." Nickolas paused. "I don't think she would be willing to do that. She's not very nice."

"Yeah," Sarah continued, "she doesn't really play well with others." Sarah thought for a moment. "But I might have another way to get you what you want. Can I have a day to try?"

"Of course, Sarah," Dr. Lucy said. "I will try to slow down Simon's immune system to keep his body from killing off the purple things. That might buy us some more time. But hurry, and let me know the instant you find anything out."

"OK!" Sarah said, rapidly throwing the mushroom solution and the notebook into the shoebox and tugging Nickolas out of the room. "Come on. Let's go find Grandma Vera. We need to get home!"

Nickolas looked imploringly at Dr. Lucy, but she merely waved them out with a quick good-bye and added, as if an afterthought,

"Perhaps it would be best if you didn't tell Grandma Vera or anyone else about this until we can determine we are on the right path."

Sarah did not hear her, as she was so intent on dragging Nickolas out the door, but Nickolas quickly promised that he wouldn't before he was swept around the corner.

◆

As soon as Sarah and Nickolas arrived back at the ranch, they ran to Sarah's room. She went straight to her desk and opened her small jewelry box. There, under several sets of sparkly beads she had won at the fair last year, was Charles's ring. She brought it over to where Nickolas was waiting, and the two sat on the carpet with the ring between them. Sparks jumped down from Sarah's pillow and sat expectantly next to them, looking intently at the ring with her head cocked as if asking about it. Sarah absently petted the puppy while she and Nickolas inspected the ring.

It was large and made of gold, too large to fit any of Sarah's fingers. The square stone on top was a dark ruby that winked in the sunlight from the window. On both sides of the stone were carved scenes in fine relief work. On one was a picture of three daggers lined up in a row, and on the other was a musical instrument that looked a lot like a shortened bassoon. Strange spiky symbols and words were carved around the stone and the two scenes, written in a language that Sarah and Nickolas had never seen before. Inside the ring was an inscription: *Clama ad me, et ego ad te volare.*

"Cool ring, Sarah." Nickolas reached for it. "Where did you get it?"

Sarah snatched it from his hand. "Charles gave it to me, and Audiva showed me how to use it on the plane."

"Why did he give it to you and not to me?" he asked, feeling a bit jealous.

"Maybe he thought you would lose it," Sarah shot back.

Nickolas thought about this for a moment and then nodded. "Probably. What does it do?"

"It calls the muses. Audiva said that we should use it if we ever needed them."

"Do you think they can help Simon?"

"Well, if they can't, I don't know who can. And they probably can help us get the ingredients for Dr. Lucy." Sarah placed the ring in her palm. "Here goes nothing."

She carefully opened the hidden catch Audiva had shown her that was under the stone, revealing a tiny space between the ruby and the gold of the ring. A small blue chip of tanzanite was attached to the gold, and Sarah pressed down on it, causing the stone to burst to life with light. After twisting the tanzanite a few times in a specific sequence, Sarah clicked the ring closed.

"Is that it?" Nickolas asked, wondering why, considering the ring came from Charles, more did not happen, like an explosion or shooting sparks.

The words were hardly out of Nickolas's mouth when the doorbell rang. Nickolas picked up the ring where it lay on the floor and slipped it over his thumb as both children dashed from the room and down the hall with Sparks right behind them. Neither noticed that Georgiana's strange box on Sarah's bookshelf glowed bright silver.

CHAPTER 7

BARD UNDER COVER

In which Bard receives an urgent message

Charles arrived at the muses' safe house in Beijing. The ancient home was of traditional Chinese architecture, and as the city had grown, the tiny house had been dwarfed by the newer concrete structures closely built on either side.

The home belonged to Walter, the Muse of Group Theory Algebra, but he graciously let all the muses use it whenever they visited Beijing. Walter was not in residence when Charles arrived, and it looked like the quiet math muse had not been there in quite some time. Stacks of papers covered nearly every surface, and half-solved math problems were written on the chalkboard on one wall and covered the paper napkins on the table. Even the linen tablecloth was marked with diagrams and symbols.

But all was quiet in the tiny house. It took Charles only a moment to realize that Bard was not within, although the large battle-ax leaning against the wall was a sure sign that he had been. Gentle Walter would hardly have owned such a weapon.

Charles peered out into the busy street. Bicycles and pedestrians clogged the narrow roadway, and houses and shops lined the road. Each shop had a bright-red sign proclaiming its name and wares in gold Chinese characters, and strings of red paper lanterns and banners crisscrossed overhead. Directly across from Walter's home was a café that was doing a lively business serving bowls of noodles and glasses of thick beer. In the middle of a group of dark-haired patrons he spotted Bard's unmistakable flaming red hair. The war muse was head and shoulders taller than all of his companions and about twice as wide. As if he wasn't conspicuous enough, he was dressed in that horrific bright-orange tunic and kilt he loved to wear.

Charles closed his eyes for a moment, once again wondering what on earth Ardus thought he would be able to teach Bard about covert operations. Huge, lumbering, *orange* Bard was simply incapable of blending into anything, and certainly not in Beijing. As if to make his point, Bard was approached by a group of schoolchildren, and one timid girl produced a camera and gestured that she and her mates would like to take a picture with him. Good-natured Bard nodded and agreed, posing with a huge boyish grin surrounded by the gaggle of girls in school uniforms as one of Bard's lunch companions snapped the picture. Charles buried his face in his hands, shaking his head.

With a sigh, Charles slipped across the street. "Are you ready to go?" he asked Bard in an undertone.

"Charles!" Bard exclaimed, wrapping one of his huge arms around Charles's shoulder and nearly crushing the smaller muse. "You are just in time for lunch. The noodles here are fantastic, and the company is even better." Bard switched to Chinese and added, "Chongan, Fang, Gen, this is my brother Charles I was telling you about. Charles, these fine men are Chongan, Fang, and Gen." Bard motioned to get the noodle shop owner's attention and called, "Longwei! A chair and some noodles for my brother!" The owner smiled cheerfully and brought over the requested items.

"Bard, we have to go. We have an appointment we can't miss. And besides, you don't even eat noodles," Charles whispered, trying to extricate himself from Bard's embrace.

"You know that, but they don't," Bard returned. "And it wouldn't be polite not to order the noodles. Surely we have a little more time, just to be friendly?" Bard's baby face looked pleadingly at Charles.

Charles was not persuaded. "Now, Bard."

"But…"

"Now or else I'll call Brigitta." Charles's tone was serious.

"OK," Bard said dejectedly. "Sorry, guys, duty calls. Maybe on my way out we could meet up again." Bard placed a small stack of Chinese bills on the table and rose to his feet, having to duck down to avoid hitting his head on the awning.

Followed by a chorus of loud farewells from all of his new friends, Bard trailed the fuming Charles across the way.

Charles turned to glare at his taller brother once they were safely back at Walter's home. "Just what do you think you were doing over there? You don't think those men will talk about the red-haired giant they met at lunch? Do you think James won't inspect his brother-in-law's house in Beijing to see if his sister or Walter are here? The chances of you being discovered by James are very, very high, and just what exactly do you think we are trying to do? We are trying to spy on James to figure out what he is doing and in the process not have him discover what we are doing. Is that clear? Or should we just announce that we are in town on a billboard so James is sure to see it?"

Bard hung his head like a dejected puppy. "I'm sorry, Charles. I was just lonely and wanted to pass the time until you came. And wouldn't it be better to have a straight fight with James and get it over with? All this sneaking around, it just doesn't make sense."

But Charles continued his tirade and didn't even hear him. "Furthermore, Bard, you don't even eat human food, and you ate at Georgiana's just last week. Surely you aren't hungry already."

"I may not eat human food, but I fake it well!" Bard brightened.

"Not really, trust me on that one." After a few moments Charles continued. "But we don't have any more time to discuss this. Ardus sent me the coordinates that Edmund lifted from James's calendar. He is expected within the hour at the labs of one Dr. Nikki Ping and her associate Dr. Elizabeth Candy. According to the memo, the labs are not too far away. Let's see what kind of transportation Walter has in his garage."

"Good, we will find James there and then have our fight." Bard's eyes gleamed with anticipation, and gathering his ax, he followed Charles out the back of the house to the alley behind. Charles did not even bother to reply.

In a ramshackle hut serving as Walter's garage were two vehicles. One was a small white van with "Manchu's Laundry" emblazoned on the side in Chinese. The second was a cargo bike, the trailer piled high, covered with a canvas tarp, and secured with ropes.

Charles checked out the van. The keys were on the front seat, and the back cargo area was neat and tidy and empty. There was even a full tank of gas. Charles sat eagerly in the driver's seat and began figuring out all of the controls. He had only driven a few motorized vehicles of this sort, and although the van was very old, it was still newer by nearly eighty years than the last vehicle he had driven. Before their capture in 1912, motor cars had been a rarity, only owned by the very rich or by car enthusiasts. Most people had still gotten around by train, trolley, or horse-drawn carriages. Charles himself had owned one of the early Fords, but with the amount of traveling the muses had to do, the car had been rather impractical. Cars had come a long way since 1912, and Charles had to take a moment to become familiar with the technology.

Bard inspected the cargo bike while Charles was fiddling with the van. The red-haired Muse of War curiously looked under the tarp to find out what Walter was transporting, but when he lifted the flap, Bard discovered that the cargo trailer was actually a cleverly disguised tent. The tarp and cargo box surrounded a fairly large empty space. Walter had furnished the area with two benches along the edges. It was fully networked, and two workstations were set up on the far end. A periscope was rigged in the center, allowing someone to see 360 degrees around the cart when it was parked without anyone being the wiser.

Bard pulled himself inside, the cart swaying dangerously under his weight. Once aboard, however, the cart stabilized, and Bard found that he could actually stand fully upright and had plenty of room to stretch out his long legs when seated at the workstation.

Bard stuck his head out of the door flap and called to Charles. "Hey, Charles, check this out!"

"Stop playing around, Bard. I have just about figured out how this van works, so I need you to get on board," said Charles, sounding rather low on patience.

"Seriously, Charles, you have to come see this. Walter is a lot cooler than I ever thought he was."

Charles grumbled to himself and stepped out of the van, approaching the bike. Bard held open the flap and reached down to pull Charles into the cart. As usual, Bard misjudged how little his brother weighed, and Charles went flying into the back of the cart to land rather indecorously in the middle of the floor. Charles opened his mouth to berate Bard, but he closed it with a sharp click as he saw the interior of the trailer. A slow smile crossed his tanned face. Walter was indeed a lot cooler than he had thought.

᪥᪥

Charles was questioning his choice of conveyance less than twenty minutes later. One look at Bard's orange clothes, flaming hair, and freckled skin convinced him that Bard should not be the one to pedal the bike, so instead, Bard was hidden from view in the back of the cart. If it had been Christina in the cargo area it wouldn't have been a problem propelling the bike through the narrow streets of Beijing, but Bard's bulk made the hills torture and the turns treacherous. From the feel of the high center of gravity, Bard was standing in the middle of the cart enjoying the ride of his life at the expense of Charles's knees and sanity. "He is probably watching the world go by through the periscope," Charles grumbled, cursing Ardus for the hundredth time that day for saddling him with Bard on this assignment.

Charles turned off Qianmen Street into a short alley and pulled the bike over. He slipped into the back of the cart, carefully looking from side to side to make sure that he was unobserved, and pulling the leather cap he had borrowed from Walter's closet lower over his eyes. Sure enough, there was Bard, with his face pressed to the periscope.

Grinning, Bard turned to his brother. "This is just so awesome," he started in a loud voice before Charles shushed him.

"The walls are paper thin, and cargo is not supposed to talk," Charles whispered, noting the swaying of the cart as Bard plopped heavily onto one of the benches. "It's not supposed to move, either. I need you to be quiet and motionless. The lab James is supposed to be visiting is in the back of that pharmaceutical building. You

72

can just see the door at the end of the alleyway. Now sit still while I get things ready."

Charles bustled around the tiny cargo area, setting the periscope to keep a close eye on the door and booting up the workstations. He removed a blue glass cube just like the one he used to enter his workroom from one of the pockets on his sleeve. He placed the cube in a square-shaped indentation on the workstation panel, and the screen instantly came to life. A few jabs at the screen and Charles was logged in to his network. There on the monitor was a three-dimensional representation of the fly he had made earlier in the day. He took the containment tin from a side trouser pocket and set the bug on the workstation table. A few more jabs and the screen glowed bright blue.

Before Bard could react, a portion of the glowing screen detached from the wall and flew straight at Charles, enveloping his hands and head in glowing blue bubbles. Charles raised his left hand, and mimicking him, the fly flew straight upward a few inches. As Charles pinched the forefinger and thumb of his right hand, the fly buzzed for a moment, and then, like an old car engine, it sputtered once, dipping toward the floor, almost choked, and then buzzed again and regained its altitude. Charles smiled and pushed the palm of his left hand forward, and the fly flew in a direct line toward the flap door in the tent.

Unfortunately, it missed the opening, hit the wall, sputtered, stopped buzzing, and fell to the floor, lifeless once more. Charles sighed and, pinching his fingers again, tried to get the fly's buzz to turn over and catch. The fly's motor caught after a few false starts and began to rise off the floor, a little shakier this time.

Bard leaped to his feet and, sounding like a herd of stampeding aardvarks, raced to the door flap, arriving just in time to sweep it open for the fly. Bard poked his red head out the flap and watched the fly buzz down the alley to the laboratory door.

⊰⊱

Dr. Elizabeth Candy sat at her desk poring over a stack of lab results, eating a ginormous slice of chocolate cake, and sipping a large frozen café latte from a pink straw. Her partner, Dr. Nikki Ping, was out for the morning, so Dr. Betty had the tiny cramped office to herself. In a fit of pique, Dr. Nikki had split the room in half with a stripe of silver duct tape, but whenever she was gone, Dr. Betty's precarious stacks of notes and books would inevitably tumble across the line into Dr. Nikki's immaculate half. It was a bone of constant contention between the two ladies. Dr. Betty could not imagine how Dr. Nikki got any work done with nothing on her desk, and Dr. Nikki could not imagine how Dr. Betty could find anything in the piles surrounding her.

But Dr. Betty could always find what she was looking for. For if she could not remember herself, she had left plates of crumbs of whatever she had been eating at the time on top of the piles. The memory of the food would jog her memory of the contents of the folders beneath.

Dr. Betty could always be counted on to remember food, for she ate copious amounts of it each day. In fact, it was seldom that she was ever seen without a plate in front of her and a fork in her left hand. In medical school she had learned how to eat left-handed so she could write notes with her right, and her lab partners had always been in constant fear that she would inadvertently eat their science experiments instead of her cakes and cookies.

Dr. Betty had been morbidly overweight in those days, spilling over her lab stool and having a horrible time finding clothing that fit. In fact, if she hadn't found Mr. Oden, who custom made her frocks, she would have had nothing to wear at all. Mr. Oden's full-time job was making fancy tents for expensive weddings and circuses, but he kindly donated his after-hours time making clothes for Dr. Betty. Dr. Betty had always been rather embarrassed that she needed Mr. Oden's services, but she pretended not to care, even when her fellow scientists made snide comments and teased her mercilessly.

But in the last year, thanks to some collaborations with Dr. Nikki's friend Dr. James, Dr. Betty no longer required Mr. Oden's services to make her clothing, as Dr. James had introduced her to a magic solution that melted her figure down from humongous to pleasantly plump in just a few months, all without her having to stop eating her favorite foods. Dr. Betty idolized the handsome Dr. James to a point of near worship, but whether it was the man or the solution that she was more enamored with could not be easily determined.

In fact, Dr. James's assistance had also changed the course of her and Dr. Nikki's research. The two women had been exploring how to lengthen the amount of time an organ could remain viable outside of a donor's body while it was being transferred to the intended recipient. The same solution that had melted her excess body weight seemed to also prolong the viability of the donated organs. The only problem they now faced was the solution's apparent limited shelf life, so with Dr. James's help, they set out to find a way to keep that alive longer as well.

Dr. James was going to be visiting them that afternoon to discuss their results, and Dr. Nikki had tasked Dr. Betty with compiling their presentation. Dr. Betty took another huge bite of cake, brushed the resulting crumbs off her paperwork, and turned to her computer to create the presentation.

A *Musca domestica* had flown, unobserved, straight through Dr. Betty's open window. Had Dr. Betty seen it, she might have been concerned about the way it flew, for unlike its meandering cousins, this fly only traveled in one direction, straight ahead. And right in the path of the fly was Dr. Betty's blond bouffant hairdo. The fly was unable to stop in time and crashed into the beehive updo, sputtered once, and remained unnervingly motionless.

⊰≒⊱

Charles tapped the screen that covered his head, and it parted in the middle, allowing the muse to focus on the workstation in front of him.

"What did you see?" Bard asked.

Charles winced as the larger muse's booming voice reverberated around the tiny room. "Shh, Bard, really we must be quiet." But upon seeing Bard's face crumple, Charles relented. "Not much. There is a short blond scientist compiling reports, probably for her meeting with James. The fly is stuck in her hair, and I can't seem to get it to start again. I think it's trapped."

"What are you going to do?" Bard asked, shifting uneasily from foot to foot, causing the bicycle cart to rock back and forth.

Charles sighed. He was making a habit of sighing when trying to make the bulky, noisy Bard into a covert spy. Really, what Ardus was thinking when saddling him with Bard on this mission was anyone's guess. Not that Charles didn't like Bard—in fact, the opposite was true, for he was probably the brother Charles liked best. Bard was honest, decent, kind, and quite good in battle. In fact, Charles could point to many occasions when Bard had stood up for him against Ardus and the rest of the elitist muses. No, Bard really was a pretty great guy, just not on a covert mission

76

where silence and stealth were more important than brawn, honor, and courage.

"Well, I am going to leave the fly there. As long as no one tries to remove it from her hair, we should have a front-row seat for the meeting with Dr. James. I just need to adjust a few things so that I can get the vision and recording devices working with the flying mechanism disengaged." With that, Charles turned to the screen and began rapidly typing and manipulating the fly's design, frowning until he got the programming just right. Then, with a touch of his hand, the screen around his face closed and glowed once more.

⊰ଧ ⋈⊱

The door to the conference room opened a few moments later, and Dr. Betty entered with a stack of stapled papers in one arm and a plate with another piece of chocolate cake in the other. Charles watched from her hairdo as she carefully placed the papers in the center of the table and took a huge bite of cake. Still chewing, she moved over to the sideboard and poured herself a large mug of coffee, adding a generous amount of cream and sugar. Charles watched things from this disembodied 360-degree viewpoint and started feeling rather ill, so he stumbled to the seat beside Bard and sank onto the bench.

He turned his attention back to Dr. Betty. She had returned to the table and placed one of her stapled handouts in front of three of the chairs. She inadvertently spilled pink frosting on one of the copies and wiped it off with a finger, placing it in her mouth. She then exchanged the pink-smeared copy for her own and sat down, flipping through the pages and polishing off her coffee and cake.

She had just returned from the sideboard with a second helping when the door opened again. A short woman with black hair and a fussily tailored suit under her lab coat entered. She looked down her short stubby nose at Dr. Betty and sniffed. "Eating again, I see. How we are ever to turn a profit with you eating all the proceeds is beyond me. I could save thousands of dollars if I just fired you."

"Oh, Nikki," Dr. Betty said with a laugh. "You can't fire me! We're partners, and without my help you wouldn't even have that grant money. And I don't eat that much. I really have cut back. And besides, with Dr. James's solution, I don't have to worry about how much I eat, and once we publish our results, you won't have to worry about grants anymore. Doctors and pharmaceutical companies will be flocking to our door throwing money at you to come work for them. Don't be such a worrywart. Try the cake—it's delicious."

Dr. Nikki sniffed again and moved to the sideboard, where she poured herself a cup of black coffee and then returned to the table. "I see you got the presentation done, at least," she said as she wiped cake crumbs from her copy and flipped through the pages. "Dr. James should be here shortly, so get rid of that plate and tidy yourself up." Dr. Nikki looked pointedly at Dr. Betty's blouse, which showed signs of dribbled coffee and cake crumbs. "Here, put this on." She removed her lab coat and passed it across the table.

The coat was too narrow in the shoulders for a comfortable fit, so Dr. Betty had to stuff herself into it. "I think I left mine in the coat closet here," she said, getting up and trying to take off the too-tight lab coat. She struggled to remove the first sleeve and ended up spinning around in a circle trying to get it off her arm. The fly in her hair spun around too and threatened to dislodge due to centrifugal force. Charles grabbed Bard's arm and closed his eyes to shut out the swirling visions.

"Oh, let me help," Dr. Nikki hissed and rose to assist her colleague. The two women were struggling with the lab coat when suddenly a noise outside the door caused them both to freeze.

"Oh hello, Matilda, you are looking lovely today," Dr. James's oily voice purred, getting louder as he approached. "Are we in the usual conference room? Don't get up. I will let myself in."

Dr. Betty flipped the lab coat back into place on her shoulders and hustled to her seat, dropping her empty plate and mug out of sight on the chair next to her just as the door to the conference room opened and Dr. James entered. Charles opened his eyes and looked straight at his least favorite cousin.

James was tall and thin and athletic-looking. If you liked men who looked like they spent hours and hours at the salon and even more in their bathrooms grooming themselves, then Dr. James was very handsome indeed. His jet-black hair was scraped back from his forehead with a generous dollop of hair product, and his nails on his long fingers were buffed to a perfect shine. He wore an expensive silk suit and English wingtip shoes. In one hand was an Italian leather briefcase, and in the other was an ebony walking stick. Charles, who honestly could say that he spent as little time as possible in front of a mirror and cut his own long brown locks with one of his knives if he cut it at all, was not impressed, but the two doctors appeared to think otherwise.

Dr. Nikki approached Dr. James as soon as he arrived and shook his hand vigorously. "Welcome back, Dr. James," she said brightly. "We have been looking forward to your visit for some time now."

"Yes," Dr. Betty added. "Help yourself to some coffee and cake. They're both very fresh."

"Hello, ladies, it is very good to see you again. No thank you, Elizabeth, I just had lunch and have no desire for dessert—seeing the two of you is sweet enough for me."

James's speech was so disgusting Charles thought he might just be sick. Well, he might be sick anyway—he needed to talk to Christina about how to stabilize the vision on this thing.

Dr. James sat at the head of the table. "How are our experiments going? Obviously yours are going well, Elizabeth—you look stunning." Dr. Betty blushed at his praise and nervously looked at her icing-stained hands, forcing Charles to peer at the screen on top of his head to keep a visual on James.

"Yes, yes," Dr. Nikki interrupted a bit impatiently, "but we just aren't seeing the returns that we want on our investment in that area. I mean really, we can't do all this work for nothing. Our spreadsheet is positively on life support. We only made half a million dollars last month. How am I supposed to live on that?"

"Half a million is plenty, Dr. Nikki. It's not about the money, but the people we can help," Dr. Betty admonished lightly, looking back up and relieving the crick in Charles's neck.

"Well it might be plenty if you would stop literally eating the profits!"

"Now, ladies, I didn't come all this way to hear about your minor issues. Please, let's get down to how the experiments are going, which in the end is why I am helping you and how you are both going to turn a profit and help people." Charles seriously doubted that James cared about either one. Muses had no use for money, and helping people really didn't seem to be James's style. Charles had no idea how he'd ever passed his final examinations to be nominated for this assignment. Just what was James after, and why?

"Of course, Dr. James." Dr. Nikki turned her back on Dr. Betty and opened the presentation. "If you'll turn to page five, I have our results here in this packet I made up for you."

Dr. Betty sulked as Dr. Nikki led James through the packet. Charles had to swivel his head to keep his eyes on the packet, as Dr. Betty alternately looked at the page and gazed at Dr. James with her head tilted to one side. From what Charles could manage to read, it appeared that James supplied the scientists with the substance that they used for both Dr. Betty's weight loss and Dr. Nikki's organ preservation experiments.

"You can see in some of our experiments that by adding saline periodically, we can keep the solution viable for up to ten days. Not quite as long as we had hoped, but better than the normal shelf life, and it should give recipients of the organs time to be prepped for surgery. We are trying, Dr. James, really we are," Dr. Nikki said.

"How did you hit upon the saline idea?" James asked, sounding intrigued for the first time.

"Oh, that was me," Dr. Betty interjected, jerking her head up and causing the fly in her hair to bob up and down, which made Charles groan, close his eyes, and clutch his stomach. Something in the sudden movement dislodged the fly, and Dr. Betty swept it off her cake plate and onto the floor. "I was eating pretzels while reviewing one of the attempts, and I guess a few grains of salt must have fallen in. Worked like a charm, though."

"And it worked even better when we used a more scientific method of adding the saline." Dr. Nikki shuddered. "Sometimes my associate's methods leave much to be desired."

"Well, Dr. Elizabeth, as long as your methods result in advances in our research, all is well." James smiled. "Not quite what I was looking for, ladies, but it is an improvement. I was hoping we could get the solution to be viable for up to a month, but we will keep trying. Now, sadly, I must go as my flight leaves early tomorrow morning. I am assuming that you will be attending the annual meeting this fall?" As the two scientists assured him that they would, Charles was able to kick-start the fly's motor and raise it up to the level of the table, slightly behind James. "Good, I will see you then," James continued, unaware of the fly spying over his shoulder.

With the meeting ended, James rose to leave. He spun the lock on his briefcase and opened it, placing the handout neatly inside. Charles's eyes widened as he observed the internals of the case. He quickly waggled the fingers on his right hand, and the camera in the fly's protruding eyes rapidly clicked away, capturing everything inside, as well as the lock combination as James's closed the case with a snap of its gold clasps.

※

The two ladies returned to the table once James had left and continued to squabble about their meeting. "Really, Betty, do you have to mention your disgusting habits of eating in the lab? We need his money and his solution if we are ever going to make the kind of return on investment we talked about!"

"Nikki, you're the one who is always worried about money and returns on investment. I thought by going into research I could leave those mundane things behind. If I wanted to make money, I wouldn't have become a scientist. Scientists don't make money—we create wonderful things to improve people's lives. Like long-lasting donor organs and simple weight-loss programs. Things that change people's lives for the better. As long as we have enough to eat and a place to do our work, who needs money?"

"Seriously, Betty, money is the only thing that matters. Why work so hard if we can't have something to show for it?"

The two women went back and forth with this argument for some time, but Charles wasn't really paying attention; he was too busy thinking about the contents of James's case. For lying on top of the papers had been a very familiar green velvet roll, and the jeweled handle protruding from a pocket in the lid had to be his diamond knife. James had his lock picks and all his other tools! The implements had been stolen from Nickolas during their escape from Lady Vivian's manor the week before, and Charles desperately wanted to recover them. He had a real affection for his various tools and gadgets, and he hated the idea of them in James's hands. Now, just how was he going to get them back?

While Charles was musing about his tools, Bard was still sitting on the bench beside him concentrating on being quiet and not moving. The latter was no easy task for Bard. In general, he was a reasonably quiet man, and being married to Brigitta, who talked a lot, had given him years of practice at not talking, but sitting still was another issue. Bard loved to be moving, and in fact, he always felt rather too bulky to be indoors or confined in small places. He had to be very careful not to knock things over or to crush them inadvertently. He felt much better out in wide-open places, where he could walk, run, and move unencumbered.

The tiny trailer on the cargo bike had been fine while it was moving and he was peeking out of the periscope as the buildings had whizzed by, but now that they were standing still and the midday sun was causing it to be stifling hot inside the canvas, Bard was anxious to find some fresh air and space. Add to that, Charles was definitely acting ill, looking dazed behind his blue bubblehead, and what skin was exposed was turning a bit green as the fly's perspective disoriented the little muse.

Bard thought Charles was looking a bit like their sister-in-law Deidre, whose skin was naturally a greenish color, and he didn't want to be in the tiny confines of the trailer if Charles did get sick. He wondered if it would stay inside the bubble. Bard shook his head.

Several times he had been about to ask Charles if he was OK, but then he bit his tongue and tried to remain quiet as ordered. Bard got more and more bored, so he took out his new cell phone, for Ardus had made sure that all the muses purchased one as soon as they were freed from Dr. Vivian Montague's home. The handheld communication devices of the current era were rather clunky and unreliable compared to what the muses were used to, but they were much better than the strange wall-mounted phones that were just coming into vogue when they had been captured.

Bard had filled his phone with all sorts of adventure role-playing apps, and after checking to make sure that Brigitta hadn't texted, e-mailed, or posted on his social media wall, he opened up his latest campaign and began sending the tiny representation of himself out on a quest. Tiny Bard had almost captured the required number of potions when he was completely covered by a message box.

Bard's eyes grew large as he read the text message, and without taking his attention from the phone, he stood up abruptly, sending the tiny cart rocking furiously under his weight.

The motion snapped Charles out of his reverie, and he just had time to disconnect the control panel around his face when Bard leaped out of the cart, staring at the tiny screen clutched in his bearlike paw. Worry etched every line of his face. "Brigitta needs me. I must go," he said by way of explanation to the startled pedestrians in the alleyway, and quickly ran to the main road, inadvertently knocking those around him to the pavement as he went.

"Who was that?" Dr. Betty asked, looking out of the window.

"No idea," Dr. Nikki said, pulling aside the drapes to see out better.

"How odd," Dr. Betty said. "He must be a tourist."

"Hmm. Yes, I agree." And with that Dr. Nikki returned to her argument, not noticing the fly buzzing straight out the window and through the flap in the back of the bicycle cart in the alley.

That was definitely interesting. Charles slipped the fly back into its tin with a click. He decided that Bard could take care of himself, and he needed to follow James and get his stuff back. A maniacal smile crossed Charles's face as he slipped out of the cart and, turning the bike around, pedaled the much lighter conveyance back onto the main thoroughfare.

CHAPTER 8

M. Craubateau

—⧈⧉—

In which Fulvio finds the stable master's condition concerning

Fulvio returned to the main servants' passageway and came across one of the maids, looking harried and frantic.

"Good morning, Peggy," Fulvio said, reaching out a hand to steady the panicked girl. Peggy had been at the manor for many, many years, but as she had arrived at the age of sixteen, she was still one of the youngest maids. And having always been young for her years, many of the staff looked on her as their little sister. She had bright russet hair that framed her face in wild ringlets that no matter what she did, always escaped the neat bun under her maid's cap by the time she had finished breakfast. "What is the hurry today?"

"Good morning, Fulvio, sir. It is M. Craubateau. I took his early breakfast tray as usual. You know he likes to eat before he has to go to the stables, and the horses rise early, so he asked me years and years ago to make up his tray before all the others," she started breathlessly.

"Yes, yes," Fulvio said gently. "I am aware of M. Craubateau's habits." Fulvio's eyes twinkled. "How is the stable master this morning?"

"That's why I have come looking for you. He is not well at all. Usually he meets me at the door of his cabin and asks what took me so long, even though I am right on time. But today I knocked on the door and he didn't answer." Peggy paused a moment. "So I knocked again, and when he didn't come then I tried the door. It was unlocked. So I stuck my head in, right? And called for him. But again there was no response."

By now, Fulvio was gently leading Peggy through the servants' corridors and back toward the kitchens. It wouldn't do for Lady Vivian to overhear them through the thin paneling that separated the servants' corridors from the main rooms of the manor.

"Well, the front room was a mess, and no fire had been laid in the hearth, and there were dishes everywhere. And his dinner tray was still on the table where the night maid had left it, completely untouched. Even the cookies, and you know how much M. Craubateau likes your cookies. Well, I was really worried then. So I went in and put the tray down." Peggy's eyes were very round at this point. "He was in bed in his riding jacket!"

Fulvio knew that the fastidious M. Craubateau would never have gone to bed fully clothed and was starting to worry a little himself. Peggy and Fulvio quickened their steps, and Fulvio opened the sliding panel to the main kitchens, ushering Peggy inside. She didn't seem to even notice their surroundings as she continued. "He was really cold when I touched his hand and didn't respond even when I shook him! I was so scared I ran all the way back here to find you."

Fulvio called across the kitchens in his booming voice, "Carole, grab the first aid basket and some food. Zac, you are in charge until I return." Zac looked faintly sick at the idea of being in charge, but one of the motherly sous chefs reassured him that she would help him out.

The efficient Carole had collected the first aid basket and a second basket of food before Fulvio had even retrieved his coat, and the pair followed Peggy out of the kitchens. Peggy was desperate to break into a run, but the two portly chefs could not keep up with that pace, so she ran forward and back like an overexcited spaniel, urging Fulvio and Carole to hasten.

Behind the stables and through a patch of woods was the tiny cottage where the stable master lived. Most of the servants had rooms in either the basement or the attic of the manor, but both the chauffeur, who lived above the garage, and the stable master did not. The little cottage had a small fenced pasture behind it, and the stable master's personal stallion, Curieux, was standing by the gate, looking at the trio expectantly.

"I doubt that the stable master has been able to care for his horse if he has been ill," Carole said. "Why don't you go see if you can find him some feed and fresh water, Peggy, while Fulvio and I see to M. Craubateau?"

Relieved, Peggy headed toward the paddock and searched for a bucket in the little lean-to beside the gate.

"I didn't want her to have to go back into the cabin. From her description, I am not sure if the stable master is still with us," Carole said quietly to Fulvio.

Fulvio pushed open the door and found the usually spartan cottage to be unkempt. "M. Craubateau? It is Fulvio and Carole. May we come in?"

But there was no answer, so Fulvio and Carole quietly entered the cottage. It only consisted of two rooms; the main served the function of both living room and a kitchen and pantry. In the back of the room was a door that led to the stable master's bedroom. Fulvio knocked and then, since there was no answer, opened the door. The bed was empty and the sheets and pillows in disarray.

"M. Craubateau?" Fulvio called louder and entered the room. A quick search found that the stable master had fallen out of the bed and lay wedged between the mattress and the wall on the far side. A quick check of his wrist revealed that M. Craubateau was still alive, though his pulse was slow and weak. "Help me, Carole," Fulvio murmured.

Together, Fulvio and Carole were able to return the stable master to his bed. The poor man was barely conscious, and his gray skin was even more wrinkled and shrunken than it had been the week before. Fulvio stared at the stable master in shock. For as long as he had been at the manor, no one had aged a day, nor had any of the staff been ill beyond small cuts and bruises. It was no wonder that Peggy was so overwrought at seeing M. Craubateau's condition.

Fulvio attempted to get a few sips of broth into the stable master's quivering mouth while Carole buzzed around the cottage setting it to rights. Before long, a cheerful fire was going in the grate, and everything was back to its usual impeccable order.

Peggy knocked timidly at the door. "I have finished caring for the horse, Chef Fulvio," she said. "How is M. Craubateau?"

"He is very ill, but still with us, thank goodness," Carole said. "No need to worry."

"I am so relieved." Peggy's shoulders relaxed. "Do you need me to stay and nurse him? I would be happy to."

"That would wonderful, my dear. I was so worried that he would be here alone when Fulvio and I had to return to our duties. I will make sure your regular chores are done for you. If anything changes, send the chauffeur to the kitchens, as he is closest. I will make sure that a tray is sent to you at lunchtime." Carole smiled fondly at the diminutive maid and slipped back into M. Craubateau's bedroom to bring Fulvio up to speed.

⊰⊱

Long after dinner had been cleared up and the rest of the kitchen staff had retired for the evening, Carole knocked on Fulvio's office door. "Come in," was the response. "Ah, Carole, did you get a chance to check on Peggy and M. Craubateau?" Fulvio welcomed Carole in and ushered her to her usual chair in his office. "I was just going to have a cup of tea before bedtime. Would you like one?" He indicated the steaming pot on his desk.

"That would be lovely, Fulvio," Carole responded, sighing as she sank into the chair. "I did just come from the cottage. M. Craubateau seems to be much better. He is sitting up in bed and was quite chatty."

Fulvio raised an eyebrow as he passed Carole her teacup. "Chatty? That isn't usually a word I would use to describe the stable master. Bossy perhaps, but not chatty. He must really not be feeling well."

"Well, he isn't making a lot of sense, but he is definitely chatting away. I am rather worried, as I think his mind is wandering. He was oscillating between subjects. First, he was very upset that all of the horses are missing and raving about how he thought that the footmen had stolen them. He was very irate, almost to the point where I was worrying about Peggy's safety, when suddenly he changed subjects and acted like we were all having a nice tea and chat about his horse, Curieux. He was telling me how proud he was that his horse had sired a little foal named Blaze and how she was the first baby horse to be born on the property in nearly one hundred years. Peggy told me that he has been doing that all afternoon." Carole looked concerned.

Fulvio poured himself a second cup, adding a large spoonful of honey. He stirred the tea thoughtfully. "I have been thinking about M. Craubateau all day and observing the other staff members as well. Have you noticed that we all seem to be aging again? There are many more gray hairs in my beard than there were before, and even Zac is showing signs of growing some blond stubble."

Carole sighed. "When Zac and I came here, I noticed that we stopped aging almost immediately. I no longer had to cut my hair or my nails. The change was even more pronounced in Zac. I don't think I ever told you, but he was suffering from a rapidly progressing degenerative disease at the time. The doctors had told me that the prognosis for his illness was very grave, but almost as soon as we arrived the progression of the disease stopped. Several times over the years I have thought of leaving, but knowing that this place somehow kept Zac's illness at bay, I always decided to stay."

"I am very glad that you did." Fulvio looked a little taken aback. He had known when he hired Carole that her son was ill—the scientist who had recommended her to him had told him so. But he had not known how seriously sick the boy had been. "You are my right hand, Carole, and I don't know how I would do things around here without you." Fulvio cleared his throat. "But about Zac—have you noticed if he is getting sicker again?"

"I have been so busy, I haven't, but I will just as soon as we finish here." Carole rose to her feet and brushed the crumbs from the tea cake off her apron. "Oh, and one more thing about M. Craubateau. I stopped by the stables on my way back just to see if he was right, and sure enough, all of Lady Vivian's horses are missing, even tiny Blaze. And more than that, all of their tack and saddles are missing as well. There is no sign of a break-in. It is as if they were all taken out for a ride and never returned. How very odd. Do you think we should have one of the men in the kitchens take over for Peggy? I worry that even in his weakened state, M. Craubateau might harm her when he is in one of those rages."

"I think that would be a good idea, Carole," Fulvio said, nodding his agreement. "Whom would you suggest?"

But Fulvio never got to hear who Carole would suggest, for at that moment, a wood-splintering crash came from the kitchens.

⊰⊱

Fulvio sprang to his feet, upsetting his teacup in the process, and dashed to the door. It was hard to see into the darkened kitchens, but by the light of the remaining coals in the roasting fires, he was just able to discern a large, lumbering shadow running toward the now long abandoned food stations. Fulvio's heart sank.

The captured guard had escaped.

Without thinking, Fulvio chased after him, catching up to the guard just as he reached the first station. The guard ignored Fulvio completely and started grabbing the remaining vials, rapidly drinking their contents. Once drained, he would smash the vials on the ground and then reach for the next. "Where is it?" he kept exclaiming as he moved from station to station, drinking and smashing as he went. "Where is it?" The desperation in his voice getting louder and louder.

Once he had destroyed all of the vials in the last station, he turned unsteadily to face Fulvio. "Where have you taken them?" he demanded, advancing on the chef. The guard grabbed Fulvio by the shoulders and shook him violently, slamming him against the wall. With his face just an inch from Fulvio's and his teeth bared, the guard asked one last time: "What have you done with the essence?"

Fulvio gasped for air. The combination of the guard's thumbs pressing into his windpipe and the foul stench of his mushroom-solution breath made speech impossible. The guard's thumbs tightened, and Fulvio felt the edges of his vision blacken, but then there was a mighty clang and the guard immediately released him and slumped to the floor.

There, standing on the other side of the inert guard's body, stood Carole, a large cast-iron frying pan still reverberating in her hands.

CHAPTER 9

SMASHING

⊰⧉⊱

In which Bard does what Bard does best

Sarah and Nickolas tore out of Sarah's room and down the stairs just as Grandma Vera opened the door. There on the stoop stood Brigitta, looking exactly as she had when they had first met her in Great-Aunt Vivian's gardens. She was wearing Grecian robes tied with gold cords at her waist and twined in her long red hair. Like Audiva, her sister, Brigitta had blue tanzanite fibulae holding her robes together at the shoulders, and in her hands she carried her golden Celtic harp.

Grandma Vera was just saying, "Why, Ms. Telyn, this is a surprise. Welcome! Please come in and make yourself at home." Grandma Vera was way too polite to comment on her lawyer's rather odd clothing, but Sarah could see the confusion between her grandmother's brows.

"Brigitta!" Sarah exclaimed, running down the last few steps and into Brigitta's waiting arms. Then looking behind the beautiful muse, she added, "We were expecting Charles. Is he coming too?"

"No, little one." Brigitta smiled and gave Sarah another hug. "Ardus asked Bard and me to keep a lookout over you three. Charles is on another assignment in Europe, and actually, Bard is with him too, so you just get me tonight. I hope you aren't too disappointed."

"Oh no," Sarah said. "I am very happy that you could come. We have so much to tell you. But first I need to introduce you to our grandmother."

"We have already met," Grandma Vera said, looking quizzically at Brigitta and Sarah. "But how do you know her? Wait, this looks like it may be a long story. Let's move into the kitchen and get out some cookies and milk."

They all followed Grandma Vera into the large country kitchen and in short order were seated around the breakfast island with chocolate chip cookies and tall glasses of milk. Brigitta graciously declined but sat between the two children and across from Grandma Vera.

Once they were all settled, Sarah quickly brought Grandma Vera up to date about how they had met the muses at Great-Aunt Vivian's manor and how they had helped them return home.

Nickolas noticed Sarah had left out a great number of details in her story. To hear Sarah tell it, it sounded like they had met Audiva, Brigitta, and the rest at a tea party in Great-Aunt Vivian's drawing room and just walked out the door with them afterward to be put on a plane and head home! Sarah didn't exactly lie to Grandma Vera, but she definitely painted a much more benevolent picture of the facts.

Grandma Vera in turn explained that it had been Brigitta who had represented them at the custody hearing in Denver, and it was her testimony that had returned Nickolas and Sarah, as well as Simon, into her keeping.

"Now, Sarah, please tell me why you called me this evening. How can I help you?" Brigitta asked once the introductions and explanations had been made.

"It's Simon." Sarah turned somber as she quickly explained bringing Simon to the hospital and about the moving bowtie cells in the cookie crumbs and their blood. Sarah paused and looked expectantly at Brigitta.

Brigitta digested Sarah's rapid-fire summary, smiling to herself as she thought that Sarah sounded very much like the creative musicians she usually worked with. "Let me see if I understand. There is something in the food at Vivian's manor that is making Simon sick?"

"Well," Nickolas chimed in, "it is something in the food that kept Simon from growing up. Actually, it kept everyone at the manor from getting older, even us. For Sarah and me it isn't a problem because we were only at the manor for a few weeks. But for Simon, who was at Great-Aunt Vivian's for years, it seems that the bowtie things are dying off, causing his cells to try to quickly age him up fifty years, which isn't working because he is growing too fast. Dr. Lucy thinks she can slow Simon's body down and reduce the rate which it is killing off the bowtie things but she can't do it forever."

"Can I see these bowtie things?" Brigitta asked.

"Maybe." Nickolas looked sheepish. "I ate all the cookies, but the same things are in the mushroom solution I made, and I still have some of that. Let's go to my workshop. Just let me grab the solution from Sarah's room."

A few moments later, Nickolas led the way out of the back door of the kitchen and across the pasture to his workshop. As they went, Brigitta stopped only for a moment to pat little Blaze and her mother, Moonstone, on the nose as they passed their fence.

Grandma Vera trailed behind, her mind in a whirl about what she had just heard. Sarah and Nickolas had told her next to nothing about their time at her sister Vivian's home, and she was beginning to suspect that a great deal more had happened there than she knew about. She was pretty sure that she would be having a word or two privately with Ms. Telyn before the night was over.

◆◄╡╞►

They arrived at his workroom, where Nickolas quickly prepared another slide of the mushroom solution, pocketing the rest, and clipped the slide under the lens of the microscope. He got the focus centered on one of the red bowties and passed the eyepiece to Brigitta.

She bent over the microscope, holding her long red hair out of the way with one hand. Her green eyes widened as she looked through the lens, and her body stiffened for just a moment before she composed herself. "I see," she said, more to herself than to the children, as she drew back.

"The ones in the food looked just like this only much more densely packed, and they were purple," Nickolas said. "Have you seen things like this before?"

Brigitta took a long time to answer; her thoughts were very far away. "I have," she said carefully, "a long time ago, when I was in school. They are tiny programmable creatures called programmable android microbiotics, or PAMs, sometimes referred to as microbios. Our scientists use them to cure disease or create robotics. I have never heard of healthy people taking them for prolonged periods of time, however."

"Dr. Lucy said that they were in every cell of Simon's body—in his tissues, in his blood, even in his tears," Nickolas said. "It would be really cool, if they weren't what was making him sick."

Sarah rolled her eyes. "Yeah, lots of things would be really cool if people didn't use them to harm others."

"Actually, Sarah, I think you have the right of it," Brigitta said gently. "Everything can be used for good and for evil. The thing itself is not good or evil, but how it is used. The microbios are not an evil invention; in fact, they have saved millions of lives. But it looks like they can be used with malicious intent as well. But more importantly, we need to figure out how to safely extract them from Simon."

⊶⊰⊱⊷

Shortly thereafter, Brigitta, Grandma Vera, and the children were all back in the living room and comfortably seated on the soft leather couches Sarah's mother had picked out years ago when the children were little. They were well worn and scuffed from many movie nights, pillow fights, reading sessions, and long afternoon naps. The slightly battered look of the room was what made it homey, and Sarah would have had it no other way.

"So what do we know about these minibots?" she asked once they were all settled.

"Microbios, Sarah, really." Nickolas rolled his eyes.

"Does it matter what they're called?" Sarah shot back. "What matters is that we can get rid of them." She stuck her tongue out at Nickolas behind Grandma Vera's back.

"I wonder if we know of anyone else who stopped eating the food at your Great-Aunt Vivian's and what side effects they experienced. It would be helpful to know what we are facing," Brigitta mused.

"We're the only ones we know of who ever left. Everyone else seemed to be there forever," Nickolas said. "Some of her servants had been there for decades. I think Mr. Fairchild had been there for over a hundred years!"

"I know Mr. Fairchild has been there for a hundred years," Brigitta said with a laugh. "I was there for a hundred years too, remember? Hmm, the only people who ever left the manor were your great-grandfather and his baby. I know that your great-grandfather ate the food for years. I wonder what happened to him."

Grandma Vera, who had been up to this time just observing and saying little, said, "When I was researching my father years ago, after Vivian contacted me, I found out that he had worked at Chicago University for about four years in the mid-1940s. He died shortly after that, but the lawyers didn't provide many details." She then turned to Sarah and added, "I gave a copy of the reports to your father at the time. I wonder if he kept them."

"I doubt Dad kept copies—he never keeps anything—but I bet Mom sure did," Sarah said, jumping up from her seat. "Let me go check her file cabinet." And Sarah dashed from the room toward her mother's office. She returned shortly with a triumphant air, waving a blue folder over her head. A neat label on it identified it as Dr. Christopher Montague, from Mom Vera.

Sarah gave the folder to her grandmother and sat down next to her. Grandma Vera opened the folder, revealing several pages of paper on a lawyer's letterhead.

WILLIAM STEWART, ESQ.

STEWART & STEWART, ATTORNEYS AT LAW

1900 WEST MAIN STREET

FLAT FALLS, MICHIGAN 44555

MAY 5, 2002

DEAR MS. MCGUIRE:

IN RESPONSE TO YOUR REQUEST THAT WE CONDUCT AN INVESTIGATION INTO THE MATTER OF YOUR ADOPTION IN FEBRUARY 1944, WE HAVE DISCOVERED THE FOLLOWING:

YOUR NATURAL BIRTH PARENTS WERE DR. CHRISTOPHER MONTAGUE AND VICTORIA MONTAGUE, NÉE ANDREWS, NOW BOTH DECEASED. THEY WERE MARRIED IN SYDNEY, AUSTRALIA, WHEN YOUR FATHER WAS TWENTY-ONE AND YOUR MOTHER WAS SEVENTEEN.

YOU HAVE A SISTER, A VIVIAN MONTAGUE, WHO WAS BORN ABOUT A YEAR AFTER THEY WERE MARRIED.

VERY LITTLE INFORMATION WAS AVAILABLE ON YOUR MOTHER EXCEPT THAT SHE WAS BORN IN SYDNEY, AUSTRALIA, AND DIED ON THE DATE OF YOUR BIRTH.

WE WERE ABLE TO DETERMINE A BIT MORE ABOUT YOUR FATHER:

- DR. MONTAGUE WORKED AT THE UNIVERSITY OF SYDNEY FOR MANY YEARS AS A PROFESSOR OF CHEMISTRY AND CEL-LULAR BIOLOGY.
- HE WAS GRANTED THE TITLE OF BARONET IN 1919, ALTHOUGH HE RARELY USED HIS TITLE.
- IN 1943 HE TRANSFERRED TO CHICAGO UNIVERSITY AS A FULL PROFESSOR OF GENETICS AND CELLULAR BIOLOGY.
- HE DIED IN CHICAGO IN 1948 (SEE ATTACHED DEATH CERTIFICATE).
- HE DID NOT HAVE A KNOWN WILL AT THE TIME OF HIS DEATH, AND ALL OF HIS PROPERTY WAS GIVEN TO THE UNIVERSITY AS NO LIVING KIN CAME FORWARD.

BY LAW, AS HIS CHILD, YOU ARE ENTITLED TO HIS EFFECTS, IF ANY STILL EXIST. I WOULD RECOMMEND GOING TO CHICAGO UNIVERSITY AND ASKING IF ANYTHING HAS BEEN RETAINED IN THEIR ARCHIVES.

WE HAVE ATTACHED DOCUMENTATION SUPPORTING OUR RESEARCH, WHICH I HOPE WILL BE HELPFUL TO YOU.

SINCERELY,
WM. STEWART, ESQ.

ATTACHMENTS:

BIRTH RECORDS FOR:
CHRISTOPHER MONTAGUE
VICTORIA ANDREWS
VIVIAN MONTAGUE
VERA MONTAGUE

BAPTISMAL RECORDS FOR:
VIVIAN MONTAGUE
VERA MONTAGUE

MARRIAGE BANNS POSTED FOR:
CHRISTOPHER MONTAGUE AND VICTORIA ANDREWS

DEATH CERTIFICATES FOR:
DR. CHRISTOPHER MONTAGUE—CHICAGO, ILLINOIS
LADY VICTORIA MONTAGUE—SYDNEY, AUSTRALIA

ADOPTION PAPERS FOR:
VERA (MONTAGUE) ALLEN

The remaining papers in the file consisted of old copies of birth certificates and church records, which Sarah and Brigitta pored over curiously. Nickolas, after a cursory glance at the pages, soon grew bored with the old, crumbling papers and wandered off into the kitchen in search of more cookies and milk. He stopped for a moment at the table, eyeing Brigitta's harp.

"Didn't it seem odd to you that Vivian was so old?" Sarah asked, pausing over Vivian's baptismal record from 1872.

Grandma Vera looked up from the marriage banns. "Honestly, Sarah, I don't think I gave it much thought. I was grieving your grandpa Patrick at the time and really was just looking to see if what Vivian was saying in her letters was true. I don't even remember all of these documents being included with the letter. I must have been quite distracted, and I certainly didn't look at them closely enough to realize how old everyone was. In fact, how on earth did my mother give birth to me? She must have been around seventy at the time!"

"Actually, she was closer to ninety," Sarah said. "But time was funny at Great-Aunt Vivian's. I think the food kept people from aging, which is why Simon looks six when he is really fifty and Great-Aunt Vivian looks twenty-five when she is"—Sarah paused to look at Great-Aunt Vivian's birth certificate—"like a hundred and forty years old. Yikes, I knew she was old, but not that old. How bizarre!"

"She is a hundred and forty years old? How is that possible?" Grandma Vera looked at Brigitta.

"I am not sure, but from what we were able to gather at the manor, your sister, Vivian, has been working on the problem of aging for a very long time, and her experiments with various substances she grew on the grounds of her manor and a substance that she extracted from Simon led to her discovery of the food, which apparently contained microbios. The microbios must do something to the cells of the person who ingests them that keeps their cells from aging. Once the subject stops taking the microbios, I would guess that the effects would reverse."

Sarah was rereading the lawyer's letter while Grandma Vera and Brigitta were talking. She interrupted them and read aloud the next to last paragraph: "'By law, as his child, you are entitled to his effects, if any still exist.' I wonder if the university has anything. It would be interesting to find out why he left Montague Manor and why he brought you to the Allens."

"It would be interesting," Grandma Vera agreed. "Perhaps a trip to Chicago is in order." She paused and looked thoughtful before adding, "But who would take care of the ranch while I was away?"

"Bard and I would be happy to do that for you," Brigitta volunteered. "You could have Mr. Drysdale look in as well. Let me contact Bard; it won't take him long to get here." Brigitta reached for her cell phone.

While Brigitta was texting Bard, Sarah and Grandma Vera had a quick conversation in hushed tones. "Sarah, I hardly know Brigitta. There are lots of children here at camp. I don't feel comfortable leaving them in the care of a stranger."

"Brigitta is one of the people who rescued us from Great-Aunt Vivian and brought us home. Surely we can trust her. The muses have already shown that they care about us and are willing to protect us. I called Brigitta to come help us because I think she is the only person who can save Simon. Please, Grandma! Your father was a scientist who worked on the very things that we are trying to fix. His papers could be invaluable to Brigitta and Dr. Lucy, and they might even save Simon's life. It is only for a couple of days, and you could leave Nickolas here to keep an eye on things too." It was a sign of how desperate Sarah was to go herself that she offered up the plum job of being in charge to her absentminded older brother. She could tell that Grandma Vera was not convinced.

"What is Bard like?" Grandma Vera asked, still thinking that leaving the ranch to relative strangers even for a day was not a good idea.

Sarah tried to be diplomatic. "Bard is Brigitta's husband. He is really big, but he's really nice too. No one would get past him to harm the campers, and he wouldn't harm a fly. You are really going to like him. He has got a great…personality," Sarah said earnestly. "Brigitta can tell you!" she added as the muse returned to the couch.

"Tell you what?" Brigitta asked.

"Tell Grandma Vera about Bard and why she should let him guard the campers while we go to Chicago University," Sarah explained.

"Hmm. I think it might help if I told you about how I first met Bard." The beautiful muse smiled. "But I warn you, the tale does not reflect well on myself!

"I was very young and in my second or third year of school. Bard was in my grade, but either he wasn't in any of my classes or I hadn't noticed him yet. Back then, I had this horrible habit of telling off the bullies at school, even if they were bigger and older than I was. As I am sure you have noticed, I love to debate and even more I love to win my debates, so sometimes I get a bit passionate about winning.

"The day I met Bard, I came across three of the biggest bullies in the school picking on a little first year girl at recess. You have met one of them, Sarah, at your Great-Aunt Vivian's. James was one of the three."

"Oh, he isn't very nice. You went to school with him? Poor you," Sarah said.

"Who is James?" Grandma Vera asked, narrowing her eyes suspiciously.

"No one to worry about, Grandma Vera," Sarah said quickly. "Please continue the story, Brigitta."

"Well, the three bullies were being really mean to the little first year, taking her doll away from her and threatening to hurt it. Quick as quick, I grabbed the doll and returned it to the little girl, and before the bullies could figure out what happened, I started to shout, taunting them so they paid attention to me while the little girl ran away.

"But then I realized that they were all bigger than me too, and they were not best pleased with some of the rather insulting things that I had said about their lack of brain capacity. They started to move in to attack me. Of course, I quickly decided that hanging around wasn't a very good idea, so I ran. Fortunately, because they were bigger than me, they were also slower getting off the start, so I had a bit of a lead before they figured out that I was running. But every time I looked over my shoulder I could see that they were gaining on me. So I looked ahead for a hiding spot, and miraculously, there in front of me, was this huge mountain of a kid with flame-red hair even brighter than my own."

"That must have been Bard," Sarah whispered to her grandmother. "Continue!"

Brigitta smiled again and went on. "Yes, it was Bard. He was just sitting there, on the ground, with a butterfly resting on his hand. He was looking at the butterfly with this rapt look of delight on his face and carefully not moving so he wouldn't frighten it. So I ran and hid behind him, causing the butterfly to fly away.

"Bard looked up to see what had happened to startle the butterfly, and he saw my three pursuers rapidly approaching and figured out what was going on. He stood up to his full height, which was much taller and broader than the three bullies. 'Can I help you?' he asked them.

"They skidded to a stop a few feet in front of us. Two of them looked up at Bard in awe and stepped back a pace, but James jutted out his chin and said, 'Hand her over, Bard. She means nothing to you, and we have something to settle with her.'

"Bard said, 'You might as well settle it with me then, because she and I are on the same team.' James knew Bard was slated to be one of the Muses of War and that no one at the school had beaten him in any of the combat sports, so he slunk away with his friends. They never bothered me again. And from that point on, Bard followed me around like a huge overprotective Newfoundland dog. He decided he was on my 'team,' and no matter what I said or thought would take him off of it. I finally stopped trying a few years later. Bard kept the bullies away, and you just can't help but like someone who is that kind and loves you that much. Once I stopped thinking boys had cooties, I fell in love with him too.

"I can guarantee that he will protect your campers with his last breath, Vera. And he will be kind and gentle with them too."

"Well, I agree that my father may have information in his papers that might be crucial to saving Simon. But I will have to meet and approve of this Bard person before I say yes, understood?"

But Sarah wasn't listening to Grandma Vera; she had just caught sight of Sparks, who was looking intently toward the kitchen. When she looked where Sparks was looking, she caught sight of Nickolas, cookie crumbs on his chin and a milk moustache on his upper lip, and in his hands was Brigitta's harp. He was absently picking out a tune with the instrument precariously balanced on his knee at an odd angle. Sarah was just about ready to admonish him to be careful with the priceless harp, when a huge, wood-splintering crash came from the foyer along with the shouted bellow of *"Brigitta!"* followed by the crunching sound of the huge oak double doors falling from their hinges onto the stone tiles below.

Bard had arrived.

⚜

Brigitta's harp dropped from Nickolas's hands and bounced unharmed to the floor as he rose to face the noise in the foyer. Unnoticed by anyone but Brigitta, and possibly Sparks, Charles's ring on Nickolas's left thumb stopped glowing silver, no longer illuminated by the music of the harp.

CHAPTER 10

BEHIND THE PANELING

⊰⊱

In which we hear some of Great-Aunt Vivian's plans

Carole had helped Fulvio return the comatose guard to the copper pot room. The instant the guard had been knocked unconscious, he had returned to his potato form again before he even hit the floor. It appeared that the guard had used one of the smaller pans to smash open the ancient door, which had not been intended to keep anything but crockery from escaping the room's confines.

"So where are the fourth vials?" Carole asked. "I know that Lady Vivian collected them several days ago, but do you know what she has done with them?"

"She took them to her office that night, but what she did with them after that I have no idea." Fulvio looked down at the unconscious guard thoughtfully. "You know, he actually hasn't been very difficult to take care of until now. Do you think if we provided him with the fourth solution he would be calm again?"

"I don't know." Carole looked shocked that Fulvio had asked her. Up until a moment ago she hadn't an inkling that Fulvio had one of Lady Vivian's guards locked up in the pot room. In fact, it had been several days since she had seen any of the guards or footmen around the manor at all.

But Fulvio didn't seem to hear her. "The other solutions seem to make him sleepy. Maybe the fourth solution is the same." Fulvio ran a hand through his mussed hair. "Carole, do you think you can handle the breakfast rush on your own? I would like to try the last solution on the guard, and I want to see if I can get into Lady Vivian's office before she arrives for the morning. That is the last place I saw the vials. Perhaps they are still there."

"Of course I can handle the kitchens, but do you think it is wise to sneak into Lady Vivian's affairs? You know how volatile she has been lately."

Fulvio sighed sadly. "Normally, Carole, I would be the first person to recommend letting the sleeping dragon lie, but unfortunately, I don't think that I have any choice."

With that, he finished screwing the new lock into place and returned the tool bag to its nook in the hallway.

"I will be back in an hour, and I promise not to do anything foolish."

Carole smiled after him. Fulvio was not one to do anything rash, she knew, but then she would have never thought he would be holding a prisoner in the pot room, either. Perhaps, after knowing the man nearly fifty years, there were still some mysteries about Fulvio that she had yet to learn.

⊰⊱

Shortly thereafter, Fulvio replaced his white chef uniform with a more somber-colored shirt and slipped silently through the servants' passageways toward Lady Vivian's office. He had rarely used this particular corridor, and if the layer of dust and lack of footprints were any indication, none of the other maids and under butlers had used it either. He would just quickly sneak into her rooms, grab a vial, and sneak out. None would be the wiser. Lady Vivian had been so distraught the night of the explosion she would not have counted the vials, and she would probably not miss just one.

But his heart sank as he approached the sliding panel that led to his goal, for the unmistakable high girly voice of Lady Vivian came from behind it.

"Louis," she said, "I just got a letter from Dr. James. He is moving up his visit. Originally he thought he would come in a few weeks, but his latest letter says that he will be here in just a few days. He's requesting we return to him a small number of gems that he had entrusted into my keeping. I need you to retrieve them from my safe and secure them here so I can get them for Dr. James at a moment's notice."

"Of course, Lady Vivian," Louis's rodentine voice responded. "Which gems would these be?"

"They are fourteen round tanzanites that I have in a blue silk pouch. They are quite large, and you should have no trouble finding them. I want you to put them somewhere where they won't be easily discovered. They are worth more than either you or me to Dr. James. To confess, Louis, I have been very foolish. Dr. James is most displeased with me, and I need to do everything that I can to rebuild his trust. The night the lab was destroyed, several things disrupted the work we were doing here for Dr. James, and he expects me to set that to rights before he arrives. I need you to help me accomplish that, and we have very little time."

Fulvio could almost see in his mind's eye Louis's tiny sunken chest puffing out with pride. The man positively lived for power, and here Lady Vivian was even giving him some over her. Lady Vivian must be very scared of Dr. James indeed for her to do such a thing.

"He was actually quite angry in his letter, Louis. In fact, the tone was one that I have never heard from him. He is threatening to withdraw his support for my research, and with the destruction of the lab, I need his grants more than ever. I was just talking with the architects, and the design bill alone is more than the annuity my father left me. If the Crown ever caught on that my father died without a male heir, we would be ruined, and the manor would have to be sold. This must not happen, because many of the things that Dr. James had asked that I do for him are protected on these grounds, so I must make sure that I retain ownership of the manor."

"I am most sorry, Lady Vivian," Louis said a trifle insincerely. "How can I be of service?"

"Well, for starters, I need you to start taking care of Mr. Benjamin and the other prisoners down in the dungeons."

Fulvio nearly fell over as he realized that Mr. Benjamin really was in the dungeons. He hadn't really believed that the rumor Carole had told him in the greenhouses could be true. He decided that he would get down there as soon as possible to see if he could help Mr. Benjamin in any way.

Fulvio pushed away his thoughts about Mr. Benjamin and turned his attention back to Lady Vivian. She had changed subjects again, and Fulvio hoped he hadn't missed anything important.

"...and speaking of the guards, they seem to be suffering from some sort of illness. They appear to think that they need the essence to cure whatever ails them, but I am reluctant to give it to them. I have very little left, and until we can rebuild the labs and obtain another source, we will have to be on very tight rations."

"If I may be so bold, my lady, I think you should give it to them."

"Whatever for?" Vivian said. "They are just servants, and if I don't find a way to restart my research soon, they will be out of a job anyway."

"Yes, but you need the guards," Louis said imploringly. "Now that the servants are no longer eating your scientific foods, they will start dying. It won't take them long to figure out why they are doing so, and you will have anarchy on your hands. Without the guards to protect you, I fear for your safety and the safety of your most loyal supporters. They may be just servants, but they far outnumber us, and people do desperate things when they are desperate."

"I hardly worry about that, Louis. Most of the staff have worked with me for years and are unwaveringly loyal, like yourself. And besides, they are still eating the synthetic foods, just without the essence. That will keep them healthy."

But they weren't eating the synthetic food, and now they couldn't, Fulvio realized. The guard had drunk and smashed all of their remaining supplies just a few hours before. Fear gripped Fulvio for a second, and it deepened at Lady Vivian's next words.

"And if they aren't eating the synthetic food, they will die in a matter of days or at most weeks—the withdrawal is very rapid. We have seen it before with servants who have left the manor for one reason or another. Which is why I am not worried at all about the head butler leaving."

"The head butler left?" Louis asked. This piece of news had obviously not yet reached his ears.

"Yes, yes," Vivian said. "He left a while ago, surely I told you. Never mind. He got some crazy offer from a publisher in New York for those horrible romance novels he has been scribbling away on for years. They are a load of rubbish, but I guess there are people who read things like that. So off he went, with no notice whatsoever. But since he didn't take a supply of the food with him, he might not even reach New York."

Fulvio was swallowing his panic. The fatigue they all had been feeling, the pains in his joints, the added gray in his hair, M. Craubateau's illness—were these all related to the withdrawal from the food? Would Carole, Zac, Peggy, and everyone else he loved and cared for in the kitchens be dead within a fortnight? What could he do? He was still working on this problem when Lady Vivian caught his attention by saying his name.

"I am thinking of promoting Fulvio to head butler. He has done well organizing the kitchens over the years, and I have never had a single complaint with his service or his loyalty. And he has that lovely way of ignoring anything he finds unpleasant, so he has never questioned too closely what I am doing. I rather like that in him. Plus, he cares so much about those who work for him, so he would be so very easy to control if he ever got out of line. What do you think, Louis?"

"As you wish, Lady Vivian. I know that the head butler usually reports directly to you, but as you are so busy these days, why don't you let him report to me. I will make sure that he does everything you wish. That will relieve you of one or two worries," Louis said.

Fulvio's despair was rapidly turning to anger. Louis was a bully, as had been the head butler, and the head butler before him, and Fulvio's own father who had been head butler before *him*. Fulvio had had enough of being bullied when he was a child and had no intention of letting anyone bully him ever again, and most certainly not Louis.

But then the full effect of her words hit him. Lady Vivian wanted him to fill his abusive father's shoes. And Fulvio had neither the desire nor the aptitude to do so. Besides, he had no time. In fact, no one at the manor had time.

Fulvio retraced his steps to the kitchens in a daze. So many things were swirling around in his head he could hardly keep his thoughts straight. Lady Vivian was thinking of promoting him to head butler. Why on earth would he want to be head butler? Being responsible for everything in the manor, the servants, the footmen, the kitchen staff, the valets and lady's maids, as well as keeping all the furniture, artwork, dishes, clothing, carpets, chandeliers, and linen clean, dust free, polished, and in good repair, to say nothing of keeping the doors from squeaking, the floors from creaking, the roof from leaking, and the servants from squabbling. The list went on and on. In fact, the only thing Fulvio felt confident of about the head butler's job was that he wanted no part of it.

But then, he had bigger problems. The staff responsible for the cooking, cleaning, de-leaking, de-squeaking, and de-creaking were all going to die in a matter of days unless Fulvio found a way to get them the synthetic food, but the rogue guard had eaten, smashed, or destroyed all of it just a few hours prior. His thoughts turned to M. Craubateau. If he was any indication, then they had even less time until the staff would have to take to their beds. Would Vivian give him more solutions? Did she even have any more now that the lab had been destroyed?

But then Fulvio stopped in his tracks. Mr. Benjamin! The one scientist who knew everything about Lady Vivian's experiments was Mr. Benjamin, and now Fulvio knew exactly where Mr. Benjamin was.

Fulvio ran the last few corridors to the kitchens and immediately pulled Carole into his office. "Carole, we have a problem."

"Only one?" Carole asked, raising an eyebrow.

Fulvio laughed. "All right, we have lots of problems. But I think I know a way to at least give us some more time to solve them. Come with me to the dungeons."

CHAPTER 11

CHICAGO UNIVERSITY

In which we are introduced to Dr. Montague's best friend

B y the time Sarah and Nickolas arrived in the foyer with Grandma Vera on their heels, Brigitta was already taking charge of the situation. With her hands on her hips, she stared down her husband, her eyes flashing murderously at him.

Bard stood in the splintered ruins of what used to be Sarah's front door, filling the space inside the double door frame with his broad form, his flame-red hair clashing magnificently with his orange Irish warrior's robes. His thick calves were buckled in leather-strapped boots, exposing only his enormous kneecaps between them and the tabs of his leather skirt. Beneath the leather armor, he wore a shockingly orange undertunic with a plaid length of fabric wrapped over his massive shoulders and tucked into his belt. Also hanging from his wide leather belt was his ginormous battle-ax, on which lightly rested one of his tanned and meaty hands. On one finger was a huge emerald ring that exactly matched in color, if not in form, the delicate emerald ring on Brigitta's left hand. Sarah thought it pretty amazing that the slight Muse of Music could stare down the huge warrior, but that was exactly what Brigitta was doing.

"Care to explain yourself?" Brigitta asked in a deceptively gentle voice.

"Sorry, Brigitta." Bard hung his head like a contrite puppy. "I just thought you were in trouble."

"Thought, did you? I am assuming that you are planning on picking this mess up," she continued, indicating the splintered doors and destroyed entryway.

"Of course, Brigitta." If it was possible, Bard's head sank even lower.

"Well, get on with it then." She stomped her foot for emphasis.

Nickolas took pity on the dejected muse. "Come on, Bard. I'll show you where the tools are kept. And I can help you, right?"

Bard nodded and followed Nickolas out of the ruined doorway and into the night.

"Seriously, that man is a nuisance." Brigitta shook her head at the mess Bard had made in the foyer. "Oh well, at least he is nearly as good at putting things back together as he is at destroying them. Come, ladies, we have much to discuss."

Brigitta led the way back to the living room and started outlining their plan for visiting Chicago the following day with an incredulous Grandma Vera and a giggling Sarah trailing behind her.

⌖

The next morning found Brigitta, Sarah, Sparks, and Grandma Vera leaving the ranch via the newly repaired front door. True to Brigitta's word, Bard had done a wonderful job of fixing the damage, and unless she looked very closely Sarah could not tell that the doors had been nearly pulverized just ten hours before.

The flight to Chicago was quick and easy, and Brigitta had a limousine waiting for them just outside the terminal. A short ride later, the car eased to a stop in front of a large brick home.

"Here you are, miss," the limousine driver said with a flourish as he opened Brigitta's door. "This is the dean's house. You will find him waiting for you inside."

"Thank you, Richard." Brigitta helped Sarah and Grandma Vera to alight and led the way up to the dean's front door. She didn't even have a chance to raise her hand to knock before the dean's short, stocky secretary, Mr. Williams, swung it open.

"Ms. Telyn? You are right on time. The dean will be down to see you in a couple of minutes. He is on a conference call, and he asked me to show you into his study. Can I get you any coffee? Tea?" Mr. Williams led them off of the main foyer and into a cozy wood-paneled library with leather couches and chairs and a huge desk buried in papers.

"Tea would be lovely, Mr. Williams. Vera, Sarah, would you like anything to drink?" Brigitta introduced her two companions to Mr. Williams, who gave them each a slight bow.

"I would love some tea," Grandma Vera said, and at Sarah's quiet nod she added, "and some for Sarah as well. Thank you so very much."

Mr. Williams bowed again and soon returned with a tea tray piled high with cookies and cakes as well as a steaming pot of tea and four cups. As he was passing out the cups and plates, he spoke warmly to Grandma Vera. "Ms. Telyn told us on the phone that you are Professor Montague's daughter. He was quite a favorite around here during the Second World War, I am told. My father had him as a professor, and when I mentioned to him that you were coming, he said to pass along his regards. My father is in a nursing home and is very elderly. Usually he doesn't have much to say, but he seemed surprisingly lucid when discussing your father. Something about Professor Montague getting him his first internship with Applied Chemical Corporation. My father retired as vice president of ACC about twenty years ago. He seemed to think that without the professor, he would have never been considered for a job there."

Grandma Vera was at a loss for what to say, for she had never met her father and knew next to nothing about him. Mr. Williams seemed to know him more intimately than she herself. She was saved from having to reply when a balding, pudgy man with a congenial smile and a broad face entered the study through the back door.

"Ms. Telyn!" he exclaimed, coming forward to take Brigitta's hand. "It is a pleasure to finally meet you! Judge Brown tells me that you are quite the young lady and highly recommended you. And you must be Professor Montague's daughter and great-granddaughter!" The man turned to Grandma Vera and Sarah in turn, giving them both warm, energetic handshakes that nearly upset Sarah's tea.

"I am Jackson Fisher, and I have been dean at the university for nearly forty years. Unfortunately, your father was here long before then, so I never had a chance to meet him, although I have heard stories about him over the years. He was much loved around here. Even my secretary, Williams, has a connection to him. It seems that while he was here, Professor Montague touched the lives of everyone he met.

"I did some digging last night to see if I could find some information for you. Ms. Telyn tells me that you were adopted when you were very small and actually never met your father, and that you were interested if he had left behind any personal effects or information that would help you connect with your past. I contacted the chair of the Chemistry Department, Professor Michaels, to see if there was anything left behind. She is eager to meet with you and has collected as much information as she could.

"We will head to the Chemistry Department first, and then we'll have lunch with the provost. Please come with me." And without pausing for a breath, he led them out of the study through the large oak doors and onto the pavement. Sarah just had time to hastily put down her teacup and hurry after the adults. "The chemistry building is just up the hill a bit. Not far."

Sarah whispered to Brigitta, "Just how do you know him? Last I checked you were a hundred-year-old statue."

Brigitta laughed quietly. "Yes, Sarah. But my brother and sister muses in other disciplines were not, and I was able to track down a few of them. They were very happy to hear from me and to help me out. The Muses of Academics have contacts in nearly every major university in the world, and Edith, the Muse of Education, is an old friend of mine. She was able to contact Mr. Williams, who told her that Dean Fisher knows Judge Brown, whom I met in Denver when I was helping your grandmother regain custody of you and Nickolas. I may not have a network of my own anymore, but I am not above using the networks of others! Besides, I did know Professor Montague, and I was sure that he would be as charming to the people at Chicago University as he was to everyone at the manor."

By this time, they had reached the ivy-covered chemistry building, and a puffing Dean Fisher led them inside. They found Professor Michaels waiting for them in a comfortable corner office with two elderly gentlemen and a few younger people.

Both of the men were over eighty years old. The first was Mr. Williams's father. He sat in a wheelchair and was attached to a canister of oxygen, and although his body appeared frail, his brown eyes were bright and shining. The other man was likewise quite elderly and seemed as eager to meet Grandma Vera, Brigitta, and Sarah as Mr. Williams's father.

"Good morning, Professor Michaels," Dean Fisher effused. He took a deep breath to continue on, but Professor Michaels cut him off.

"Dean Fisher, how good of you to escort Ms. McGuire, Ms. Telyn, and Miss McGuire up here yourself. Really, you shouldn't have. I know you have thousands of important things to do down in your office. It is amazing you had the time to walk them up. Mr. Williams called to let us know you were on your way and begged me to send you back just as soon as I could possibly spare you. There is some question about a donation from a prominent alumnus that he needs your help with. I know how much you would like to stay, but with important issues like that waiting for you back at your office, I am sure you really must go."

Dean Fisher opened and closed his mouth a few times, and looking like a child who has been denied a treat, he quietly slunk out of the room.

Professor Michaels closed the door with an overly dramatic sigh. "Sorry, ladies, but if he stayed he would have talked the whole time, and we would not get to hear anything that these gentlemen have to tell us. Come in and find a seat." They all quickly joined the circle and sat down, Sarah sitting between Grandma Vera and Brigitta.

"First let me introduce you to Tom Eckles," Professor Michaels continued, indicating the elderly man sitting next to her. "Tom was one of our GI Bill students in the 1940s. He had your father as a professor, and I think he even worked with Professor Montague on a summer project."

For a man in his late eighties, Tom Eckles seemed very healthy and active and launched directly into his tale without prompting. "I remember your father as the coolest of professors. I was an undergrad at the time and thought that I was pretty smooth. I had this dog, Cocoa, who came back from the war with me. I just couldn't stand to be apart from her. She saved my life in Germany more than once, and until the day she died, I kept her by my side. Professor Montague would always let me bring Cocoa into lectures with me. He never asked why, never pried, just let her come in, and he even greeted her by name. He seemed to love that dog as much as I did.

"Like Professor Michaels said, I worked on a research project with Professor Montague the year before he left. I went back through some boxes I had up in the attic to see if I had any of his papers among mine, and I found these." He handed a bound stack of yellowing pages to Grandma Vera. "They're my notes from that project. Professor Montague was trying to isolate some rogue cells that were attacking other cells in one of his lab mice, causing it to age prematurely. We spent all summer trying to isolate them, but the cells kept dying before we could finish the experiments. It was fascinating work, but also frustrating, because we couldn't come up with a solution. He had indicated that he would like to work on it again the following summer, but he passed away before we could get started.

"I do remember the last day I saw him. It was in June, right before he left, and I was throwing a tennis ball in the quad for Cocoa. When she spotted him, she stopped chasing the ball and went right up to him. Didn't jump on him or anything, just sat at his feet and let him pet her. I think he knew he wasn't going to live through the summer, and I think Cocoa knew it, too. She just wanted to stop and say good-bye to the old man.

"A few days after that, I got a letter from him, out of the blue. It was really strange. I kept it because it didn't make a lot of sense at the time, and I felt pretty special that he had trusted me. It might be a help to you. Let me read it." Tom pulled a fragile envelope out of his pocket and withdrew two sheets of crumbling paper.

Dear Tom,

Thank you so much for your assistance on the quad yesterday. It was very important that I deliver that package to the library, and I would not have been able to do so without your and Mr. Williams's help.

If I could be so bold, I want you to do me another favor, as I don't think I will get a chance to return to the university for some time. I forgot to put a little book in that box. It is extremely important that it is placed there, and I know that I can trust you to help me. I have enclosed the key to my rooms in this letter, and I beg you to go and retrieve the little brown leather book that you will find on my bedside table and give it to Miss Anne at the library. She will know what to do with it.

I will be forever indebted to you if you can do this for me. Please do not share the contents of this letter or the book with anyone besides Miss Anne. I know that you understand that sometimes something is so important and secret that you cannot explain it to anyone, you just need to do it, whether it is against the rules or not.

Give Cocoa my love and tell her thank you for me. I know she plays an important role in your life, far more important than any role anyone else could ever play, and she does it faithfully and silently as only a good friend could do.

Sincerely,
Professor Montague

"Gosh," Tom said, dashing tears from his eyes, "I still miss that dog, and it has been seventy years. Anyway, I did as the professor asked. I snuck into his rooms and took the book to the library. I asked the head librarian if I could talk to Miss Anne, whom I had never met, not surprising, as I spent as little time as possible in the library in those days. The head librarian looked at me like I had grown three heads, led me to the records room, and introduced me to 'Miss Anne.' She was all of six years old and quite full of herself. Once the head librarian had left and the little girl's grandmother was busy with another student, I slipped Anne the little book and whispered what Professor Montague wanted her to do with it. She nodded her curls very seriously and skipped off with it, promising me that I could rely on her. I never saw her again."

"What does the second page say?" Brigitta asked, breaking the protracted silence after Tom finished his story.

"That was the funny part; it was a letter to the head chair of the Chemistry Department. I asked him if I could keep the letter once he read it, and he said that I could. Could you please read it aloud? I am not sure that I could get through it without breaking down." He handed the letter to Brigitta to read.

Charlie:

I want you to know that several of the professors have not been letting Private Cocoa accompany Private Eckles into classes.

I have it on very good authority that Private Cocoa is one of our war heroes. In fact, she holds several medals for valor for her service to her country; you can check with the war department for confirmation.

In 1944, she was injured in a raid in Germany while protecting her squad from hidden explosives detonated by a trip wire. She identified the wire and pushed her squad into a protected position before detonating the wire herself, sustaining extensive injuries. Private Eckles used his own funds to return Private Cocoa stateside for treatment in his hometown. His father, a veterinarian, was able to return Private Cocoa to full health, and she was waiting for him at the end of the war.

From my own observations, both Private Cocoa and Private Eckles need each other to recover from the atrocities that they faced overseas, and their combined service to our country should warrant them a little bit of special consideration.

As a favor to me and with my taking all responsibility for the outcome, I would like a policy to be passed that Private Eckles and Private Cocoa should be allowed to stay in company in any classroom, lab, library, or building on campus.

I am sure you will agree with me that Private Cocoa deserves a GI Bill education as much if not more so than Private Eckles. She does seem to be the brighter of the two.

Sincerely,
Christopher Montague

Brigitta quietly folded up the letter and returned it to Mr. Eckles.

"From that day on, they all let me take Cocoa with me everywhere. No one ever said a word about it; they just welcomed her in and let her sit at my feet. Even the really fastidious head librarian let Cocoa come into the library. She had lost both of her sons in the war, and I think she appreciated Cocoa for protecting us.

"Cocoa lived to a very old age and died a quiet and peaceful death. I buried her on my parents' farm. Never had another dog that could hold a candle to her; she was something special, that is for sure." Tom Eckles put the letter in his pocket and took his leave. "If you ever need anything, Mrs. McGuire, anything at all, you can count on me."

After a moment filled with much eye wiping and sniffles, Professor Michaels introduced the second elderly man as Howard Williams. They already knew he was Mr. Williams's father. After breathing deeply a few times, he began to speak, pausing often to administer more oxygen.

"Tom has the measure of Professor Montague. He was one of the kindest, most amazing gentlemen I ever met. He got me my first job. Recommended me for an internship that, without his letter, I wouldn't have had a haystack's chance in a wildfire of getting. He gave me good advice too, told me to work hard when the job was boring so that they would recommend me for a job that wasn't. He was right. The other three interns moaned and groaned about the menial tasks they asked of us and I didn't. I was the only one they kept on after the summer. I never left that firm until the day I retired. All because of Professor Montague. Great man, he was, the greatest of men.

"I don't know what I can tell you that Tom didn't, except that I remember that last day too. Professor Montague was getting pretty frail by then, could hardly walk, and here he comes, shuffling up the hill from his apartment, carrying this heavy box. Tom carried it for him across the quad and then asked me to take it into the library for the professor.

"I was happy to do it. My girl, Elizabeth, worked in the library, so it just gave me a good excuse to go in and see her. So I helped Professor Montague up the stairs and into the library and handed him off to the head librarian before I went to see Elizabeth. I overheard him ask if he could put the box in storage in the records room. Lots of professors kept stuff in the records room—their important papers, journals, and things like that. But I had never seen anyone put a box of stuff in there. I don't think it was full of papers; it kind of rattled like there were glass and hard objects inside. I remember thinking how odd it was. And then the professor never came back. He went on his vacation, and the next fall there was a new professor in his classroom. We all missed him. All the professors here are wonderful, but there was something special about Dr. Montague, something really, really special."

Mr. Williams seemed tired and almost nodded off. His nurse suggested that they take a break for a while, and if Grandma Vera had any questions, she could meet with him after lunch. Professor Michaels glanced at the clock on her desk. "We need to head up to the commissary. The provost wants to meet with you for lunch in his private dining room, anyway."

"Thank you so much, Mr. Williams," Grandma Vera said as she rose with Brigitta to leave.

Sarah stopped by Mr. Williams's chair before they left and squeezed his hand. "Thank you so much for helping my great-grandpa that day, Mr. Williams. You are pretty special too." And she kissed his cheek before leaving with the rest of the party.

Howard Williams blushed. "Been a long time since a pretty girl kissed me," he said to his nurse. "Not since Elizabeth died five years ago. You don't think Elizabeth will be mad at me for getting kisses from other girls, do you? She can be frightful jealous."

⋈

Lunch with the provost turned out to be seriously dull. The pompous man just droned on and on and on until Sarah was afraid that lunch would last until it was time to fly back home.

She was pretty sure that the information that they needed was in the library somewhere, and certainly not in the provost's private dining room.

When the clock started reaching toward two thirty, Sarah could see that even Brigitta was getting nervous about how much time they were wasting. The muse had tried over and over again to wrap the luncheon up, but the provost would just launch into another long and boring story about the history of the university, and Brigitta would smile her beautiful smile and tap her toe impatiently under the tablecloth.

"What time to we need to leave to catch our plane?" Sarah whispered in Brigitta's ear.

"Within the hour," Brigitta whispered back. "He just doesn't seem to take a hint."

"How about if I sneak out to the library and see if I can get the box. He doesn't seem to notice me," Sarah whispered back, and without waiting for an answer, she slipped away from the table, whispering, "Bathroom?" to one of the servers, and feigning desperation as she scooted out of the room.

Once free of the provost's dining room, Sarah dashed out of the commissary and across the quad. It was easy to recognize the library, as it was a large white-columned building with lots of stairs leading up to the front doors.

Once through the double doors, Sarah found herself in a cool and quiet rotunda with a large, imposing front desk in the middle. A severe-looking librarian stood guard, and she looked down her long nose at Sarah in a way very reminiscent of her great-aunt. But Sarah knew how to charm adults, and so she skipped up to the desk and put on her most innocent air.

"Hello!" she said.

"Shh!" the librarian scolded.

"Hello," Sarah whispered. "I'm looking for the records room."

The librarian pointed to a small room off the rotunda and was just about ready to let Sarah go on her way when she called her back. "Little girl, do you have an ID?"

Now if you really want to annoy Sarah, call her little. That makes her blood boil in an instant. But Sarah was also very smart and knew that it was much easier to get adults to do what she wanted with sweetness and respect than by railing at them for calling her little, so she took a deep breath with her back to the librarian, wiped the scowl from her face, and turned around, all sweetness and innocence once more.

"No, I am just here visiting my grandmother. She works in the records room," Sarah lied, hoping that the records room librarian wasn't twenty-five years old.

"Oh, you are Ms. Jones's granddaughter. I see the resemblance now. Off you go." And the librarian waved her away.

Sarah was amazed at her luck and spun on her heel, walking as quickly as she dared into the records room.

The room was small and narrow with a tall counter at one end. It seemed deserted, until Sarah worked her way down to the far end and saw that there was a small office door behind the counter. The door was ajar, and Sarah could just see an elderly woman sitting at a desk drinking tea and eating cookies. She looked up and saw Sarah, and a bright smile crossed her face. She immediately stood up and came out of the office.

She was short and plump with a mass of gray curls and twinkling blue eyes surrounded by copious amounts of smile wrinkles. "Hello, my dear," she said as she came around the corner, and then she stopped dead still. "As I live and breathe," she whispered, staring at Sarah, one hand grabbing at the counter for balance.

CHAPTER 12

Professor Chambre's Lab

⊹ ⫶ ⊹

In which Charles boils over

Charles had secreted himself in the abandoned attic apartment for the sole reason that it faced the five-star hotel where James planned to pass the night after his meeting with Drs. Betty and Nikki.

From his vantage point, Charles could observe not only the hotel's front entryway, but also the fourth-floor room that James had been assigned. Through the smallest of gaps in the curtains, Charles was able to position his *Musca domestica* in such a manner that he could watch James in his room. James reviewed several documents, and the *Musca domestica* obediently transmitted their contents. They were various rather dry lab reports from scientists all over the world. James also placed multiple phone calls, which were equally banal, and finally, he retired for the evening.

Charles was half tempted to sneak into James's room as he slept and retrieve the knife and lock picks, and he had actually gone so far as to climb James's window ledge with his mini crowbar in hand to force the window when James's cell phone had started buzzing.

"Hello?" a rather too awake James had answered. "Edith, I have been waiting for your call. Did Brigitta arrive at Chicago University?"

Charles had nearly fallen off the window ledge at the mention of his sister-in-law's name. If someone named Edith was discussing Brigitta, then she must be Edith the Muse of Education. A vision of a rather diminutive, bespectacled muse with gray hair pulled up into a messy bun on the top of her head came to Charles's mind as he strained to hear the other end of the conversation.

"Two humans, you say? What did they look like?" James paused for the reply. "The elderly one must be Dr. Montague's daughter, and the young one sounds like Dr. Vivian's great-niece. Did they find any of Dr. Montague's papers?"

Again James paused, and Charles wished even harder that he could hear Edith's reply.

"I need to get my hands on those papers. Can you detain them at the university until I can send you reinforcements?" After the reply he added, "No, don't tip your hand—Brigitta needs to trust you. She can't know how many of us are involved in this. If we can just keep the Muses of Music and War in the dark, we can recapture them all at once and keep them from reporting us. Just keep putting obstacles in their path so that they don't leave. And whatever you do, don't let them take any of Dr. Montague's effects off campus. I will talk to you soon. Thanks, Edith, excellent work." And with that James hung up and instantly dialed another number.

"Karina? James here. We've found where Dr. Montague hid his research. It is at Chicago University. Can you take backup and retrieve it? Brigitta is there with Dr. Montague's daughter."

Charles could hear yelling coming from the other end of the phone, and James held the receiver far away from his ear. Between the curse words and the berating, Charles was able to decipher a couple of sentences. "How did Brigitta get involved in this? I thought you had them safely imprisoned in Australia."

Karina's shrill voice had not mellowed one whit in a hundred years, Charles ruefully noted.

"Thanks to Lady Vivian's lax guardianship, they escaped."

"All of them?" James was holding the phone quite far from his ear by now.

"Yes, all of them, and the Muses of War too. But we will recapture them. Right now I need to make sure that our experiments are all secured. Once that is accomplished, we can work together to recapture Ardus and his lot. They cannot possibly suspect the extent of our work here, so the element of surprise should buy us some time."

Suffice it to say, Karina did not seem convinced.

"Please, Karina. We do not have time to discuss who is to blame. We just need to contain the problem. Take the least obvious of our guards and retrieve the information. Kill Brigitta and the humans if necessary, but for goodness' sake keep it quiet, and definitely don't tell Joanna."

"Joanna doesn't know?" Karina yelled loudly enough that Charles thought even if Joanna didn't know, half of Beijing did by now. "You are in so much trouble, James. What is in it for me to help you? I don't need Joanna to think I was involved in your mistakes."

"You are hardly blameless in this, Karina. Do I need to remind you that it was because of your bumbling that Charles found out about the essence in the first place?"

"That was not my fault, and you know it," Karina shot back. "I will help you, just this once, but if a breath of this reaches Joanna's ears, I will make sure she knows that you were responsible for every bit of it. I will call you when this is contained."

And the phone went dead. James had gotten out of bed and started pacing the room. He was so distracted that he didn't notice as Charles and his *Musca domestica* removed themselves from his window ledge and returned to the attic across the street.

Now Charles was in a bit of a quandary. He needed to warn Brigitta, but perhaps Brigitta already knew and had called Bard as backup, which was why the ax-wielding muse had left the rickshaw so abruptly. He decided it couldn't hurt to make sure. So Charles got out his cell phone and texted Brigitta.

> Do not trust Edith and
> Karina. Get far away
> from Chicago
> University. Contact me
> when you can.

He was just about ready to send a similar text to Bard when he glanced out the window and noticed that James had left the hotel. Stashing his phone in his pocket and grabbing his few belongings, Charles slipped into the shadows and followed, not realizing that his text message would never reach Brigitta in time, as it had been flagged for review by the Chinese government before being transmitted overseas to Chicago.

⠿

Charles poked his head out of the wheel well of James's private jet, just in time to watch as two men loaded a long, heavy wooden crate from the plane's hold into the waiting trunk of a black stretch limousine. Since the crate was too large for the trunk to close properly, one of the men secured it with ropes, leaving the lid of the trunk open by several inches.

Charles slipped from under the plane as soon as the two men had moved off and he had ascertained that the coast was clear. He barely fit into the tiny space between the crate and the edge of the trunk. It wasn't the first time that Charles had been happy that he was the smallest of the Muses of War, and he was certain that it wouldn't be the last. None of his brothers would have been able to fit half their girth into the small spot.

Charles discovered a black blanket in the trunk, and with much finagling, he was able to free it from under the crate and spread it over himself, effectively hiding from all but the most persistent of observers.

He had barely gotten situated when he heard the door of the jet open and James descend the stairs. James paused for a moment by the back door of the limo. He was only a few paces away, so Charles heard every word that James exchanged with the chauffeur.

"Dr. James, Master Chambre would like me to take you directly to the new chateau," the chauffeur said with a heavy accent. "The route will take us through the worst of the slums, so Master Chambre has asked that I let you know that you should not open the windows or give out any money to the locals. That will just mean that more of them will swarm the car, and we will never get to our destination. I beg you humbly to follow Master Chambre's warning."

Charles could almost feel James stiffen. "I am not in the habit of handing out money to anyone," James said coolly. "Nor do I need your advice. You are wasting my time. Your job is simply to take me to Dr. Chambre's home and to return me to the airport as soon as humanly possible after our meeting. Are we clear?"

"Yes, sir," the chauffeur stammered and hastily opened the door for James. He shut it with a click once the muse was aboard. The chauffeur then dashed around the back of the limo, right past

Charles's hiding spot, giving him a good glimpse of the chauffeur's pale face before he took his seat behind the steering wheel.

The chauffeur drove expertly through the afternoon congestion, liberally applying his horn to hurry along the traffic be it animal, machine, or human. They turned off the main road, and the houses became increasingly smaller and more run-down.

Although the inhabitants of the area were obviously very poor, Charles was amazed by the chorus of sounds that reached his ears. Dogs barking merrily in the distance mingled with the shouts of children at play. Roosters crowed, and there was the sound of some men singing in accompaniment to music played on crude instruments. They passed a few women chatting out their back doors as they did their chores. Everyone seemed rather content if not happy.

As soon as they spotted the limo, however, the children, dressed in filthy rags, paused their games and swarmed the car along with cows, stray dogs, and the occasional chicken, pressing far too close for safety and clamoring for James and the chauffeur to help them. The cries of the children were piteous in sharp contrast to the boisterous shouts a few moments ago, and their rags and pinched, hungry faces broke Charles's heart. They looked like they had not had a bath, clean clothes, or a decent meal in years.

A few of the children and one of the cows noticed Charles where he peeked out from around the blanket, but most of the children must have assumed he was either there to guard the exposed crate or was a fellow street urchin and left him alone.

However, one little boy did approach Charles. He didn't beg for money, but instead he leaned in close and whispered urgently, "Going to the chateau?" He was furtively looking around at his mates to make sure they didn't notice him.

Something about the little boy's state compelled Charles to answer, even though he didn't want to draw any attention to himself that might alert James to his presence. "Yes."

"If you see my sister, could you tell her I miss her and want her to come home?" The boy looked near to tears.

"How will I recognize your sister if I see her?" Charles asked.

"She's a little younger than me, and she has the sparkliest eyes. Oh, and she's always dancing. Her name is Abha. Please?"

Charles nodded, and the boy was swept away into the crowd, which only got thicker the deeper they went into the slums. The smell of unwashed bodies, communal latrines, and fetid livestock was overwhelming, drowning out the sounds of music and laughter that had filled the area just a few moments before, and just as soon as Charles thought about diving under the blanket to escape the smells, the limousine drew up to a set of high golden gates.

Beyond the gates was an entirely different world than the slums on the other side. A huge expanse of perfectly manicured lawn bordered the precisely graded gravel drive. The limousine crunched to a halt in front of a sweeping marble staircase that led to a five-story red brick mansion. Charles again bided his time until James had been led into the house by a liveried butler. Charles secreted himself under the car before the trunk could be unloaded. Sure enough, not a minute later, two footmen exited the house and carried the crate toward a side door, taking the chauffeur with them.

Now that the drive was deserted, Charles stealthily made his way around the other side of the mansion and through an unattended open window. He used his aura glasses to make sure that no one was in the hallway, and Charles was able to slip undetected into a broom closet under the main staircase. Once he was safely ensconced in the closet, he sent his *Musca domestica* in search of James. Charles seemed to be getting a bit better at manipulating the fly's controls, for with only minimal problems and a few minor crashes into walls and bric-a-brac, he was able to find the salon where James and his host were meeting.

"Dr. James," a hook-nosed, dark-haired man was saying, "I am very glad that you were able to come and visit me today. I know you are very busy, but I thought you would like to see my new chateau. The old one was just too small for my needs, and since I will be starting a whole new set of experiments, I needed a whole new lab. Would you like a glass of cognac? I just opened a bottle of 1858 Croizet Cuvee Leonie."

Charles rolled his eyes as James accepted an exquisitely cut glass with the dark amber liquid inside. James slowly swirled the cognac as he cupped the glass in the palm of his hand. Charles noticed Master Chambre did the same after taking the seat across the low coffee table from James.

"Why did you need me here in person, Neville? Surely whatever you have to say could have been sent in an e-mail with your annual report." James swirled his glass again and sniffed at the liquid.

"Well, I not only wanted to show you my chateau, I also wanted to discuss certain changes that I desired to make in my experiments. Last time we met, you informed me that Lady Vivian in Australia was doing experiments with human test subjects and delivered to me that wonderful sample of essence she extracted. Of course, I have to admit that I got a little jealous. Here you were trusting her to use human test subjects while only allowing me to do animal testing. At the time, you said you wanted to find an animal subject that gave similar results to human ones, as it was much easier to procure animals without garnering unwanted government attention.

"So I said to myself, what if I could find a way to get human test subjects without having to worry about government interference? Wouldn't that solve both of our problems? You could get the quality you wanted, and I could get the prestige that I wanted. So I looked far and wide for a way to circumvent our issues.

"And voilà." Master Chambre spread his arms wide, being careful not to spill his cognac. "I have found it!"

James leaned forward, very interested at this point, and placed his untasted cognac on the coffee table. "What, exactly, have you found, Neville?"

"I have found this corner of the world, where the lives of the cattle out there are more valued by the community than the lives of the children. You may have wondered why I built my magnificent chateau in the middle of one of the worst slums of the world. Well, I have two reasons. The first is that I look ever so much richer when you compare my mansion to the hovels around me. There are no contenders for thousands of miles who could come close to matching my wealth and prestige. Secondly, all I have to do is take one step out of my gates with ten dollars in my hand and I can purchase as many test subjects as I could ever need. Parents line up at the servants' entrance with their youngest sons and daughters, begging me to take them in and give them work at the chateau. As long as they are paid what they feel is a fair price, they never ask any questions about their children ever again.

"I don't know what the parents are telling the children, but they come willingly into my laboratory and kiss my feet when I show them to their cells. Here they have plenty to eat, a clean bed, space to themselves, and no hard work or beatings. They gladly give me all the essence that I want. And if the children who live in adjoining cells occasionally do not return from their latest extraction, it is of no concern to them."

Charles felt rather ill in his tiny closet, and he was pretty sure that it wasn't vertigo from the *Musca domestica*. How was it possible that this overdressed, hook-nosed, poppet of a man could be so vile? He positively made James look warm and fuzzy by comparison. Charles was pretty sure that little Abha was one of those children Master Chambre spoke of. Charles reasoned that the townsfolk must have thought they were providing their children a chance at better life, never dreaming that Master Chambre was turning them into lab rats. Charles was just about to leave his hiding place to find and rescue the imprisoned children when the *Musca domestica* transmitted more of Master Chambre's words.

"Would you like to see my experiments?"

"I would," James replied. "And I would also like to discuss your security detail. Are you still using the guards I sent you?"

"Oh yes, they have been most effective. Speaking of which, did you bring more of those vitamins they need? I am starting to run rather low."

"I am afraid that Lady Vivian will not be able to provide you with those vitamins anymore, as she has had a rather unfortunate accident at her labs. But now that you will be producing your own high-quality essence, you should be able to create your own vitamins with a little assistance. Also in light of the accident at Lady Vivian's, I have brought some additional suggestions to beef up security. Both of which we can discuss in your lab. Shall you lead me there?"

The two men rose from their chairs. Master Chambre drained the last swallow of his cognac and placed his empty glass on the table next to James's untouched one. The scientist frowned at the full glass, but he said nothing and led the way out of the room, unaware that a tiny black housefly was tucked unobtrusively in his cuff.

⊰⊱

Charles slipped quietly from shadow to shadow behind James and the scientist as they made their way to one of the far wings of the mansion. They arrived at a locked steel door. Master Chambre unlocked it with a swipe of a white plastic card and with a flourish motioned for James to precede him inside. He didn't notice a moment later when the door quietly swung open a fraction to allow a dark figure to slide in behind them.

Charles found himself confronted by a series of hallways, lined with closed doors and mousy brown-haired guards stationed every few feet. All eyes were on Master Chambre and James, so Charles was able to slip into the shadows, unobserved once more. Carefully extracting two pairs of suction spheres from one of his pockets, Charles attached them to his palms and knees. They were another of his inventions that he was rather proud of for they allowed him to climb straight up walls and hang from any surface. He used them now to scale the high concrete walls of the corridor and lost himself among the pipes that traversed the ceiling.

The well-trained guards kept their attention riveted straight in front of them; none bothered to look up while Charles passed overhead. It was almost too easy sometimes to do his job, Charles mused as he followed James and the scientist toward the large double doors at the end of the hallway.

The doors proved tricky, as they created a lot of movement and required Charles to be in the guards' line of sight. By carefully timing his movement with the return of the guards' attention once James and Master Chambre had passed, he was able to slip through the doors before they swung closed once more. If the guards detected an odd shadow, they merely assumed that it was caused by the swinging doors.

Finally, Charles found himself in a large warehouse-like room lined floor to ceiling with cages. The upper cages were accessed by a series of catwalks and ladders, and at the head of each was an armed guard. They looked identical to the guards in the hallways from their pristine uniforms to their mousey brown ponytails and dull brown eyes.

Most of the cages were unoccupied and sparklingly clean, containing a twin-size bed made up with white sheets, a fluffy pillow, and a thick blue blanket. A screen hid a small shower, sink, and toilet, and each was furnished with a small wardrobe and stool. The cages that were occupied held a small child dressed in a spotless white gown. Unlike their counterparts outside the gates, they were freshly scrubbed with hair and teeth brushed. But also unlike their counterparts, these children were dull-eyed and unnaturally quiet, sitting on their beds staring blankly forward.

Charles found a small space to hide as Master Chambre showed James around. "I could not abide by the living conditions these children were raised in. I had to make sure that I had uncontaminated test subjects in order to obtain uncontaminated results. So you can see that their lives really have improved by being here. Once a day they go outside for exercise classes, and they also spend time learning to clean and cook and care for the mansion. They are taken to the lab once a week and spend an hour on the extraction table. I am hoping to increase that to every three days, but the results with that have been spotty. Some of the newer children who are more malnourished don't seem to tolerate more than one extraction a week. So I will be waiting until they are healthier to increase the number of extractions. Follow me to the lab."

Charles remained behind while Master Chambre led James through another set of double doors that must have led to the extraction room. The doors had hardly shut behind the two men when a bell tolled and all of the cages swung open of their own accord. Tables and benches rose up out of the floor in the center of the room. The children filed out of their cells and moved smartly to one edge of the room where there were pass-through windows to a room beyond. The smell of curry reached Charles's nose, as he noticed each child returning from the window with a large steaming bowl of rice and vegetable mash in one hand and a full glass of milk in the other. The children placed their food on the tables and stood behind the benches as if waiting for a signal.

Once the last child had brought his lunch to the tables, a bell pealed and all the children sat down and silently began their meals. A few of the thinner and more ragged children ate as if they had never seen food before, but the rest showed more restrained behavior. The guards made rounds and gently reminded those children eating voraciously to slow down. One look at the guards' weapons and even the newest children, those who still showed signs of years of ground-in dirt and bruises, began to mind their manners.

Charles noted that all the children acted like automatons, and there was not a set of sparkly eyes or a pair of dancing feet among them. Either Abha was no longer among the children, or she had been reduced to the same somnolent state as the others.

When the final child ate his last bite and drank his last sip of milk, another bell tolled and they all took their trays back to the windows. Most of the children then queued at a set of doors at the far end. A small number went into the room behind the windows, and an even smaller number lined up outside the door that James had entered a few moments before. Another bell, and all the children filed out with the guards following them, leaving Charles and the empty tables alone in the room.

⇥⇤

Immediately, Charles started exploring and determined where all the doors and exits were. He ensured that he was truly alone and there were no security cameras. He inspected the cage doors,

143

which were all automated to be opened remotely with a code. Of course it was only a moment's work for Charles to decipher it, and a quick test later, he had the ability to open all the cages from his phone, no matter where he was in the world. He smiled with satisfaction, and he installed a tiny security camera of his own in the ceiling, positioned facing a small section of the cages and the doors to Master Chambre's lab. He then moved to the lab doors and was just about to slip through them when he heard James on the other side and quickly returned to his tiny hiding place to observe.

"Everything seems to be in order. I am rarely impressed, but today you have surpassed my expectations. As I stated before, security has to be your number one priority—not just to keep the children in, but to keep the details of our experiments from leaking out. I will be sending you more guards to help you secure your compound, and I have brought you a shipment of new weapons to arm them with." As James spoke, two footmen carried the crate into the room and placed the box on the nearest table. With a large pair of lock cutters, they snipped the metal straps that held the lid in place, and then they opened the box. James removed the layer of straw covering the contents within and pulled out a large black weapon.

Unlike the weapons Ardus had sent Charles to catalog and review just the week before, these were not made of any metal available on earth, nor did they contain any earthly ammunition, for they were not created by human hands. Charles had not seen their like in nearly three millennia. In fact, the only place he had ever seen weapons like them had been in the hold of his parents' smuggling ship. They were atomic blasters, illegal in every corner of every galaxy known and cataloged by any species.

Charles felt the rage and fury begin to build from his toes and roil upward to the very top of his head. Thunder rolled in his ears, and his vision turned red and tunneled directly on James. Knives sprang unbidden to his hands, and his weight shifted in anticipation of his coiled attack. His mouth was opening to roar his rage when a strong hand grabbed the back of his collar and yanked him to the top of the nearest column of cages, and a second hand clamped itself over his mouth and obstructed his airway. Charles struggled mightily in the iron grip of his assailant to no avail. He was captured once again, and he hadn't even enjoyed two full weeks of freedom.

CHAPTER 13

THE FIRST BOX

-Э日Ӻ-

In which we discover what Dr. Montague left Grandma Vera

Sarah reached out to steady Ms. Jones. "Are you all right, ma'am?" she asked, worry creasing her usually smooth brow.

"I'm fine, dear," Ms. Jones said. "Just a little startled. You look exactly like someone in an old photograph I have—you could be her twin. For a minute there I thought I was having a dream. How often I have wished that her husband would come through that door. In fact, I was just thinking about him when you walked in. I must be getting very old." Her smile returned, and her gray curls started bouncing again. "Here, let me show you and you tell me if you don't agree." She fished a long old-fashioned chain from under her neckline. Attached to the chain was a black oval locket inscribed with gold leaves and art deco designs. Ms. Jones carefully slipped her nail under the catch and opened it. Both sides of the locket were covered with tiny glass panels that caught the light, temporarily obscuring the pictures they contained.

Sarah accepted the locket from Ms. Jones and peered into its depths. On the left side was a young man in a fancy suit. It was a very old photograph, older even than the ones that Sarah had seen in Great-Aunt Vivian's library. But although the man was younger than in any of those pictures, she knew at once that it was Professor Montague. The warm eyes and rakish hair were the same, although he hadn't yet grown the beard that he wore in later years. He was probably no more than twenty in the photograph, and his formal attire led Sarah to think it was his wedding or engagement photo. On the other side of the locket was a beautiful girl, only a few years older than Sarah. And Ms. Jones was right. If you replaced the woman's eyes with Sarah's father's, and her chin with Sarah's mother's, the woman would be her twin—same nose, same smile, same unruly hair, and same tiny ears.

"It's Victoria Montague!" Sarah exclaimed. "How on earth do you have a picture of her?"

"I never knew her name, but she was the wife of my favorite person in the whole world when I was a child. She had died by then, in childbirth I believe. The man is Professor Montague, although by the time I met him, he was very old indeed." Ms. Jones seemed lost in her memories for a moment. She suddenly shook her head and gave Sarah a rueful smile. "Now where are my manners? I am Anne Jones, head records keeper here at Chicago University. And you are?" She held out her hand for Sarah to shake.

Sarah shook Anne's hand warmly. "I am Sarah McGuire, Professor Montague's great-granddaughter."

Anne's smile grew very broad, even as tears formed in her eyes and she folded Sarah into a warm grandmotherly hug. A few moments later, she released her and dashed the tears away, so much like a little girl that Sarah had to laugh, and Anne joined in. "One thing you find, Sarah, is that when you get as old as me, you start getting very sentimental about your childhood, and Professor Montague was a huge part of mine. Come, let's have some tea, and you and I can talk about him." Anne bustled Sarah into the office, produced another teacup, and poured Sarah tea, adding generous amounts of milk and sugar without even asking. She then placed a pretty floral plate in front of the girl and took the last cookie from the tray, carefully breaking it in half, placing the larger portion on Sarah's plate and the smaller on her own.

"There we are—all set for a long chat." Anne settled herself comfortably into her chair. "I assume you are here to learn about your great-grandfather," she said, tucking the locket back under her shirt. Sarah nodded and picked up her teacup, blowing on the steaming contents to cool it. "Well, I can't remember the first time I met him, as I must have been about two years old. So we were fast friends from my earliest memories. I used to work here in the records room with my grandmother. My father died in the war, and my mother worked in a factory and couldn't take me with her. So my grandmother essentially raised me here in the library. Many of the professors befriended me and talked to me when they came in to do research or deposit things in the records department, but there was something very special about Professor Montague. He always made me think that he came here just to see me, and frankly, I think sometimes he did. He told me once that I reminded him of his own little girl. He had had to put her up for adoption when he moved here, since he didn't have a grandmother to take care of her like I did. He carried her picture in his pocket all the time and would show it to me. It was just a baby picture with her in a christening gown, but you could tell that he loved her very much and regretted that he couldn't raise her himself.

"So he had to suffice with seeing me. According to the stories my mother and grandmother told me, I was quite the talkative and precocious child, so I doubt the poor professor could get a word in edgewise. But even now, when my memory is getting very dim, I can remember our conversations, tea parties, and exactly how he looked." Anne paused to pour Sarah another cup.

Sarah nodded her thanks and picked up the tea. "I wish I had gotten to know him. Everyone seems to think he was fabulous, but he died years and years before I was born. Grandma Vera never even met him. I think he died when she was four. She's here with me, but she got stuck in a long, boring lunch with the provost."

Anne laughed. "One thing you learn here is to never accept a lunch date with the provost if you have anything else to accomplish that day. I always take my lunch here so I don't get buttonholed into anything like that. Did you come to find out about Professor Montague?"

"Yes. My grandmother is trying to research some of my great-grandfather's experiments. We met earlier today with some of his old students, and they were very helpful, but I came to see if he left anything in the library. Some of his students said that he had placed a box of things here before he left the university."

"I remember that day," Anne said, nodding. "Professor Montague was getting very frail, and he brought this huge box in and left it with my grandmother. We had tea. That was the last time I saw him. After he died, I used to go find that box in the basement and go through it, just so I could feel close to him again. There were all sorts of interesting things in there, if I remember correctly. That's where I found this locket. I hope you don't mind that I've been wearing it all these years, but when I was little I wore it to remember my friend, and as I got older, I just didn't feel complete without it around my neck." Anne removed the locket and slowly and deliberately put it in Sarah's hand, closing Sarah's fingers over it firmly. "But it's yours, and you should keep it or give it to your grandmother." She was silent for a moment, but then her ready smile returned and she stood up, brushing the cookie crumbs from her skirt and cleaning up the tea settings. "If you're done, we should see if we can find that box. I haven't looked at it since I was a child, and I have no idea where it is now. We've been going through a major recataloguing of everything in our records, scanning papers and the like into the computer and destroying the originals unless they have historical value. I've been very careful with the under-graduates who have been helping me to make sure they don't inadvertently destroy something important, and I'm fairly confident that Dr. Montague's things have not been catalogued yet. Let's check the computer."

Anne led Sarah back into the records room and behind the counter where there were several sleek new computers. She logged in to one of them and started typing rapidly. "No, nothing under Professor Montague here. Let me check the old files." She took Sarah into a back room lined wall to wall with old-fashioned filing cabinets. There were old wooden ones against one wall, and as the rows marched across the room, the cabinets became newer and more crowded. Anne stopped in front of one of the oldest wooden ones and pulled out a drawer labeled "M: 1925–1950."

The folders and papers inside were yellowed with age, and the labels were typewritten in uneven letters. Anne muttered as she flipped through the files, until she triumphantly pulled one out labeled "Montague, Dr. Christopher." There were several sheets of paper inside, all of them written on in strange faint bluish-purple ink by a strong hand.

"These are all referencing his experiment notes. He used to come in whenever his research was completed and would file his notebooks with us. There are about twenty of them downstairs. Aha!" She pulled out one of the forms and handed it to Sarah.

Squinting at the page, Sarah was just able to make out the words:

Name: *Dr. Christopher Montague*
Date: *June 9, 1947*
Depositing: *One box of artifacts*
Retain until: *Indefinitely*
Authorized recipients: *Dr. Christopher Montague, Miss Vera Allen*

Notes: *Please keep this box secured until called for by Miss Allen or myself. Please make sure that identification is checked carefully. Under no circumstances is this box to be released to anyone else, especially anyone claiming to be Dr. Vivian Montague of Sydney, Australia, or Dr. James of Oslo, Norway. Upon verification of Miss Allen's death and my own, this box is to be destroyed.*

Signed: *Dr. Christopher Montague*
Received: *Eleanor L. Martin 7/9/47. Filed in Bin B, Row 2, Shelf 3*

"Vera Allen. That's my grandmother's maiden name! I'll have to fetch her," Sarah said, getting excited.

"Let's see if we can find the box first," Anne said. "Things downstairs have gotten rather jumbled over the years, and I am concerned that the box may be lost in the mess. Do you want the research books as well?"

"Yes, definitely, they might hold the information we're looking for." At Anne's quizzical look Sarah continued. "My cousin is ill, and Dr. Montague was researching the same illness all those years ago. We're hoping that some of his research will help the doctors cure our cousin."

"I hope so," Anne said simply and gathered all of the papers together. "Come with me."

Anne led Sarah to the back of the file room, through a door, and down several flights of stairs, far beneath the library. The door at the bottom of the stairs led into a cavernous room. Anne flipped on a switch as they entered, and ancient light fixtures flickered to life far above their heads. There was a small area just inside the door that was separated from the rest of the room by a floor-to-ceiling chain-link fence. It contained a metal desk, a lamp, and two disintegrating chairs. There was a padlocked and chained gate in the fence behind the desk. Anne removed a ring of keys from her pocket and soon had the gate open, and she ushered Sarah through.

"The notebooks should be over here," Anne said, pushing a rickety metal cart. She turned down an aisle labeled "1945–1950: Experiments—Chemistry." There were neat folders, some as large as dictionaries, lined up on shelf after shelf, from the floor to way over Sarah's head. Anne stopped in front of a set of shelves about halfway down the corridor. There, about eye level, was a shelf neatly labeled "Professor Christopher Montague, 1943–1947." A dozen notebooks lay on the shelf, and Anne carefully placed them on the cart.

"Would the box be here too?" Sarah asked, looking at the emptied shelf.

"No, this section is only for research results. Larger items are stored over in Bin B." Anne led Sarah out of the aisle and deeper into the storage room. Bin B turned out to be another huge area enclosed in a locked chain-link fence. Anne's keys soon opened the door, and they entered. The area was positively packed with boxes, crates, suitcases, and trunks. It resembled the lost and found area in an airport, only much, much bigger and more crowded with a huge assortment of items. Among the boxes were also pieces of furniture, odd metal contraptions that looked like they hadn't worked in years, and Sarah was sure she even saw a birdcage among the flotsam and jetsam around her. Just how were they ever going to find Dr. Montague's box?

"I seem to remember it was over here, on the floor where I could reach it," Anne said, carefully picking her way around the stacks toward the far end of the bin.

"The page says row two," Sarah said, looking at the sheet in her hand. "How can you tell what is row two in all this mess?"

"There once was more order to this area, but when my grand-mother passed away and before I took over, the records area was run by students, and obviously they weren't as meticulous as my grandmother was. Unfortunately, I have been so concerned with preserving all of the paperwork and files of the professors that I haven't gotten back here in years. We stopped storing things of this nature a long time ago, and I guess I just haven't found the time to clean this out." She moved a lampshade out of her way and climbed over a stack of steamer trunks.

Sarah was pretty sure that the seventy-year-old woman shouldn't be clambering around and hoped that she didn't injure herself. However would she get Anne out if she did?

As Anne helped Sarah over yet another pile of boxes, and Sarah was just coming to the conclusion that "Row 2, Shelf 3" would never be found, Sparks poked her nose out of Sarah's pocket. Sarah had almost forgotten that the little dog was in there, as she had not made a sound or a movement the entire day. But now her paws curved over the top of the pocket, and her little nose was twitching rapidly, tast-ing the air. With a happy woof, Sparks launched herself out of Sarah's pocket and scrambled over the piles of objects, tail wagging, following whatever had caught her nose's attention.

"Let's try this way," Sarah suggested, following where Sparks had gone.

"Did you see something?" Anne asked, hitching up her skirts to climb after Sarah.

"Just a hunch. I think I saw something labeled 'Row 2.'"

Fortunately, Sparks seemed to think that the section they were in was Row 2 as well, for she ran straight down the tiny clearing between two huge piles. She paused for a moment halfway down, lifted a paw, and sniffed the air first to the left and then to the right. Finally she dashed to the left, pushing her way between two boxes to get to the center of the pile. Sarah heard another muted woof, and then Sparks returned with a tiny scrap of paper in her mouth, which she laid at Sarah's feet. Sarah stooped to pick it up just as Anne caught up with her.

"What did you find?" Anne asked.

Sarah smiled and handed Anne the tiny scrap. "Bin B, Row 2, Shelf 3—Professor Montague" was written in Anne's grandmother's neat handwriting. "It's somewhere around here. Shall we dig?"

It took Sarah and Anne quite some time to shift the boxes that were obscuring the shelves that once were neatly placed in Bin B. When they reached the metal shelves, they were rewarded by finding—right where it should have been on the now label-less shelf—a dusty corrugated box. Sarah pulled it out and was surprised by how heavy it was. She and Anne were just about ready to open it up, but then the cell phone at Anne's waist began to buzz.

"Records," Anne answered. "Yes…Yes…She is right here with me…Yes…We will come right up." Anne ended the call and then said to Sarah, "That was the head librarian. Your grandmother is in the records room and is quite worried about you. Let's take this upstairs and show her what we've found."

Sarah scooped Sparks up from where she sat next to the box, and together, Sarah and Anne carefully extricated themselves from Bin B. Sarah put the heavy carton onto the cart with a sigh of relief and headed for the main exit to the records room, Anne carefully locking the gates behind them.

⹅⹆

Grandma Vera and Brigitta were anxiously waiting in the records room. Sarah made introductions, and soon Anne and Grandma Vera were chatting away like old friends. Sarah and Brigitta opened the box and started putting its contents on the counter. Inside was an old greatcoat, several notebooks, some framed photographs, a curious wooden box that was locked tight, a handful of leather-bound books, a small diary, a bundle of letters tied with a red ribbon, a legal-looking document with a pale-blue cover, a folding knife, a ring of keys, a pipe, some chemistry equipment, a few old vials, an empty peppermint tin, and a gold pocket watch.

Anne picked up the watch and held it carefully in her hands. "I remember this. It was the last thing Dr. Montague gave me. He almost forgot to put it in the box, as it was still in his pocket after he dropped the box off with my grandmother. He asked me to put it in for him, which I thought was odd, as he never went anywhere without his watch." She opened the front lid, revealing the long-stopped face. "I think it was then that I knew he wasn't ever coming back." She turned it over in her hand. "It never worked. I remember wanting to keep it wound for him until he returned, but the winding mechanism was broken. See?" She showed Sarah how it turned smoothly without catching on anything.

"I guess this is yours now." Anne sadly handed the watch to Grandma Vera, who held it carefully, looking it over, and then passed it to Sarah, who slipped it into her pocket. A tear rolled down Anne's cheek unchecked. "Your father was such a wonderful man. I miss him to this day. I cannot tell you what a joy it has been to meet you and your granddaughter. It is almost like he has come back to say good-bye to me once more before my own days are done. I am so glad that these items are finally with their rightful owners. I know he really wanted you to have them, and now you do." Anne helped them to pack up the box, placing everything inside and sealing it for its journey back to Colorado.

Brigitta held the box in her hands, Grandma Vera carried several of the notebooks, and Sarah took the rest. A few hugs later, they were on their way out of the library while Anne sadly waved good-bye from the top steps.

Suddenly, Brigitta stopped dead in her tracks, for coming up the stairs were three people, two of whom she instantly recognized. Brigitta pulled Sarah and Grandma Vera back into the shadows of the library's rotunda, whispering frantically to Anne, "Is there another way out of here? I need to get Sarah, Vera, and these documents to safety."

"What?" Sarah asked. "Who are those people?" She had just gotten a glimpse of the short gray-haired woman with the pinched face, a tall elegant woman with straight auburn hair and ice-cold blue eyes, and the nervous-looking man with skin so pale he resembled an albino snake.

"I don't have time to explain right now, Sarah. Just know they are friends of James."

"Got it," Sarah said, taking the box from Brigitta's hands and turning on her heel. "Miss Anne, please get us out of here pronto. I will explain on the way."

Anne nodded and, without a word of protest, led Grandma Vera and Sarah across the rotunda and through a hidden door in the paneling. The passageway beyond led deep into the old service corridors of the library and headed underground. Anne then turned to speak. "These lead to the old fallout shelters. They were built during World War II, and in fact, some of the projects Dr. Montague assisted with were conducted down here. Once the war was over and I was a young child, I explored down here. There is a way out in the very back that leads directly to the 'L.' I'll get you on a train to the airport. The tracks end there, so you will not have to worry about missing your stop. Here, take this." She pressed a small plastic card into Sarah's hand. Anne looked around frantically. "Wait, where is Ms. Brigitta?"

"She didn't come with us. She went to distract the people on the stairs so we could escape," Sarah said, worry coloring her voice. "I think they recognized her, but they wouldn't recognize us as they have never met us before. I'm sure she'll meet us at the airport if she can. If not, she'll meet us back at the ranch."

"Sarah, what is going on?" Grandma Vera stopped and turned to face her granddaughter.

"I promise I will tell you when I can, Grandma, but right now we have to get to the airport and get home. I'll tell you more once we are back safely with Bard." Sarah hoped that Bard would be able to tell her grandmother more, because frankly she had no idea how to tell her grandmother about the muses, Dr. James, and the imploding brown potato fairies. No idea whatsoever.

⧉

After what seemed like miles and miles of hiking in the dripping gray tunnels beneath the city, Anne led them up a series of steps and opened a rusty metal door that looked like it hadn't been used in fifty years. It led to a city street with the yellow Chicago "L" tracks clanking above their heads. "Just head up these stairs to the station. Swipe the card at the booth and get on the next northbound train," Anne directed them, giving Sarah a quick kiss on the cheek and Grandma Vera a warm hug.

"Wait a minute." Sarah stopped suddenly halfway up the stairs and handed Grandma Vera the box she was carrying. "I'll be right back." Sarah dashed down the stairs, removing both the locket and the watch from her pocket as she ran. She looked at the watch and then the locket, and then nodded to herself.

"Here," she said to Anne, pressing the locket into her hand. "I know Dr. Montague would want you to have something of his. Keep this, and please keep in touch." Before Anne could protest, Sarah kissed her wrinkled cheek and dashed back up the stairs, putting the watch into her pocket.

CHAPTER 14

KARINA'S TALE

In which Charles debates James's fate

Charles found that not only had his assailant managed to block his nose and mouth with one meaty hand, but as he had been yanked upward, his unseen attacker managed to wrap one huge calf up and around his body, hooking the foot of the same leg behind the knee of the opposite one, effectively pinning Charles's arms to his sides and rendering the knives in his hands completely useless.

Pinned, trussed up, and silenced, Charles struggled for a moment to figure out what he *did* have at his disposal—he determined that his legs and his teeth were the only weapons he could use in spite of the hundreds more he had hidden in his pockets. If he banged his legs against the cage, it would make a racket and bring others to the scene, but considering that the chateau contained many who would view Charles as an enemy, it didn't seem like a good idea.

Charles could not see anything in the darkness above the cages. Carefully wiggling his hands, he was able to activate the nearly forgotten *Musca domestica* lying dormant in Master Chambre's cuff, and the control screen formed around Charles's head. His attacker, sensing his movements, tightened the vise grip triangle around his middle to the point where Charles could hardly breathe, but now through the eyes of the *Musca domestica*, he could see just the tiniest bit of the person holding him prisoner, for one foot hung over the edge of the cage.

But that tiny bit was all that Charles needed to identify his assailant, for there was only one person in the entire world that Charles knew had that particular shade of greenish skin. He allowed himself to go completely limp in Deidre's arms, and as she sensed the change in his behavior, she tentatively loosened her grip on his mouth and nose. Just enough for Charles to get a complete breath. She growled warningly in his ear, in that deep-throated almost imperceptible growl that only Deidre had. Having had years of learning to decipher her grunts, growls, and raised eyebrows that were the Amazonian muse's main forms of communication, Charles could tell that she was informing him to keep quiet. Considering she didn't release the death grip her legs had around his middle, it was also clear that she didn't trust him yet to behave himself.

"Deidre," Charles whispered so low that only Deidre's bat-like ears would pick it up. "You really can let me go. I won't do anything foolish, I promise. And it would really be nice to breathe."

With a grunt that communicated how much Deidre doubted that Charles was capable of behaving himself, she undid the lock of her legs and released Charles, who collapsed in a panting heap on the top of the cage. It took him a few minutes to catch his breath and recover from the anaconda constriction of Deidre's legs. Charles pushed himself up to his knees and deactivated the *Musca domestica* so he could look up at his sister-in-law.

Deidre was nearly twice as tall as Charles. Of all the Muses of Music and War, Deidre was only shorter than David, and then only by less than an inch. She was muscular to a point where world-class body builders would be jealous of her arms, and her dark-green skin and wide-set and tilted black eyes gave her an alien look, which she accented by pulling her long greenish-black hair up into an eye-wateringly tight ponytail high on her head. Never one to worry overly much about her appearance, her Grecian robes, once pristine white, were now gray with dust and torn and tattered around the hem above her bare and dirty feet. Her ponytail was matted with knots and filled with twigs, leaves, and feathers that she either didn't notice or hadn't bothered to remove.

Charles smiled lopsidedly at Deidre. "Thank you for rescuing me from myself, Deidre," he whispered, placing his right fist to his chest and bowing slightly to her in the formal bow of the Muses of War. Squashed as he was on the top of the cage, it didn't look nearly as imposing as when Ardus or Galahad executed it with military precision and just a touch of the ancient honor and duty his brothers attached to the movement. Charles was far too irreverent—and short—to give the bow the same level of dignity, and even stoic Deidre's lips twitched with amusement at his attempt.

Charles ignored her smirk and leaned over the side of the cage to view what was going on below. James had fortunately been so wrapped up in showing his weapons to Master Chambre that he hadn't noticed Charles and Deidre's overhead scuffle. He was placing the huge black gun back into the crate. "These should keep you protected for now. I am currently negotiating to get a stronger protection force for all of my laboratories, so expect reinforcements soon. They won't be as inconspicuous as your current guards, but they will be much better fighters."

Master Chambre looked confused. "Why do I need such a huge protection force? I am surrounded by poverty and weakness. Anyone trying to approach the chateau will have to deal with the street urchins impeding their progress, giving me ample warning. Really, Dr. James, your experiments are quite safe here."

"Just humor me," James growled. "I know what I am talking about. You will be thankful at some point for the protection. You might even consider purchasing a helicopter for a quick exit. You certainly have room for it on that lawn of yours."

"An excellent idea," Master Chambre said, stroking his chin. "It will make the perfect statement. None of my associates have one, and I do always like to be first…"

Master Chambre might have gone on for quite some time, but James held up his hand to silence him, pulling his ringing phone from his pocket. "Yes," he answered, and listened intently to the other end for a while.

"Is she dead?" he inquired, and Charles felt himself tense. Brigitta! How could he have forgotten?

"Please, please, please," Charles begged, gripping his hands tightly, Deidre staring at him quizzically.

"And what about the two humans she was with?" James continued, no indication in his tone or body language to give Charles a clue as to the answer to his previous query.

"Meet me in the lobby of the American Royal Hotel in an hour. I will send you the coordinates." James disconnected the call and returned his phone to his pocket. "I shall have to end my tour of your chateau prematurely, Neville. A rather urgent situation has arisen that requires my immediate attention. Please show me to my limousine."

⸙

James and Master Chambre had left the room through the double doors that led to the main section of the chateau, freeing Deidre and Charles to climb down from the cages and slip out the back.

As Charles had suspected, it led to the elaborate gardens behind the chateau. The sound of children being led in calisthenics reached them from over the nearest hedges, so Charles led Deidre on the path to their left. Deidre, from her great height, was able to see over the garden hedges, and after only a few moments of following Charles, she grabbed his arm and dragged him down an adjacent path.

They arrived at the doors of the chateau's stables several moments later, and Deidre commandeered two mounts from the frightened stable hand. The bay had already been saddled, as if one of the chateau's occupants had requested her to be ready to ride, while the towering midnight black stallion wore neither saddle nor bridle.

Deidre threw the reins of the smaller horse at Charles and then, not bothering to see if he caught them, grabbed a huge fistful of the stallion's mane and gracefully hauled herself onto its, back urging it into a gallop immediately.

Charles endeavored to keep up with her on his tiny horse. The mare's legs were a blur as she struggled valiantly to catch her stablemate, whose ground-eating lope seemed deceptively lazy. At last, at the far end of the gardens, Deidre halted and dismounted next to the wall. She had already removed the locked garden door from its hinges and led the way through by the time Charles had caught up.

Along the back of the garden wall was a rarely used dirt access road, and Charles could just hear the rumblings of an approaching Jeep. Deidre flattened Charles against the wall with one massive hand, obscuring him in the ivy growth and fixing him with a dark "don't move" stare. Deidre leaped to the top of the wall and waited with such feline grace that Charles half expected to see a swishing tail beneath her muddy robes.

They didn't have long to wait, for almost instantly, the Jeep rounded the corner and bounced along the road toward where the two muses were lying in wait. The unsuspecting gardener had no warning before Deidre landed in the seat beside him and knocked him out with one blow of her danso, dropping him neatly over the side of the Jeep and into the gutter. Charles grinned at her from where he had swung himself into the backseat, and without so much as a grunt of acknowledgment, she slid into the driver's position and continued along the dirt track.

Charles turned to his companion. "Deidre, I need to send the information that I gathered at the Chateau to Galahad and Ardus." Deidre's only response was one of her usual raised eyebrows.

Interpreting correctly, Charles added, "I am sending it to Galahad because he will make it his duty to free the children in a timely manner. Ardus would waste precious moments debating whether or not it was the proper time to show our hand to James, and those children don't have time for that kind of delay."

Deidre grunted, which Charles took to mean she agreed, whether about Ardus or Galahad or the need for the children to be freed immediately or all three, Charles didn't bother to worry about. He quickly transmitted all of the pictures taken by the *Musca domestica* of Master Chambre's facilities, the code to open the cages, the live feed from his camera, and the coordinates of the chateau to both Ardus, leader of the Muses of War, and Galahad, the most chivalrous of Charles's brothers. Deidre, in the meantime, expertly maneuvered through the heavy traffic toward the hotel.

⊰⊱

They reached the opulent lobby of the American Royal Hotel long after James had already secured a private dining room in the center of the modern restaurant. Round tables were sprinkled around the room draped in long white linen tablecloths, and the tables at the center of the room were each surrounded by thick walls of glass and chrome so the privileged occupants could be seen but not heard by the dining room's other less important guests. The well-dressed James sat alone at a private center table, his back to the restaurant's door.

The maître d' looked down his nose at Charles's matted hair and Deidre's torn and dirty dress. He thought for a long moment about refusing them entry into his pristine establishment, but either the generous tip that Charles slipped into his hand or the snarl the imposing Deidre gave him a second later changed his mind. He led them to a secluded table right next to the kitchen door; it was obscured by a half wall and several potted palms.

Charles ordered an expensive bottle of wine that he hoped wouldn't kill the palm trees and turned his attention to James's table. A tall, striking woman had joined him, and with a flourish, she placed a rather battered old cardboard box onto the table in front of him. Karina took the chair opposite James and crossed her long legs. As the tablecloth shifted to allow her feet access, Charles saw something that made him salivate more than Georgiana's craggleberry pie, for there, under the table, was James's exquisite leather briefcase.

Charles sent his *Musca domestica* across the room and under the glass doorway into James's private dining room. He adjusted the controls so only the tiniest of blue strips covered his ear, and then Charles deactivated all but the fly's audio feed, hiding the tiny bug in one of the two unoccupied chairs at James's table.

"Karina," James was saying. "I want to hear everything. Do not leave one detail out."

Karina looked a little discomforted, which Charles took as a good sign. "When we arrived at Chicago University, Edith met us and took us to the library where Brigitta had been meeting with the head records keeper. It took us rather a while to persuade the old bat at the reception desk to let us in, and by the time we got to the records room, we just saw Brigitta slip out the back door with this box under her arm.

"Fortunately, she isn't too hard to follow with that red rat's nest she calls her hair. So we were able to track her to the front of the university, where she ducked into a cab and sped off. Of course we were able to procure a second cab to follow, and the driver was very easy to persuade to try to catch her up. She headed to Union Station.

"The cab driver was rather rule bound about dropping us off in the loading zone, so we lost precious moments, but we arrived in the ticketing area just in time to see Brigitta leave the counter and hand off the box to the Red Cap agent. She was well across the room from us at that time, but again we were able to see her red hair heading toward the trains. That pale-faced associate of yours and I split up at that point. I sent him after the luggage while I followed Brigitta.

"She headed toward the 4:45 Cardinal—which was the next train to New York. As it was 4:40, I hastened my steps so not to miss her. I just saw her hair disappear into the first car of the train. It was a first-class cabin, and the conductor at the door was very hesitant to let me enter without a ticket, but money persuaded him otherwise. He wanted to issue me a ticket on the spot, but he was taking ever so long to do so, insisting all the while that I could save money by returning to the ticket counter. Frustrated at the delay, I shut him up. Hopefully he didn't have a family.

"I barely got away from him in time to see Brigitta pass into the next carriage. The train was full of holiday travelers who kept blocking my way as they tried to cram all of their ginormous luggage into the microscopic overhead compartments. One little old lady even had the audacity to ask me to help her put her over-sized purple handbag into storage for her; she held me up for over a minute.

"It seemed every time I entered a carriage, it was just in time to see Brigitta exit it at the far end. How she managed to get through the throng so effortlessly is beyond me. I reached the doors to the last carriage, only to find them blocked by another of those odious conductors. This one was wide enough to fill two crossways, and he would not let me pass without a ticket. Once again I was informed how much money I was wasting by purchasing my ticket on the train, but there were far too many people in the carriage for me to dispatch him. As I was trying to get past, your man caught me up with the box triumphantly under his arm. So I left him to deal with the conductor as I elbowed past, entering that last carriage as the train pulled away from the station. I just caught sight of Brigitta on the platform surrounded by the crowd of disembarking passengers from the neighboring train. She gave me one of those overly toothy smiles of hers before she covered her hair with a black scarf and completely disappeared.

"We could not get off the train until the next station, and by then we had lost all track of her. At least we were able to procure the box for you. I brought you the box and sent your man to search for Brigitta before her trail went completely cold."

Charles breathed a sigh of relief that Brigitta had escaped, but he feared that whatever the contents of the box were, it was not good that it was in James's hands, so carefully, going from table to table, hiding in the folds of the linen cloths, Charles crept closer to James's room, and when the waiter entered to take their order and commanded their complete and rather irritated attention, he slipped in their enclosure and slid under the table.

James dismissed the waiter curtly and turned his attention to the box. He slipped his knife under the messy packing tape and slit it open. The first yellowing sheet on top quickened his pulse, for it was the form Dr. Montague had filled out when he deposited the box in the record keeper's care. He dove with great anticipation into the box's contents, scanning each page with growing annoyance. "What is this that you have brought me?" he asked Karina, his knuckles whitening on the edge of the ancient box. "Fax cover sheets, scribbles, junk mail, misfiled forms, leftover copies, a first draft of a horrific novel, and unused napkins from a fast-food restaurant? You brought me the records room recycle box! You fool!" And with that James threw the contents of the box at a startled Karina, grabbed his briefcase, and stormed out of the dining room.

Karina pulled herself haughtily together and, grabbing her handbag, followed him out of the room. Charles grinned in his hiding spot beneath the table and returned his diamond knife to its sheath in his boot. He placed the roll of golden lock picks in a pocket in his shirt before crawling out from under the table. He gave the startled busboy a few bills and disappeared behind the potted palms to bring Deidre up to date.

⋇

Still fuming, James reached for his briefcase as the limousine entered the highway toward the airport, intending to review his rather unsatisfactory meeting notes from visiting his scientists around the world. Why couldn't they see how urgent and important their research was? Wasn't he paying them enough to solve these minor problems for him? Perhaps he should just silence them all and start again with a new batch of scientists. He already needed to do so with Dr. Vivian. She had seriously disappointed him, and she'd opened him up to exposure not only to the local authorities, but to the Muse Council as well. And not only that, but his do-gooder cousin, Brigitta, was sticking her pert little nose where it definitely did not belong. He was surrounded by amateurs.

Just as James was thinking things could not get worse, he noticed a scrap of paper attached to the pocket in the lid of his briefcase.

James—

Don't ever take something from someone who is a better thief than you. You really should know that by now.

—C

The blood drained from James's face, and his jaw tightened in anger. Yes, things could get worse, indeed. He slammed the lid of his briefcase down and glowered out the window of the limousine into the jungle. Just how long had Charles been following him? How much did he know? And how much time did he have to silence Charles before he got around to telling that other goody-goody Ardus? But then a thought came to James that turned his glower into a grin. Oh, he knew how to persuade Charles to keep his peace—nothing like a little family pressure to help tip the balance.

"Joanna," he said silkily into his cell phone a moment later. "Do you happen to know when Olivia is expected to arrive? I will need to speak to her when she does…"

CHAPTER 15

DR. MONTAGUE'S DIARY

In which Nickolas finds the key

Sarah and Grandma Vera arrived home late in the evening to find that Nickolas and Bard were waiting up for them in the living room. They were playing a game of marbles, with Brigitta sitting calmly in a nearby chair. "It was the only game that we had that he knew how to play," Nickolas whispered to Sarah. But Sarah wasn't listening, and she went straight to Brigitta.

"Are you OK?" she asked, searching the pretty muse's face for any sign that all was not well.

But Brigitta laughed. "Oh, Karina is no match for me. There is no chance that she followed me here. In fact, I think she's halfway to New York by now."

It took only a moment for Bard to update Grandma Vera that all had been quiet that day and that the camps had run just perfectly in her absence. Now that she was assured of Brigitta's safety, Sarah could not contain her excitement and proudly retrieved Dr. Montague's box from the van and placed it with a flourish on the coffee table. She wouldn't let Nickolas or Bard touch it, but instead pulled out the contents item by item to show them.

The greatcoat, which smelled of old pipe smoke and mothballs, was far too long for Nickolas, but he tried it on anyway and dug his hands into the many pockets the coat contained. To his disappointment, he found them all empty, not a coin or an old receipt to be found. He quickly lost interest in the coat and placed it on the floor in a heap, for Sarah had just revealed the first of Dr. Montague's notebooks.

Excitedly, Nickolas took it and its 11 mates to a corner, once he was able to convince his sister to give them to him, and began reading, ignoring the rest of the party. The notebooks outlined four years of Dr. Montague's experiments. They all had to do with his attempting to manipulate the life span of the microbios in his blood. By using the very limited supplies he had brought with him from Australia, Dr. Montague had been able to inject lab mice with the tiny creatures. He had performed endless experiments, trying to keep the microbios alive and manipulate them into repairing the cell wall damage they had caused while rejuvenating the cells and then, once the cells were repaired, slowly decrease their number in mice's bloodstreams. Experiment after experiment failed, leaving the mice with the tiny inactive creatures hiding in their lymph systems and only partially repaired cells.

While Nickolas was deeply engrossed in the notebooks, Sarah pulled out the leather diary. The first entry was dated July 1, 1943. "Listen to this, Brigitta," Sarah said, taking the little book over to where the muse sat on the couch with Grandma Vera.

July 1, 1943: Today I have had the most worrisome news. Dr. Ansley came at my request and examined Victoria. At first I had feared that her cancer had returned because she has become so tired of late and has been unable to keep down her breakfast. I worried that, in my attempts to wean us off the age-halting food that Vivian developed with Dr. James, I had also exposed my dearest darling to a relapse. Foolish, foolish man that I am. I had been so happy with my progress, celebrating each haircut and nail-trim, and forgetting the other things that had been frozen in time as well by those heinous microscopic creatures. For it appears that Victoria is in a delicate condition, and a child will be joining our family in December.

July 15, 1943: I am in even deeper anguish than last time I wrote. Victoria is determined to have the child. No amount of pleading on my part has moved her. She insists that her life is nothing compared to the life of the unborn baby. I understand that she has seen the full course of her life, even cheating death once with Vivian's serum. But I am not ready to let her go. What will I do without her? She is the very substance of my existence.

July 21, 1943: Dr. Ansley visited again today. Although he was very encouraging to Victoria, as soon as he left her rooms and entered mine, his mien changed. There is very little hope that she will survive the birth, and he fears for the tiny new life as well. He has recommended that I set up for a wet nurse as soon as possible and hire a midwife to stay at the manor full time. I am torn—to hire these ladies will require that I inform Vivian of Victoria's condition. Something I am not ready to do. She and I have not been on good terms since the death of Mrs. Alcott. Vivian absolutely refuses to stop her experiments and will not stop using the manor staff as her unwilling and unsuspecting guinea pigs. As fast as I can develop means to safely eradicate the creatures, she is developing ways to increase our dependence upon them. Her latest efforts have been in not just stopping cell degeneration, but she and Dr. James are starting to work on experiments to reverse the aging process as well.

August 10, 1943: I have engaged the help of Chef Fulvio, and he assures me of his strictest secrecy. It seems that we already have a midwife living in the manor, for Mrs. Craubateau held that office before retiring here with *her husband to care for the stables. Fulvio informs me that he will have a private word with her and make sure that she is ready and willing to step in should the need arise. He will also be working on developing a type of artificial baby milk. He tells me that he read of such things while he was in London at culinary school. He believes that he can create something that will do until the time is right to bring Vivian into the loop.*

August 19, 1943: Today is Victoria's and my anniversary, so I slipped into town to see if I could find a suitable gift to give her. I had just about given up finding anything appropriate, when I ran into a man selling puppies on the street corner. The man himself was rather nondescript—being neither tall nor short, thin nor fat, young nor old, fair nor brown. In fact, I am not sure I could describe him at all beyond the fact that he wore a great black trench coat. He approached me and asked if I knew anyone in the market for a puppy. He said he had sold all but one, and this last one was so tiny, no one wanted it, for it could not be a good guard dog, nor a hunter, nor a worker. He pulled it out of his pocket, and it barely filled his hand. She had floppy black ears and twinkling brown eyes so full of intelligence that I knew she would be just the thing for Victoria. The man placed her in my hand and told me that her name was Sparks. I was so enthralled with the puppy that I didn't notice that the man had left. When I looked up to ask the man how old the puppy was and if he knew anything about her parents, he was gone. The street was deserted in all directions. It was very strange, but I guess he really wanted that puppy to have a home, and he saw that I was enraptured with the little thing. So Sparks has come to join our family, and as I surmised, she and Victoria are already fast friends.

"So that's how Sparks came to join our family," Sarah said, interrupting her reading. "I always wondered where she came from."

At that moment, Sparks was curled on Dr. Montague's discarded greatcoat, and when Sarah mentioned her name, her little head came up and she gave Sarah a happy wag of her tail. "So some mystery man sold you to Dr. Montague, did he?" she asked the puppy, and Sparks happily yapped her reply. Sarah went back to reading the diary.

Bard looked ready to say something, but Brigitta shook her head and he kept silent.

September 7, 1943: Well, the secret is out. Vivian came to our quarters today with Dr. James, under the guise of discussing their latest developments. Victoria had been feeling a little better and was sitting on the settee in front of the fire with a quilt draped over her legs. It was as if that man could see right through the blankets, for he instantly asked Victoria when the baby was due to arrive. Vivian got a rather strange and calculating look on her face like the news pleased her especially in some way. She could not help smiling the entire time, even when I was discussing the risks that her mother faced in the coming months. The pair of them have always made me uneasy, from the earliest days of Dr. James joining us in my lab at the University of Sydney. Vivian's relationship with the much younger Dr. James has led to salacious gossip among the professors and students at the university, and I am not comfortable with the direction his experiments are taking. But Vivian is an adult and is no longer willing to be ruled by her foolish father.

September 21, 1943: Fulvio arrived at my office today with two very welcome surprises. The first was a completed baby food recipe, which he went over with me, and it seems satisfactory in every way. The second was a large plate of his amazing oatmeal raisin cookies. It was wonderful to have some good news for a change. And I ate every last one of the cookies.

October 31, 1943: *I have been distracted lately, but it has come to my attention that little Sparks is not growing at all. She still fits in the hollow of my hand. I wonder if she is not actually a puppy at all, but a full-grown dog. I was worried that she wasn't eating, but I think I have solved that mystery. I have it on good authority that she sneaks down to the kitchens regularly to visit with Chef Fulvio. Perhaps he gives her those oatmeal raisin cookies.*

November 15, 1943: *We are rapidly approaching the time for the little one's arrival. Victoria is having more and more problems moving and breathing. I fear for her so very much. Then she will place her hand on her growing stomach and smile that beautiful smile of hers and with wonder announce that the baby is moving. I feel caught between joy and sorrow every day. How I wish I could wrap the two of them in my arms and keep them safe for always.*

December 18, 1943:

"Wait a minute," Sarah said, looking up from the diary. "He missed your birthday, Grandma Vera."

"I gather he was rather busy at the time. He doesn't seem to be the most regular of diarists, and babies have a way of taking up all available time. Also, remember, my mother died that day, so he was probably too overcome to record it. Perhaps he tells us what happened in his next entry."

"This next entry is really hard to read," Sarah said, passing the diary over to Grandma Vera. "Can you make it out?"

"I can try."

December 18, 1943: I hardly know what to write. It is as if everything that I know and love has been destroyed and trampled on in the last two weeks. First, at the very moment that my precious new daughter Vera took her first breath, my dearest darling took her last. Words cannot express how all alone I am. Victoria was everything beautiful and good in my life, and now it is as if darkness surrounds me. The one light is little Vera. She looks at everything around her with wide eyes and wonder and almost never cries. Between Mrs. Craubateau and myself, the little princess has constant attendance, and she seems to be thriving. Thank the heavens she is healthy, the poor motherless girl.

December 19, 1943: What on earth prompted her to do this? Vivian has gone completely mad. I went to my rooms today to take over for Mrs. Craubateau so she could get her luncheon. When I entered, I found not Mrs. Craubateau giving Vera her noon bottle, but Vivian in the rocking chair feeding the little mite! I was so astonished, as I have never known Vivian to be interested in babies—in fact, just the opposite. And then I espied the tray beside her. On it was not Fulvio's usual warm jug of baby milk, but the three vials of solution that Vivian uses to make her scientific food! The milk in the bottle was laden with the microbiotics. Oh the row we had then. Didn't she realize that if the baby ate those things she would never grow up? She would be trapped at two weeks old for all eternity! Vivian hardly looked sorry. In fact, if anything, she looked rather pleased with herself, as if that was what she wanted the whole time. I shall have to keep a very close eye on what baby Vera is fed in the future. Once I had calmed down enough, I went to see Fulvio and find out his side of the story. He was extremely apologetic, saying that Vivian had led him to believe that I wanted the baby's food to be synthesized. He promised me that he would not let it happen again.

January 1, 1944: Mrs. Craubateau has come down very ill and has had to retire to her bed, leaving me with no nursemaid for little Vera. Fulvio has recommended a handful of the maids that he says can be trusted, so I have put them on a rotation schedule to help me. Vera seems to have suffered no ill effects from the few bottles of synthesized baby food that she was fed. There were just the smallest number of microbiotics in her bloodstream, but they have all died out. I am hoping there are no lasting effects. On a happier note, she seems to have taken notice of Sparks at last. I caught her looking at the little puppy and smiling. Her baby vision must be improving.

"So you have always been able to see Sparks, Grandma Vera," Sarah interrupted. "It must be because you were at the manor."

"We were never at the manor," Nickolas said, looking up suddenly from the corner where he sat. "And we have always been able to see her. Hey, can you see her, Brigitta?"

"We have always been able to see her, Nickolas. Even when we were in the gardens and your great-grandfather and great-grandmother would walk among us, we could see little Sparks," Brigitta said, her brow furrowed in confusion.

"Yes, all the muses can see her," Bard added. "Can't everybody see her?"

"No, very few people can see her, actually," Grandma Vera said. "Until the children went to the manor, the only people I knew who could see her were my husband, Grandpa Patrick; my son, John; and Sarah and Nickolas. The horses that the children brought back from the manor are the same way. The children and I can see them, but no one else here can. Well, all except little Blaze—everyone can see her."

Brigitta and Bard met eyes over the children's heads, and Bard raised an eyebrow. Brigitta motioned for him to remain silent, nodding to the tiny black lump that had fallen asleep on Dr. Montague's greatcoat and was gently snoring.

"Perhaps Dr. Montague has some answers for us in his diary. Please keep reading, Vera," Brigitta said.

January 15, 1944: I am on my way to Chicago. So much has happened in the past two weeks since I last wrote. The day after my last entry, I returned to my rooms to find Peggy, the young parlor maid, snoozing in the rocking chair and the crib empty. Peggy was quite frightened when I woke her, but she said that Vivian had come and taken the baby for an airing. For an airing, my eye! I raced to her lab. Vivian had the baby in a tiny bassinet on her lab table, and she and Dr. James were preparing an experiment to extract something from baby Vera's tiny spine! I snatched up the baby and ran, so upset that I didn't even know where I was running to until I found M. Craubateau on the main horse path riding my stallion. He stopped when he saw me and asked if there was anything he could do to help. I commandeered the horse and took off toward the front gates and never looked back. By the time the sun rose and I had had time to calm down, I realized my foolishness. I had nothing with me for baby Vera and myself to live on. Just the clothes on our backs, very little money, and nowhere to go. At a loss, I headed to the university, and fortunately, I chanced on kindly Dr. Johnson and his wife. They took me into their home and swore themselves to secrecy. Their daughter, Phoebe, worked in the kitchens at the manor, and she arrived late the next night with a jug of Fulvio's baby food and a copy of the recipe. She even had slipped into my rooms and gotten my checkbook, passport, and other important papers. Bless her. The Johnsons soon got me in touch with other professors and old friends at the university who were able to help me transfer my money to an untraceable account in Switzerland, and they helped me make connections with some scientists who were working on a top secret project at Chicago University for the war effort. One of the professors had contacts in the government. They helped smuggle me out of Sydney. We took an ocean liner to America and are now on a train to Chicago. I am praying that our efforts at subterfuge are enough to keep Vivian and Dr. James from ever being able to find us again.

February 10, 1944: I am safely settled in Chicago with baby Vera. She is doing well with the sweeping changes in her life. Far better than her old father is, I must admit. In my haste to leave the manor, I left most of my research on eradicating the microbiotics locked in my laboratory. Nothing there is of interest to Vivian, so I am not concerned that my notes will help her, but I need that research to continue to eradicate the microbiotics from my own system. I will most likely die within the next few years if I am not successful. I don't care so much for myself. As Victoria said, I have lived a full life and have little left to accomplish. But poor baby Vera only has me in this whole world, and if I do not live, she will be on her own. I am sure that Vivian had reasons for conducting experiments on the baby, so I must hide her as best I can from Dr. James and Vivian. I have decided to put Vera up for adoption, as much as it pains me to do so, but I think it is for the best.

February 20, 1944: I have found the perfect place for little Vera to live. I won't write it down for fear that someone will read my notes someday, but suffice to say I found a childless couple in a faraway place, which is the last place that Vivian would ever look for her. They are kind and sweet and wonderful and are willing to adopt Vera and have agreed never to tell her she is adopted or who her parents really are or where they come from. I will be finalizing the adoption next week.

February 27, 1944: It is with a heavy heart that I returned home today. Baby Vera sleeps tonight in another home and in another cradle. Another man calls her daughter, and another woman sings her to sleep. I shall miss her. I can only hope that it is for the best.

Grandma Vera looked down at the little book. "You picked a wonderful family for me," she whispered to the pages. "And yes, I think it was for the best. You protected my family and me for nearly sixty years. You did very well indeed."

"But how did Sparks end up with you?" Sarah asked. "Did the Allens adopt her too?"

"Oh no, Mom and Dad Allen couldn't even see Sparks. An old man gave her to me when I was little," Grandma Vera said, and then her eyes widened with understanding. "That must have been my father. I wish I could remember more about him, but the only memories I have are of wrinkled hands giving me Sparks and warm blue eyes smiling at me." Grandma Vera waved her hands in exasperation.

"There are some pictures in the box," Nickolas said. He had stopped reading the journals and now was rummaging through the remaining contents of Dr. Montague's belongings. He pulled out a handful of old photographs and handed them to Grandma Vera.

"This is him," Sarah said, pointing to a picture of an old bearded man holding a baby in a christening gown. "That same picture was at the manor in a photo album Nickolas and I saw. I bet the baby in that picture is you, Grandma!"

Brigitta nodded. "Yes, that is how he looked about the time he left the manor, and this one is his wife, Victoria." Brigitta handed Grandma Vera a framed picture of a beautiful woman with her hair piled up on her head and a long silk gown in the fashion of over a century ago. The other pictures were of Dr. Montague's colleagues at the University of Sydney and Chicago University. The last picture was of a little girl about six years old with masses of curly hair and wearing a pinafore.

"Who do you think this is?" Grandma Vera asked.

"Is it you?" Nickolas peered over Grandma Vera's shoulder at the pretty little girl.

"No, and it couldn't be, because I wasn't this old at the time Dr. Montague died. Plus I have pictures of myself at this age, and I look nothing like this girl. Do you recognize her, Brigitta?" Grandma Vera asked, passing the picture over.

"It isn't Vivian. The clothing is the wrong era for her, and the picture is too new, plus she doesn't look at all like Vivian. Or Victoria, for that matter. I don't think I have ever met her. Perhaps she was the child of someone he knew." Brigitta handed the picture back to Sarah.

"I know who she is," Sarah exclaimed. "It is a picture of Anne from the records room. See, she even signed the back! I wonder if she slipped it in the box later or if she gave it to Dr. Montague before he left."

Nickolas had returned to the box and pulled out the pocketknife and the keys to examine them. "Ow!" he exclaimed as the sharp blade of the pocketknife sliced his thumb.

"Give me that," Sarah said as she grabbed the knife from his hands. "Really, Nickolas, can't you ever be careful?"

But Nickolas was distracted again, and he absently sucked on his cut thumb and inspected the ring of keys.

"You don't think those are to his rooms at the manor, do you?" Sarah asked.

"No, I don't think so. They don't look anything like the keys at the manor," Nickolas said, showing them to Sarah. "These are all Yale keys, which were popular in the 1940s and '50s. Our modern keys look a lot like them, only bigger and thicker. The keys at the manor were all old-fashioned keys, and most of them were made out of precious stones, not metal. I bet these were Dr. Montague's keys at Chicago University. Probably to his car, apartment, office, and labs." He held up a tiny key. "This one is probably to his luggage or briefcase."

"Are there any more entries in the diary?" Brigitta asked Grandma Vera, who was still reading it to herself.

"Just a few entries about his experiments on removing the microbiotics from his system and finally admitting defeat," Grandma Vera said. "He felt that if he had a few more ingredients from the manor's gardens he might have been able to make more progress. He even lists them here as well as his ideas for next steps, but he wasn't willing to return to the manor and potentially expose me to Vivian and Dr. James. After that there is only one last entry." Vera read it aloud.

June 8, 1947:

Dearest Vera,

If you are reading this, then I have passed away and you have come to Chicago University to find out something of your past.

I know not how you would find this, but I wanted something to be there if you came looking. For if you know that you were adopted, then you should also know why.

My elder daughter—your sister, Vivian—has been conducting experiments that require her to find a close relative to extract ingredients from. With you being her closest possible relative, that meant that you were her first choice. She tried to conduct experiments on you when you were just a baby, and of course I could not allow that. So to keep you safe and untraceable to your sister, I put you up for adoption and had the records sealed so only you could access them.

I hope and pray that this has protected you, and I warn you never to have anything to do with your sister, Vivian, or her associate,

Dr. James. I have left many things in this box that should allow you to get to know who you are and where you come from.

I have already left you my two most prized possessions, dear one. My heart is yours and always has been; the other is the tiny puppy, Sparks, whom you hopefully remember from your childhood. She is a strange little dog, never eating in my presence and never seeming to grow older or lose her puppy antics. Many people claim that they cannot see her, and I am not sure if they are pulling an old man's leg or if they truly cannot. In fact, the only person in America that I have found who can see her is you, my little one, which is why I trusted her to your care when you were so very young.

I wish I had been able to see you grow into a woman. Even as young as you are, you remind me of your beautiful mother. I wonder if you will inherit my love of science or her love of art, or perhaps you will be something else altogether, uniquely you.

I wish you long life and happiness, and know that you were loved so very much by your natural father and mother. If we could have lived longer and assured you of safety, we would have never put you up for adoption, but I know the family I have picked for you will care for you and love you deeply and will be the best of parents to you. I have already seen that they are.

Best of everything and all of my love,
Father

⟨⟩⟨⟩

About halfway through Grandma Vera's reading of the last letter, Nickolas had picked up the pocket watch, and just as Anne had done, he opened the cover on the face of the watch and observed the nonworking hands. Nickolas, unlike Anne, did not accept that the watch could not be fixed, and he immediately turned it over to discover if there was a way to look at its innards.

Nickolas retrieved a tiny screwdriver from one of his pockets and carefully pried under the watch's back. With careful pokes and twists, he was able to remove the back cover. In the dim light of the living room, Nickolas could just discern that a velvet pouch was affixed to the inside of the back. He opened the silk ribbon strings of the pouch, and a tiny ruby key fell out into his hand.

Sarah looked up and saw the watch in pieces in Nickolas's lap. In horror she said, "Nickolas, what are you doing? Don't break that!"

Nickolas guiltily shoved the key back in the pouch and returned the back to the watch. Sarah snatched it out of his hands and stuffed it into her jeans pocket. "Can't you touch anything without breaking it?" she admonished.

"I wasn't breaking it. I was just examining it," Nickolas retorted, and probably a fight would have broken out between the children if they hadn't caught Brigitta's look and their protestations died on their lips.

⧉

After rereading the journal and cross-referencing it with the notebooks, Brigitta and Bard decided that it would be best to return to the manor and retrieve the ingredients listed in the diary. Since all of the needed items were in the gardens (tree roots, gems, and mushrooms), they felt they could slip in, gather the ingredients, and slip out again without anyone at the manor being the wiser.

Sarah, of course, wanted to go with the muses, but they—and Grandma Vera—insisted that she stay at home.

"That is totally unfair," Sarah huffed. "Who found the notebooks and the diary in the first place?"

"I know, Sarah," Brigitta said. "But we really won't be there long, and we don't have time to add thirty-two hours of air travel to the schedule."

"How are you going to get there then?" Sarah asked, still miffed at having to stay home.

"Muses can travel in ways that humans cannot. Bard and I can get there almost instantaneously. We can leave from here and be back in no time. You will hardly miss us. Why don't you take all of these notebooks to Denver General and bring Dr. Lucy up to speed. Tell her we will bring you the ingredients tomorrow afternoon at the latest. Between her abilities and ours, we should have a cure for Simon very soon. At the very least, we can keep the microbios alive in his system until we find a way to slow them down."

Sarah reluctantly agreed to the plan, appeased by the fact that she would at least be doing something to help Simon. Perhaps it was her absolute hatred of airline food that tipped the balance.

"Do you have Georgiana's satchel handy?" Brigitta asked.

"Yes, it's up in my room, under my bed." Sarah bounced up and led the way upstairs with Bard and Nickolas behind them. She pulled the satchel out from its hiding spot and handed it to Brigitta.

Brigitta searched the satchel thoroughly and then turned to Sarah. "Was there a box in here? A pretty one with lots of inlays and carvings?"

"Yes!" Sarah exclaimed, grabbing the box off the shelf above her bed and handing it to Brigitta. "Sparks showed me where it was hidden and wouldn't calm down until I had retrieved it and put it up here." The muse looked a bit startled at this but said nothing as she turned the box over in her hands. Nickolas watched in fascination as she began to slide and move hidden panels on the box until she was able to slip it open. Inside was a silver bar with buttons and dials on its top. Brigitta adjusted the dials and pressed one of the buttons. Then she quickly closed the box and returned it to its solid state, placing it on the bed.

"We will be back very soon," she said and gripped Bard's hand, shooting the last panel into place and putting her left fist on the top of the box, knuckles flush to its lid.

The box glowed silver, bathing both muses in its light. The glow seemed to become entrapped inside the muses, and they too began to glow, brighter and brighter until Sarah and Nickolas had to avert their eyes.

When the silver glow dissipated enough for Sarah to look back at where the muses had stood, they were gone and the box had returned to its normal ornate wooden state.

⊰⊟⊱

Brigitta and Bard rematerialized near Georgiana's plinth in Great-Aunt Vivian's gardens, startling a squirrel that had found the stump to be an ideal sunning spot that morning. The box, hidden in its roots, began to dim from its sudden glow, and Brigitta only had a moment to realize that something was horribly wrong as she felt herself returning to her statue form once more. She was rooted to the spot, still staring at the squirrel, with her hand entwined with Bard's marble fingers.

CHAPTER 16

THE DUNGEONS

⊰⊱

In which Fulvio and Carole sincerely hope they don't turn purple

Carole followed Fulvio through the narrow servants' corridors, moving deeper and deeper beneath the manor carrying the large basket of food she'd insisted on bringing. It was quite cold and damp in those forgotten passageways, and Carole was wishing that she had brought her shawl as well when Fulvio suddenly halted.

Peering over the rotund chef's shoulder, Carole saw the reason for their sudden stop. The passageway in front of them had been boarded over.

"This is new," Fulvio said, appraising the rotting boards.

Carole was not so sure of that, because the boards were covered in dust and cobwebs. She shuddered as a particularly large spider scurried to safety from the light of Fulvio's torch. "Here, hold this please, Carole," Fulvio said, passing the torch to her and reaching into one of the long side pockets of his chef uniform. He extracted a huge spatula that Carole recognized as the one he used to ice the dramatic cakes he made for Lady Vivian's parties. Its thick blade was quite sturdy, and she watched in fascination as he used it to pry the nails from their boards. In short order, Fulvio had the doorway cleared enough to be accessible.

Fulvio grasped the knob, only to find that the door was locked fast. With a mischievous twinkle in his eye, he reached again into his pocket and withdrew a large ring of keys.

"You have the keys to the dungeons?" Carole asked incredulously. "How did you ever get those?"

Fulvio selected a particularly crooked iron key and inserted it into the lock. "When I was a child, I really wanted to see the dungeons. The only person I knew who had a key was my father. So late one night, I crept into his rooms as the manor slept and pressed my father's key into a bar of soap and crept back out with none the wiser. The blacksmith's apprentice—we had a blacksmith behind the stables in those days—was a particular friend of mine, and he helped me to fashion this key from some leftover iron. It isn't much to look at," Fulvio said as the key reluctantly turned in the old lock, "but it does the job." He shoved the door open with his shoulder, and a blast of cold air came through. "Welcome to the dungeons."

Carole declined to go first, letting Fulvio have the honors of clearing out the cobwebs, and followed him into the dank corridor beyond. This was not part of the servants' passageways, but a wide stone walkway, slightly tipped downward.

A few paces further on, the passageway opened into a circular room, with several archways leading out of it. A large wooden table that was crumbling to pieces dominated the center. The walls were decorated with rusty chains and other disintegrating tools, the nefarious purposes of which Carole could only guess. She shuddered and quickly followed Fulvio through one of the archways.

A short corridor led to another large, dank room. This one was full of gigantic cages. It reminded Carole of when the circus had come to town when she was a youth and they had parked all of the cage train cars that contained lions and tigers and elephants around the fairgrounds. All of these cages, however, were empty, save one.

The cage in the middle of the dungeon had three occupants blinking rapidly in the torchlight: a round, balding, middle-aged man whom she recognized as Mr. Benjamin; a stooped, broad-nosed gentleman who she thought was named Dr. Trowle; and a third younger man whom she had never laid eyes on before. Carole was pretty sure she would have remembered the teenager if she had ever seen him, for his blond hair was partially dyed black. Silver rings glinted in the torchlight from multiple piercings in his eyebrow, nose, and ears, with remnants of black makeup smudging his eyelids and lips, having not been reapplied in days. All three gentlemen were barefoot and wrapped in thin woolen blankets. Dr. Trowle and Mr. Benjamin were visibly shivering. Carole was aghast. She hadn't thought that even Lady Vivian could treat people so cruelly.

Fulvio ran toward the cage. "Mr. Benjamin!" he exclaimed. "Are you all right?"

"Fulvio, my good man," Mr. Benjamin said, holding out his hand to greet the chef as if they were casually meeting in the manor library and not separated by steel bars.

Fulvio clasped Mr. Benjamin's freezing fingers in both of his warm hands, rubbing them together to impart some heat. "We have brought you some food," he said, indicating Carole and the large basket she carried, "and were hoping you might be able to help us and we help you, of course."

Dr. Trowle grabbed the loaf of bread that Carole held out and retreated to the cage's lone bench to eat it, curving his body around the loaf protectively and darting furtive glances at his cellmates as if they would steal it from him. Shocked, Carole gave Dr. Trowle a disapproving glance, but she merely handed Mr. Benjamin and the teenager some of the other provisions she had packed.

Mr. Benjamin took a large bite out of the lump of cheese and a swig of lemonade before passing the flask to the teen and addressing Fulvio and Carole. "Thank goodness Lady Vivian sent you, Fulvio. It has been a while since she last delivered food to us. We were beginning to think she had forgotten we were down here."

"Sadly, Mr. Benjamin, Lady Vivian did not send us. I overheard her talking to Louis about your being here, and I immediately set out to see for myself if she really had prisoners in the dungeons." Fulvio took in the condition of the captives and paused for a moment. He removed his jacket, passing it through the bars to Mr. Benjamin. Even though she was shivering, Carole did the same with hers. The teenager gratefully accepted it and walked over to Dr. Trowle, draping the jacket around the scientist's thin shoulders. Dr. Trowle merely grunted at the teen, who responded with a lopsided smile as if he had expected nothing else.

Mr. Benjamin noticed the quizzical look on Carole's face as she observed the teenager. "Fulvio, Carole, I think you know Dr. Trowle," he said, nodding toward the scientist. "And this is Alec. He had the misfortune of being in the wrong place at the wrong time, and when Lady Vivian captured us, she captured him as well."

The teenager sauntered over and held out his hand. "I am Alderic Alexander Anderson the fourth, but please call me Alec as the rest is rather pretentious. My parents couldn't break the family habit, but I try to bring it down a few notches." Carole noticed that the line had an oft-delivered quality, like it was what he always said when he met somebody, but the flat delivery seemed new, like he used to say it with a twinkle in his kohl-rimmed eyes. "I'm not one hundred percent sure what happened, but one minute I was in the airport getting ready to board a flight to the States, and the next this crazy lady and her henchmen started lobbing vials of who knows what at a couple of kids. I tried to stop them, and for my pains I ended up here. But I think the kids got away at least."

"Sarah and Nickolas?" Fulvio directed his question to Mr. Benjamin, who nodded.

"Yes, Lady Vivian was most anxious to recapture them, and their cousin Simon, too. She got the vials from Dr. James, and she told us that they would capture the children, but that she didn't really know how they worked. When one of them shattered on my chest, I found myself here. Don't ask me how, for I have no idea." Mr. Benjamin shrugged his shoulders underneath the blanket and jacket.

"I don't think she was successful," Carole assured him. "We've seen no sign of the children at the manor." Mr. Benjamin seemed pleased.

Fulvio inspected the lock on the cage. "I never did figure out how to open these. To my knowledge, my father did not have the key on his ring. But we have to get you out of here."

"I am not sure that that would be wise, Fulvio," Mr. Benjamin said.

Dr. Trowle immediately made a huff of incredibility. "Why ever not, Benjamin? I have no idea why Lady Vivian keeps us down here anyway, unless it is something that *you* did. *I* have been nothing but loyal to her for years."

Mr. Benjamin ignored the scientist and continued. "I am hoping that Vivian will realize that keeping us here is not in her best interest. But if we mysteriously escape, she will definitely be alerted to your involvement, and Lady Vivian is not known to be forgiving to those who cross her."

"Well, we can at least keep you fed and clothed," said Carole, disapproval etching every line on her face.

"Yes, and unfortunately, we need some assistance from you, as well," Fulvio said urgently. He then explained the withdrawal effects from the synthetic food and how all of their supplies had either been taken by Lady Vivian or destroyed by the guard. "I overheard Lady Vivian saying the servants wouldn't survive long without it." From the shocked look on Mr. Benjamin's face, Fulvio could tell he had no idea of the addictive properties of the food. "Do you think you can help us create some more of the three solutions to keep the staff healthy?"

Mr. Benjamin thought for a long moment, looking very grave. Then he gave himself a little nod, and a smile spread across his face. "Actually, we don't need to make more of the three solutions. I have just the thing in my quarters."

⊰⊱

Carole and Fulvio, with the now empty food basket, picked their way back to the door to the servants' corridors. "That is disgraceful," Carole said, shaking her head.

Fulvio nodded, opening the door and ushering Carole through. "I am not sure I understand what Lady Vivian is thinking. Mr. Benjamin is one of her most trusted associates, and it is obvious that Dr. Trowle is one of her supporters as well. And keeping that child down there in those horrid conditions? Wish I had a key to those cells."

"Who does have the key?"

"I don't know. I am sure that Lady Vivian does, and probably Louis." Fulvio looked thoughtful for a moment. "I think

I have a plan for getting the key and being put in charge of their welfare. If Lady Vivian really does make me head butler, then I am sure that Louis would be happy to let me care for the prisoners." Fulvio's eyes twinkled mischievously. "Especially if he thinks I don't want to."

"You know, Fulvio, I always thought you were so honest and straightforward. I am beginning to find that you really are quite devious," Carole said with a combination of shock and admiration in her voice.

"You are supposed to think that I am kind and straightforward, because for the most part I am. But I also don't have any problem with persuading people to do the right thing, especially if it affects the people I care about, and most especially when they don't want to. Ah, here we are—Mr. Benjamin's quarters." And with that, he opened a hidden panel in the wall that led to a large suite of rooms.

Mr. Benjamin's rooms were like all the suites in Lady Vivian's manor, consisting of a sitting room, a bath, a dressing room, and a bedroom. Mr. Benjamin had transformed his sitting room into a small laboratory, complete with marble-topped tables, sinks, and cabinets full of chemistry equipment.

The two chefs started their work in the dressing room, selecting clothing they thought would keep the prisoners warm until the time was right to release them. Carole carefully folded everything and placed it neatly in her basket, then returned to the sitting room/laboratory.

In the center of the room, on the largest table, a complex experiment was set up, with a leather-bound notebook open beside it covered in grease pencil markings. Fulvio opened the cabinet beneath the table and pulled out several brown glass bottles with cork stoppers. He searched for the bottle Mr. Benjamin had specified, while Carole perused the notes in the leather book.

By using the principles developed by Lady Vivian and her father, I hope to be able to create a supplement that provides all nutrients and calories necessary for one day of sustenance. If we can get this into a pill form that can be easily stored in a small space, produced at an economical price, and with a reasonably long shelf life, it could be exported to eliminate hunger in countries where food is scarce.

Each page of the notebook contained the results of various experiments with the supplements. At the end of each experiment Mr. Benjamin listed his results.

Resulting pill is much too large. It would be impossible to swallow unless the subject was an elephant. I will experiment with making the pills smaller or requiring more pills to be taken throughout the day.

Resulting pill only has a two-week shelf life before it turns toxic. Back to the drawing board.

Resulting pill meets all requirements for size and shelf life. Trials in animal test subjects resulted in unsatisfactory side effects. Vomiting...profusely.

Vomiting corrected. The resulting pill meets all requirements for size and shelf life. Trials in animal test subjects resulted in unsatisfactory side effects. Now the other end is messed up.

Bowel issues corrected. Resulting pill meets all requirements for size and shelf life. Trials in animal test subjects resulted in unsatisfactory side effects. Skin and fur turned purple and patches of fur fell out. They are vomiting again.

If Carole hadn't felt sorry for the test animals, she would have found the ever-increasing list of scary side effects to be humorous as she pictured tiny balding, purple mice trying to swallow a pill bigger than they were. And there was a portion of the sous chef's heart that was happy that Mr. Benjamin hadn't found a way to replace food entirely; her love of food, its taste, its smell, its beauty, just couldn't be replaced by a tiny one-a-day pill. Or a gargantuan one-a-day pill, for that matter.

Fulvio interrupted her reading with a cheerful "Aha!" as he found the bottle of pale-blue pills he had been looking for.

"Are you sure those won't turn us purple and make our hair fall out?" Carole asked, showing Fulvio the experiment results she had been reading.

"No," Fulvio said with a laugh. "These are from a different experiment. Lady Vivian needed some pills for her guards that provided no nutrients, just extracts of the tonza tree roots and the fourth ingredient. The only side effect is that they make you very thirsty. Hopefully, they will do the trick and keep us from having the withdrawal symptoms from the synthetic food."

Carole looked dubiously at the small bottle. The pills were tiny, about the size of a grain of rice. "Nevertheless, we should probably test them just to be sure. Who did you have in mind to be the guinea pigs?"

"We probably should try them on ourselves first," Fulvio said gravely.

"I thought you might say that." Carole sighed and then added resolutely, "I always wanted a way to get rid of my gray hair, although purple would probably not have been my first choice."

CHAPTER 17

Return to Montague Manor

-⊰꒰꒱⊱-

In which Sarah and Nickolas get tired of waiting

S arah and Nickolas sat in Sarah's room waiting, and waiting and waiting…

They had returned from Denver General hours ago, after briefing Dr. Lucy on the contents of Dr. Montague's box. She had been very intrigued and kept saying things like "No way," "This is so cool," and "Imagine what we could do with this technology!" To the point that Sarah had started to feel a bit uncomfortable that Dr. Lucy wanted to continue Great-Aunt Vivian's experiments rather than stop them.

When Nickolas started agreeing with Dr. Lucy, Sarah had had enough. "You do realize that this 'amazing technology' killed Dr. Montague and is killing Simon at this moment? I don't know about you, but anything that Dr. James and Great-Aunt Vivian think is a good thing should be a bright-red warning sign flashing 'Stay Away.'"

Sheepishly, Dr. Lucy agreed. "You are right, of course, Sarah. We don't know enough about this technology to use it safely, and we know that it has been abused by the people who do know about it. We should be focusing on getting Simon well."

Nickolas looked less convinced than Dr. Lucy. "Sarah, just because Great-Aunt Vivian is evil doesn't mean that the microbios are. I bet Dr. Lucy and I could come up with lots of ways to use them for good, like keeping you from having to cut your hair or fingernails. Think of how much we could increase productivity for people!"

"Oh please, Nickolas, you never cut your hair or nails unless someone makes you. And you would spend that spare time playing video games, not saving the world. Be reasonable."

"Let's talk about Simon," Dr. Lucy interjected, heading off the siblings' row. "You said that Mr. and Ms. Telyn would be able to bring me some of the ingredients that are mentioned in the notebooks? When will they arrive? I can set up the beginnings of Dr. Montague's suggested next steps without them in one of the labs here at the hospital. I will reserve a room and get started right away."

"I think Brigitta said that they would be back by the time we returned to the ranch, if all goes well. So we will bring you the ingredients later today. Do you really think you can save Simon?"

"Yes, at the very least we can stop the withdrawal effects he is suffering from now. Curing him will take more work, but if Dr. Montague is correct, he was very close to a solution seventy years ago. I only hope that I am good enough of a scientist to pull this off."

"Of course you are!" Nickolas exclaimed. "And I will help you, so we should have Simon better and back home in no time."

Sarah was not as confident as Nickolas, but she thought it best not to mention it.

⋈

But that had been hours ago. They had expected the muses to be at the house when they arrived, as they had returned well after noon. But now it was nearing 3:00 p.m., and there was no sign from the box that it would start glowing again and deposit the muses on Sarah's rug loaded down with mushrooms and tree roots.

In his boredom, Nickolas picked up the box. He had watched Brigitta carefully when she manipulated it, and now he tried to replicate the steps she had followed to open the intricate puzzle. At first, he was not able to get any of the panels to slide like he had seen Brigitta's nimble fingers do. But then, to his great joy, one of the tiny side panels moved under his touch.

He racked his brain trying to recall the exact sequence of movements Brigitta had used to open the box, and step by painful step he found he could remember them. After each movement he felt the box give a little click, so he knew he was on the right path, and after only two false steps, he got the box open.

Sarah and Sparks had been playing on the bed and didn't notice what Nickolas was doing, but once the box was open, it emitted a faint silver glow, which caught the little dog's eye, and she quickly trotted over to Nickolas and dragged his hand away from the box by pulling his shirtsleeve with her teeth. "Stop that, Sparks! I almost have this figured out!" Nickolas said, trying to remove his shirt from the tenacious dog's mouth.

While Nickolas was distracted, Sarah grabbed the box from his lap. Turning it over in her hands and looking at the various dials and buttons, Sarah said, "Wow, how did you get this open?"

"That was easy—I just remembered what Brigitta did and did the same."

"Easy for you and that freakish memory of yours. Do you think we can get it to work?"

"I don't know. The knobs are all marked with strange symbols that don't make any sense to me. I can't even guess what they mean."

"Maybe we don't need to set the knobs. Maybe they are set correctly already. Unless you changed any of them. You didn't, did you?"

"No?" Nickolas didn't sound so sure. "I touched them, but I don't think I moved any of them. Here, let me see. That freakish memory of mine might remember how they were before."

Sarah stuck her tongue out at Nickolas, but she handed the box back to him all the same. Nickolas looked at the knobs, his face screwed up in concentration like it always was when he tried to remember something. And then his forehead cleared. He carefully turned one of the knobs two clicks counterclockwise and set it gently on the bedspread. "That is how it was," he said with conviction. "And this is the button Brigitta pressed." He indicated it with his pointer finger and was just about ready to press it when Sarah snatched his hand away.

"Do you think it would work for us?" Sarah asked. "Brigitta didn't think so."

"I don't see why not," Nickolas said.

"Well, we aren't muses for starters," Sarah replied. "Didn't Brigitta say it only worked for muses?"

"Yeah, but everything else has worked for us, so why not this? Besides, what is the worst that can happen? Worst case, it glows and we stay here until it stops glowing."

"Do you want to try it?" Sarah asked.

"Beats sitting around here waiting, doing nothing."

"OK, let's press the button. Which one was it?"

Nickolas indicated the right button, and Sarah pressed it.

Nothing happened.

"I think Brigitta closed the box and put her fist on it," Nickolas said after a long pause.

Sarah picked up the box and tried to fit the cover back on it. It only slid partway and refused to go on any farther. She struggled with it for a minute and then looked at her brother's smug face and outstretched hand. "Oh, just do it already, and don't give me that look," she snapped, handing him the box.

Nickolas closed it up by reversing the steps he had taken to open it and placed his fist on top. Sarah quickly grabbed his arm so she wouldn't be left behind, but she needn't have bothered, for once again, nothing happened.

"What are we doing wrong?" Sarah asked rhetorically, fiddling with the box and trying to open it once more.

"Maybe Brigitta is right, we do need to be muses to use it."

"Probably, but I have this sneaking suspicion that we're doing something incorrectly. Brigitta did something that we aren't."

Nickolas looked down at his hands, thinking hard. He absently turned Charles's ring around his thumb as he did so. The children's eyes met over the shiny ruby, realization making both pairs widen with excitement.

Brigitta had been wearing her emerald ring on the hand she had placed on top of the box, and the ring had glowed silver when she did! What if they tried it again, only this time with Charles's ring?

⇥⇤

Surprisingly, it was Nickolas who stopped them from trying to leave immediately. "I need to get some things first. If we really do go to the manor again, I want to be prepared this time. Just give me a second." And he dashed to his room.

He grabbed a backpack from the floor and began filling it from the overstuffed drawers in his desk. He packed tools, wire, nails, a flashlight, extra batteries, a sweatshirt, a spare bridle he had lying on his bed, some interlocking parts from various toys, his baseball and mitt, a remote-controlled car and its controller, and his toothbrush. He double-checked that the mushroom solution was still in his pocket and added a box of matches. He then headed quietly downstairs, tiptoeing so as not to alert Grandma Vera, who was reading in the living room. He slipped into the kitchen and packed some cookies and a thermos of lemonade.

Once he had gathered his provisions, he returned quietly to Sarah's room. She was standing by her desk, searching through the piles stacked on its surface.

"Ready?" he asked her.

"Just one more thing. I need to find that key Charles gave us." She dug furiously through one of the desk drawers.

"Didn't you give it back to him before we left Australia?" Nickolas absently picked up Dr. Montague's watch from where Sarah had set it on her dresser and stuffed it into his jeans' pocket, where it made a soft *clink* when it hit the mushroom vial.

"Nope," Sarah said, turning triumphantly from the desk with a large golden key in her hand. The front end of the key was all jointed, but instead of being floppy like it had been the last time Nickolas had seen it, it was stiffly holding an old-fashioned key shape. "I kept it. You never know when something like this would come in handy. He didn't ask for it back, so I didn't remind him that I had it. If he wants it, all he has to do is let me know. I also have the key to our rooms," she said, holding up the tiny sapphire key the valet had given them their first day at the manor. She pocketed the two keys and placed Georgiana's satchel strap across her body, settling it safely against her hip. "Shall we try the box again?"

"Definitely," Nickolas said, his eyes bright with excitement. Nickolas checked to see that Charles's ring was still on his hand, and grasping Sarah's with the other, he took a deep breath.

"Here goes nothing," he said, and placed his fist on top of the box.

At first, nothing happened, but then the box began to glow, just as it had for Brigitta and Bard. Nickolas felt an odd cold sensation rising from the box and into his arm. It spread upward, engulfing his whole body and spilling over into Sarah's through their clasped fingers. When the light reached Sarah's hand, she gave a gasp so much like the one Nickolas had given when the glow had first touched him that he laughed. Soon the cold and light intensified, so Nickolas could neither see anything around him nor feel anything but the cold—not the carpet beneath his feet nor the touch of Sarah's hand. Just when Nickolas thought he couldn't take the cold and glaring light anymore, it suddenly stopped.

⧉

Grandma Vera rushed into Sarah's room just in time to see the children start to glow. Sparks's barking had woken her up from where she was dozing on the couch. She had run to the stairs with such urgency that she hadn't even bothered to grab her shoes from the floor before dashing toward the sound of the little dog. She looked in horror as the glow engulfed first Nickolas and then Sarah as she and Sparks raced toward the children. Sparks jumped the last few yards from Sarah's bed and landed on Sarah's satchel, as Grandma Vera grabbed her granddaughter's free arm.

Sparks began to glow just as the children did as soon as she touched Sarah's clothes, but the silver light did not jump from the children to Grandma Vera. "Nickolas, stop!" she yelled, but the only answer she got was silence from an empty room and a firmly closed and unlit wooden box.

CHAPTER 18

THE GARDENS

In which we find everything in disarray

Lady Vivian stormed into the kitchens just after the noon meal and approached Fulvio menacingly, obviously in a very foul temper.

"Lady Vivian! This is a surprise. You have just missed luncheon, but I can have something made up for you in an instant." He turned looking for Carole and caught his sous chef's eye and nodded. She returned his nod and bustled off to the larder to whip up a tray for their mistress.

"I am not here for food, Fulvio," Vivian snapped. "I need to talk to you in my office immediately and could not find anyone on duty to deliver my message. But we will talk about that problem and several others in my office. Now!"

"Of course, Lady Vivian," Fulvio said to Vivian's back, for she had already reversed course and was stomping toward the kitchen doors. Fulvio followed her, only pausing to accept the basket that Carole rushed out to him. Fulvio gave Carole a confident smile of thanks and hastened to catch up with Lady Vivian's train.

A few moments later, Fulvio found himself standing before Lady Vivian's massive oak desk in her father's old office. When Dr. Montague had occupied these rooms, it had been filled with books and comfy chairs, with a warm, cheerful fire always in the fireplace and a welcome smile for any visitor. But Lady Vivian had long since removed all the cheerfulness and warmth along with the chairs, leaving only her own chair, the desk, and little more than a chilly reception.

"Fulvio," she begun.

"Yes, ma'am."

"I just had a message from Dr. James. He is expecting to arrive very soon. He is quite concerned with all the happenings here, and he wants us to make sure that things are back to rights immediately. He is most displeased with our progress."

"How can I help, ma'am?"

"I need you to make sure that the food you serve Dr. James is impeccable. I am trusting you with one of my precious vials of essence for that purpose. Under no circumstances is anyone other than Dr. James or myself to be fed food made with this vial." She passed Fulvio one of the tiny hand-topped vials from a locked desk drawer. "Promise me, Fulvio. This is very important."

Fulvio took a deep breath, pocketing the vial. "My staff and I will be happy to produce an excellent feast for you and your guest."

Vivian nodded curtly, locking the drawer that contained the other vials of essence with the ruby key she wore on a black ribbon at her wrist. "Dr. James's rooms will need to be aired and prepared for his visit. You may be wondering why I am asking you to take care of this task personally. It is because I am promoting you to head butler. Your father held that position, I recall, and I am sure that you will do an adequate job. Here are your keys"—she handed him a large ring of keys that Fulvio recognized as his father's—"and your uniforms will be delivered to your rooms. I expect that you will move quarters as well. You can't very well maintain the order of the household sleeping in the kitchen."

"Yes, ma'am," Fulvio said, pocketing the keys. Perhaps Lady Vivian had just given him the keys to the prisoners in the dungeons! First the fourth ingredient and now the keys? Fulvio had to control his features carefully not to let his relief show. If she kept this up, she might just give him solutions to all of his problems, possibly including the cure for Zac's incurable disease and a fool-proof way to keep hollandaise sauce from curdling.

Lady Vivian scowled down her long nose at him. "I assume that you will pay attention to your duties more appropriately than your predecessor, who just ran off with no notice. I further assume it would be redundant for me to tell you that such behavior is unacceptable?"

"Of course, Lady Vivian," Fulvio said, sobering.

"You will be reporting directly to Louis, who will inform you of my commands. Promote whomever you wish to head chef, and try to get this place back under control before tomorrow. I don't know exactly when Dr. James will arrive, so we need to be ready as soon as possible. Dr. James, to say nothing of myself, will be most displeased if you are not."

"Yes, Lady Vivian. May I ask one thing?"

"No, you may not ask anything. Just get it done, Fulvio. Understand?"

"Yes, ma'am." And with that, Fulvio bowed and exited the room. In the outer chamber he found Louis sitting at his desk, a smug smile curled across his lips.

"So, you report to me now, Chef. Won't that be special? You can start by getting those lazy maids of yours to actually clean this house, top to bottom. Since the explosion, things have been lacking around here, to say the least."

"Of course, sir, but perhaps it is less a fault of the maids and more due to the lack of footmen. What are your plans to replace them?" Fulvio kept his tone pleasant and subservient.

"There are no plans to replace them. Make do, Fulvio. We all are doing our part"—he pointed to the neat stacks of paper on his desk—"and I expect you to do the same. I want the manor spotless by morning. When Lady Vivian's guest arrives, I expect the whole staff to be turned out to greet him."

Louis frowned upon noticing the luncheon stains on the tea towel attached to Fulvio's waist. "In freshly laundered uniforms, I might add."

"Yes, sir."

"So what are you waiting around here for? Get going, man. You have work to do. And make sure the first thing you do is change your uniform. Head butlers do not wear that ridiculous hat."

Fulvio bowed and slowly left the room to return to the kitchens, quietly removing his favorite toque.

⊣⊨

After the interview with Louis, Fulvio returned to his old rooms and placed his chef's hat upon its shelf of honor.

He was no longer head chef. He was losing far more than his hat, and he knew it. He was leaving a job that he loved for one that he knew he had no aptitude for, nor desire to do.

The old head butler had been cruel and harsh, doing Lady Vivian's bidding no matter how vicious her commands. Many a maid had rushed to Fulvio's office for cookies and sympathy after being yelled at, beaten, or worse by the old butler for the smallest infractions.

And now he was supposed to fill that odious man's shoes. He was sure that he could eventually, with the right staff and enough time, bring the manor into the same calm oasis that he had made in his kitchens. But surely not by tomorrow.

He did know, however, that sulking about it wouldn't get anything done, so Fulvio turned to his closet and, digging far in the back, pulled out his father's old uniform.

Just the smell of it, dusty and mothballed, brought back unpleasant memories. Fulvio fervently hoped that the cruel and vicious behavior of his predecessors didn't go with the job. He was horrified to discover that the jacket fit perfectly, and with an extra yank on his belt, the trousers were acceptable as well. He carefully tied the bowtie at his neck and started packing his possessions.

⊣⊨⊢

Several hours of packing later, Fulvio arrived at the doors of the head butler's rooms with two ancient suitcases and a large packing box in his arms. He shifted the luggage and pulled the ring of keys Lady Vivian had given him from his pocket. He didn't have to look twice at them to identify the key he needed. He had used the turquoise key so many times in his youth. He squared his shoulders and opened the door.

The room had changed little from when Fulvio's father had lived here. Young Fulvio had frequented his father's rooms only when he was in trouble, usually for being caught exploring the manor with Lord Myers's two boys, for he had lived in the kitchens with his mother. Fulvio noticed that the switch his father had used so liberally on Fulvio's boyish backside still stood in the corner behind the desk. Had the interim butlers used the switch as well?

Fulvio set down his luggage just inside the door, and with purposeful strides, he crossed the room and seized the switch and repeatedly snapped it across his knee until it was reduced to matchstick-size kindling, which he resolutely deposited in the old metal trash bin under the desk.

He then set to work removing all signs of the previous owner's sadistic décor and replacing it with his own cheerful possessions.

⚞⚟

The first things Sarah was aware of after the nothingness of the silver light were the pressure of ground beneath her feet and the death grip that Nickolas had on her left hand. Her other senses returned to her slowly. She heard birds calling to one another and the sound of a breeze running through leafy trees. She smelled the loamy smell of green lawn and the perfume of flowers. In addition to the ground and Nickolas's death grip, she felt the cool wind pulling at her hair. The silver glow dissipated enough so that it no longer blinded her, and she found herself looking at a green floral hedge, dappled with sunshine.

Sarah looked around and recognized that she was in one of the statue clearings on Great-Aunt Vivian's grounds. The relief of familiarity was short lived, however, for the clearing also contained one plinth, one pesky brother, one faintly glowing box, one small black puppy, and two muse statues.

Sarah shook her hand out of Nickolas's and rubbed feeling back into her fingers as she approached Brigitta's statue. Unlike her earlier pose, playing her harp and looking stunningly beautiful, Brigitta looked like she had been just on the verge of telling someone off. Her brows were pulled together, and her blank marble eyes flashed. Her mouth was open as if she was yelling,

"Look out!" and her free hand was raised above her head as if blocking a blow. Her other hand was firmly clasped in Bard's massive marble paw. His free hand was on his ax hilt, as if he was preparing to draw his weapon, and his usually gentle boyish face was hardened into a battle-ready scowl.

Sarah carefully touched Brigitta's face, and her heart sank. How was she ever going to free them?

"I wonder if there is a tanzanite in the fountain," Nickolas asked, tilting his head as he looked at Bard.

Sarah had almost forgotten that her brother was there, and she gratefully whirled toward him. "Yes, that's a perfect idea! Let's go see." But before she left the clearing after her brother, she turned once again to face Brigitta. "Hold tight, Brigitta. We will free you, don't worry!" She hustled up the path with Sparks at her heels.

The children arrived at the fountain after quickly traversing the forest and flower gardens. To their surprise, the fountain was not running. Only once in their previous trip had the fountains been quiet, and that was in the middle of the night. The fountain itself looked neglected. There were dead leaves floating in the water, and some green algae grew along the sides and bottom of the basin. Even the nymphs had algae growing in their giant urns, and one had a white sticky substance dripping down her cheek.

"Wow, what a mess!" Nickolas exclaimed.

"The flower garden was all weedy, too. I wonder what happened to the gardeners." Sarah looked quizzically at the stagnant fountain.

"I think we may have turned them into potatoes in the lab. All of those Faeries had to come from somewhere," Nickolas said, fishing a clump of leaves from the water. "Wish we still had Charles's glasses to see through all this gunk. Well, guess I'll have to do this the old way." And with that, he swung his leg over the edge of the fountain with a splash and began pulling golf ball–size gems from the bottom.

Nickolas had done this so many times before when he had looked in the fountain for the daily tanzanite that it was obvious that he had it down to a pattern. Sarah thought about joining him, but the cold winter air, the slimy dirty water, and Nickolas's splashing dissuaded her, so she walked around the perimeter of the fountain and used her eyes and not her hands to look for an elusive tanzanite gem.

Sparks seemed to agree with Sarah, for she stayed close to her and occasionally peered into the fountain's depths, only to shake her floppy ears and move on.

It took Nickolas several minutes and much splashing to determine that there weren't any tanzanites in the fountain. In fact, he was pretty sure that no new stones had been added to the fountain in some time, as they were all dirty and covered in plant growth. If new gems had been added the night before, he figured, they would still be sparkly and clean.

To check his theory, the three returned to the flower garden. Nickolas stopped in front of the first flower plant, and oblivious to the large puddle of murky water forming at his feet, he inspected it from tips to roots. There were flowers in various stages from tiny buds to full bloom, but unlike their previous visits to the flower garden, there were also blooms that had passed their prime and were turning brown and shriveling up. Nickolas plucked one of these from the plant and opened the petals to look inside. A horrid stench emitted from the open flower, and in the place where the gem should have been was nothing but a shriveled prune-like sphere reeking of rot.

"I didn't know that gems rotted," Nickolas said, trying to hand the smelly flower to Sarah.

Sarah dropped it immediately and wiped her hands on her jeans. "Maybe they aren't really gems. I always wondered why Great-Aunt Vivian felt that she had to sell her experiments for money when she had all these precious stones in her possession. Just one of those diamonds must be worth a fortune. But if they rot over time, then they wouldn't be worth anything."

"How depressing. I was hoping to bring some home so I could buy a Bunsen burner and more equipment for my lab," Nickolas said, looking dejected.

"Yeah. But I bet Mom will be really glad that you can't do that. You probably would just have burned the stable down if you had a Bunsen burner, so maybe this is a good thing," Sarah said.

"Maybe." But Nickolas did not look at all convinced.

After a long pause, Sarah stood up from where she sat on the path. "Well, sitting here isn't helping anything. We need to find where Great-Aunt Vivian put the tanzanites. They aren't on the plinths, and they aren't in the fountain, so they must be somewhere!"

"Unless Great-Aunt Vivian destroyed them." Nickolas still sounded dejected.

Sarah paused but then shook her head. "I don't think she did since they obviously still work. She is too practical to destroy them. We have to find the tanzanites if we hope to go home, as we don't know how to use that box thing to go back, so we only can go forward. We can worry about how when we get to that point."

"You know, you sound annoyingly like a grown-up when you say things like that," Nickolas grumbled.

"Well, one of us has to be," Sarah shot back.

Sparks interrupted their spat by barking sharply and running up the trail.

Both children knew Sparks well enough to know that it was usually a good idea to follow her when she told them to, so with one last glare at each other, they turned and ran after the little dog.

Sparks led them through the maze garden and the mushroom garden, pausing only a moment at the top of the stairs to the Zen garden to make sure that the children were following. The general disarray that they had noticed in all of the gardens was most pronounced in the Zen garden. The wind and weather had washed away all of the neat swirls in the garden's sand beds, and in several places there were holes and footprints. In fact, the only part of the garden that was still pristine was the small portion directly under the invisible pathway, making it easy for the children and Sparks to see where they needed to go.

The manor loomed gray and forbidding over them once they had gone through the path in the Zen garden. There was a deserted feel to the mansion that they had not noticed before, as two weeks prior the home and the grounds had been teeming with footmen, servants, and scientists.

Sarah paused in the middle of the breakfast garden and looked at Nickolas. "Where should we go?"

In response, Nickolas's stomach growled. "Let's find Fulvio. He should be able to help us find the tanzanites…and some lunch as well.

"Ugh…I don't want to eat anything here. It's killing Simon as we speak. If a lot of it will kill you, why would you eat even a little of it?" Sarah pulled a face of disgust.

"Because I'm hungry and it tastes good," Nickolas replied. "Come on, Sarah. You don't have to eat anything, but I'm sure you want to see Fulvio. And the sooner we find him, the sooner we can find the tanzanites, free Brigitta and Bard, and get out of here. I'd forgotten how much this place creeps me out."

"Me too," Sarah agreed, leading the way to the hidden staircase to the kitchens.

⊰⊱

Sarah and Nickolas met no one on the staircase, but when they rounded the bend to the double doors that opened into the main kitchen, the sounds of activity reached their ears. They peeped through the round kitchen door windows and were amazed by the number of cooks and drudges who were working inside.

The last time they had visited the kitchens, the cooks had little to do unless Great-Aunt Vivian was throwing a party, as nearly all the food was created by her footmen from the vials. But now the kitchens were busy with people chopping, mixing, boiling, baking, kneading, roasting, basting, sautéing, plating, serving, and cleaning.

Sarah took one last peek to determine that Great-Aunt Vivian was not in the kitchens before she pushed the doors open. Sparks slipped out of Sarah's arms and dashed inside ahead of them. The puppy paused for a moment, sniffing the air, and then made a beeline across the room toward a pair of workers in white uniforms. Nickolas also sniffed the air, and he was ready to make a beeline of his own for one of the tables laden with fresh bread rolls, but then Sarah grabbed his arm and propelled him after Sparks.

Sarah stopped up short when she realized that neither of the people Sparks was leading them to was Fulvio. One was a short motherly-looking chef wearing a tall toque and carrying a wooden spoon just like Fulvio used to. The other was a tall lumbering man in his early twenties who was bending over to pet Sparks with exaggerated care.

The woman noticed the two children, and her eyes grew wide. "Mistress Sarah? Master Nickolas? Whatever are you doing here?" Then she clamped a hand over her mouth and looked furtively over the kitchens. "Come in here," she whispered, leading them into a little room behind them. "Zac, guard the door and don't let anyone in except Fulvio," she said to the large man holding Sparks in one hand with a bewildered look on his gentle face.

"OK, Mama. Is Chef coming down to the kitchens then?" he asked, looking hopeful.

"I don't know, but if he does, tell him to meet me in here, OK?"

"OK, Mama."

And with her son standing sentry, she closed the door behind her, giving the children a nervous smile. "I'm Carole," she whispered. "Up until today, I was Fulvio's head sous chef, but with his promotion, I have been elevated to head chef. Why are you back? Mr. Benjamin told us that you had escaped to America."

"We had," Sarah said, also whispering. "But we had to come back. Simon, another child who was here, escaped with us, and he is very ill. We were hoping to get some ingredients that would help him get better, but we kind of have bigger problems now. The two people who can get us back home, well, they need some help, too. So we were hoping to find Fulvio. Do you know where he is?"

"He is in the head butler's rooms," Carole informed them.

"The butler? But he is really, really mean. What is Fulvio doing there?" Nickolas exclaimed loudly.

"*Shh!*" Sarah and Carole admonished him together.

"In the head butler's rooms," Nickolas repeated in a much quieter voice. "What did Fulvio do? Is he in trouble?"

"No, no, nothing like that," Carole said soothingly. "Fulvio isn't in any trouble. Lady Vivian just promoted him to head butler and ordered him to clean out his predecessor's things and move in there. Anyway, I think we may have something that will help Simon. All of us here at the manor are feeling the withdrawal effects of the food, and Mr. Benjamin—you remember him, right?" They nodded and she continued. "Well, he is helping us work out a solution behind Lady Vivian's back. Are you feeling the effects as well?"

"No," Sarah assured her. "The doctor who is helping cure Simon, Dr. Lucy at Denver General, says that because we weren't here very long, there shouldn't be any adverse effects. But wait, if you aren't eating the scientific food, what are you eating?"

"Regular food. All of the synthetic food ingredients were either destroyed or confiscated by Lady Vivian. We are having to cook everything again. Fulvio was able to set up a weekly delivery for supplies from town, and I am sure you noticed the increased activity in the kitchens. It is a lot more work, but it is definitely better for us. Are you hungry?"

"Starving," Nickolas said before Sarah could shush him again.

"Come this way." Carole led them back out the door and around the kitchens to another room. As she went, she had a few whispered words with one of the younger cooks, who scurried off toward the laden food tables.

The second room was more of an office, filled with cookbooks, toques, aprons, and scribbled bits of paper. It was also filled with packing boxes in various stages of unpacking. "I'm sorry for the mess. I just moved in here this afternoon from my other quarters. It will take me some time to get everything buttoned down." She looked disapprovingly at the boxes.

Sarah had the impression that Carole was normally a very organized and orderly person, and that all of the disarray around her was causing her a great deal of stress. But Sarah didn't have very long to ponder about Carole, for following a knock at the door, two servants entered with trays full of food. Carole removed several stacks of books and papers from the desk, and the servants quickly placed their trays upon it.

"Now you are sure that this is safe to eat?" Sarah asked as she tentatively filled her spoon with stew. Nickolas felt no such compunction and was rapidly cleaning his tray. Carole reassured Sarah, and after one last cautious sniff, she took a bite. The food was delicious, and after a cautious start, Sarah was soon matching Nickolas in scraping down their soup bowls with fresh crusty bread as Carole talked.

"After you're full, I'll lead you to the head butler's rooms, and then we will go visit Mr. Benjamin in the dungeons."

"What?" Sarah exclaimed. "Why is Mr. Benjamin in the dungeons?"

"It's a long story, but if you are done, I will fill you in along the way," Carole said calmly. "The sooner we get the two of you out of here the better. Lady Vivian has been in a seriously bad mood since you left, and now she's in a tizzy over Dr. James's planned visit to assess the damage to the labs. She has given Fulvio, to say nothing of the kitchens and staff, an impossible task. To have the manor prepared to perfection with half the staff missing."

"Why is half of the staff missing?" Nickolas asked around a chocolate cupcake.

"All of the footmen and guards left after the explosion in the labs. They're the ones responsible for the grounds and the cleaning and care of the manor. Without them, the grounds are overgrown, the manor is dusty and neglected, no fires are laid, no stairs are swept, and no rooms are aired. Fulvio was able to fix the problems with the kitchens, so now Lady Vivian thinks he can fix the problems with the rest of the manor. Next she will be putting him in charge of weeding the gardens, and then the man will drop of exhaustion for sure."

Sarah got the idea that Carole was fiercely protective of Fulvio. She instantly decided that she liked Carole. And since Carole had immediately fed Nickolas, Sarah was pretty sure he liked her as well.

⚎

Fulvio was nearing completion transforming the old butler's rooms into a homey and comfortable space, and as a final touch, he placed his toque in the center of the mantelpiece and stood back to admire the effect.

Sarah could hold back no longer and rushed into the room to embrace her old friend. "Oh Fulvio, it is *so* good to see you!" Sarah exclaimed into his lapel, barely audible as she was holding him so tight.

"Mistress Sarah! Master Nickolas! What are you doing here?" Fulvio's arm wrapped around Sarah, tucking her head under his chin, and he reached out his free hand to pull Nickolas in for a squishy hug as well. It took some time for Sarah to relinquish her hold on Fulvio, and when she did, the whole story poured out of her, starting with Simon's sickness and finishing with Brigitta and Bard's stone forms. Sparks and Nickolas interrupted every so often to add their own barks and comments to Sarah's tale.

Fulvio listened carefully, worry lines appearing between his brows and deepening with each sentence the children said.

"So we need to get the tanzanites to free the muses and the ingredients from the gardens to help Simon," Sarah finished up.

"I think I know where the tanzanites are," Fulvio said slowly, "and we need to see Mr. Benjamin. He may be able to help you with Simon, as we are facing similar problems here. Mr. Benjamin was able to provide us with some pills that are arresting the withdrawal symptoms until he can develop a permanent solution. In fact, I promised to take this box of science equipment to him to help him with his experiments in that area. I was planning on taking it down to him with some more food this afternoon."

"Couldn't I take the food and the box to the dungeons while you and the children find the tanzanites?" Carole asked, thinking that she didn't want the children anywhere near the freezing cold cells.

"Can I go with Carole to the dungeons?" Nickolas asked eagerly.

Sarah looked thoughtful and said, "I agree that splitting up is a good idea. We can get everything done faster that way. How about I go with Fulvio and get the tanzanites, and Nickolas can go with Carole to the dungeons. He can tell Mr. Benjamin everything that we learned from Dr. Montague's papers, and Mr. Benjamin can tell Nickolas everything he thinks Dr. Lucy should know to help make the cure. Then we can return to the gardens and get the ingredients that Dr. Lucy needs on our way back to Brigitta and Bard."

Fulvio could tell that Carole was not happy with the plan, but he saw its merits and readily agreed. Just as long as he could keep both children far away from Lady Vivian and Louis.

After loading Nickolas down with the box of science equipment and seeing him on his way to the dungeons with Carole, Fulvio and Sarah headed out of the butler's rooms and into the servants' passageways.

Carole led Nickolas into the servants' passageways as well, but in a different direction and deeper into the manor than he had ever traveled before. When Nickolas was pretty sure that they couldn't go any lower without hitting the water table, Carole opened the door that led into the stone dungeons. She grabbed a torch off the walls and led Nickolas rapidly across a room filled with nightmarish equipment and into yet another passageway.

They soon heard voices coming from up ahead, and Nickolas nearly broke into a run when he heard Mr. Benjamin's gentle baritone, but he slid to a stop when he saw Mr. Benjamin trapped in the cell. Carole arrived a moment later, puffing slightly with the effort of keeping up.

"Master Nickolas, whatever are you doing here?" Mr. Benjamin sounded equally horrified at seeing Nickolas in the dungeons as Nickolas was to see Mr. Benjamin in the cell. "I thought you were safe!"

CHAPTER 19

LADY VIVIAN'S DRESSING ROOM

⟨⟩

In which we discover Fulvio has hidden talents

Mr. Benjamin shook Nickolas's hand through the bars. "I am very glad to see you again, of course, although I was hoping that you had escaped the manor for good and would be well away from your great-aunt's experiments. Why on earth did you return?"

"I hope I won't see Great-Aunt Vivian while I'm here, either. In fact, I'm hoping she won't even know I came back. But I have a bit of a problem that I'm hoping that you can help me out with," Nickolas said.

"Of course I will help you any way I can, Master Nickolas."

"Sarah and I came here with two of the muses, Brigitta and Bard. You remember them. The beautiful redhead and the big guy with the battle-ax," Nickolas explained but didn't wait for an answer. "Well, as soon as they set foot in the statue garden, the two of them turned back into statues. We need to free them, but there aren't any tanzanites in the fountain. So Sarah and Fulvio are off looking for the tanzanites, but I thought I could work with you. Simon is experiencing the same symptoms as everyone here, only worse since he doesn't have the pills you gave Fulvio."

Mr. Benjamin looked thoughtful for a moment. "I am not sure the pills would work for Simon as they are based on the solution we extracted from him. I would think, since the DNA involved is his own, that his body would just absorb the pills without the chemical reaction occurring. We could certainly try them, but I don't think we will have very good results."

A loud "Humph" came from Dr. Trowle's bench.

Nickolas noticed Mr. Benjamin's cellmates for the first time. "Who are these guys?" he asked, pointing to the scientist who sat sulking on the bench and the pierced and dyed teenager slouching against the bars a few feet away from where Nickolas and Mr. Benjamin were talking.

The teenager came to the bars and held out his hand. "This is Alec," Mr. Benjamin said, making introductions.

Nickolas vigorously shook Alec's offered hand. "Nice to meet you," he said. "I'm Nickolas." He was intrigued by Alec's eyebrow ring and was completely unaware that he was staring until the teenager raised the eyebrow in question at him sardonically, causing Nickolas to drop his gaze.

The reception from the sullen Dr. Trowle was far icier. The scientist didn't even bother to get up to meet Nickolas when Mr. Benjamin introduced him.

Once the introductions were done and Carole was busy giving food to the prisoners, Nickolas began poking in the large cardboard box that Fulvio had sent to Mr. Benjamin. It was packed full of science equipment and various vials full of powders, liquids, and gasses, all labeled in Mr. Benjamin's neat purple handwriting. He was just thinking about pocketing a small vial of sparkly substance labeled "Gem Extract" when Mr. Benjamin interrupted him. He nearly dropped the bottle but was able to catch it at the last moment.

"Yes, Mr. Benjamin?"

"You were telling us that you are attempting some of the same experiments to heal your cousin Simon that I am working on to save the rest of the occupants of the manor. Did you and your sister suffer any ill effects from being on the food?"

"No, we were eating it for such a short time, nothing happened to us." Nickolas absently placed the solution back in the box and returned to the bars.

"I must admit that the withdrawal issues are something that I didn't foresee. I always assumed that once we stopped eating the food, we would return to our normal timeline. But that does not seem to be the case," Mr. Benjamin said, more to himself than Nickolas.

"Dr. Montague did a lot of similar experiments before he died, but he was never able to solve it either. It was all in his papers he left Grandma Vera."

Mr. Benjamin's eyes lit up with hope. "You didn't by any chance bring Dr. Montague's papers with you?"

"No, but I can help," Nickolas said. "I read them all cover to cover, and I have a pretty good memory." And with that Nickolas and Mr. Benjamin launched into a long, detailed conversation.

⧓

As they walked along, Sarah asked Fulvio some of the questions that had been concerning her. "Why does Great-Aunt Vivian have Mr. Benjamin locked up in the dungeons? I thought Mr. Benjamin was her right-hand man?"

"They seem to have had a bit of a falling out," Fulvio said.

"Yes, I gathered that," Sarah answered, her eyes twinkling. "Last time I saw him he took one of those vials that Great-Aunt

Vivian was throwing at us in the chest. When the vial hit Mr. Benjamin, he just disappeared!"

"I talked to him about that last time I visited him. He said something about the vials being from Dr. James and containing markers. How he was transported here was as much a mystery to him as it was to me. I have to admit that I am rather shocked by the whole thing. Ah, here we are. If my memory serves me correctly, if we turn down this corridor and then up these stairs, we should be right outside Lady Vivian's quarters."

"Why do we want to be outside Lady Vivian's quarters?" Sarah's eyes were wide, and she stopped dead in her tracks. "I thought the plan was to avoid her."

"True, but if we want to get the tanzanites, we will need to get them from her safe. I am fairly confident that she is not in her rooms at the moment. Dr. James is returning soon, and she is in a state that everything in the lab and manor be perfect for his return. Since her rooms are the one area of the manor where I can guarantee Dr. James will not be visiting, I think we can rest assured that she will not be here." Fulvio carefully depressed the latch that opened the sliding door in the paneling. It slipped aside smoothly, and Fulvio ushered Sarah inside.

The door led them into what must be Great-Aunt Vivian's dressing room. Sarah had always thought that the rooms that Great-Aunt Vivian had assigned to Nickolas and her when they visited were ginormous, but they were nothing compared to the dressing room she had assigned herself.

The room was lined floor to ceiling with mirrored cabinets, and there was a row of mannequins in front of the mirrors, all dressed in fantastic gowns of every color and description, complete with matching gloves, jewels, and shoes. The room was lit by a series of large crystal chandeliers, each with hundreds of candles. The light sparkled off the crystal fobs and swags and was reflected in the mirrored cabinets, giving the whole room a warm golden glow.

Between the wardrobes and cabinets, there were alcoves that were used for displaying ostrich feather hats on elaborate hat stands or expensive cosmetics on silver trays or displays of fabulous jewels in locked glass boxes or exquisite-cut glass perfume bottles arranged neatly on mirrored ovals. Behind these displays were either elaborately framed mirrors or masterfully painted artworks. In one alcove, among the perfume bottles, there was a small framed picture that Sarah recognized. It was the same one from the photo album in the library, only this copy had not been handled nearly as often. It showed Great-Aunt Vivian standing beside a tall, handsome man in a time before her experiments had made her young. Since in this copy the face had not been worn away, Sarah could see that her suspicion had been correct: it was Dr. James with Great-Aunt Vivian in the picture. He wore a satisfied smile, like he had just been given a fabulous gift that he had always wanted and had schemed for years to obtain. The much older Vivian looked like a besotted schoolgirl, if such girls had wrinkles and gray hair.

As Sarah studied the picture, Fulvio moved from alcove to alcove until he found one containing a magnificent peacock-blue hat, complete with matching feathers held at the brim with a sapphire brooch and blue netting cascading in swags all over it. He carefully removed the hat and its stand, setting them on the floor and reached into the space above the cabinet. Curious, Sarah moved to his side. On the wall in the back of the alcove was a still life picture of a collection of antique Bunsen burners, all glowing and reflecting their flickering flames. Although an appropriate piece for a scientist to own, Sarah thought that it was a bit odd that the artist had chosen this subject when most still lifes she had seen contained fruit and crockery.

"It was painted by her mother, your great-grandmother," Fulvio said as he swung the painting away from the wall on hidden hinges. Behind it was hidden an old-fashioned wall safe. "Now I need you to be quiet for a moment while I open this."

Fulvio put his ear to the safe and carefully turned the combination lock clockwise. He paused for a moment, nodded, and then swung it back around counterclockwise, slowing down after one full revolution and stopping again on another number. He turned it one more time clockwise, and a wide grin crossed his face as he stopped at a third. "That should do it," he said as he turned the large silver handle and opened the safe.

"Fulvio! Where on earth did you learn to crack safes? Should I be calling the police?" Sarah said, half appalled, half amazed at her friend's hidden talent.

"Ah, Mistress Sarah, didn't I tell you that I was a bit of a scamp when I was younger? There was not a lock or a safe or a door or a fence that could keep me out if I wanted to go somewhere back in those days. And it's like making a pie—no matter how many years it has been since you have done it, you never forget how." At Sarah's scandalized look he laughed. "Just kidding, Mistress Sarah. I observed Lord Myers opening this safe from the servants' passageway when I was very small, and luckily, it appears that Lady Vivian has never changed the combination. Regardless, I am not entirely sure if my mother sent me off to culinary school in England to educate me or to protect me from the wrath of my father and Lord Myers! Oh, those two poor men were run to distraction by the antics that Lord Myers's sons and I got into. And since I was just a servant's boy, I am sure that I got blamed for more than my fair share. They probably all breathed a huge sigh of relief when I left."

He said all this with a twinkle in his eye, which left Sarah thinking that his childhood pranks were more curiosity and good fun than maliciousness and thievery. "Have you met Charles, one of the muses?" she asked. "I think the two of you would get along great."

"I only met your muses briefly as they visited my kitchens two weeks ago. Perhaps the day will come that you can properly introduce us, only this time, perhaps they can leave a few less dead potato people around for me to clean up." Fulvio pulled jewel boxes and papers from the safe as he talked, carefully piling them on the floor. Sarah sat at his feet and went through them quickly, making sure that none of the boxes contained the tanzanites. There were tiaras and necklaces, bracelets and earrings, ropes of pearls and strings of diamonds. It was like going through the queen's jewels, and Sarah wished she had had more time to inspect them, but hardly had she opened one box when Fulvio was placing three more in front of her. The papers were mostly deeds and wills, including an old will of Dr. Montague's. She had seen a similar one among his papers in the box from Chicago University. At the time, she hadn't bothered to read it, but now she opened the thick sheaf of papers and glanced through them.

This copy of the will was dated long before Grandma Vera's birth, but obviously after Dr. Montague had been made a baronet. There were pages and pages of legalese outlining what belonged to the baronetcy and therefore would revert back to the king if he died with no male heir versus what belonged to himself, and therefore he could pass on to Vivian and any of her heirs. Sarah was no lawyer, so she understood only about a third of what she was reading, but it appeared that Dr. Montague didn't own the manor in his own right and that it legally now belonged to the Crown along with the title, several medals, and endowments, which should have been boxed up and sent back to England years ago. Sarah highly doubted that Great-Aunt Vivian had done so, and she was pretty sure she had seen some of the medals and grants among the boxes and papers around her knees.

From what she read, Sarah gathered that the rules of succession meant that her father would not be the next baronet, though she doubted that her father would care that he wasn't Baronet McGuire. In fact, his personality was such that she was pretty sure he would have laughed at the whole thing, thrown it all in a box, and never given it another thought. The idea of her mother—who usually wore old jeans and T-shirts from the various half marathons she had participated in—in one of the sparkly tiaras from the safe nearly set Sarah into giggles.

Sarah was brought out of her paperwork by Fulvio. "That's everything. Sarah, did you find the tanzanites?"

"No, just jewels, medals, and papers. Are you sure she said that she had them in here?"

"Positive. Louis must have taken them already. Let's put everything back and head down to Lady Vivian's office. Maybe we will find them there."

Sarah and Fulvio placed the boxes and papers back into the safe. When they were done, Fulvio spun the lock and swung the picture back into position. Finally, he put the elaborate blue hat and hat stand back in place, careful to position it just as it had been before.

They had just reached the door in the paneling when they saw that someone was turning a key in a lock just outside the dressing room. Fulvio quickly pushed Sarah through the opening and slid the panel silently back into place behind them. And just in time, too, for Great-Aunt Vivian entered the dressing room not a moment later, muttering to herself. "I wonder who locked that door. It is never locked…"

Sarah watched through a peephole as Great-Aunt Vivian removed her bracelets and set them on one of the counters. Her long black gloves followed, and she began to remove several old-fashioned sparkly rings from her gnarled fingers. Sarah had only caught a glimpse of Great-Aunt Vivian's hands once before, and what she saw now confirmed her suspicions. Not all of Great-Aunt Vivian had been affected by the rejuvenating properties of Simon's essence, and although her face and body appeared to be no more than twenty-five years old, Great-Aunt Vivian's hands appeared to be much closer to their true age. Sarah quickly looked at Fulvio. He appeared to be in his forties from the top of his head to the tips of his fingers, and he had been eating the food for as long as Great-Aunt Vivian had. Why wasn't he affected in the same way?

When she looked again, Great-Aunt Vivian was wrapped in a silk robe with her hair bound up in a fluffy towel. Piles of silk dress and underclothes were strewn all over the dressing room floor, and she was heading out the door toward the bath across the hall. The dressing room door clicked firmly behind her, and Sarah whispered to Fulvio, "Why are her hands old and gnarled like that?"

"I'm not sure, but I know that they have been that way for many, many years. Come, we can talk as we walk toward Lady Vivian's office." Fulvio took a few steps down the hidden corridor and then stopped. "Wait here, I need to get something." Fulvio snuck back to the entrance to Great-Aunt Vivian's dressing room and slipped through the door. Sarah could just see him grab something off the dresser and put it into his pocket before he returned to her side. "This way, Mistress Sarah," he said as he led her down the passageway once more.

Sarah followed Fulvio down several corridors before he started into his tale again. "Lady Vivian made an alteration to the food composition many decades ago, which is when certain members of the household began to show signs of getting younger. Alas, it did not happen to me, and I have looked as I do now for as long as I can remember.

"At dinner one night when I was serving, Lady Vivian and Mr. Benjamin were discussing some of the less desirable side effects of their experiments, and one of the things they mentioned was that the rejuvenating process was incomplete, but they were working on how to address that. Something about needing a closer DNA match. It all meant nothing to me. Now if they were talking about how to make bread rise more evenly, then perhaps I would have understood, no?"

Fulvio paused before another door panel. "Right this way, Mistress Sarah. Here is Lady Vivian's office. She seemed like she was going to be indisposed for quite some time, so let's take the opportunity to search her study, shall we?"

Sarah was pretty sure that this wasn't the best idea, but she desperately wanted to free Brigitta and Bard, get the ingredients that they needed, and return home, so she quietly followed Fulvio into the study.

"Sarah, why don't you search the desk, and I will search the file cabinets," Fulvio said, pulling a ruby key on a black ribbon from his pocket. He quickly used it to unlock all the drawers on the filing cabinets behind the desk and then handed it to Sarah.

The desk was what her mother, who loved old furniture, would have called a partners desk as it was wide enough for two people to use it facing each other. There were drawers on both sides so each "partner" would have his or her own set. Sarah started on the side where a large leather upholstered chair had been drawn up to the kneehole. Once unlocked, the center drawer revealed some thick cream writing paper with the

Montague family crest embossed on the top, as well as several fountain pens and small vials of ink. Sarah closed that drawer and moved to the two drawers on the left-hand side of the desk. Both of those contained various writing supplies and a ledger with neatly balanced numbers marching in columns down the pages. Sarah moved to the other side, where there were two additional drawers.

The top one was covered with a writing surface, which once removed contained a shallow area that was filled with neatly placed vials. Sarah recognized them, for they had the hand-topped stoppers that she had seen the footmen making food out of in Fulvio's kitchens. Sarah was pretty sure that the milky-white substance in the vials was all that remained of Simon's essence. The lower drawer contained a row of hanging files. The labels were all neatly written in Great-Aunt Vivian's girlish handwriting and appeared to be her personnel folders. There were files for each of the servants in the manor who reported directly to Great-Aunt Vivian. Fulvio was there, as were Mr. Benjamin, M. Craubateau, and Mr. Fairchild. There were lots of other people listed on the folders whom Sarah did not know. Then Sarah's eyes caught a folder tucked away in the back of the drawer labeled "Dr. James."

Curious, Sarah pulled out the folder. It was very thick and heavy, and as she pulled it out, a slim leather-bound diary fell out from the file and landed heavily on the carpeted floor at Sarah's feet. Still holding the file, she was crouching down to retrieve the diary when she heard something that made her freeze beneath the desk.

"Just what are you doing in Lady Vivian's private office, Fulvio?" a nasal man's voice called from the vicinity of the room's main door.

CHAPTER 20

THE TANZANITES

In which Sarah finds she is handy with a letter opener

Fulvio calmly turned from the file cabinet. "Why, Louis, this is a pleasant surprise. I am just tidying things up in here for Dr. James's visit. Lady Vivian made it perfectly clear that she wanted the manor to be spotless, and I figured that she didn't want one of the under maids cleaning her room and would be much more comfortable if I were the one to do it personally."

Fulvio walked casually around the desk and carefully closed the open file drawer with his knee, while pretending to straighten papers and knickknacks on Great-Aunt Vivian's desk. Sarah slipped deeper into the alcove, and Fulvio straightened the chair so that she was all but hidden in its depths. She hardly dared to breathe.

"I am surprised that she asked you to clean up in here, as that is usually my job." Louis sounded suspicious.

"Really? I was unaware," Fulvio said, still sounding calm and reasonable. "I must have been mistaken in her directions. I will clarify it next time I see her. But if that is all, I really must be heading back to my other duties." Fulvio quietly removed and pocketed Lady Vivian's key from where it rested in the file drawer lock, while deftly picking up the dirty teacup and pot that lay on her desk.

"What did you just put in your pocket?"

"Nothing," Fulvio replied. "I was just gathering these tea things. I am sure you meant to do it soon, but I will be happy to take them back to the kitchens for you."

"I am sure that you would, but unfortunately you will be accompanying me back to my office for a moment and turning out your pockets."

"Seriously?" Fulvio said, letting amusement color his words. "Am I a child again to be brought to the principal's office for punishment? My understanding was that as head butler, I had been promoted to one of the two highest positions in the household. Or am I mistaken and I have really been demoted to the level of newest kitchen drudge?" Fulvio asked. Sarah could tell that Fulvio would only allow Louis to push him around so far. She couldn't imagine Fulvio ever being disrespectful, but she had seen how he ran things in the kitchens, and although everyone loved him dearly, he was rarely, if ever, crossed by his peers and staff.

"Yes, you are the second-highest position here, Fulvio, but you seem to have forgotten that *I* am the highest and that *you* report to *me*. It seems that you have gotten above your station all those years hiding out in your kitchens, and it is time you realize that there are limits to what you can and cannot do here." Louis was losing his temper.

"Well, shall we go to your office then? Do you wish to use the main door or go through the servants' corridors?" Fulvio still stood behind Great-Aunt Vivian's desk, and Sarah could see him indicate the sliding door in the panel just behind them.

"I never use the servants' corridors. Those are not intended for the likes of me. You shouldn't be using them either. They are only for the parlor maids so that they won't be seen. You and I are meant to be seen about our tasks. You shall not be using them from here on out. Is that clear?"

"Of course, Louis. After you, sir?" Fulvio rounded the desk and motioned for Louis to precede him out the door.

"Not a chance, Fulvio. You shall lead the way and keep your hands where I can see them." The two men exited the room, and Louis closed the door with a sharp click behind them. Sarah heard him turn the lock from the outside, and for a moment she panicked that she wouldn't be able to get out of the room, but then she remembered the passageway and eased her way out of her hiding spot.

Fulvio had locked the drawer to Great-Aunt Vivian's desk when he had removed the key, so Sarah had no place to put the folder and diary she had removed. She certainly didn't want to leave them lying around, for they would have gotten Fulvio in even deeper trouble if they were discovered by Great-Aunt Vivian. The folder had been so far back in the drawer that Sarah doubted it would be missed anytime soon, so she slipped the diary and folder into Georgiana's satchel, which was still slung over her shoulder. She then returned the chair to its correct position and quietly slipped through the sliding panel.

Once inside the servants' passageway, she could hear Fulvio and Louis talking through the opposite wall. The secretary's office must be just on the other side. Worried about her friend, Sarah pressed her ear against the paneling.

"Turn out your pockets, Fulvio, or I will take you directly to Lady Vivian," Louis was saying.

"This is ridiculous," Fulvio said with a sigh, but Sarah could hear the jingling and clinking of items being put on the desk. "My keys, a vial of pills, and a spatula."

"What are the pills for?" Louis asked.

Sarah could almost hear Fulvio thinking, and then with a deep sigh he told Louis the truth—well, almost the truth. "The pills are to keep the staff healthy. They each contain enough of Lady Vivian's synthesized food to give the staff one day's worth of nutrients. Since the footmen are no longer coming to the kitchens and Lady Vivian took the fourth vials away, those pills are keeping the staff healthy until she can get her labs up and running again."

"Intriguing. So if you take these, you don't have to eat the food? Does it have the same antiaging properties as the food?" Louis sounded almost awed.

"I believe so. But there are only so many pills, and once they run out, the staff will become ill again."

"You won't mind if I take over the ownership of these pills and their distribution now will you, Fulvio?" Louis didn't really wait for an answer.

Sarah took in a sharp breath and fervently hoped that Mr. Benjamin was close to a solution or had additional pills hidden somewhere, but Fulvio seemed unruffled. "Not at all, Louis. The staff have already had their pills for today, so please plan on starting distribution tomorrow morning. We usually do it at the morning meal in the kitchens."

Louis wasn't listening to Fulvio. He had been sidetracked by something else from Fulvio's pockets. "How is it that you came into possession of Lady Vivian's personal key? I know for a fact that she doesn't let it leave her wrist under any circumstances. Even I do not have a key to her desk and am not privy to its contents, so I am certain she did not give you that key to 'straighten up' her room!" Louis had started out quietly, but by the time he finished he was yelling.

Still in his calm and reasonable voice, Fulvio answered, "But alas, that is what happened, Louis. Ask Lady Vivian yourself if you so please. I don't need to warn you that Lady Vivian does not take kindly to people who question her rules and authority, but it's your risk to take."

"Well, perhaps you are right, but I am still going to write you up and put it in your file. That way if I find that you are snooping around where you shouldn't be in the future, I will have it well documented." Sarah heard a drawer being opened and the sound of paper being withdrawn. "Now let's get this filled out properly. What is your full name?"

"Fulvio de Silvia, as you well know, Louis. I have been here longer than you have." Fulvio sounded weary.

"Don't talk back. What is your title, and how long have you held that title?"

"Head butler, which I have held for about eight hours, as you also know."

"Only eight hours on the job and already getting into trouble, tsk, tsk. Not going to be a very smooth ride for you is it, Fulvio?" Louis sounded gleeful. Sarah took his obvious enjoyment of his task as an opportunity to slide the panel open an inch so she could see what was going on.

The panel was behind Louis's desk, just as Sarah had suspected by listening to the voices in the room. Over the back of Louis's head, she could see Fulvio standing with his hands behind his back. Fulvio's voice betrayed none of his emotions besides weariness with the proceedings, but Sarah could see two spots of pink on his cheekbones, and she saw the flash of his eyes when Louis's head was bent over the paper he was filling out. Something sparkling caught Sarah's attention as she was looking at the secretary. The top drawer of his desk was ajar, and something in it was refracting the light with blue glints. It was just the right color to have come from a blue gem! Could the tanzanites be in that drawer? If only she could catch Fulvio's attention!

Louis continued to ask Fulvio many more questions that he most likely already knew the answers to. Between questions, Sarah tried to catch Fulvio's eye. She opened the panel door just a few more inches and waved her hand at him. Immediately Fulvio's eyes widened, and he mouthed the word "GO!" at her. She shook her head and pointed to the drawer next to Louis and mouthed "Tanzanites" back at him. Realization dawned in his face as Louis looked up at him sharply.

"Fulvio, you are not paying attention. I asked you what your salary was!"

"I am very sorry, Louis, I was woolgathering. I do know this is important, but shouldn't we be discussing how we are going to get things prepared for Lady Vivian's guest and worry about this after he has left? I would not like to disappoint Lady Vivian. Knowing her as I do, I am sure that she wouldn't be very happy with my superiors if the reason I was waylaid from my duties was because of paperwork you decided absolutely must be filled out right this instant."

Sarah could tell that Louis was weighing Fulvio's words, for his pen hovered above the paper forgotten for several moments. "I think you may be right this time, Fulvio. But don't think for a moment that I will forget this."

"I wouldn't dare to think anything of the sort," Fulvio said dryly, and that might have been the end of it, but unfortunately, Fulvio's luck that day was just not very good, for as Louis went to stand from his chair, the door to his office burst open and one of Great-Aunt Vivian's guards stormed in.

The guard's uniform was completely rumpled, and most of his mousy brown hair had escaped its ponytail, framing his face in snarled mats. He half ran, half walked into the room, his body contorted into a crouch as he went. The guard halted in front of Louis's desk, and pointing a shaking hand at Fulvio, he struggled to catch his breath. "You!" was all he was able to growl for several moments. Then he sputtered, "You!"

"Him, what?" Louis practically begged, excitement gleaming in his eyes. He had rarely seen any of the guards since the night of the explosion, and he had figured that most of them had run off when Lady Vivian had refused to give them the essence. What did this one remaining feral guard have to do with Fulvio? "Out with it, man! What has Fulvio done? Is it something *bad*?"

The guard ignored Louis and advanced on Fulvio, his hand still shaking. "I...need...the...essence...you...promised...me... when...you...locked...me...up! Must...find...Lady...Vivian!" he gasped out.

"You have been keeping this man locked up against his will? Fulvio, I would have never thought this of you." Louis rubbed his hands together with suppressed excitement. "Guard, seize him!" The guard needed no further urging and yanked Fulvio's arms behind his back with a maniacal laugh of triumph.

"Shall...we take...him to Lady...Vivian?" The guard's eyes glittered at Louis.

"No, she is far too busy right now," Louis said, smiling maliciously. "We shall take him to the dungeons. Perhaps a little time there will convince him to behave. Follow me." And Louis left the room in such haste, pocketing the vial of pills and the ruby key into his waistcoat and with the guard and Fulvio behind him, that he forgot to lock his desk.

⋈

Sarah waited until the door closed behind Fulvio and then counted slowly to ten, taking calming breaths as she did. Once she was sure that the coast was clear, she carefully opened the door in the paneling and slipped into Louis's office.

The drawer to the desk was still open, and Sarah pulled it wider. She removed a large stack of papers headed "Disciplinary Action Forms," and found the bottom of the drawer contained several sparkling gems from the fountain, but none of the tanzanites. Couldn't anything be easy today?

Sarah tried all of the other drawers in the desk and found them all locked tight. She checked all of the other pieces of furniture in the room and found them either locked or devoid of tanzanites. She dejectedly sat down in Louis's chair to think things through and plan her next steps. She found herself staring at the open drawer. Something didn't look right about it. Just why would Louis have those gems in there?

On a hunch, Sarah removed all of the gems and carefully placed them on the desk, and then she tried to pull the drawer out of its slot. As she pulled on the now empty drawer, she heard something rolling around, like a dozen golf balls in a box that was too big for them. The noise stopped when she stopped moving the drawer and started up again when she slid the drawer back in.

Sarah began to inspect more closely. She measured the depth of the drawer sides with her hand and found that the inside measurement was more than an inch smaller than the outside. The drawer must have a false bottom! Like most well-made pieces of furniture, there was a catch on the track beneath the drawer that kept it level and attached to the desk, so it could not be completely pulled out. Sarah crouched beneath the drawer and attempted to release it from the track.

After much fiddling and the assistance of a fancy silver letter opener, Sarah was able to remove the drawer. She sat on the floor and turned it over in her hands, causing the rolling noise to start up again. Both bottoms of the drawer (the inside false bottom and the underside of the drawer box) were perfectly smooth and did not show any indication of having a way to gain entrance to the space between them. Sarah then looked at the drawer itself. It was made of thick hardwood, using tongue-and-groove construction throughout. Sarah could not perceive a way to get into the hidden space between the two bottoms short of breaking the drawer.

But then she remembered the box that had contained the travel mechanism that had been in Georgiana's satchel. Nickolas was able to slide portions of the box in a given sequence to open it. Perhaps the drawer worked on a similar principle.

Inspired, and feeling a bit more like her brother than she'd care to admit, Sarah began pushing and pulling on various parts of the drawer to no avail. When she was just about ready to give up, she felt a tiny strip on the back of the drawer give way. Excited, Sarah tugged and tugged on the strip, and millimeter by millimeter it began to slide. Sarah was able to use the letter opener, once the strip passed the edge of the drawer frame, to pry it open just a little bit wider until she got a square opening about an inch in each direction.

The opening was too tiny for Sarah to slip her fingers into, but by standing the drawer up on its end, she was able to shake the drawer's contents down to the bottom of the hidden opening, and with only a little more shaking and finagling, one perfectly round tanzanite fell out and onto the carpet.

Sarah gave a whoop of success before clamping one hand over her mouth and glancing furtively toward the door. Hopefully no one had heard her! Sarah realized that she had wasted a great deal of time getting the drawer off of its track and finding the opening to the secret compartment. Just how long would it take for

Louis to secure Fulvio in the dungeons, and how soon would he be back?

Panic made Sarah fumble-fingered, but as she shook and tilted the drawer, tanzanite after tanzanite fell out. At first Sarah had thought to only take two of the stones down to free Brigitta and Bard, but then she figured she should take as many of the stones as she could. Certainly she would rather have them in her possession than let them fall into the hands of someone like Dr. James or Great-Aunt Vivian.

The last tanzanite stubbornly rolled around in the bottom of the drawer and refused to emerge from the opening. Finally, using the letter opener to give it a bit of persuasion, the fourteenth tanzanite landed with a plop onto the carpet.

Sarah looked dubiously at the large pile of stones. She feared that they would roll out of the satchel's open top, and she couldn't chance that even one would be lost. But the ever-resourceful Sarah stripped off one of her riding boots, removed her purple striped sock, and returned her boot to her bare foot. She filled the sock with the tanzanites and tied a quick half-knot in the remaining leg to secure them and popped the lumpy lot into the satchel. She pushed the tiny strip of wood back into position, closing the opening in the false bottom, and then, after a few unsuccessful tries, she returned the drawer to its track, replaced the drawer's contents, and slammed it closed. Grabbing Georgiana's satchel and settling it across her body once more, Sarah slipped back into the servants' passageway and closed the panel behind her.

⧎

Sarah leaned against the cool stone of the passageway and caught her breath. What on earth was she going to do next? Louis was dragging Fulvio down to the dungeons. She needed to warn Nickolas and Mr. Benjamin that they were coming, but how could she get there? She didn't even know where the dungeons were. In fact, she wasn't even sure how to get back to the kitchens.

For the most part, Sarah was perfectly content to be the girl she was. She was smart, confident, funny, and she owned her own horse. What more could a girl want? But at the moment she would have given up that horse for her brother's photographic memory. He would not be sitting in the passageways wondering how to get back to the kitchens. He would remember everything, and he'd probably be able to figure out how to get to the dungeons by extrapolating fundamental spatial geometry concepts and follow it all up by giving her a confused look saying, "What, you don't get this?" It was a sign of just how desperate she was that this thought didn't even make her mad.

But being Sarah, she couldn't stay defeated for long and figured that standing around inside the wall waiting to be discovered was definitely *not* the answer to her problems, so she started down the corridor in what she hoped would be the right direction.

She wandered around for several minutes, going down narrow staircases and up winding corridors, and then she suddenly came to a familiar bend in the passageway. She was right outside the sitting room where she had first overheard Dr. James and Great-Aunt Vivian talking the night of Great-Aunt Vivian's party. With that realization, a smile crossed Sarah's face. She now knew exactly where she was, and with just a few more turns and one more staircase she found herself outside of the kitchens.

⊰⊱

Once again, Sarah faced a dilemma. Did she go into the kitchens and try to find Carole and Nickolas, or should she go down to the gardens and free Brigitta and Bard? Thinking of being seen by all of the cooks and servants in the manor didn't seem like the smartest idea when trying to be clandestine, so Sarah decided to slip up the stairs to the landing that led to the breakfast garden. Brigitta and Bard would know what to do, and the three of them had a much better chance of rescuing Fulvio than she did alone.

⇥⇤

As she was making her way across the bridge over the Zen garden, a sudden thought crossed her mind. Where was Sparks? Usually the little puppy would pop out of her pocket and help her through the twists and turns of the maze. So where was she? Sarah checked in the pocket of her jacket where Sparks usually slept and found nothing but a pack of chewing gum.

Just what she needed, Sarah thought as she entered the maze. Someone else to worry about. Where could that puppy have gone?

Sarah could not remember the last time she had seen Sparks. She had been with them as they had traveled up to the manor from the gardens, and Sarah was pretty sure that she had seen Sparks in the kitchens. She had definitely greeted Fulvio in the butler's rooms, but after that? She just couldn't say.

Sarah racked her brain all the way down the path to the statue gardens. She had already passed several of the empty plinths when she arrived at Charles's clearing and realized that in her contemplation she had walked right past Brigitta's pedestal. She backtracked and placed one of the tanzanites from her sock in the divot on the plinth labeled "BRIGITTA," whispering a prayer that the tanzanites still worked. She dashed past Charles and Francesca's clearings and placed a second tanzanite on Bard's plinth and slipped through the opening in the hedge to where Georgiana's statue had once stood.

⊰⊱

Only Brigitta's quick warning kept Bard from hacking Sarah into two pieces as she emerged from the foliage. "Really, Bard," Brigitta admonished. "Will you please learn to keep that ax in your belt until I tell you it is time to smash things? Seriously, you almost killed Sarah. I can't see Ardus being all that happy about that."

"I'm sorry, Brigitta." Bard hung his head and quickly slipped his battle-ax back in its holster.

"It's not me you should be apologizing to," Brigitta said, still scolding her husband. "It is Miss Sarah to whom you should apologize."

"I'm sorry, Sarah."

"Oh, don't worry about that," Sarah said, her heart still thudding. "But I do need your help," she said before quickly rattling off her current problems. "Fulvio has been captured, and they took him down to the dungeons where Nickolas was visiting Mr. Benjamin, and I'm worried that they are going to capture him too, and Sparks is missing, and Dr. James is on his way to the manor!"

"Slow down, Sarah. One thing at a time!" Brigitta embraced the girl. "First of all, thank you for freeing us. Second of all, how on earth did you get here?"

"Oh, that's easy—we used Georgiana's box." Sarah then launched into telling the whole story. Brigitta listened while Bard patrolled the edged of the clearing, ax at the ready.

It was a full fifteen minutes later before Sarah had gotten everything out, and Brigitta looked very grave. "Well, the first thing we need to do is make sure that the tanzanites are secured to the plinths and cannot be removed."

Bard stopped his patrolling and returned to Brigitta's side. "Does that mean I get to smash something?" he asked, a twinkle in his green eyes.

Bard looked at the tanzanite in the divot on his old plinth, but when he raised his battle-ax, Brigitta stopped him. "I don't think that is going to work, Bard. If you shatter it, then you will most likely turn back to stone. I have a better idea. Give me a second." Brigitta sat down on the grass and primed her harp on her knee and began playing a lilting song. Sarah watched as the marble plinth began to shimmer and congeal like a large white tree stump made of Jell-O. Not pausing a moment in her playing and singing, Brigitta caught Bard's eye and nodded.

Bard swung his ax over his head and was just about to bring it down on the tanzanite, but then Brigitta suddenly stopped playing. "Not with the ax, Bard, with your hand."

So Bard sheathed his ax and, once Brigitta had resumed playing, brought his hand down flat on top of the tanzanite. With a slight squelching sound, the plinth swallowed it up as if it were being pushed into a mound of vanilla pudding. Brigitta stopped playing as soon as the stone was buried completely in the plinth, and then the stump solidified, leaving it as solid as before. In fact, the only discernible change was that the divot on the smooth top of the plinth was completely gone!

"Come on, Sarah," Brigitta said as she moved toward the next clearing. "We need the rest of the tanzanites."

Sarah, Brigitta, and Bard repeated the process on each of the thirteen remaining marble stumps. The last tanzanite disappeared into Georgiana's plinth, and Brigitta wearily returned her harp to its holder on her back and with Bard's assistance regained her feet.

"I always forget how exhausting that is without my sisters' assistance. The more of us that are available to play, the easier it is on each of us. Simple things like this I can accomplish on my own, but for more complex things like healing I would need additional help. But enough, we need to get back up to the manor and find Nickolas. I am not sure how you two managed to get here via the transport box, but we need to get you home safely before Dr. James arrives."

CHAPTER 21

THE POCKET WATCH POEM

-⊰⊱-

In which Nickolas has to hide

Once Carole had fed and cared for the prisoners, she informed Nickolas that it was time to return to the kitchens. Nickolas begged to be allowed to remain with Mr. Benjamin. Reluctantly, Carol agreed when Mr. Benjamin had added his requests to Nickolas's, and she packed up her basket.

"Fulvio or I will come to collect you shortly, so be ready," she admonished Nickolas and then turned to Mr. Benjamin. "And I am expecting him to be safe and in one piece, Mr. Benjamin."

Both Nickolas and Mr. Benjamin assured her that no harm would befall them, and with a disbelieving tut, Carole left the dungeons.

Nickolas and Mr. Benjamin continued their talk about the experiments Dr. Montague had described in his notebooks. As they talked, Mr. Benjamin began assembling some of the equipment that Fulvio had sent him from his lab.

"It seems that Dr. Montague had the same goals for his experiments that I hope to accomplish with mine," Mr. Benjamin said, fiddling with a beaker stand and adjusting its height. "I never dreamed that the food was making us dependent. It never entered our equations that someone would want to stop the antiaging effects. The fact that it makes your cells unable to support themselves—leading to accelerated death—is astounding. I truly thought we were accomplishing just the opposite."

Mr. Benjamin continued to question Nickolas about the details of Dr. Montague's experiments. Much to Mr. Benjamin's surprise, Nickolas did indeed remember most of what he had read, and Mr. Benjamin began scribbling furiously in his lab book while Nickolas recited what he remembered.

When they were only about two-thirds of the way through Dr. Montague's experiments, there was a commotion in the hallway leading to the dungeons. Nickolas frantically looked around for a place to hide. But the cavernous room was only filled with cages that offered no plausible hiding spots, and the room's only exit was soon to be blocked by the newcomers. He was trapped.

Mr. Benjamin looked just as bewildered as Nickolas felt, so he would be no help. Nickolas was just about to despair when Alec, holding one of the dark blankets near the back of the cell, whispered, "Over here." Hope flaring inside him, Nickolas dashed around the back of the cage and approached the teenager.

"So what's the plan?" Nickolas whispered back.

⊐⊨

With a sigh of relief, Nickolas removed the blanket from over his head and rose from the crouched position he had assumed behind the cell. "Thanks, Alec, that was quick thinking. I thought I was going to be caught for sure." But then Nickolas really took in his surroundings, and his heart sank. Fulvio was now imprisoned inside the cell with the original three prisoners.

"Fulvio, what happened?" Nickolas exclaimed.

"Louis caught me in Lady Vivian's study searching for the tanzanites. Fortunately, your sister did not get caught. As far as

I know, Lady Vivian still does not know that I was in her study, nor does she know that you are here. But she will know very soon that I had one of her guards under lock and key in the kitchens, for somehow he has escaped."

"Having one of Dr. James's spies running around the manor is not a good development, for they have always observed way more than I thought was humanly possible," Mr. Benjamin added.

"Well, since they aren't human, that makes sense. The muses told us that they were Faeries—some sort of potato people who work for Dr. James," Nickolas said.

"They have been here for years. I had no idea that they transformed into potatoes until I fought them with your muses in the kitchens two weeks ago," Fulvio said. "The one who remained alive has been a very strange prisoner. He would eat nothing for days and then drank only the solution bottles that we used to make the food from. They seemed to put him in some sort of stupor. And then he just went insane, smashing everything in the kitchens and demanding that I give him the essence. I even had managed to procure the essence he wanted, but I didn't have a chance to give it to him." Fulvio pulled the bottle Lady Vivian had given him from his pocket and turned it over in his hand. Louis had been so excited by the discovery of the pills and Lady Vivian's key that he hadn't even made sure that Fulvio had emptied all of his pockets. "And how he escaped the second time, I have no idea."

The group was silent for several moments, but then Nickolas, who was rarely silent even when he had no one to talk to but himself, asked, "Well, where do we go from here?"

"We need to figure out a cure for all of the occupants of the manor and hopefully one for Simon as well," Mr. Benjamin said. "I have been looking over the notes that I took concerning Dr. Montague's experiments, and I don't think I can complete them successfully here in the dungeons. Ideally, I would like to get into Dr. Montague's lab and see if he left any additional clues in there. I just wish I had all the information in one place, not scattered all over the world."

"It is even more important that we create a cure, for Louis stole from me the bottle of pills you made. He said he would take over the distribution of them to the staff, but I am not sure that I trust him to do that." Fulvio hung his head. "If only I had been smart enough to give him the key first, I might still have the pills."

"Can't you make more of those pills?" Nickolas asked Mr. Benjamin.

"I can, but I need to get to a well-stocked lab to do that. And we need to get the rest of the bottles of essence. The one bottle that Fulvio has will only go so far."

"How can we get into Dr. Montague's lab? Where is it?" Nickolas asked.

"In the observatory tower," Fulvio said. "But no one has been in there for years. Dr. Montague locked it when he left, and even Lady Vivian does not have the key."

"Yes," Mr. Benjamin interjected. "Many years ago she tried to get into the tower, and even called in a locksmith, but she was told that the lock was especially complex and that the only way to break in would be to literally bulldoze the door. Lady Vivian contemplated this, until a structural engineer told her that it would most likely result in the destruction of the tower if she tried. She was working on a number of different things at the time and must have eventually lost interest."

"Do some of your servants' passageways go there?" Nickolas asked Fulvio, hopeful that there was a back way into the tower.

"No, that tower and the wing beyond are actually newer than the rest of the manor and were never added to the passageway network." Fulvio shook his head. "Dr. Montague and his wife were very private people, and they chose that wing for their quarters specifically because they were cut off from the rest of the manor. They never had any maids or valets, and from my understanding at that time, Dr. Montague did most of the cleaning up there himself. He always was uncomfortable with the idea of being a baronet. He never introduced himself by the title and always insisted that we address him as Dr. Montague, not Sir Montague or Baronet Montague. Unlike Lady Vivian, who enjoys the title and its trappings very much, I always felt Dr. Montague was happiest in his office at the University of Sydney. He certainly always made himself scarce whenever Lady Vivian threw her parties and balls."

Nickolas felt his affection for Dr. Montague growing more and more and could see where his gentle grandmother and kind father were related to this man. He had a very hard time picturing the relationship between them and Great-Aunt Vivian, however. Just what had caused her to be so self-absorbed and nasty, he had no idea.

Dr. Benjamin looked thoughtful. "There wasn't a key among Dr. Montague's things, was there?"

"Yes, there was a ring of keys, but they weren't from the right time period. I think they were his keys from Chicago University. None of them were old enough to belong to the manor," Nickolas said, but then a thought tickled at the back of his brain. "Wait, there is a key, but it is very, very small, and nothing like a door key at all."

"The locksmith said the same thing about the lock in the door, that the keyhole was very small," Mr. Benjamin said, sounding excited. "You didn't by any chance bring the key with you?"

"Yeah, it's here in my pocket." Nickolas pulled out the old pocket watch.

Tears sprang to Fulvio's eyes. "I never thought I would see that again," he said. "The staff and I all pitched in to give him that watch when your grandmother was born. It was our congratulations gift as well as condolences, as he lost your great-grandmother at the same time. If you look inside the front cover, you will see that we engraved it with the crest of the manor. I am touched that he kept it."

Nickolas was busy prying open the back cover of the watch with his tiny screwdriver. When he had it open, he pulled the small key from its velvet bag and showed it to Mr. Benjamin through the bars. Mr. Benjamin reached for the key, which was still attached to the velvet pouch by the ribbon ties. The pouch gave way, leaving both pouch and key in Mr. Benjamin's hands and the rest of the watch still in Nickolas's.

"I am so sorry..." Mr. Benjamin began, but Nickolas was not listening. He was looking intently at the back of the watch. There, previously hidden by the key bag, was a poem etched in gold.

"Listen to this," Nickolas said, reading out loud:

Opening Time

I was the happiest of men when it began,
But time reversed while earning angel's wings.
For your sake, I forced it forward again,
To be stopped forever,
As another your lullaby sings.

"That is new—we didn't inscribe that," Fulvio said, looking perplexed.

"Are you sure?" Nickolas asked.

"Positive. I was the one who purchased the watch and paid for the engraving. We barely had enough money to get the crest," Fulvio said, reaching for the watch.

"So if it wasn't engraved when you gave it to him, Dr. Montague must have had it engraved later." Nickolas was going to say more, but at that moment he heard voices in the corridor once again, and he ran to the back of the cell and dove beneath the blanket.

⚜

Nickolas needn't have worried, for it was only Sarah, Brigitta, and Bard being led to the dungeons by Carole.

"Nickolas!" Sarah exclaimed, rushing to his side. Then she remembered that he was her pesky older brother, so she stopped awkwardly next to him without giving him the hug she had first intended.

Bard's relief that Nickolas was safe showed on his broad face as well, but he didn't stop himself from giving the boy a bone-crushing squeeze. "I am glad to see you again, Nickolas. You had us worried."

"Sorry, Bard," Nickolas said once air had returned to his lungs. "Sarah, how did you get the tanzanites? Did you get them all?"

Sarah brought everyone up to speed with what had happened since Fulvio was captured, and Brigitta added how they had placed the tanzanites into the plinths so the muses would no longer turn to stone while on Great-Aunt Vivian's grounds.

In turn, Fulvio told the muses everything that had been happening in the manor since they had left two weeks ago, and Mr. Benjamin told what he knew about Lady Vivian, Dr. James, and his experiments to neutralize the effects of the dying microbios.

Once everyone was on the same page, they began to discuss what they should do next.

"I think that it would be better for Mr. Benjamin to do Dr. Montague's experiments rather than Dr. Lucy," Brigitta said. "Mr. Benjamin knows far more about the microbios than anyone else working on this problem."

"It would be very helpful if I could get to a real lab to do the work, though. I just don't have the space or equipment here," Mr. Benjamin interjected, indicating the attempts he had made to turn the dungeon into a laboratory and the less than satisfactory results.

Bard loosened his battle-ax in its holster and then paused and turned to his wife. "Brigitta, is this a good time to smash?" he asked innocently.

Brigitta smothered a laugh, and eyes twinkling she said, "Yes, Bard, this would be a very good time to smash."

Permission granted, Bard gave a mighty swing of his ax on the cell door, and with an echoing clang, the heavy metal burst open and hung precariously on only one hinge.

"Well, that was efficient. Thank you, Bard." Fulvio nodded to the muse as he picked his way over the smashed door and into freedom, with Mr. Benjamin following right after him.

"Do you need your things, Mr. Benjamin?" Alec asked, placing the science equipment that was strewn all over the cell back into the packing box that Nickolas had left outside the door.

"Oh yes," Mr. Benjamin said. "Thank you, Alec. We can leave all of that here, but I will need my notes."

Before climbing out of the cell, Alec handed the notebook to Mr. Benjamin. "Coming, Dr. Trowle?"

"No, I think I will stay right here, thank you very much." Dr. Trowle sat firmly on the bench in the back of the cell. "Lady Vivian may not be pleased with me for failing to capture the children at the airport, but I will give her no reason to be displeased with me again. I need my position with her at the manor to pay for my son's college education, and I will not jeopardize that in any way."

"Come, Trowle," Mr. Benjamin said. "Surely you can see that staying here will only further incur her wrath. You can help me with the experiments, and once we are done, we can look for work together. I don't think Lady Vivian will have use for either one of us for some time yet. So much of her research is gone. I don't think she has money to pay anyone, especially personae non gratae like us. Come, now."

"No, Mr. Benjamin," Dr. Trowle said resolutely. "I won't."

Mr. Benjamin shrugged and said, "Suit yourself, Trowle. But feel free to come running to me if Lady Vivian turns you out. I will always have need for excellent scientists like yourself."

Sarah had been curiously watching everything that had happened and was especially curious about the teenager whom Mr. Benjamin was calling Alec, so once Alec had climbed over the door and out of the cell, she approached him, arm outstretched. "I'm Nickolas's sister, Sarah," she said with a warm smile. "I gather you are Alec. You were at the airport, weren't you? I think I remember you."

Sarah was expecting him to greet her in the same way most of the teenagers at camp did. Usually they said hi and then ruffled her hair, treating her like she was a lot younger than her ten years and promptly ignoring her unless they had a question that would be easier to ask a kid than a counselor or a grown-up, like where the bathrooms were. But that was not what Alec did.

"Delaney," he said half to himself, his eyes widening as if he had seen a ghost. He backed away from Sarah as quickly as he could, bumping into the toppled door of the cell. He stumbled and sat down hard. His eyes never left Sarah's face. Slowly he found his voice. "I'm sorry, you look just like my little sister. She is…she was…the most important person in my life."

"I get that all the time," Sarah said kindly. "Just two days ago someone mistook me for my great-grandmother. I hope Delaney isn't ninety years old, or else I think I'm going to start getting a complex."

"No, Delaney was ten," Alec said.

"What happened to her?" Nickolas asked, coming over to stand next to Sarah.

"Nickolas! That's not polite," Sarah exclaimed.

"That's OK. I'm sure you'll find out anyway," Alec said in a flat voice. "Delaney was killed in a car accident three years ago."

"I'm very sorry to hear that," Sarah said. "I'm glad that I remind you of her then, because I can tell you loved her very much. Maybe we can be good friends. Then you can find out that Delaney couldn't possibly be as annoying as I am. Just ask Nickolas—he can tell you."

"Don't believe her," Nickolas said in a stage whisper. "She's only really annoying about four or five times a day. The rest of the time she's pretty cool."

Sarah dug her elbow in to Nickolas's ribs. "Ow! What did I say now?"

The party slipped out of the dungeons and followed Fulvio to the servants' passageways. "As I said before, these don't lead directly to the observatory, but we can use them to get close enough that we should not be observed entering the tower. Once we get you there, Carole and I will need to return to the kitchens. I am concerned that once Vivian finds out about the guard, her first step will be to capture Zac and Carole to use them to persuade me to reveal all that I know. I would feel much better if the kitchen staff were warned and Zac was in my keeping."

Brigitta and Bard nodded their agreement, and then the party fell silent as they followed Fulvio through the passages.

Several minutes later, after they had climbed multiple staircases and followed innumerable corridors, Sarah whispered to Brigitta, "Is it safe leaving Dr. Trowle alone down there? Won't he just tell Great-Aunt Vivian our plans?"

"Probably," Brigitta whispered back. "But hopefully we will be out of here quickly enough that it won't matter. My hope is to get Mr. Benjamin started on the experiments, safely locked in the tower, and then return the two of you to your home within the hour. We can come back and get his results later, and there is nothing wrong with having Dr. Lucy working on the problem at the same time as Mr. Benjamin. I am sure that Ardus and Audiva will be interested in knowing that James is here and will have plans for how to neutralize him. My orders from Audiva are to keep the two of you safe, and having you here at the manor makes that directive infinitely more difficult to follow."

"Sorry, Brigitta," Sarah said, bowing her head contritely. She pretty quickly realized that she must look a lot like Bard did when he apologized to the beautiful muse, and she began to laugh, looking up to see the twinkle in Brigitta's eyes as well.

"No worries, Sarah," she said in her musical voice. "Just as long as you don't smash anything, we should have no further troubles."

"You don't have to worry about me smashing things. Maybe you should worry about Nickolas though."

They all followed Fulvio out of the passageways and into the breakfast garden right next to the observatory tower. Using the key from the watch, Fulvio inserted it in a keyhole that was nearly hidden between two of the large gray stones that comprised the tower walls. The key turned easily, making a noise like the winding of a clock. Fulvio turned the key several times before the mechanism stopped. A slight ticking sound emitted from the keyhole, and the key slowly unwound on its own power. The key finally stopped, a sharp click was heard, and a seam in the stonework appeared. Nickolas was just able to get a grip on the portion of the wall that opened, but even with Alec's help, they were unable to open the door more than an inch. Bard gently shouldered past the two boys and easily opened the door.

"Well, we had best be returning to the kitchens now," Fulvio said once the tower was accessible. The children quickly hugged Fulvio and Carole and wished them luck.

Sarah held tight to Fulvio and whispered, "Please let Brigitta and Bard know your plans once this is all over. I'm sure that Dad could help you get a job in Colorado. There are lots of resorts and hotels in our area that could use good chefs like you. Please say you will come once Mr. Benjamin gets you the cure. Please?"

"I cannot imagine anything more perfect, Mistress Sarah. I doubt that your great-aunt would want to keep me on after everything that has happened. I will see you soon—you can count on that." And with one last hug, Fulvio and Carole headed back into the passageways.

CHAPTER 22

THE OBSERVATORY

In which we discover Victoria had a sense of humor

The three children and Brigitta were able to slip through the tower door quite easily, but the portly Mr. Benjamin and enormous Bard were a tight fit. For a moment it looked like poor Bard would have to wait outside, but then he gave the door a second tremendous shove and was able to widen the opening enough for him to squeeze through.

Once on the other side, the counterweight mechanism was visible, so Brigitta quickly retrieved the key, and all it took was Bard leaning on the weights for the door to be easily closed.

Nickolas lit two of the torches with the matches that he had packed in his pocket. Brigitta took one and led the way up the winding stone staircase, while Bard retrieved the other and took up the rear.

Sarah found herself next to Alec on the long climb upward. She had been intrigued by the teenager ever since he had called her "Delaney," so Sarah decided to try to find out more about him.

"Where were you heading when you were at the airport and Great-Aunt Vivian so rudely interrupted your travels?" she asked.

"I was heading to the home of some friends of my parents in LA. My father sent me on an Outward Bound trip to the outback of Australia to try to get me to…well, I don't know…find myself I guess? I've been rather lost since my sister died, and my parents are kind of fed up with me. I know they want to help, but they don't understand. They weren't there when it happened. They weren't responsible. I was." Alec looked at the floor and wouldn't meet Sarah's eyes.

Sarah decided to return the subject to safer ground. "How was the Outward Bound trip? I want to go on one of those when I get older. It sounds like fun."

"It was fun. At first I didn't want to participate and made rather a jerk of myself, but once I realized that no one was going to do the work for me, I started actually having a good time. I didn't want to go on the rest of my trip, though. Having to answer lots of questions from my parents' busybody friends didn't sound pleasant. I guess it was a better plan than going home to Delaney's ghost and spending the summer with my father's anger and my mother's weeping."

"Maybe your parents took some time to get over things while you were gone. Do you have a good relationship with them?" Sarah thought about her own parents and how she could tell them anything and they wouldn't get mad, just help her figure out how to move forward from her problems. Her easygoing father had never yelled at her, and her mother only cried at sappy movies, and then she was laughing at herself at the same time.

"No, not really. It was always Delaney and me against the world. Our parents were always working or on business trips or going out with their friends. Delaney and I were left alone a lot, or with nannies until I got too old, and then it was just the two of us."

"What was she like?" Sarah asked, sensing that Alec wanted to talk about her.

"She acted a lot like you, bossing me around even though she was the little sister. She was smart and funny and full of life. Looked a little bit like you too. Hair all over the place and her eyes always sparkling and mischievous."

"Poor girl, if she looked like me!" Sarah teased. "At least she didn't look like you—or worse, like Nickolas."

"I didn't look like me when she was alive," Alec said sadly. "I didn't want to look anything like myself after she died. I figured if I looked on the outside the way I felt on the inside, then people would leave me alone. It works, you know—dye your hair, pierce your nose and eyebrows, and wear black makeup and clothes. People back up right away. They only see the outside and decide they don't really want to talk to you or find out about you at all. Works like a charm."

"Well, I'm talking to you," Sarah said pointedly. "And I want to know about who you are."

"That's because you're different, like Delaney was, you don't care about the outside. But trust me, most people do."

"Interesting. Do you still want people to leave you alone?" Sarah tilted her head and looked up at Alec quizzically.

"Most people, yes."

"Do you want me to leave you alone?"

Alec thought for a moment. "Surprisingly, no I don't. I kind of like you bothering me."

"Good, because I plan on bothering you as much as I can. At least until you get rid of that ring in your eyebrow. It's kind of creepy." And with that Sarah dashed up the stairs to catch up with Brigitta.

Alec smiled after her. It hurt the muscles of his face to do so as it had been too long since they had been used. She did remind him of Delaney. Delaney would have told him to lose the eyebrow ring as well, and before he could change his mind, he reached up and unhooked its clasp, letting the silver ring fall to the floor behind him.

⚎⚎

The stairs ended at the very top of the tower. Unlike the library tower, there was nothing on the lower three floors; in fact, there weren't any lower three floors, just the winding staircase going up and up and up. The top floor was a giant circular room dominated in the center by a huge telescope on a revolving platform. They had seen some of the mechanisms that moved the platform in the space beneath the floor as they had come up the stairs. The cogs and pulleys reminded Nickolas of giant clockworks. Since the observatory had been built in the time before electricity, everything moved via gears and wheels and weights.

The section of the ceiling that retracted to allow the telescope access to the night sky had been left partially open for the past seventy years, so leaves and other debris littered the floor in mounds beneath the sliver of blue sky. Puddles of rainwater and signs of water damage were everywhere, from the observation platform, to the telescope, to the planks of the floor. In some places, the floorboards had rotted out, leaving holes to the chasm below.

Sarah was careful to step wherever Bard stepped, being pretty sure that her much lighter weight would not pass through the flooring if Bard's did not.

"Dr. Montague's rooms are over here," Mr. Benjamin announced as he stood next to a door in the wall. "They are unlocked."

Everyone followed him through the door and found themselves in Dr. Montague's sitting room. The room was covered in dust, and it looked like it hadn't been disturbed in many years. There were still books on the desk, a fire laid in the fireplace ready to light, and fresh candles in the sconces around the room with a box full of long matches on the mantle waiting to light them. Nickolas went around the room, lighting candles as he went and opening curtains to let sunlight filter through the dirty windowpanes.

Sarah could imagine what a cozy place this would have been before the dust and dirt had engulfed it. There were quirky artworks on the walls, all oil paintings of science equipment. Sarah would have bet her favorite bridle that they were all painted by Victoria Montague. She particularly liked the one behind the desk that showed the back of a scientist at his table surrounded by a plethora of beakers, Bunsen burners, pipettes, and other equipment. The male scientist had wild hair the same burnished copper color as Great-Aunt Vivian's, although it was sticking out at odd angles from his head. It reminded Sarah of the way Nickolas and their father looked first thing in the morning before they had found time to wash and comb their hair into place. It must be Dr. Montague, and the way Victoria had painted him—all arms and legs and wild hair—made Sarah smile.

While Sarah was exploring the sitting room, the others had moved through the room's one door out to the corridor beyond. There were three doors off of it. One led to a bath, another to a large dressing room that was filled with old-fashioned men's clothing on one side and women's clothing on the other. The dressing room was not nearly as grand as Great-Aunt Vivian's had been, for the neckties were all jumbled next to the purses and hats, giving the impression that neither Dr. Montague nor his wife cared much about appearances or fashion. Sarah noted that there weren't any mannequins in this dressing room.

The last door led to Victoria and Dr. Montague's bedroom, which again was small and warmly decorated. There was a crib and changing table set up in one corner and a rocking chair was placed in front of the bay window. Sarah noticed that there were disarrayed blankets in the crib, and the covers on one side of the master bed were pulled back with dusty slippers neatly placed under the box spring.

Off of this room there were two more doors. Mr. Benjamin opened the first, revealing a large artist's studio, one wall of which was floor-to-ceiling windows. Had they been cleaned, the room would have been bathed in natural light and made a perfect place in which to create. There were half-finished canvases strewn around the room, and rows of paint tubes filled the cabinets. A painter's smock and hat hung neatly by the door, and there was even a painting on the easel in the center of the room.

Curious, Nickolas approached the painting. It was covered with a sheet to protect it from dust and light, but when Nickolas lifted the covering, the painting was revealed to be a picture of Great-Aunt Vivian. Her sapphire eyes bore into Nickolas through her pince-nez, and he could just picture her saying something about rules and how they were not to be broken. It wasn't a very flattering picture; she looked decades older than the Great-Aunt Vivian Nickolas knew, and the scowl on her face, even though it hadn't been completely finished, looked very lifelike and menacing. Why would her mother paint her this way? Did Victoria suspect what Great-Aunt Vivian would become?

Nickolas did not have any time to ponder these questions, for Brigitta called him back into the bedroom. They were standing before the other door, which was locked tight.

"Nickolas, do you have the key to this door?" Brigitta asked, and Nickolas handed over the key that had opened the tower. But it didn't fit the lock, being far too small.

"Here, try these," Sarah suggested, handing over the two keys she had packed, but neither worked, and the keys were returned to the children's possession. Without Charles in the party, they had to resort to Bard's way of opening locks, and with one blow from his ax, the door splintered and fell away, revealing an impenetrable wall of bricks behind.

Bard was just going to try to smash his way through that, but then Brigitta stopped him. "Let's try to find another way in first, Bard. And then you can smash through it, OK?"

"OK, Brigitta," Bard replied, reluctantly putting his ax back in its holster.

Nickolas was looking around the room, taking in the dimensions. When he compared them with the other dimensions of the rooms in Dr. and Mrs. Montague's wing, it dawned on him. "Wait, I bet there's a door in the dressing room that goes to the same room. See how this room is the same width as the bath and the hallway? Well, the room through that door should also border the dressing room. Let's go see." And with that he hurried out of the bedroom and into the dressing room with the others following.

Nickolas pointed to the wall on his left. "It should be through there."

Alec and Mr. Benjamin searched the wall indicated and found that there was a door hidden in the back of a huge wardrobe. This door was also locked, and none of the keys worked for this one either.

Bard offered to smash the door down, but again Brigitta held him back.

As Brigitta and the rest of the adults were discussing the door lock, Nickolas was sitting on a pouf in the dressing room turning the pocket watch over in his hand. Dr. Montague had put the key to the tower inside the watch. Why would he leave the key to the outer door and not the key to the inner doors? It didn't make any sense. So if one key was in the watch, maybe the other key was in it as well. Nickolas took out his mini screwdrivers and tried to get to the inside of the watch where the watch works would have been housed. But the case appeared to be seamless, with no access panels at all.

As he was fiddling, Sarah sat down next to him and observed what he was doing.

"Find anything?" she asked.

"No, it doesn't seem to open," he replied, handing the watch to her.

"It has to—these old watches needed maintenance to keep them running right. They didn't have batteries to replace, but the winding mechanisms would break and they would need to be adjusted. Remember that old watchmaker who used to have a shop downtown?"

"Yeah, I used to go and bother him all the time when I was little. He went out of business, though. I guess people didn't have enough antique clocks to keep him busy," Nickolas said with a sigh.

"Or maybe he got tired of all of your questions," Sarah teased. Nickolas stuck his tongue out at her. "Wait a minute, what's this?" Sarah pointed to the poem.

"I just found that. It's a poem that Dr. Montague had engraved in the back of the watch."

"'Opening Time'—that's an odd poem title. Unless..." Sarah got a thinking look on her face that Nickolas recognized immediately and waited. "Unless it's how to open the timepiece!" she said, her eyes going wide.

"Possibly," Nickolas agreed. "Let's look at the poem."

"Let's start with the obvious. Who is 'I' and who is 'you' referring to in the poem?" Sarah asked, chewing on her lip in concentration.

"The 'I' is a man, and the poem was most likely written by Dr. Montague. So I would bet that 'I' is Dr. Montague," Nickolas said.

"If that is the case and the 'I' is Dr. Montague, who would the 'you' be? The words 'your lullaby' indicates that it's a baby or a small child, so it could be Great-Aunt Vivian or Grandma Vera."

"I think it would be Grandma Vera, because Great-Aunt Vivian was an adult when this was written and Grandma Vera was a baby or little girl," Nickolas said. At Sarah's questioning look he added, "Fulvio told me that he gave this watch to Dr. Montague right after Grandma Vera's birth, and the poem wasn't inscribed in it then. Four years later he put it in the box, and the inscription was there. So it was inscribed sometime in Grandma Vera's first four years."

"OK, I can see that. So we know it's about Dr. Montague and Grandma Vera. It makes even more sense that this would be how to open the watch, because he would want Grandma Vera to know how. So how would you open it?" Sarah asked.

"The only thing on the watch that works is the screw that sets the time, so perhaps there is a time you can set it to that makes the watch open. Are there any times mentioned?"

"'I was the happiest of men when it began.' That sounds like a time, but I have no idea when. How would we know when he was the happiest of men? OK, moving on. 'But time reversed while earning angel's wings.' Isn't earning angels' wings a euphemism for death? So who died...?"

The two children looked at each other and then said in one breath, "Victoria!"

Sarah continued: "'For your sake, I forced it (time) forward again, to be stopped forever as another your lullaby sings'. Who sang Grandma Vera's lullaby? Well, Victoria didn't—she was dead. Dr. Montague might have for a while, but then she was adopted and Great-Grandma Olsen did. So we have Victoria's death, Grandma Vera's adoption, and one other date. How do you show dates on a watch?"

"You don't, Sarah," Nickolas said, his eyes widening, "but those things have times associated with them too. The time of death is always recorded. And I don't know much about adoptions, but I bet they have a time too."

But Sarah didn't look like she was listening. She was thinking hard for something that she thought she had heard only once and quite a while ago. Something about a sappy movie and her mother's tears—something she had thought about earlier when she was talking with Alec. The phrase "happiest of men" kept swirling around in her brain and conjuring up a picture of her mom sitting with her on the couch watching an old movie. Then she got it! "Remember when we watched that old Jane Austen movie with Mom last Christmas?" she asked.

"Vaguely." Nickolas looked nervous.

"You know the one where the girl hero fell in love with one guy and hated the other and then found out that the first guy was a cad and so she married the other one because he really was OK?"

"No, not a bit."

"And they wore all those pretty dresses and funny hats and walked everywhere. You remember, we joked about it afterward."

"I'm pretty sure I slept through it, and I wasn't the only one—Dad was snoring too, if I remember correctly." Nickolas looked perturbed. "Did I miss something important?"

"Yes! The boy hero—the good guy, not the cad—told the girl hero that on their wedding day she would make him the happiest of men. It must be Dr. Montague's wedding day—or rather, his wedding time." Sarah was excited now.

"I'll take your word for it, and it does make sense. But we don't know those times, and they could be anything."

"We know what they are, Nickolas," Sarah said, really grinning now, "or rather, you do. If you can just use that crazy memory of yours to remember. They were all with the letter Grandma Vera's lawyer wrote her when Grandpa Patrick died. It had her parents' marriage license, Victoria's death certificate, and Grandma Vera's adoption papers. You did look at them, didn't you?"

"I did!" Nickolas screwed up his face in concentration, pulling the pieces of paper from his memory. "Marriage was eleven thirty a.m. on August 19, 1871…Death was three fifty-three a.m. on December 4, 1943…Adoption was five p.m. on February 27, 1944. Got it! Eleven thirty, three fifty-three, and five. Let's try it."

Nickolas pulled out the knob on the top of the watch and set it to eleven thirty. For good measure he clicked the knob back in. Then he pulled it out and set the watch to three fifty-three and clicked it again. Finally, he set the watch to five o'clock and clicked it a third time. And nothing happened.

"Are you sure about the times?" Sarah asked, looking at her brother doubtfully, but then laughed. "Silly question. I should more question that I got the dates right than you got the times right. Sorry, Nickolas. There must be something we're missing." She looked over the poem again. "I got it! Time reversed when she died, so you are supposed to set eleven thirty clockwise, three fifty-three counterclockwise, and then time goes forward again, so set five clockwise. Try it!"

So Nickolas did exactly as Sarah said, and when he clicked the watch down on five o'clock, the whole face sprang open, revealing the space where the clockworks should have been.

It was no wonder that the watch didn't work anymore, for there were no gears, wheels, or springs in the cavity. They had long been removed, and fitted in their place were three small vials containing a red, a blue, and a green solution, and a tiny golden key.

CHAPTER 23

PIXIES AND SPRITES

In which Deidre is exposed as a muse

Charles and Deidre had made their way to the small Parisian flat that the Muses of Music and War kept as a safe house when they traveled to France. It was outfitted with everything necessary to assist the muses in their work. The small study was stocked with all the tools that Charles needed to re-create the invitation he had seen in James's briefcase. It was to a ball that was to be held that very evening, and it only took a short phone call for Christina to deliver his formalwear. Fortunately, men's fashion had not changed much in the past one hundred years, so his old tuxedo—equipped with hidden pockets to house all of his regular supplies—would work quite nicely for the evening's event.

Once he had wrestled the white bowtie into a close approximation of a proper knot, he returned to the study to find Deidre studying the invitation that was drying on the drafting table. Charles peered around her elbow and admired his handiwork.

The Grand Duke and Duchess Henri
request your presence at a ball
to be given in honor of their daughter,

Alicia,
and her fiancé,
Marquis Johann de Marsilleaux,

in celebration of their engagement.
June 29 at 8:30 p.m.

Invitation required for admittance.

"Not bad, if I do say so myself. Now let's just hope that they don't have a master guest list they are checking against," he said as he removed the invitation from Deidre's hand and tucked it into his jacket's breast pocket. He shot his sleeves and straightened the bowtie. "How do I look, Deidre?"

Deidre snorted and rolled her eyes at him.

"I will take that to mean I look presentable. I will return here around midnight, and then we can figure out what to do next. Hopefully I will have some additional information when I do."

Deidre shrugged, and Charles took his leave.

James, neatly attired in his own couture tuxedo, kept looking furtively over his shoulder as if he felt that he was being followed. His instincts weren't wrong, for less than a block behind him, Charles was blending into the shadows and keeping just out of sight along the busy Paris street.

Once again, James paused, looking left and then right before jogging up the front steps of a white stone row house. The mansion was quite old and over five stories tall, identical to the four other mansions that lined the block and faced the Seine.

A tail-coated butler opened the door and accepted James's invitation. "Dr. James, you are very late," the butler admonished. "They should be finishing dinner soon."

"Don't worry, August, I will slip quietly in, and no one will be the wiser." James clapped the man on the shoulder and started to enter into the home. "Has everyone else already arrived?"

"How would I know?" The butler sighed wearily. "There are people here whom I have never met before in my life. The marquis seems to be related to half of Paris. And not the best half, if you get my meaning, sir."

"How is poor Henri holding up?" James asked. Charles got the distinct opinion from the conspiratorial way the butler talked to James that they had a long-standing acquaintance.

"As well as can be expected, sir. Alicia is happy with the young man, and her mother is happy with his title, so the grand duke has no choice but to be happy too."

"It is very important to keep the wife happy, as I know well. Henri is a very smart man." James gave the butler a reassuring nod and disappeared inside the house.

Across the street, Charles smiled to himself. It looked like he would fit right in, at least with the marquis's relatives. He gave James several minutes to settle into the house before mounting the stairs himself.

The same tail-coated butler answered the door. First, he looked right over Charles's head, and seeing no one, he made to close it again. Charles cleared his throat. "I am here for Lady Alicia's party," he said in his most pleasant voice.

The butler looked down his bulbous nose at Charles, taking in his spotless clothes and tangled brown hair. "I am sorry, sir, but the ball is by invitation only."

"Ah, but I have my invitation," Charles said, making a great show of patting his pockets before "discovering" the invitation exactly where he knew he had placed it. "I am Charles, cousin to the marquis." He presented the butler his invitation with a bow.

The butler looked over the invitation carefully, as if he didn't want to believe that it was genuine. Charles knew his forgery skills would have made a KGB agent of old positively green with envy, so he did not worry that the butler would see through his deception. Besides, he had other ways to gain access to the house if things turned ugly.

Charles gave his most innocent smile to the butler, only to find that the man was distracted by something behind him. Charles whirled around only to share an identical dumbfounded look, for there, coming up the stairs in a sparkly black evening dress and six-inch stiletto shoes, was Deidre.

Charles looked her over from her hair, which she had wrapped, twigs and all, around her ponytail holder to form an updo held in place by what looked suspiciously like a pair of takeout Chinese chopsticks, to the dress, which was several inches too short at the ankle, as Deidre was well over six feet tall, and the dress had been made for a much shorter woman. The backless, haute couture dress exposed an extensive amount of muscular green flesh. He worked his way down past the hem of the dress to the exposed ankles and the large wide feet, now elegantly shod in towering stilettos that must have been at least a size fourteen. Where Deidre had found the dress and the shoes, Charles was too afraid to ask, but he was pretty sure that one of the fashion houses on the rue would find themselves missing the items in the morning.

A strangled noise from behind him brought Charles back to the present. "Deidre, darling," he said, trying for an endearing tone to cover his surprise. "You look stunning. I was just heading in." He extended his elbow, at a severe upward angle to reach Deidre's hand. "Thank you, sir," he added to the astonished butler. Charles was just about ready to sweep past him through the door, but the butler shot out a restraining arm.

"Your invitation is for one," the butler said coldly, his voice quivering a bit toward the end as Deidre bared her teeth and growled at him.

Charles was spared having to make an excuse by the strangest of happenstance, for just at that moment an odd, skinny little man in a black tux showing nearly as much ankle as Deidre's dress passed though the hall near the entryway. His body kept walking, but his head stayed riveted on Deidre. He only stopped when he was in serious danger of toppling over.

"My muse!" the strange man exclaimed, pushing at the heavy fringe of platinum hair that covered one dark-brown eye. "You have finally arrived!" He ran up the stairs to the doorway and grabbed Deidre's arm, oblivious to the snarl and withering stare she gave him. He led her into the mansion, completely ignoring the butler's protests, and with a shrug to the pompous servant, Charles slouched after Deidre and her admirer. Was the man really one of Deidre's students, or did he just call her a muse for some other reason? Charles didn't realize that Deidre had any students. Well, not ones that weren't green anyway.

Once they were out of the doorway and down the grand hallway, Charles slipped to Deidre's other side and hissed, "Just what do you think you are doing? You are not going to blend in." His words were accented by the crash of a tray of wine glasses. A servant had just entered the hall and caught sight of her.

Deidre easily broke his grip on her arm and shrugged, heading straight for the double doors on their right and allowing the blond stranger to lead her through. Music from a string quartet floated out when he opened the door for her, and Charles could glimpse the overflowing ballroom beyond. He was thankful for the crowd, for it would allow Deidre and himself better cover to blend in. Well, blend in as much as possible with a six-foot-tall, green, sequin-clad Amazon by his side. Charles sighed and followed Deidre and her "date" into the crowd. Her date had just introduced himself as M. Chandler and was inquiring after Deidre's name. Deidre, of course, gave him no answer beyond a snarl.

From her great height, Deidre spotted James almost immediately where he stood talking with an elderly man in a rumpled tux. More than a hundred dancing guests stood between Deidre and James, but she immediately began elbowing her way through, pulling the unprotesting M. Chandler along with her, upsetting drinks and treading on trains as she went. Indignant guests turned to reprimand her, only to find their words dying on their lips as they stared up and up and up into her stony glare.

She had only gone a third of the way across the ballroom when she bumped the arm of a flamboyantly dressed man with shaggy silver hair and a purple velvet tuxedo. The man turned and, instead of being enraged by the plate of canapés that had spilled down his front, seemed awestruck at the sight of Deidre. He hurried after her and plucked at her free arm.

"Darling," he said, pulling on her formidable biceps. "Where have you been all my life? We must talk." He kept pestering her until she turned to face him, her frown deepening into a scowl that would wilt braver men than the one who stood before her. But there is a saying that fools rush in where brave men fear to tread, and M. Cormier was definitely the former. "You must dance with me," he continued, attempting to sweep Deidre onto the dance floor.

"You can't dance with her—I saw her first," M. Chandler protested, trying to disengage M. Cormier's hand from Deidre's arm.

"You are just a two-bit designer. Her beauty would be diminished by your puny clothes. She shall be the inspiration for my next line. I shall call it 'Amazonian Verde,'" M. Cormier shot back, releasing Deidre's arm to gesticulate wildly as he spoke.

"My clothes are far superior to your old stuffy house's tripe. You haven't been trendy in decades. My clothes are worn by all of new Hollywood. Yours are worn by aging matriarchs. Surely your clientele won't understand this beautiful muse's attraction." And M. Chandler pulled Deidre toward the dance floor with the protesting M. Cormier following loudly behind.

Deidre shot Charles a bewildered look that nearly put him into giggles. He had never seen Deidre look uncomfortable, but when being the object of the two designers' adjunct attentions, there was no other word for it. Charles shrugged and pointed to James and continued his way across the floor.

M. Chandler had not missed a beat, and he continued to talk and dance with Deidre, firmly ignoring M. Cormier. "Of course you have heard of me. I work for Madame and am one of her main designers this season. Madame has asked me to personally create something new and fresh for the upcoming fashion week, and you, my dear, will be my muse. No, no. You don't have to thank me yet, but with your looks and my fashions, you will be the talk of the town. Of the whole world. No one looks as amazing and stunning as you, my dear, and with the right dress and shoes, there is nothing you cannot do, and no price you cannot ask. I see an amazing future for you as a model—as my model. Just say yes and you will be the 'it' girl to overshadow any 'it' girl before you or after you. No one will be able to fit in your shoes."

Charles had to stifle his snort as he passed out of hearing, for truly no one normal would be able to fit Deidre's shoes without M. Chandler's help. It would be like Cinderella's slipper only in reverse.

Through a gap in the dancers, Charles could just see James wrapping up his conversation with the elderly gentleman, and perhaps he sensed Charles's gaze, for James looked his way. But as usually was the case with people, James looked right over Charles's head and straight at Deidre and her two escorts.

James's eyes grew very round, and he turned on his heel, rapidly heading toward one of the smaller doors behind the quartet. By the time Charles got through the tangle of guests, he watched the door quietly close and click locked behind James.

Charles turned to catch Deidre's eye, as she still danced with M. Chandler, looking more and more frustrated in the enthusiastic man's arms. M. Cormier kept trying to cut in, and the three were the complete center of attention.

Deidre saw Charles's nod, and she abruptly broke M. Chandler's hold on her and stalked through the remaining dancers. As she passed the quartet, she noticed that one of the players had a danso lying on the floor by his side. The instrument was far finer and newer than the one she had left in the apartment, and with a grunt she picked it up and inspected it.

"Hey!" the musician started to protest, but one look at Deidre's towering form and snarling face and he freely offered for her to borrow it for as long as she liked.

Charles had picked the lock by the time Deidre joined him. They found a narrow staircase on the other side of the door. It must be for the servants to use, as it was not nearly as grand as the one in the front foyer. The two muses rushed upward and arrived in the long corridor above just in time to see a silver flash coming from under one of the many doors.

Charles tried the handle and found it locked, but his lock picks soon had it open, and they entered the formal guest bedroom beyond.

It was completely empty save for a large four-poster bed covered in embroidered white linen and mounded with pillows. There, nestled among two oblong neck rolls, lay an intricately carved wooden box.

Charles deftly opened it and pressed the activation button, closing it up once more. He placed his fist on top of the box and was surprised when nothing happened. He was just about to open it up again to determine that everything was functional when he was startled by a noise behind him.

Deidre had cleared her throat and was pointing to the mannish gunmetal ring encircling her middle finger and then indicating Charles's bare hands.

"Oh, right, I gave it to Sarah." Charles shook his head and then continued. "Would you do the honors, Deidre?" He bowed to the tall muse and indicated that she should take his place next to the box.

Deidre shrugged and brushed past Charles. She grabbed his hand crushingly in her left and, making a fist, jammed her right onto the box. Still nothing happened.

Charles reopened the box and, using several of his lock picks, lifted the front panel, exposing the inner workings. He poked around the chips and connections for a while and then noticed something strange. The frequency chip had an attachment that wasn't usually in the transport boxes. He pulled some tweezers from a pocket in his boot cuff and removed the pale-green attachment, reassembling the box. "Looks like James doesn't want a record of his movements."

Turning to Deidre, he gave her a roguish grin. "Well, that will either do the trick and allow us to follow James, or it might just blow us up into miniscule unrecognizable pieces. Want to give it a go?"

Deidre did not bother to reply and just palmed Charles's head like a basketball in her huge green hand and jammed her ring onto the top of the box. The two muses glowed silver for just a second, and then the room was quiet and empty with the box still nestled among the pillows.

⊰⊱

Charles had to remind Deidre to let go of his head and then rubbed feeling back into his cranium for several minutes. She, of course, ignored him and surveyed their surroundings. They had emerged on a quayside. From the looks of the large white building on their right and gigantic semicircular bridge on their left, they had arrived in Sydney Harbor quay.

It was early morning, and all was quiet around them. Only a few runners were out, bundled against the winter chill in the air as they jogged the path along the harbor's edge. Apparently, they were so deeply engrossed in their workout that the runners were oblivious to the oddly dressed pair standing in the shadows.

Only one of the quay slots showed any signs of life. A sleek black yacht was starting its engines, and two attendants were casting off their mooring ropes preparing to move out into the still, dark harbor. In the bow of the boat, Charles spied James, hands clasped behind his back, surveying the hills on the opposite side of the bay. James was chatting with a well-dressed man who Charles assumed was the yacht's owner.

Charles was looking about him for a boat or ship that he could commandeer when Deidre caught his arm and pointed to their left. Sitting on the side of a nearby quay lay a four-person racing scull, complete with oars at the ready.

Doubtfully, Charles whispered to Deidre, "You think we can keep up with the yacht in that thing?"

She raised her eyebrows and then decisively shook her head. She jabbed a thumb at her own chest and nodded curtly.

"Thanks for the vote of confidence, Greeny," he said under his breath and then headed for the scull.

Deidre dropped the racing boat into position on the water and removed all but two of the oars, unceremoniously throwing them on the dock beside the boat. She shoved the danso into the neckline of the back of her dress for safekeeping, and she grasped the skirt of her gown just above the knee. With one sharp pull, she ripped it off at that height and dumped the remaining skirt into the water. Her gigantic stiletto heels soon followed the skirt into the harbor with a splash. She gestured for Charles to sit in the coxswain's spot, and once he was settled, Deidre plopped in facing him and reached her great hands to grasp the two remaining oars.

"You can really row a four-man scull by yourself?" Charles asked, looking at the awkward position Deidre held.

In response, he got only a snort from Deidre as she tightened her grip on the oars and pushed off from the edge of the quay. Charles watched as the two stiletto heels floated past them. They were so wide and so big that they hadn't sunk when Deidre had thrown them into the water. Charles wryly thought that they might have been a possible alternate form of transportation had the scull not been available.

The two disproportionate ships left the quayside at roughly the same time, with the yacht taking the lead position. Deidre, with powerful strokes and tireless arms, slipped right into the yacht's wake and maintained a quiet distance behind.

They crossed the harbor and slowly worked their way south, eventually turning west onto the Lane Cove River. All Charles had to do was lean back and keep an eye on the yacht to direct Deidre's turns. He thought about picking up the microphone and chanting her strokes, but he was pretty sure that would just result in him getting a danso in his gut, or possibly thrown overboard, so he kept his peace.

⟞⧲⧳⟝

A tall cliff appeared on their right several miles up the river, and not much farther on they heard the yacht cut its engines. Deidre quietly slowed her strokes until the scull sat calmly in the water a few yards from where the yacht was docked against the cliff. Charles could just make out one person disembarking onto a narrow dock in the predawn dark. The yacht departed, leaving its passenger behind as it circled and headed back toward Sydney Quay. The tall thin man on the shore could only be James, so Deidre and Charles waited until he had started up the cliff face via a small stone stairway.

Deidre quietly eased the scull up to the dock and jumped ashore, nearly swamping Charles in the process. Shaking the water from his hair and goatee, Charles followed suit.

Deidre looked expectantly at Charles, holding on to one of the scull's oars to keep it from drifting away.

"No, I think we should set it adrift. It will go downstream and end up close to where we found it. Someone will pick it up and get it back to its rightful owners via the registration numbers. Wait, though—let me leave payment for its use." Charles reached into one of his pockets and withdrew a leather bag of gold coins. He shook a few out into his hand, and they instantly changed into plastic Australian dollars, which he hid in the pouch under the coxswain's seat. "That should do it. Let her go, Deidre."

The scull slipped silently back into the water and slowly reversed her course toward Sydney Harbor.

⧊⧈

By the time the boat had rounded the first bend, James was no longer in sight on the stone staircase. Charles and Deidre hastened upward, keeping quiet and hugging the shadows as before. The stairs wound up and up and up until they were nearly at the crest of the cliff.

There the staircase abruptly stopped. There was no landing before the door in the cliff face, so Deidre slammed right into the back of Charles, nearly sending him toppling off the stairs and plummeting down to the river below. Only Deidre's huge hand on the back of his neck kept Charles from falling. He wasn't sure if he should be thanking Deidre for saving him from the fall or admonishing her for nearly sending him over the edge, so he decided to take a leaf out of her own playbook and say nothing. He turned his attention to the round green door that was closed and locked in front of him.

Charles confidently pulled out his silver lock picks, but before he could insert them, the lock suddenly clicked and opened of its own accord. Astonished, Charles found himself in a familiar clearing. Right in front of him was the marble tree-shaped stump engraved with **ARDVS**. They were back on Vivian Montague's grounds.

⚑⚐

Charles and Deidre traversed the familiar statue garden, passing the plinths of all Charles's brothers and Deidre's sisters as they went. Charles paused a moment to touch the smooth top of the plinth where he had stood all those years, noting that the divot that had been intended to hold the tanzanite stone was now smoothed over. Curious, he slipped the aura glasses from his pocket and noted that the area where the divot had been now glowed golden as if a small golden orb was embedded right below the surface. Traces of muse magic hung in pearly white wisps around the stump. Someone had fused the tanzanites and the plinths recently. One of Deidre's sisters must be here at the manor.

The realization quickened Charles's pace, as perhaps his sister-in-law was unaware that James was back, and needed his assistance. "There is another muse here at the manor," he whispered to Deidre. "I think it is one of your sisters. We should hurry."

Deidre nodded her agreement, and when they arrived at Audiva's plinth, Charles turned to head toward the hidden passageway in the wall that would lead directly to the kitchens. He pulled back the vines with his dagger tip and was just about to pick the lock when he saw a pearly white aura out of the corner of his eye.

He dropped the vines and dashed after the little glow, with Deidre in tow. The glow stayed just out of Charles's line of vision,

294

so all he saw was the tiny wisp of an aura zipping up the path ahead of him. The glow took an unexpected turn in the forest garden onto a path that had not appeared on the map that Sarah and Nickolas had given him. Charles had no time to ponder the question of the new path, as keeping the pearly aura in sight took all his concentration and skill.

Suddenly, Charles heard voices up ahead, and he stopped behind a great oak tree to peer into the clearing beyond. He had to take off the glasses in order to see clearly, for through them all he could see was a rainbow of swirling auras so bright that it blinded out everything else. He placed the glasses safely back in his pocket and focused on the clearing.

In a small circle of giant oaks, an archway formed between two of the trunks and the intertwining branches above. The archway glowed faintly blue, and the area within the arch swirled with mist that shimmered and pulsated as if it were alive. James stood before the archway with a strange contraption in his hands that looked similar to the travel boxes but was much smaller and thinner. He was tapping instructions into the device, and the mist swirled faster.

"What news have you brought me, James?" The voice came from the mist. It sounded tinny as if it came from a long way off through imperfect technology.

"I have some news and two requests for you," James said in a far more respectful tone than Charles had ever heard from the science muse.

Charles practically jumped out of his own skin when Deidre touched his hand. He looked up at his sister-in-law, her face glowing faintly in the reflection from the mist. She carefully pointed upward and then began to scale the nearest tree, climbing high into its limbs. Charles nodded and followed her up, and the two of them settled on a branch hidden in the canopy where they could hear and observe what happened below without being seen or detected.

"What is your news?" the voice inquired as they climbed.

"We have made some progress since the last time we talked, but not as much as I would have liked. I will be terminating my relationship with the scientist at this location since her results have not been satisfactory. The crossbreeding to get the required combination of quality, quantity, and ease of extraction seems to be well on target, and we have found a renewable source of human subjects, something that we have been looking for. On the bad news side, we are still having difficulties with stabilizing the extractions for more than a week, so we are continuing our experiments in that area and are looking at alternatives to perhaps taking the human subjects off-world to see how they adapt and observing the resulting effects on the quality of the essence."

"Hmm, and what are your requests?"

"First, I will need two more transport boxes—the untraceable ones, not the normal muse networked boxes. Unfortunately, when Lady Vivian blew up her lab, the one I had here was buried in the blast. I have another one in Sydney proper that I used today, but it would be much easier to have a gateway here on the manor grounds. The other is for the chateau where the children are to be housed."

"That should not be a problem," the voice replied. "And your second request?"

"Since I will be taking over the operations here at Montague Manor, and since I cannot be here at all times, I will need a better security detail. The Faeries are acceptable for patrolling and caring for the grounds, but about a fortnight ago their guarding abilities were tested, and they were found to be quite lacking.

So I need a more battle-ready force to truly protect these grounds from intruders and snoops. I would also like to place one or two at the various installations I have doing our research and extractions. I was thinking a battalion of Sprites would do for now."

"A whole battalion to protect one off-world manor and a handful of labs? Seriously, James, I might be able to provide you with a squad of Sprites, but no more. And the cost will be three times the cost of the Faeries." The voice sounded annoyed.

James pondered this for a moment and then nodded. "I think a squad would suffice. However, I will need a Pixie to command them."

A Pixie! Charles nearly fell out of his tree. If James was bringing a Pixie to guard the manor, Ardus would need to be informed immediately. Then Charles shuddered. He hated Pixies.

"When do you think that the Sprites and the Pixie would be available?" James asked. "My need is urgent, so as soon as they can be spared and transported the better."

"A rush job, hmm," the voice droned, and Charles could imagine the unseen person greedily rubbing his hands together. "What kind of weapons will the squad require?"

James thought for a moment. "As you know, these portals are programmed to only allow approved substances to be transported through them, and most of our weapons are not approved. So I will have to arm them with local weaponry until I can procure a shipment by other means. Send them with swords and other melee weapons that the portal cannot detect. Once they are here, I will take care of upgrading their armaments."

The voice sounded pleased. "If that is all you require, I think we can safely say that you could have the squad within the hour and the Pixie by midmorning if you are willing to pay five times the usual amount."

"Five times is robbery," James protested.

"You want a Pixie and a squad of Sprites who are ten times as effective a fighting force as your hundred Faeries. You say that five times the price is too much, but I say that it is a bargain. And if you wait too long to make a decision, the price will change to seven times."

Grudgingly James agreed. "And you will deliver the Sprites now?"

"Of course. Have I ever not upheld my end of the bargain?" The voice implied that James had not been so successful keeping *his* promises. "But I do expect payment up front as usual."

"I have your payment now; that is not a problem." James tapped into the rectangular device in his hands. "I have transferred the credits to your account, and you will find your payment waiting for you at the usual drop-off point. I sent it off-world this morning, so by the time you reach the rendezvous my transport should have delivered it." James reached into his jacket's breast pocket and withdrew a medium-size vial filled with pearly white liquid. "I had intended it for another client, but he can wait until I send this shipment out tomorrow." He returned the vial to his pocket.

Charles's eyes grew round at what he suspected was in the bottle. James was dealing in essence! And the voice's next sentence confirmed Charles's worst fears.

"Now, I assume that you are only providing me with the essence extracted from the highly evolved animals on that planet and not the low-quality essence from the lesser animals. And it is only extracted from the juveniles of the species?"

"Of course. It is pure human essence extracted from children under the age of thirteen, as you requested. It is very difficult to obtain, as you know, but the one I sent this morning was extracted yesterday, so it should be fresh until the end of the week." Charles barely heard the end of James's speech, for he was now shaking. Not only was James trading in human essence, but he was extracting it in large quantities! Just how much was he taking from those children at the chateau? And did he have other instillations doing similar extractions? Just where was James doing all these extractions? And who was sending them off-world for him? James had not been out of Charles's sight for three days, so he couldn't have sent it.

Charles heard a low growl from the tree limb beside him and turned to see Deidre's eyes flashing and teeth bared. James's behavior went against everything that the muses stood for. How could he?

Far beneath them in the underbrush just outside the reach of the light of the clearing, the little pearly white aura that Charles had followed had her hackles up and was growling deep in her throat as well. Sparks was no happier with the revelations that she had just seen than Charles and Deidre were; in fact, if truth be told, Sparks was even angrier.

CHAPTER 24

DR. MONTAGUE'S LAB

⊰⊱

In which we discover we don't have enough ingredients

Sarah awoke the next morning with sunshine streaming through the dirty windows and onto her face. For a moment she wasn't sure where she was, but then memories flooded back to her. She was sleeping in Dr. Montague's huge bed where Brigitta and Bard must have tucked her in. The last thing she remembered was sitting on the floor in Dr. Montague's lab watching Nickolas and Mr. Benjamin assembling glassware to begin the experiment.

She thought back with some satisfaction to how she and Nickolas had gotten them into the laboratory after they had found the key...

"Brigitta! I think we've found it!" Sarah had shouted, running across the short distance to where Brigitta and Bard were discussing the hidden doorway. "It was in Dr. Montague's watch."

Mr. Benjamin had taken the key from Sarah and inserted it in the lock. It had been more than seventy years since the door had been opened, so it took some fiddling for Mr. Benjamin to get the key to turn. He had almost given up when with a squeak of protest, the lock gave way. When he turned the handle to open the door, he found that it would not budge. Sarah had tried after Mr. Benjamin, but considering she weighed a good hundred

301

pounds less than the portly scientist, her added determination had not been enough to open the door.

Bard had gently moved Sarah aside. "Let me try. I won't smash, I promise, Brigitta," he added with twinkling eyes when Brigitta opened her mouth to caution him. She had closed it again without uttering a word and smiled her dazzling smile. Sarah was rapidly realizing that this was an old joke between them and that Bard was only half serious when he asked if he could smash something and Brigitta was only three-quarters serious when she warned him not to.

Bard had grasped the door handle in his large paw and carefully turned it while pushing with his massive shoulder. Sarah had heard something heavy being moved with the door as he pushed. Slowly and carefully he had opened the door wider until it was wide enough for Brigitta and Sarah to slip through. It had been very dark inside, and the small amount of light that came into the room from the doorway had not been enough to illuminate beyond a few feet.

"Nickolas, do you still have that flashlight you packed?" Sarah had asked, and her brother had quickly pulled the large black torch from his backpack and passed it through to her.

She had clicked it on and shined its light around the room. They seemed to have been in a small, cramped closet that had another door just a few feet on. This door was not locked, and Sarah had been able to easily open it, revealing a sun-bathed laboratory. The bright sunlight had temporarily blinded Sarah and Brigitta, but their eyes soon adjusted, and they were able to determine that a whole stack of toppled boxes was impeding the opening of the first door.

They'd soon had the boxes moved out of the way and the door opened wide enough to allow Nickolas and Alec to enter. Bard had been only able to fit by ducking low and turning sideways, looking very much like a crab scuttling out of its hole. Sarah had stifled a giggle; poor Bard just wasn't made for tiny spaces.

The laboratory hadn't been much bigger, and it was crammed full with equipment set up on marble-topped tables. There were signs that Dr. Montague had left in great haste. Experiments were still set up on most of the tables, with notebooks open and pencils expectantly beside them. Long-evaporated substances left residue in the beakers, and long-burned-out lanterns and candles lined the walls.

Brigitta had sent Sarah and Alec out into the main rooms to collect candles to replace the stubs while Mr. Benjamin and Nickolas had searched the room. In short order, Mr. Benjamin had announced that everything he needed was in the laboratory and that it was obvious that at the time of his departure from the manor, Dr. Montague had been working on solving the same problem of the dying microbios that they were.

Mr. Benjamin had picked the cleanest of the tables and began instructing Nickolas on helping him pick up the mess left by Dr. Montague and the supplies he needed from around the room and closet to get started. They had talked in a kind of shorthand: "I need a 100ml burette" and "Can you get me a 2G crucible?" and "See that small separatory funnel? No, not that one—the one by the extraction apparatus." It had made Sarah's head spin, but Nickolas had seemed to understand all of Mr. Benjamin's requests and quickly found and brought what was needed.

Mr. Benjamin and Nickolas were soon so deep in building what looked like an intricate glass Rube Goldberg machine that Sarah had started feeling sleepy. She must have lost the battle with her heavy eyelids, and either Bard or Brigitta had moved her to the bedroom to sleep out the night.

Concerned that she might have missed something important, Sarah sprang out of bed and rushed into the sitting room.

There she found Alec fixing a makeshift breakfast out of the chocolate chip cookies Nickolas had brought from home and some hot tea made from some old dried tea leaves he had found in a tin in Dr. Montague's desk.

"How old are those tea leaves?" Sarah asked, helping herself to a cookie.

"Near as I can guess they're about seventy-five years old," Alec said unconcernedly, drinking a large cup of it. "It tastes a bit bland and could really use some sugar, but it's better than nothing."

"Are you sure it's safe?"

"Nickolas and Mr. Benjamin gave me about a twenty-minute lecture on how if you keep tea away from light and moisture and air it can last indefinitely. They threw in some facts about room temperature and the pros and cons of refrigeration as well, but the bottom line was that it probably wouldn't kill us. Besides, Mr. Benjamin needed the caffeine after staying up all night on the experiment, so I brewed it anyway. Care to live dangerously and join me in a cup?"

Sarah agreed, and Alec poured her some in a pretty blue flowered teacup. If Nickolas and Mr. Benjamin were drinking it and thought it was OK, that was good enough for her.

She settled into a chair and blew on her tea to cool it while eating another cookie. "Did everyone get some sleep last night?" Sarah felt a little guilty for taking the only bed in the tower.

"I slept out here on the couch in front of the fireplace." Alec indicated where a blanket and pillows still adorned the settee. "I think Nickolas and Mr. Benjamin were too enthralled with what they were doing to sleep, and I'm not sure that Brigitta and Bard need to sleep. They look just as fresh and ready to go as they did yesterday. Just what exactly are they, anyway? And why do they look like they're going to an ancient Greek costume ball?"

"They're muses," Sarah said, and when Alec raised his now ring-less eyebrow at her, she continued. "I know it sounds crazy, and it'll only sound crazier if I tell you more. I find it is best to just accept them as they are and not try to figure it out too much."

"Considering I was magically transported from the airport to a dungeon cell a couple of weeks ago, I'm more willing to accept things than you would think. Try me."

"Well, when we were here last, we found the muses in the garden. There are fourteen of them. Seven are Muses of Music— Brigitta is one of those—and seven Muses of War, like Bard. They were trapped as statues when we first found them. We think it was another muse, a Muse of Science named James, who trapped them here. Nickolas found these stones in the fountain that freed them. And then they helped us escape our great-aunt Vivian and get back home. It really does sound fantastic, but it's true." Sarah finished her tea and rose to get another cookie.

"I've met your great-aunt, and if the muses are on the side against her, I'm on that side too," Alec said ruefully. "Do you think they could get me home?"

"That I'm sure of, since all Brigitta wants to do is get us home as soon as possible. If Nickolas wasn't helping Mr. Benjamin, I'm pretty sure they would have already taken us back to the States. Grandma Vera must be beside herself with worry."

For some reason, this seemed to upset Alec, for he turned away from Sarah and glared into the fireplace. His shoulders were hunched as if he was remembering painful things.

Sarah would have asked him if he was OK, but at that moment, Brigitta and Bard entered the room from the direction of the laboratory.

"Morning, Brigitta," Sarah said, rising to give the beautiful muse a hug.

"Good morning, Sarah. Did you sleep well?"

"Extremely. I don't even remember you putting me to bed. Thank you for that, by the way."

"You are most welcome. I think you were completely worn out."

"What are Nickolas and Mr. Benjamin up to?" Sarah asked, changing the subject.

"They are still in the lab, huddled over Dr. Montague's notes. I think it will be some time before they emerge."

While Sara and Brigitta were talking, Bard had gone over to stand next to Alec, and together they were inspecting a ceremonial sword that hung above the fireplace. It rested on a framed backing, which had a brass label affixed to it:

This sword is presented to
Baronet Christopher Montague
for his contributions to medical science
by
His Majesty, King George V
July 23, 1919

"Wow," Alec said upon reading the plaque. He carefully lifted the sword down from its hooks. The handle was gold and heavily engraved with golden ropes and tassels attached to it. The blade, however, was much more functional, and Alec pronounced it surprisingly well-balanced as he took some practice strokes, discussing its design with Bard.

Surprised, Sarah interrupted. "Where did you learn to use a sword? Ardus tried to teach Nickolas some things when he was here, but Nickolas didn't catch on very quickly."

"I'm on the fencing team back home," Alec said. "I've studied it since I was very little. Sabre is my favorite, and this isn't much thicker than what I'm used to, although it is quite a bit sturdier."

"You're a fencer?" Sarah looked at his goth hair and multiple piercings and raised her eyebrow. "You don't look like a stereo-typical fencer. I thought they walked around in white pajamas and funky helmets."

"I do, it goes well with the black nail polish," Alec said, and Sarah was almost sure that the melancholy young man was teasing her. She decided to test it a little.

"Really, I heard that red polish was the more tradi-tional choice."

"Only for épée," Alec replied, still testing the balance of the sword.

"Brigitta, can I borrow your daggers?" Sarah asked, getting an idea.

"Of course," the muse answered, unhooking the two ser-pentine blades that she always wore at her hip and passing them to Sarah. The emeralds in the pommels winked in the early-morning light, but they felt surprisingly comfortable in Sarah's hands, reminding her of the two curved blades Charles had let her borrow in Great-Aunt Vivian's laboratory.

"OK," she said, facing Alec and holding the two blades up in a defensive pose, "teach me."

"Well, I know almost nothing about fighting with daggers," was the reply, but Sarah and Brigitta could sense that Alec was not opposed to the idea of practicing with Sarah, and both young ladies thought it would be a good idea to try to bring the morose young man out of his shell.

"Bard and I certainly do," Brigitta said, unfolding herself from her chair. "I will coach Sarah, Bard will judge, and you two will make sure you remember that those weapons are real and have sharp blades. I am not the best of my sisters at healing, by a long shot, so keep it to minor wounds please, as I cannot patch up anything worse than a deep scratch. Agreed?" When both children nodded, she placed them in the center of the room facing each other while Bard moved the furniture out of the way.

"Now salute each other." Alec did this smoothly, and Sarah did her best to copy his move. "Alec, let's have you on offence and Sarah on defense. Start with a simple overhead blow. Sarah, you will bring your left-hand dagger up like so and block it between the blade and the guard on the handle. If you catch it right, you can use the curve of the blade to trap it, and hopefully disarm your enemy. But let's just focus on blocking it and keeping it from cutting you for now. And begin."

Sarah found that the blocking exercises came easily to her and that the well-balanced daggers were merely extensions of her arms. At first, she could tell that Alec was being extremely cautious, and his sword barely touched her daggers with enough force to make a noise. But Sarah's natural grace and speed helped her immensely, and soon Alec was picking up the pace of his blows and mixing up the direction that they came from. Brigitta started adding offensive moves to Sarah's repertoire, even teaching her to twist her arm at just the right time to disarm her opponent. Alec allowed her to disarm him once or twice, but once she understood the move, she found that he had counter moves that would quickly reverse his blade before she had time to capture it.

He smiled slightly as he thwarted her attack, and Sarah felt her annoyance rising. "Use his momentum against him, Sarah," Bard called from where he observed by the fireplace. "And don't get angry. Angry fighters make mistakes. You can only win if you stay coolheaded."

"Easy for him to say," Sarah muttered, but she took a deep breath and continued, trying to put into practice Bard's words. Every time she felt her temper rising, she shoved it firmly down to her toes, and she tried to figure out how to use Alec's momentum against him, but just about the time she figured it out, the moment she should have acted had passed.

Bard called a time-out at one point and approached Sarah. He put his arm around her shoulders in a fatherly manner and drew her away from Alec and Brigitta. "Sarah," he said quietly, "you are overthinking this. When I watch you fight, I can see in your eyes that you are trying to guess his next move and respond accordingly. You need to stop thinking. Fighting well has less to do with thinking and more to do with feeling and responding. Try to take your brain out of the equation and just use your eyes to command your arms. Don't think about doing, just do it. I should know—no one has ever accused me of overthinking, and I do fight rather well." Bards eyes twinkled kindly at her, and she nodded.

Telling Sarah not to think was kind of like telling her not to breathe, but she promised to try, and they returned to the practice ring where Brigitta had compiled a whole new list of drills. Sarah practiced the new drills two or three times to get them into her muscle memory and then tried to do as Bard had recommended. After two or three spectacular failures, Sarah suddenly found that by watching the center of Alec's chest and not his arms or legs, she could determine when he was going to strike, and by trusting her arms to be where she needed them, she found she could turn off her brain, sort of, and gained a few precious moments of time, which gave her that critical edge over her opponent. The astonishment on Alec's face every time she scored a point and the pride in Bard's left Sarah feeling like she was floating on air.

Brigitta and Bard kept them at it until Sarah was breathing heavily and even Alec was starting to sweat a little. Neither the muses nor humans noticed when Mr. Benjamin entered the room.

"Excuse me," he said timidly. "Ahem, excuse me!"

Sarah looked up and dropped her guard immediately. It took a herculean effort on Alec's part to adjust his stroke to keep it from passing through Sarah's shoulder, wrenching his own wrist in the process. Sarah noticed nothing as she approached Mr. Benjamin, but Bard gave the boy an approving nod and clapped him on the back, nearly knocking Alec flat. "Well done," the muse whispered.

Alec massaged his wrist and was just about ready to return the sword to its holder on the wall when he noticed that Sarah had slipped the daggers through her belt, and he decided to do the same with Dr. Montague's sword. After years of training, it felt comfortable there anyway.

"We are making lovely progress," Mr. Benjamin was saying. "And I could not be achieving as much without the help of young Nickolas. He has the makings of a brilliant scientist. But, sadly, we need more ingredients. Could I bother you to slip into the gardens and get two of the red mushrooms, two diamonds from the fountain, and a small handful of the tonza tree roots from the forest garden? The roots look like this one." He handed Sarah a small brown piece that looked similar to the bulbous ginger roots her mother bought from the store to cook Thai food. "Also, please collect a little of the solution that the gems are kept in from the fountain. I will need that as well."

"Sure, Mr. Benjamin, we can get those for you," Sarah said, accepting the root, a stoppered vial for the diamonds and solution, and the collecting tin for the mushrooms that he handed her. "Come on, Alec, you can come with me."

Sarah was halfway out the door, with Alec slouching behind her, when Brigitta stopped them. "Sarah, I don't think it is safe for you to be wandering the gardens. What if you were discovered by your great-aunt or one of her guards?"

"Bard can come with us," Sarah said quickly. "Please, Brigitta, I need to get outside. This waiting is killing me. The sword work was really fun—in fact, I want Alec and you to teach me more—but I do need a break, and we promise to go straight into the gardens and straight back. Please?"

Brigitta looked at Sarah's begging face, the hint of a smile on Alec's, and Bard's eager countenance and she relented. "OK, but you are to listen to everything Bard tells you, and come straight back." Brigitta looked sternly at the two children and then turned to Bard. "Bard, you are to get the ingredients and nothing else. No smashing, and no getting into trouble."

"Don't worry, Brigitta. Alec and Sarah will protect me." Bard winked at Sarah.

"You three are incorrigible." Brigitta threw up her hands in mock dismay, but she handed the key to the tower to Sarah. "Hurry back!" And with that she followed Mr. Benjamin toward the laboratory.

⧤⧥

Clearly dismissed, the three headed out into the observatory and down the stone steps of the tower. As they went, Sarah secured the key in her pocket. Bard swung the heavy mechanism on the

311

inside of the door to let them out, and then he leaned against it, pushing with his massive legs to close it from the outside. Sarah heard the locking mechanism spin and click into place once the door was closed.

Bard started heading on the path to the stables, whistling in an absentminded out-of-tune way as he went.

"Bard," Sarah called. "The gardens are this way." She indicated over her shoulder toward the Zen garden.

"Oh, you lead." Bard turned and followed Sarah across the breakfast garden. "Glad you came."

Sarah laughed. "Me too, Bard. How about I lead, Alec gathers, and you protect. I know that isn't what Brigitta suggested, but I think it's for the best." She handed Alec the collection tin and vial.

"Yes, that does seem to take advantage of our talents a little better," Alec said with a grin.

Sarah grinned back, satisfied. She did not like how depressed Alec had seemed when she had first met him, and she had been doing her best to make him laugh and bring him out of his melancholy ever since.

Sarah had a reputation on the ranch of always gravitating to the quieter, more withdrawn campers. She had a knack for making everyone around her comfortable, and she could make even the most hesitant of campers laugh and join the group in no time. When she was very young, her mother would point out the shy ones and send Sarah over to them. It was funny to see four-year-old Sarah leading reluctant teen campers to the fire and convincing them to join in the camp songs just because Sarah enjoyed them so much. This became her official job during the summer by the time she had turned nine, and Sarah loved it. She would look at each opportunity as a challenge, and she had a special wink she used with her mother to let her know when Sarah had accomplished her mission.

Alec was no different than the hundreds of wounded campers Sarah had worked with before. She was sure, with the confidence that only a ten-year-old could have, that she could get him out of his depression. Perhaps not right away, she reasoned, but over time she knew she could and maybe even be able to get him to dye his hair back to blond. He really did look ridiculous striped like a skunk. To say nothing about that nose ring...

❄

By this time, they had arrived in the mushroom garden, and Sarah pointed out the red mushrooms to Alec and recommended that he pick them up with the sleeve of his shirt covering his hand. "They contain some pretty nasty acid. Nickolas got burned by one of them when we were here last time." Sarah noticed that Alec did exactly as she said and didn't seem as fascinated by the properties of the mushrooms as her older brother was. Perhaps Alec had a bit more sense than Nickolas.

She urged them onward down the path to the maze garden once the mushrooms were safely in Alec's pouch.

Sarah found, much to her relief, that she no longer needed Sparks or Nickolas to guide her through the maze. Alec and Bard confidently followed her into its depths, and she had to grin to herself that they really wouldn't be so confident if they realized that her sense of direction in the maze was suspect at best.

Thinking about Sparks reminded Sarah that the dog was still missing, and Sarah was still quite worried about her, but her thoughts were interrupted when they arrived at the silent fountain and Alec let out a low whistle of appreciation. "Delaney would have loved this."

It was the first time he had mentioned her name without tears springing to his eyes, so Sarah quickly said, "You should see it when it's running. The dolphins throw water and gems toward the nymphs, and the nymphs pour water from their urns back into the fountain. It's pretty spectacular. And Charles, one of Bard's brothers, has these glasses that make the whole thing glow silver and gold. It was amazing." Sarah fished in the water for diamonds as she talked.

"Charles is pretty amazing, too. You know how huge Bard is? Well, Charles is like one-fourth his size. Honestly," she added when Alec looked skeptical. "I don't think the seven Muses of War are really brothers, for they look nothing alike. Ferdinand is short and dark, Ardus is tall and blond, Bard is wide and red-haired, and Charles is, well, tiny. He's smaller than me! But they call each other brothers, so whatever." Sarah shrugged. "Found one!" She held up an algae-covered diamond in triumph.

"I found one too!" Bard called from across the clearing where he had been looking.

"Me three," Alec added, cleaning his diamond off on his shirt.

"Mr. Benjamin said he only needed two, but there is no reason not to bring an extra," Sarah said, handing her diamond to Alec to put into the vial. "Don't forget to add the liquid," she reminded him. "I'm not sure why he needs it, but he's the scientist. Two down, one to go. Let's go to the forest garden. It's just through the maze and past the flowers." Sarah jumped down from the edge of the fountain and led Alec and Bard to the correct opening in the hedge that surrounded the clearing.

The flower garden was even more decayed and cloying than it had been the day before, and Sarah covered her nose with her hands to keep out the smell of decomposing flowers. The gardens seemed to be dying at an alarming rate without the Faeries' care.

Sarah looked over at Bard and saw his perplexed frown. "The gardens are dying," he said, stating the obvious. "Georgiana will know what to do."

"Georgiana likes gardening?" Sarah asked, remembering the thin, dainty muse who was so prim and proper. She tried to picture Georgiana in her pristine white dress kneeling in the dirt with gardening gloves, floppy sun hat, and a hand rake weeding a garden and found it impossible to imagine.

Bard nodded. "Georgiana is excellent at working with magic. This place is magic. Georgiana would set it to rights."

Alec pulled Sarah aside. "Magic? Like for real magic?"

Sarah shrugged and whispered back, "Jury's still out on that. There are a lot of things here that seem like magic, but some of them are just science masquerading as magic, so I don't know. Magic, maybe...odd, definitely."

⁍⁍⁍

By this time they had reached the stairs to the forest garden, and Sarah was just about ready to skip down them when Bard lifted her by the waist as if she were a rag doll and pushed her behind him. His whole easygoing demeanor had changed. His body was tense and his face stern. One arm was flung wide to keep Alec and Sarah protected, while the other twirled his giant battle-ax as if it weighed nothing.

And then Sarah heard what Bard had. Something or someone was coming toward them from the depths of the forest.

CHAPTER 25

LOUIS TELLS ALL

In which Great-Aunt Vivian learns the truth

Carole and Fulvio dashed through the passageways back to the kitchens. "You don't think Lady Vivian has done anything to Zac, do you?" Carole asked anxiously as they ran.

"Of course not, Carole. I am not even sure that Lady Vivian knows that Zac is your son. She isn't the most observant when it comes to the people who work in the manor. There are times when she even forgets my name. Don't worry, we will get Zac to safety before Lady Vivian even knows that I was imprisoned."

Even with Fulvio's assurances, Carole still quickened her steps.

They arrived in the kitchens soon after, to find that all was as it usually was at this time of day. Staff were putting away the cleaned dinner dishes into their cupboards, and the drudges were wiping down the huge tables and mopping the floors.

Carole found Zac washing the last of the pots and pans at his station by the sinks. Tears were running down the huge man's cheeks, and such an air of misery hung around his shoulders that Carole ran to his side. "Zac, what is wrong, my child?" she asked, gently removing the large copper pot from his hands and leading him over to the nearest table.

Zac sniffed and rubbed the tears from his eyes. "I got Chef into trouble. It's all my fault."

"I'm not in trouble," Fulvio said kindly, just catching up to Carole and a bit out of breath. "See, here I am, all safe and sound."

"Chef!" Zac exclaimed, standing so quickly to hug Fulvio that he knocked the bench and Carole onto the floor. "Oh, Chef! I was so worried!"

"There, there," Fulvio gasped, patting Zac on the back and trying to loosen his hold at the same time. "But I won't be for long if you don't let me breathe, my friend."

"Sorry, Chef." Zac let him go. "But I am so glad you are OK. You are OK? Yes?"

"Right as rain. So why did you think I was in trouble?"

"The soup cook asked me to get him a copper pot from the storeroom. So I tried, but the door was locked. But I knew where Mama kept the key, so I got it and opened the lock. There sitting in the middle of the floor was the funniest little creature you ever saw. It looked like a huge potato with arms and legs and everything! I wanted to see him closer, so I picked him up. And guess what he did? He bit me! See!" Zac rolled up his sleeve and showed Fulvio a nasty red mark.

Without pausing a breath, Zac continued. "I dropped him, and he ran away! But then he turned into a footman with a uniform and a ponytail and everything. How did he do that? And where did he get clothes? When he was a potato, he wasn't wearing anything. He was a potato, and potatoes don't usually wear clothes. He said something about getting Chef into trouble. I was so worried. You didn't come to dinner. I was even more worried. I am so glad you are OK, Chef. So glad." Turning to his mother, Zac added, "Am I in trouble?"

"No, Zac," Fulvio said. "You are not in trouble. But we do need to find a safe place for you and your mother to hide until I get this all sorted out. Carole, let's pack Zac a bag."

"But where will we go, Chef? And who will do my job?" Zac looked very worried.

"Have no fear, I will make sure your job gets done, and you won't be gone long. Actually, I think I have another job for you to do while you are hiding. Mr. Benjamin will need someone to wash his lab equipment for him. And I can think of no one who would do a better job than you. Some of the glassware is very delicate, but I know what an excellent job you do washing Lady Vivian's best goblets. And the lab equipment cannot be any more fragile than those."

Zac looked appeased and followed Fulvio and Carole to the apartment behind the head chef's office. What Fulvio thought would be a quick process turned out to be anything but. Carole, it appeared, was a very particular packer, and Fulvio found himself getting more and more nervous as Carole continued to pack well into the night and Zac fell asleep on his bed.

⧽⧼

Louis had found Lady Vivian in her quarters. She was already not best pleased, as he had instructed her lady's maid to pull her from her bath to speak to him.

"This had better be very important, Louis," Vivian snapped. She wore an elaborately embroidered silk robe, and her hair was twisted up in a fluffy pink towel on top of her head. Louis had never seen Lady Vivian without her makeup on, and he was surprised by how clean and shiny her skin appeared without its usual coat of powder.

"It is, Lady Vivian, I assure you. You might want to have a seat, though." Vivian perched imperiously on one of her sitting room chairs, clutching her robe closed at the neck.

"Continue," she commanded.

"I found Fulvio snooping around your office earlier. He said it was on your command, and he had this on his person." Louis handed Vivian her ruby key.

Vivian's eyes grew round at the sight of it. "Did he take anything?"

"No, I made sure of it. But while I was interrogating him, this guard came running in." Louis moved to the side so that Lady Vivian could see the disheveled guard lurking in the doorway to her rooms. Vivian hardly gave the guard a glance before returning her steely blue eyes to Louis.

"And…" she prompted.

"And he accused Fulvio of holding him captive in the kitchens for the past fortnight. I immediately took Fulvio into custody and locked him in the dungeon with the other prisoners. Of course, I then hastened up here to let you know and to ask for further instructions. Shall we visit the kitchens and interrogate the new head chef? I understand that she and Fulvio are quite close friends. Perhaps she would persuade Fulvio to be more truthful about what he was doing in your office." Louis looked positively gleeful at the prospect of the interrogations.

Vivian looked very thoughtful for a moment, and her scowl deepened. "First," she said, "we need to determine that nothing was taken from my office. Where exactly did you find him snooping?"

"He was looking in the lower right-hand drawer of your desk."

The color drained from Vivian's face, and she stood so suddenly that the towel on her head toppled to the floor. "Let me get dressed, and we will go to my office immediately."

Lady Vivian, with Louis and the guard in tow, arrived at the door of her office fifteen minutes later. Vivian immediately crossed the large room to her desk and opened the file drawer with her ruby key.

She scanned the files quickly and then glared through her pince-nez at Louis. "You idiot! One of my most important files is missing! Are you absolutely certain he had nothing else in his possession?" She frantically searched beneath and around the desk and then thumbed through the files once more, making sure nothing had fallen behind.

"I am certain that he had nothing on him. Perhaps he had an accomplice?" Louis asked.

"Where could the accomplice have gone? The door was locked, and it is the only way in or out of this room," Vivian snapped, still searching the drawer, even though she knew that Dr. James's file was gone.

"Actually, Lady Vivian, there is another entrance to this room. The servants' passageways," Louis said as he skirted the desk and approached the paneling behind it. It took him several minutes to find the hidden catch and open the door to the passageway, as it had been a very long time since he had done so. But in the end, he got it open, and sure enough, there were recent footprints in the dust on the floor. Two sets, one large and one very small, led to the door, and only one, very small, led away.

Charles and Deidre watched in horror as Sprite after Sprite came through the portal and lined up in squad formation in front of James. The Sprites looked just like Charles had remembered them, beast-like creatures as tall as an average-size man and about twice as thick.

Like most humanoids, they had two legs and two arms. The Sprites' appendages were massive and hairy. They had almost no neck, and their heads were rather cubical in shape and covered with matted brown fur except for their bulbous and squashed noses. Their eyes were small and beady, and two large yellow tusks emerged from their wide, thick lips.

The Sprites held crude spears in their paws and had curved swords at their hips. They wore leather armor, but Charles knew from experience that their own tough hides were better protection than any armor they could wear. Sprites were definitely better trained, more intelligent, and better fighters than the Faeries who had defended Great-Aunt Vivian's lab. That fight had almost not been fair, but a battle with a squad of Sprites would be another thing altogether.

Charles was pretty sure that Deidre and he could hold their own against them. The unarmed humans living in the manor and one of Deidre's sisters on her own, however, would pose no competition for the Sprites. Whoever had placed the tanzanites in the plinths might still be on the manor grounds and needed to be warned. Charles touched Deidre's hand and indicated that the time had come for them to leave.

Deidre nodded her consent, and the two of them slipped down the tree's trunk and merged silently into the forest's shadows.

Charles chanced a whisper once they were several yards away from the clearing. "We should use the hidden passageway to the kitchens so we arrive at the manor before the Sprites. Perhaps the chef who helped us last time will be willing to assist us in finding your sister." Again Deidre nodded, and they turned their steps toward the statue garden.

All twenty-four of the Sprites assembled in front of James, and the leader handed him two elaborately inlaid boxes. James then deactivated the portal and slipped the controller and the two transport boxes into his pockets. He was quite satisfied with his work. Vivian would stand no chance of escaping with the Sprites positioned around the manor. And with the new transport boxes he could come and go as he pleased with none the wiser.

He gave his orders to the leader of the squad. The Sprites' leader was nearly indistinguishable from his squad mates with the exception of a small extra twist of leather nearly hidden in the hair at his shoulder. The leader nodded his understanding and then growled orders to his squad. James had never bothered to learn the language of the Sprites, and he frowned, hoping that his commands were being relayed correctly. His wife, Joanna, had always been the one with the aptitude for languages, not he.

The squad moved out smartly along the path to the flower garden with James following in its wake. The squad halted about 250 yards before the path branched. One of the Sprites growled quietly to the leader, and the leader growled back. Two of the Sprites broke off from the squad and headed along the main path.

"What was that all about?" James asked the leader.

The Sprite smiled maliciously around his tusks. "They smelled something ahead, so I sent those two to take care of it. Pity that they will get all the fun."

CHAPTER 26

BATTLE IN THE ZEN GARDEN

❧

In which Charles creates a pincushion

The bushes to the side of the path shifted from within, and Bard raised his ax to the ready. The leaves moved faster, and the ax rose a hair higher and then began its decent.

"No, Bard, stop!" Sarah yelled. "It's Sparks!"

The ax landed with a thud, burying its blade in the dirt an inch from the little dog's nose. Sarah dashed around Bard's great bulk and gathered Sparks into her arms. "Are you OK, Sparks?" she asked, checking the little dog from tip to tail.

Sparks gave an affirmative yap and glared over Sarah's shoulder at Bard for a moment before returning her intent gaze to Sarah's face. The dog began barking rapidly and wiggling to get out of Sarah's arms in such an insistent way that Sarah laughed. Sparks barked furiously at her and stamped her little paw as if to say that the situation was no laughing matter, which of course made Sarah laugh even harder.

Bard retrieved his ax and returned it to its holster. "Good to see you again, Sparks," he said as he patted the little dog, who disappeared entirely under Bard's great hand. When Bard moved to stride into the forest garden, Sparks started barking even more insistently and grabbed at the leather tabs securing Bard's boots, attempting to pull him back toward the stairs.

"I don't think Sparks wants us to go that way," Sarah said, rescuing the puppy from being dragged along after Bard.

Bard shook his head. "We need the roots for Mr. Benjamin."

"Sparks has never steered me wrong. When she says to do something, it always turns out to be a good idea to do it." Sarah looked after the puppy, who now was standing on top of the stairs to the flower garden urgently whining.

"OK, we will get the roots later." Bard sighed and started walking back up the path toward Sarah and Sparks.

Alec looked quizzically between Sarah and Bard. The whole conversation would have made sense if there had been anything that even remotely looked like a spark that they had been talking to. From his perspective, Sarah had rescued nothing from Bard's ax, she had pointed to nothing on the path, she had picked up nothing in her arms, and they were now following nothing back toward the manor. To say that his life had become very strange since he decided to play the hero back in the airport was putting it mildly, and although his instincts told him that both Bard and Sarah were people he would trust with his life, he wasn't so confident about their sanity. Or his own, come to think of it. With a shrug, he decided just to go with it. And to think, less than a fortnight ago, he had been complaining how boring and pointless his life was.

"Thanks, Bard," Sarah said, and the three of them followed Sparks (well, Sarah and Bard followed Sparks, and Alec followed Sarah) toward the manor. They had only gone a few paces into the flower garden when Sparks paused and sniffed the air. She started racing up the path with a squeal that sounded like someone had trodden on her paw, pausing only to turn back and bark at her companions to hurry.

Sarah had never seen the puppy so agitated. She quickened her step until she was flat-out running. She realized as she careened after Sparks that she had completely forgotten about Alec and Bard. Sparks's panic was catching. She threw a glance behind her only to find Alec loping silently less than a stride back with a bemused expression on his face. She thought of her brother, Nickolas, and how he could never keep up with her, despite being more than six inches taller and two years older than she was. Sarah was the best runner in her grade, and none of her classmates could ever catch her in the spring field races. She had to admit, it kind of miffed her that Alec could keep up with her so effortlessly, and so she concentrated on adding an extra turn of speed to her pace as they entered the maze.

Bard crashed behind them, using the hedges on either side as buffers to allow him to turn his bulk faster as they rounded the corners. His keen ears caught the sound of something—or several somethings—far behind them, and if he wasn't mistaken, they were gaining. Noting how quickly they were racing through the maze, Bard suspected that what was behind them was either fleeing the same threat that Sparks had warned them about or *was* that threat.

They burst out of the hedges and dashed up the stairs to the mushroom garden. By this time, even Sarah and Alec could hear their pursuers crashing like a herd of wild horses through the maze. The mushroom garden disappeared behind them in a blur of adrenaline, and Sarah dashed along the invisible path over the Zen garden. She had only gone halfway when she heard Alec cry her name. She turned to find him floundering in the sand behind her.

Louis followed Lady Vivian wearily. She had kept him up all night.

First she had had him try to follow the tiny footprints, but for some reason, as soon as they entered the servants' passageways, a stiff breeze had whipped up and blown all the dust on the floor into tiny tornados, obliterating the trail of footprints. The breeze also slammed shut a door across the passageway only a few feet from Vivian's office, and when he tried the handle, Louis found it locked tight. None of the keys on his ring or even Lady Vivian's ruby master key opened it.

Lady Vivian took the reality of the impervious locked door better than Louis would have thought, instantly offering that the dusty passageways were no place for a lady anyway and that the dirt would ruin her gown.

Then she put him to work turning her entire office upside down in search of the missing file. She was so upset by that time that she had dumped every drawer and emptied every bookshelf in her hunt. The dust and dirt they kicked up in the frantic search had surely done more damage to her dress than walking in the servants' passages would have. Lady Vivian seemed not to notice that as they were pulling books off shelves and searching even behind the very pictures on the wall, the guard had been quietly helping himself to her private stash of essence bottles in the top drawer of her desk.

Louis had been startled to find that with every vial that the guard drank, his appearance altered from disheveled and disoriented to crisp, sharp, and alert. It was like he had taken a shower, shaved, washed and ironed his clothes, and tied his hair neatly back—just from drinking the essence. Louis was fascinated and stared at the transforming guard until Vivian had noticed his inattention and had yelled at him for not working.

Lady Vivian moved to destroying his office once she had completely turned over her own. She assumed Fulvio had somehow secreted the folder in there while Louis had interrogated him. Louis had always found that letting Vivian do whatever she wanted was the best recipe for maintaining his position at the manor, so he swallowed his aversion to trashing his office and gaily began sweeping books off his shelves and into a heap in the middle of the floor.

Lady Vivian searched his desk as well, and Louis watched as all his neat files and forms were scattered and trampled. He tried manfully not to care as Lady Vivian destroyed his belongings. But then something happened that filled him with deepest dread. Lady Vivian pulled out the drawer where the tanzanites were hidden. She did not notice anything amiss as she dumped the contents on top of the ever-growing pile at her feet, but Louis could tell by the drawer's silence that the Tanzanites were gone. And if Lady Vivian was this upset about the missing file, what would she do when she found out that he had lost the gems she specifically told him to keep safe?

The miserable night had ended in the dungeons, where there had been more mysterious disappearances. Three of the prisoners were gone, the cell was demolished, and there sat Dr. Trowle, alone in the open cell, shivering under a blanket.

Once Lady Vivian had vented her anger on the scientist for a full forty-five minutes, she finally allowed him to speak.

"It was awful, Dr. Vivian," he had said. "This huge red-haired man destroyed the door to the cell with a mighty blow of a battle-ax. A battle-ax, can you imagine! And he was wearing this shocking orange-skirted kilt outfit. It was hideous!"

"Yes, yes," Vivian had said impatiently. "But where are Fulvio and Mr. Benjamin?" She was about an inch away from Dr. Trowle's cowering face.

"F-F-Fulvio said something about going to the kitchens to get one of the drudges while…" But Lady Vivian had not let him finish his sentence. She'd turned on her heel and marched out of the dungeon with Dr. Trowle wailing, "But what am I to do?" behind them.

No one noticed when the poor bedraggled Dr. Trowle slipped out of the manor grounds several hours later and made his weary way home.

⊰⊱

"And just where are you planning on going?" Lady Vivian's girlish voice came from the doorway of the kitchens.

Fulvio whirled to find Lady Vivian, Louis, and the guard blocking the only exit to his old quarters. "You weren't planning on escaping, were you? Just when I wanted to chat with you about why you were in my study. That wouldn't be very polite, now would it? Guard, seize him!" She pointed her finger menacingly at Fulvio, and the guard moved around Louis and headed toward the chef.

"No!" Zac yelled, clambering out of his bed and lumbering over, putting himself between the guard and Fulvio. The tall boy's face scrunched in determination. "You will not hurt Chef! You are a bad guard. Chef is a good man. You belong locked up in the pot room. You leave us alone!"

The guard was momentarily taken aback, but then he came to his senses and took a mighty swing at Zac's head with the pike he had picked up in the dungeons. The sound of wood meeting skull rent the air, and without another sound, Zac crumpled to the floor.

Though he was normally calm and cool, Fulvio's eyes glittered dangerously. "Was that really necessary?" he asked, kneeling next to Zac's collapsed form on the floor. Zac was still breathing, but shallowly, his eyes rolled up into his head. "There is no reason to interrogate me or my staff. We have been nothing but loyal to you for decades."

"Really, Fulvio? I have no reason to think that you are less than loyal? Then perhaps you can explain why you stole my key from my dressing room while I was bathing, why you were found going through my desk in my private office, and why one of my files from the desk has gone missing?"

Fulvio rose and looked Vivian straight in the eye, which was impressive as he was several inches shorter than she. "I did not search through your desk, nor did I take any files from it." That much was true—Sarah had searched the desk, and she had taken the file.

"And the key, Fulvio? Do you deny taking that?" she snapped.

"No, I do not deny taking that. You specifically asked that I make sure that everything was in order for Dr. James's visit. I knew that you would be entertaining him in your office and would want it spotless for his arrival. You neglected to give me a key to that room when you gave me the butler's keys, so I went to your rooms to ask you for it. You were in the bath, and I assumed that you did not want me barging in on you to ask you for the key. I saw it lying on your dresser, so I borrowed it to clean your study. Louis here interrupted me as I cleaned, and he refused to believe that what he saw with his own eyes was the truth. He relieved me of the key and locked me in the dungeons." Fulvio was relying on his usual quick wit to get him out of trouble. It had worked for him for years, and he could see that Lady Vivian was wavering. Until Louis piped up, of course.

"How did you get out of the dungeons? And why are you packing to leave?" Louis asked, his whiny voice grating on Fulvio's ears.

"You neglected to relieve me of *my* keys when you took Lady Vivian's key from me. When I was a child and exploring the manor with Lord Myers's boys, I created a copy of the dungeon key." Fulvio pulled the crooked key from his pocket, knowing Louis would have no way of knowing that his dungeon key didn't really open the cells. "I have carried it ever since as a memento of my rather mischievous youth. I never dreamed that I would have cause to use it again, but thanks to you, Louis, I did. And knowing that it was very important to Lady Vivian that I finish my tasks, I returned to them."

Louis looked at Lady Vivian, seeing that she was rapidly becoming bored with the conversation and no longer bothering to match his words to things she had observed in the dungeons with her own eyes. She was on the verge of letting Fulvio off so that she could return to more important duties. "That still doesn't explain why you are packing," Louis said, his voice rising in frustration.

"I am not packing," Fulvio replied. "Carole and Zac are packing. As you know, these are no longer my rooms. And as to why they are packing, that boy your guard just knocked out is suffering from a degenerative disease that has returned now that we are no longer eating Lady Vivian's synthetic food. His mother was taking him to the local hospital for testing to see if anything can be done."

Fulvio knew he had misstepped the instant the word *hospital* had left his lips. Lady Vivian's bored expression changed to fury before the third syllable had been uttered. "Guard!" she hollered, and then, after a brief, sharp pain in his temple, darkness enveloped Fulvio and he knew no more.

⊰⊱

Deidre paused as she and Charles traversed the narrow passage-way between the statue garden and the kitchens and sniffed the air. She stood as still as a cat, with only her nose twitching slightly as she caught the scent.

"What do you smell, Deidre?" Charles asked, his voice low, daggers appearing in his hands as if from thin air.

Deidre growled and then, taking in their cramped quarters, began to run.

Charles wished for the umpteenth time in their long relation-ship that Deidre would communicate using more than grunts and growls, but if she was running from something, it probably would be best if he ran as well, so he instantly turned and fled down the passageway, following Deidre's silent footfalls. As he ran, Charles thought about Deidre's choice to flee their pursuers. How odd, he thought. He had never known Deidre to flee anything.

But then he had no more time to think, for he had reached the door to the kitchens. He was about to pull out his lock picks, when Deidre's large green arm swept him out of the way. Next, she slammed her shoulder into the door, reducing it to matchsticks.

"Well, that works, too," Charles muttered, following her into the wine cellar.

They were just in time, too, for Charles barely had a moment to take up his position next to Deidre, daggers drawn, when the first of the Sprites emerged from the passageway.

⊰⊟⊱

"Grab my arm," Sarah commanded, reaching over the edge of the walkway. Without pausing to think about their disproportion-ate heights and weights, Alec did so, grasping Sarah's thin wrist with his left hand. She gave a mighty, adrenaline-fueled heave, pulling Alec from the sand and onto the path. They sat panting for a moment, looking at each other, and then they heard a roar from behind them. It was Bard's battle cry. He pulled his ax from his hip and twirled it into the ready position. An entire squad of huge furry monsters was coming from the mushroom forest, swords and staves drawn. And behind them, striding confidently, was Dr. James.

"Oh, fiddlesticks," Sarah said, rapidly regaining her feet and drawing her daggers. Alec thought "fiddlesticks" was a rather mild word for their situation, but he chose to draw his sword rather than debate the point with her.

⊷⧆⊷

The first Sprite dodged Deidre's danso after taking only a few well-placed whacks from the muse, and then it ran headlong into Charles's dagger. The hilt protruded from the Sprite's chest, but it didn't slow down the beast one whit. A combination of the Sprite's claws and spear advancing toward him kept Charles dancing just out of its reach. The muse threw dagger after dagger into the Sprite's chest. It looked like a furry pincushion before the multiple dagger strikes seemed to take their toll on the creature, and it shook its head repeatedly as it tried to focus on the weaving muse before it.

Charles heard something heavy hit the floor behind him, and he hoped that it was a Sprite and not his sister-in-law. But he didn't dare take his eyes off his opponent for a moment, for even though the Sprite was dazed, it wasn't dead yet. Experience had taught Charles that Sprites weren't easily killed, and sometimes when you thought they were dead, they were only mostly dead and still rather dangerous.

Throwing one more knife into the Sprite, Charles hazarded a look over his shoulder and found that it was indeed the second Sprite on the floor at Deidre's feet, and she was using some sort of mixed martial arts move on its neck to finish it off. Her borrowed danso lay in pieces at the Sprite's feet.

His own Sprite howled in triumph as it lunged at Charles, trying to take advantage of the muse's momentary distraction. But the beast misjudged Charles's agility, and the muse simply wasn't there when the Sprite landed. The lack of contact overbalanced the Sprite, and it fell face-first on the cobblestone floor of the wine cellar, jabbing the daggers deeper into its chest. The extra inch of blade must have severed something important, for a large puddle of green ooze formed beneath the Sprite, and it moved no more.

Deidre kicked the Sprite over with her toe, checking to see if it was dead.

"I think it is," Charles said, panting a little. "Yours isn't looking too lively either." He nodded to the Sprite by the passage door, its neck and spine at odd angles.

Deidre only smirked.

"Any more?" Charles asked as he began to retrieve his daggers, wiping them thoroughly on wine cloth he grabbed from a nearby stack before returning the blades to their hidden sheaths in his pockets.

Deidre checked the passageway and shrugged.

"The rest of the squad and James must have taken the garden route to the manor. Come, we must find the others." He had not gone three strides when he realized that Deidre was not following him.

He turned to find she had gone still once more, sniffing the air and frowning slightly.

"Another Sprite?" Charles asked, and Deidre shook her head, pointing to the spot where they had fought the Faeries two weeks before and grunted. "A Faerie?" Charles guessed, and Deidre nodded. Without a glance to see if Charles was following her, she strode purposefully toward the kitchens, picking up a cleaver from one of the tables as she went.

Now Charles had personally never been able to determine the difference between the stink of a Sprite and that of a Faerie. They both smelled equally putrid to him, but if Deidre smelled a difference, all the more power to her. Charles preferred fighting Faeries to Sprites anyway; as it only took one dagger to take out a Faerie.

⊰⊱

"Retreat!" Bard yelled at the children as he inched his way along the elevated path of the Zen garden. "We need to get to higher ground!"

Higher ground? The breakfast garden was at most only a foot or two higher than the Zen garden. But then it dawned on Sarah what Bard was saying. The sooner they got off the bridge, the harder it would be for the monsters to find it. And if the monsters didn't find the bridge, then they would be floundering around in the sand just like Alec had been, slowing them down and giving Bard, Alec, and Sarah time to regroup. Better yet, if they did find the bridge, it would limit the number of monsters that could reach them, allowing Bard to pick them off one by one as they crossed, leaving any who slipped through for Sarah and Alec to get. Not that Bard was planning on any slipping through.

"Come with me," Sarah said to Alec, grabbing his hand and rushing across the remaining yards of bridge to the breakfast garden. As they ran, Sarah outlined her thoughts about Bard's plan.

Alec nodded. "I think you got it, Sarah. Do you still have the key to the tower? You should take the collection tin and run and warn Brigitta and the others. Stay in the tower, and if Bard and I need to retreat, you can let us in."

"How about I give you the key and you take the collection tin and warning to Brigitta and wait by the door to let us in?" Sarah said in a sweet voice that Nickolas could have warned Alec was Sarah's "don't treat me like a little kid if you don't want to lose" voice.

By this time they had reached the end of the path, and Bard was pressing them back behind him.

The three turned to watch their attackers floundering in the sand and making little forward progress. It would only be a matter of time before they found the bridge, but for the moment, Bard, Sarah, and Alec were safe.

"I need Brigitta," Bard said. "You two go and get her for me. Tell her we have Sprites. I will stay here and smash them."

Sarah thought about arguing, but then she got a really good look at the monsters. What was it Bard had called them? Sprites, floundering in the sand. They were the stuff that her nightmares were made of. Ugly, hairy, smelly, huge monsters didn't get any worse than these guys. In fact, Sarah was pretty sure they hadn't combed their fur or brushed their tusks in decades—definitely something her mother wouldn't have invited over for dinner. They looked like pretty competent fighters, too. So her protests died on her lips, and she grabbed Alec's hand and dashed for the tower door, little Sparks running behind them.

⚜

Charles and Deidre burst into the main kitchens to find them full of cowering cooks and drudges. They hadn't spotted Deidre yet, so Charles knew that they were cowering from something else besides two fully armed muses showing up unannounced in their midst.

Looking his green companion up and down for a moment, Charles determined that he would have a better chance of getting information out of the kitchen staff. So he approached the first knot of servants.

"Excuse me," he said confidently. "I am looking for the head chef. You know, the round one with the bunny slippers and the rolling pin. Have you seen him, by any chance?"

It was a sign of how scared the servants were that they didn't even give Charles a perplexed glance before pointing to a corner of the kitchens where a thick door stood slightly ajar. "Fulvio is in there," one of them managed to squeak.

"Thank you," Charles said, and he and Deidre picked their way across the crowded floor to the indicated door. Charles grasped the handle and opened the door wide. "After you, my dear," he said, giving Deidre a formal bow.

Deidre shook her head. Charles was enjoying himself just a shade too much. In her training, there had been no place for idle chitchat and levity. Her job was to be taken seriously. Charles and his lot were just a bunch of amateurs.

⇥⊟⇤

Deidre walked inside. Her nose told her that there was only one Faerie and several humans. Two of the humans she had smelled before—the chef and Nickolas's great-aunt Vivian were inside. The remaining smells were new. Sure enough, Deidre's nose was accurate, for there were two unconscious humans on the floor, three conscious humans standing over them, and an armed Faerie guarding Great-Aunt Vivian. All three humans turned with identical looks of horror and shock on their faces at the sight of her, but Deidre's attention was on the Faerie, and she readied her newly acquired cleaver to take it out. Before she could initiate her attack, however, a flash of silver flew past her head and embedded itself into the guard's chest.

The Faerie fell to the floor and rolled away in its potato form. Deidre was just reversing her attack's direction to face Vivian when Charles stepped between her and her quarry. "Not yet, Deidre. I know you can't stand that I have two kills to your paltry one, but we need to know what is going on here before you even the score. Sorry, but that's the way it is. Besides, this one here"—he indicated Great-Aunt Vivian—"is only worth half a point."

Deidre grunted and crossed her arms, positioning herself by the door.

Satisfied that Deidre would let Sarah's great-aunt live, for the moment, he turned and faced the scientist. "Hello, Vivian," Charles began. "We haven't been formally introduced, but we have mutual acquaintances. I am Charles, and I think you know my cousin, James. We met a few weeks ago in your lab—you remember, right?"

"You!" Vivian yelled, rushing at Charles with fingers extended like claws at his face.

"Ah yes, I see you do remember me." Charles easily captured her wrists in one of his hands and produced a length of rope from a pocket in his shirt, rapidly tying them together. "Always nice to see old friends."

Still holding on to Vivian's wrists and appearing indifferent to her struggles and shrieks, he extended his free hand toward the remaining two conscious occupants of the room. "Charles, at your service. And you are?"

Louis screamed and ran toward the door, only to be captured in Deidre's embrace.

Carole rose from where she sat next to Fulvio and Zac's unconscious forms and wiped her hands on her apron. "I'm Carole," Carole said timidly, shaking Charles's offered hand. Then gaining confidence she added, "Fulvio has told me much about you and how you helped Sarah and Nickolas escape the first time from the manor. I hope you can help them escape again. But first I need your help with Fulvio and my son."

"Wait, Sarah and Nickolas are here?" Charles asked.

"Yes, with a fellow named Bard and his wife Brigitta. They are in the observatory tower with Mr. Benjamin. Would you like me to take you to them?"

CHAPTER 27

THE THREE VIALS

⁕

In which Mr. Benjamin tells
Great-Aunt Vivian everything

The tower lock only stopped Alec and Sarah for a moment, and, as soon as they were through it, Alec pushed the counterweight to close the door. They dashed up the stairs, across the observatory, and into Dr. Montague's rooms.

"Brigitta!" Sarah called as she entered the laboratory through the tiny storage closet. "Bard needs your help." She then proceeded to blurt everything out, her words tripping over one another, rendering them incoherent.

Brigitta immediately stood from the lab stool where she sat peering through a microscope. "Slow down, Sarah. What happened?"

"Sprites," Sarah said, panting and doing her best to slow down. "A whole lot of them. Dr. James is here, and they are crossing the Zen garden toward Bard. The sand is hindering them, but not for long."

Brigitta looked concerned and rapidly crossed the sitting room. "May I please have my daggers back?" she asked, holding out her hand toward Sarah as she strode.

Sarah was reluctant to give up her weapons, but she pulled them from her waist and handed them hilt first to Brigitta as she asked hopefully, "You don't by any chance have any spares I could borrow?"

Brigitta smiled. "No, I am not Charles with hundreds of knives hidden on my body. Most of the Muses of Music don't even carry weapons, but I have grown rather fond of my daggers, and they have gotten me out of many a scrape or two. Did Dr. Montague have anything else hanging on the walls?"

Sarah was just about to return to the sitting room to check when they all heard the sounds of battle coming from the open observatory roof. A loud keening cry that could only have come from Bard's mighty chest reached their ears, and Brigitta sprinted across the floor toward the stairs, her blades at the ready.

⧊⧊

Charles was not surprised that the kitchen staff moved swiftly out of their way as they exited the head chef's quarters. If the sight of him with his dagger covering the back of their bound mistress followed by Carole wasn't enough to concern them, Deidre with Zac and Fulvio's unconscious forms thrown over her shoulders and her cleaver pointed at Louis's back taking up the rear certainly was.

Carole led them to the entrance of the servants' passages in the back of one of the storage rooms and into the corridors that led toward the observatory tower. At first, Charles found it humorous to watch Vivian wrinkle her nose in distain at being in the dark, dank passageways, and he took a great deal of pleasure watching her try to keep the train of her dress from sweeping up too much dust without the use of her hands. But as they moved deeper into the manor, other sounds reached his ears that made him wish Carole would pick up her pace.

The obvious sounds of battle brought a second dagger to Charles's hands. "How much longer before we exit the passageways?" he asked Carole a bit impatiently.

"Not too much farther," Carole assured him, her eyes wide. "What is that sound?"

"If I am not mistaken," Charles said, his head cocked in the direction of the noise, "that is the sound of my brother, Bard, having a very good time using that ax of his. Unfortunately, I think it is also the sound of him being rather outnumbered. Is there any way I can get there faster? A shortcut, perhaps?"

"I don't know these passageways as well as Fulvio does. If he was awake, I am sure he would know how to get out of here, but I only know the path he took me today. Even so, I am really just following our footprints in the dust." Carole indicated the prints on the floor.

Charles nodded. "Deidre, I need to go on ahead and get to Bard. Can you handle this on your own?"

Deidre's only response was to dump Fulvio and Zac on top of the tiny muse, nearly flattening him under their combined bulk, and then she dashed up the passageway, cleaver in hand.

"Great." Charles's voice was muffled under the mass of unconscious bodies. "Thanks for the help."

Unnoticed by Charles, Vivian, or Carole, Louis took their momentary distraction as the perfect chance to escape and silently slipped down a side corridor.

⊣⊨⊱

Nickolas and Mr. Benjamin were poring over Dr. Montague's old notes. The delicate labyrinth of glassware was complete, with several beakers of solution bubbling over Bunsen burners. The first distillate that they needed was steadily dripping into a dish at the far end of the counter.

"Dr. Montague says here that he needed more of the root solution from the cupboard in his lab mixed in at this point," Mr. Benjamin said.

"I'll get it." Nickolas dashed over to the cupboard and found the tree-topped bottle in no time. "How much do you need? There isn't very much left."

"He says that we only need a few drops. It's highly concentrated." Mr. Benjamin's nose nearly touched the page. "These notes are so hard to read. I hope I am doing this right."

Mr. Benjamin took the bottle from Nickolas and added three drops to the final dish.

"I'm sure you are, Mr. Benjamin. See, the distillate is separating just like Dr. Montague describes. What do we need to do next?"

Mr. Benjamin turned the page and pointed to a complex diagram. "We need to build this next contraption. Let's clear off this table here, leaving what we just built bubbling away. We might need more of that first distillate later."

Together, Nickolas and Mr. Benjamin cleared off the second table, filling the sink with more dirty glassware. Nickolas eyed the unstable tower warily before adding a few more beakers to the pile.

Nickolas really liked working with Mr. Benjamin on the experiments. The older man was quiet and kind, never yelling at Nickolas for his occasional clumsiness, and he always asked Nickolas's opinion when he tried to figure out Dr. Montague's notes. It was almost like working alone in his workshop in the stables, only better. For here was someone who shared Nickolas's passion for science, appreciated his eccentric ways, and in fact might just be even more eccentric than Nickolas was himself.

There was something very exciting about watching Dr. Montague's theories become reality. And something very satisfying about knowing that he was potentially saving hundreds of lives in the process, to say nothing of saving Simon.

Nickolas had always dreamed of being a hero, but he knew that his sister's personality lent itself more readily to being the traditional hero than his own bookish one. Yet here he was able to save the day in a way that his sister never could. Perhaps, he thought, heroes didn't always wear long red capes and fly into the thick of battle to save the day. Perhaps heroes also worked in labs, quietly discovering solutions to problems far more complex than a robbery or a cat stuck in a tree.

⊶⊐⊏⊷

Charles had been forced to leave Carole with Zac and Fulvio in the passageway and continued on with Great-Aunt Vivian. Very rarely did Charles worry about his lack of stature and brute strength. He had a great deal of self-confidence that his stealth and brains could make up for any need of heft. He had people like Deidre and Bard to do things like that for him, yet here in the span of less than two days, he had been painfully aware of just how tiny and weak he really was, and it didn't exactly make him feel all warm and fuzzy inside.

Well, as soon as he could find Brigitta, he could send her back to Carole and let her heal Fulvio and Zac.

It was obvious Deidre had been this way, for the door to the passageway hung precariously from one hinge.

Charles, pulling Vivian behind him, emerged through the destroyed doorway onto the breakfast garden's edge that was farthest away from the kitchens. Just to his left rose the large stone observatory tower. In front of him, the sounds of battle, which had been muffled by the walls of the manor passageways, was raging full tilt. Bard and Deidre stood shoulder to shoulder, battling a huge number of Sprites as they tried to exit the Zen garden path. Deidre had lost her cleaver somewhere, probably embedded in one of the Sprites who littered the ground in front of her. She had taken a sword off of one of her opponents and was using it with every bit as much skill as she usually used her danso. The funneling effect of the glass pathway enabled Bard and Deidre to pick them off one by one, and they seemed to have things well in hand for the moment.

So Charles turned his attention to the tower, which, according to Carole, contained Dr. Montague's lab. He found the small keyhole in the tower wall, and, still keeping Vivian covered with his dagger in one hand, he pulled out his lock picks and began to pick the lock with the other. Charles's brow furrowed in concentration, for the lock was more difficult than any he had ever encountered, and that included his own practice lock set to its highest level: nine-nine-nine. Intrigued rather than worried, Charles pulled two more picks from his pockets, and with a warning glare at Vivian to stay put, he sheathed his dagger and used both hands on solving the lock problem. It took him several moments to figure out what he needed to do. It would have taken less time if he hadn't had to pause twice and demonstrate to Vivian just how fast he could retrieve a dagger if she twitched a muscle. After those two demonstrations, she decided that it was a better plan to stand still.

Using his teeth in conjunction with his hands to maneuver a particularly intricate move, he felt the lock click, and the door popped open a crack. He used his dagger as a wedge and was able to open the door enough to slip through, pulling Great-Aunt

Vivian behind him. Perhaps Vivian would have put up more of a fight if she hadn't gotten a really good look at the monsters that Deidre and Bard were battling. Seeing them made her think a good thick stone wall between her and them was fine by her.

⊰⊱

Brigitta was running down the stairs as Charles started up them. She was relieved to hear that Deidre was already battling by Bard's side and that as far as Charles could tell both muses were unharmed. They quickly conferred and decided that Brigitta should take over possession of the prisoner, and Charles should return outside to the fight.

Once again, Great-Aunt Vivian thought about trying to escape. Brigitta was much shorter than she was, but Vivian soon learned that Brigitta was no less deft with her own daggers than her tiny brother-in-law, so Vivian grudgingly complied with Brigitta's commands.

Great-Aunt Vivian was surprised to find her great-niece and one of her prisoners from the dungeons were waiting at the top of the stairs. "What are you doing here?" she demanded.

"Trying to avoid meeting you, actually," Sarah replied. She had never been as cowed by her great-aunt as Nickolas, and with her hands tied and Brigitta's daggers trained on her back, Sarah was pretty sure that the threat of becoming Great-Aunt Vivian's newest lab rat was fairly slim.

"Sarah, I need to get outside to the battle. Do you think that you and Alec can keep an eye on your great-aunt for me? Perhaps if we tie her up in the laboratory with you and Mr. Benjamin, it would be safe. I hate to leave you here with her, but I really do need to get out to Bard."

347

"Don't worry, Brigitta. Alec and I have this under control," Sarah assured her, a mischievous twinkle in her eyes as she turned to her great-aunt. "Now dear Great-Aunt Vivian, shall we discuss the rules?"

⊰⊱

The next thing she knew, Vivian found herself trussed up to a chair in the laboratory. It was with great interest that she observed what Mr. Benjamin and Nickolas had been up to. The second experiment was bubbling away by this time, and neither looked up from their work to notice her.

"The next step requires those solutions you found in Dr. Montague's pocket watch," Mr. Benjamin was saying. "The red one seems to reverse the aging process, and the green one appears to speed it up. In the right combination, the two solutions can be used to stop the microbios from supporting the cells, providing them with the necessary nutrients to start supporting themselves again. It is very important that we get the solution just right, for too much of one will cause the aging process to reverse again and too much of the other will cause it to speed up too much. He recommends two drops of the green and one drop of the red for every fifty milliliters of solution we get from the second distillation."

"We have two hundred and fifty milliliters," Nickolas said, reading off the graduated cylinder. "How are we going to make sure that the drops are accurate? Eyedroppers and pipettes aren't very good at that."

"I would suggest we use these syringes." Mr. Benjamin handed two to Nickolas from a drawer beneath the cabinets. "Fill one with each of the solutions for me, would you? Careful now, we don't have very much—those vials are tiny."

Nickolas carefully removed the syringes from their sterile packaging and assembled the plungers in each. He then opened the red vial and carefully filled the first syringe with all of the solution it contained. He repeated the process for the green vial. "What does the blue solution do? Do we need it?"

Mr. Benjamin flipped through the notebook. "Dr. Montague doesn't say, and it isn't needed for the experiment we are working on. Leave the solution in the watch for now. We can get it later if need be."

Nickolas returned the tiny blue vial to the pocket watch, leaving it open on the counter. He picked up the two syringes and handed them to Mr. Benjamin. "Here you are, Mr. Benjamin. All set."

"Thank you, Nickolas. Here goes nothing." And he carefully added the drops of solution to the distillate turning the clear liquid a pale-amber color. Neither scientist noticed the look of longing that crossed Great-Aunt Vivian's face as she locked her eyes on the red syringe in Mr. Benjamin's hand.

⚬

The sound of great wings beating the air filled the breakfast garden, and Bard looked up from battling the two Sprites in front of him to follow the sound. There, rising from the trees of the mushroom garden, was a sight that filled him with dread.

A fully grown Pixie was emerging from the treetops, its huge black leathery wings straining against the air. Once it reached a high enough altitude to clear the trees, it headed directly toward the opening in the observatory tower roof. Dangling from her talons with a look of triumph on his face was James.

Bard turned instantly and was poised to dash toward the tower wall, an anguished yell ripping from his throat. *"Brigitta!"*

Charles caught Deidre's eye and she nodded, stopping Bard's advancement with her borrowed sword.

"I can't stay here," Bard moaned. "Brigitta needs me."

A great crash of stone came from the tower as if to accent his words. The Pixie tore savagely through the roof, sending stone and tiles crashing to the floor and leaving a huge pixie-shaped hole in the observatory dome.

Charles faced his brother and pleaded: "Trust me, Bard. We need you here more. I will save Brigitta with my last breath if necessary. I promise."

And with that, Charles raced to the tower door, while Bard and Deidre returned to battling the Sprites. Neither Bard nor Deidre would have let Charles go alone if they had known just how prophetic his promise would turn out to be.

CHAPTER 28

JAMES'S PLAN

⟨⟩

In which Great-Aunt Vivian gets her heart's desire

Brigitta was just exiting the laboratory after seeing that Great-Aunt Vivian was securely bound to the lab stool when a strange noise came from the observatory. It sounded like an avalanche of stone falling from a great height. The next sounds, however, were particularly unnerving, for a deafening animal roar followed close on the heels of a great swoosh of wings.

Brigitta gripped her daggers defensively and hurried out of the room. A quick look passed between Sarah and Alec, and as one, they headed after the muse, Alec drawing his sword and Sarah grabbing the knife off the counter that Mr. Benjamin had been using to cut up the red mushrooms. It wasn't particularly long or sharp, but it was better than facing whatever was in the observatory unarmed.

Nickolas watched his sister's back disappearing into the dressing room and decided that this time he wasn't going to stay put and allow her to walk into danger without him. "I'll be right back, Mr. Benjamin," he said as he left the laboratory. "Make sure Great-Aunt Vivian doesn't move, OK?"

Mr. Benjamin wasn't sure he wanted to be left alone with Vivian. For years he had adored and followed her, doing everything and anything that she had asked of him. Only recently, as if he had been waking from a strange dream, had he begun to realize how much of his own beliefs and hopes he had given up in his attempts to make Vivian happy. But now he was pretty sure that no matter what he did, Vivian would never be happy and certainly would never be happy with him. Her ambition and pursuit of youth were all-consuming, leaving no room in her life or heart for a balding, aging, portly man whose only gifts were his devotion and love. Neither of which Vivian wanted.

At first he had been angry, hating himself and Vivian for allowing what had started as his honorable devotion to become corrupted by her ambition and his weakness. Over the years, he just had not seen—or had not chosen to see—what was happening to Simon as they extracted from the boy the essence that was so necessary for Vivian's experiments.

But his eyes had been brutally opened when Vivian had proposed repeating their experiments on two new children and disposing of Simon once he was no longer of use to her. Arguments, reasoning, anger, persuasion, and even tears had not worked to sway her from her path, and Mr. Benjamin had found that he had no choice but to actively work against her to free the children.

Even then he found he could not openly defy her, weakly helping the children behind her back and relying on their greater courage than his to free themselves. Looking in the mirror and finding himself far less than what he had hoped he would be had been most humbling. And in the end, he had failed in the two things that he had wanted most in life: to love and be loved by the beautiful brilliant woman who sat bound before him, and to be of use to the world at large through his science. Perhaps if he could conclude Dr. Montague's experiments and cure the manor's inhabitants and Simon from the negative effects of his own work, he could find just the smallest bit of redemption for all the ills he allowed to happen around him.

With sadness, Mr. Benjamin turned his back on Vivian and knelt below the sink to gather the supplies he needed for the third phase of the experiment.

❃❧

Brigitta burst through the door to the observatory to face one of her worst nightmares. For there in the center of the room stood a Pixie and her cousin James. Sarah and Alec silently took up positions behind the muse, but the two humans might as well have been statues for all the notice the Pixie and James gave them.

"Brigitta," James said, approaching her. "What a pleasure to see you! I knew when I saw your Neanderthal husband below fighting my Sprites that you could not be very far away. For truly, Bard has never been able stray far from your leash, now has he?"

"Bard is hardly my lapdog, James. Joanna is more likely to have a leash and collar on you than I have on anyone." Brigitta's fear of the Pixie was rapidly being overpowered by anger and loathing for James. She had never liked James at school, and she'd been relieved that he had been partnered with Joanna and not herself. For a while, the school governors thought she had more aptitude for being a Muse of Mathematics than a Muse of Music, and perhaps she would have been, if she hadn't been revolted by James so much that she practiced extra hard on her harp to be assigned far away from him.

She hadn't been wrong in her assessment of him all those millennia ago, either. The muses were here for a reason, and it wasn't to conduct experiments on the people they were supposed to protect. And turning her into a statue for a hundred years didn't really put James at the top of her dance card, either.

She gripped her daggers more tightly and then opened her mouth to use her favorite weapon. "Just what are you and your friends"—she indicated the Pixie—"doing here anyway?"

"Wouldn't you like to know." James smiled his oily smile. "But since you won't live long enough to tell anyone, I may as well let you in on my little secret. I never bought into all that do-good rubbish they tried to sell us at school, but when I was very young someone informed me of all the opportunities that existed if I stayed in school and excelled. So I played nice and did what my teachers wanted me to do. I sweet-talked them and convinced them that I was the perfect little muse, all ready and eager for my assignment. But I made sure I had all my contacts in place before I was shipped out to this little backwater planet. And over the years I have been cultivating those contacts. Isn't that what they taught us at school? How to build relationships and to exploit them for our own purposes? Is that not why you are here? Just because I work for different people than you does not mean that they don't have the same goals. You want to change this world to suit your designs, and I want to change it to suit mine. The only difference is that I am willing to harvest its wealth, and you are feebly trying to protect it."

James approached Brigitta and continued. "Really, my dear, I remember a time when they were thinking about making you my wife. We would have made quite a pair." He reached to touch her flame-red curls, but he had to snatch his fingers quickly back to avoid the sweep of Brigitta's daggers as they stopped an inch from his nose.

"That would not have lasted very long, James, as I don't suffer fools very well," she said, green eyes flashing.

"And yet you are married to that buffoon. Interesting."

"Bard is neither a fool nor a buffoon," Brigitta said firmly. "His honor alone is worth ten of you."

"We shall see." James stepped away from Brigitta and gave her a sweeping bow. "It has been very pleasant chatting with you, my dear cousin. But I must continue on my mission, and you have a date with my friend here. Pixie, she is all yours." And with that, James moved toward the door to Dr. Montague's apartment.

The Pixie, who had been standing in the middle of the room quietly surveying the two muses and two humans with one of her beady hawk-like eyes, grunted in response. She unsheathed her six-inch talons and began to circle Brigitta, Sarah, and Alec.

⌐⌐⌐

Nickolas had heard everything from behind the door and dove under Dr. Montague's desk when James approached. He overheard James muttering to himself as the muse headed toward the hallway that led to the lab. "Now I wonder where Dr. Montague left those solutions. He knew that I wanted them for my own research when he left. Fool thought that he could hide them from me. Silly man. In the end I always win, even if it is only because I can wait for those short-lived humans to die."

Solutions? Nickolas was pretty sure he knew which solutions James was talking about. Why else would Dr. Montague hide them so carefully in his pocket watch? And he, Nickolas, had left them lying out on the counter in plain sight! And what of poor Mr. Benjamin? Nickolas had to warn him! So instead of returning to the observatory to help Sarah and Brigitta, Nickolas crept after James toward the laboratory.

⌐⌐⌐

Sadly, the battle between Brigitta, Sarah, Alec, and the Pixie was short lived. The huge winged creature's hide seemed impervious

355

to their weapons, and it was far faster and far more agile than they were.

The Pixie knocked Sarah and Alec away from the muse with one sweep of her wings and captured Brigitta in her massive talons, squeezing the muse around the waist like a four-year-old squeezes a fashion doll. Brigitta let out a long scream that died slowly as the Pixie shook her furiously until her daggers clanged to the floor and she hung limply in the Pixie's fist.

The Pixie turned on Sarah and Alec, using her wings to shield Brigitta from their view. Without thinking, Alec swept Sarah behind him and stood at the ready, sword poised.

The Pixie just laughed her nasty, snarling laugh. "You, boy. You think you can take me on with a toy sword? Drop it." The Pixie then addressed Sarah, who was trying to find a way around Alec's outstretched arm: "And you, drop that puny knife, or I will snap your friend in two."

Sarah and Alec looked like twins as they raised their chins in defiance and gripped their weapons tighter. Both glared at the Pixie, neither intimidated in the least by her ginormous size.

The Pixie merely laughed again and brought Brigitta out from under her wing, squeezing the muse around the middle like a tightly strung corset. The Pixie squeezed until Brigitta's waist reached an impossibly small size and Sarah was sure that an inch more would kill the muse. Both the knife and the sword hit the floor of the observatory at the same second.

⚍⚎

Nickolas peeked around the door of the closet to see that Dr. James had already spotted the syringes and the pocket watch. Mr. Benjamin was nowhere in sight.

"Yes, James, the notes said that the red solution caused cells to grow younger and the green solution made them grow older. They didn't mention the blue solution, but I am sure that we could discover its properties in my lab." Great-Aunt Vivian was trying vainly to appear beautiful and composed despite her hands tied behind her back and her legs bound to the stool.

"Which were the notebooks they were working from, Vivian?" James asked, inspecting the various notebooks open on the lab tables.

"It will be easier if you free me, James," Vivian said, trying not to sound annoyed.

"Of course, how silly of me." He spent a moment undoing her bindings.

Vivian stood and shook her skirts back into position and then rubbed feeling back into her gloved wrists. "Thank you, James. The notebooks are over here. But first, do you really think that the red solution will solve the side effects we have been experiencing?" She looked eagerly at the syringe in James's hand.

A calculating look crossed James's face, and then a broad smile replaced it. "Why don't we find out, Vivian."

Eagerly, Vivian extended her hand for the syringe. "How much should we begin with? It seems quite potent. My father only recommended a drop or two for more than twenty-five doses. Perhaps two CCs to start with?"

"Let me do the honors," James suggested, his voice silky once more. And as Vivian rolled up her sleeve, he plunged the needle into her arm and depressed every last red drop it contained into her system, throwing the empty syringe onto the nearest tabletop.

Vivian looked at it in shock. "Do you think that dosage is safe?" she asked faintly and then was distracted by whatever the solution was doing to her. She stripped off her gloves and looked at her hands.

Before her eyes, the skin on them was tightening and plumping. The fingers were straightening and the knuckles were shrinking. In a matter of seconds, her hands had returned to a youthful glow. Vivian turned, exalted, to show James her hands. "It is working! Look! Look! I am beautiful once more!" She flung her arms wide and twirled in her long dress, spreading its skirts and giggling with joy. "It is what I always wanted! What we worked for so long! James, this is fantastic!" She embraced him happily and would have kissed him full on the mouth if the look on his face hadn't caught her off guard.

Gone was his usual flattering manner and indulgent smiles. James looked cold and disgusted. "James, darling, whatever is wrong? I thought you would be happy. We are the same age now. We can be married like we always planned. It will be..." The words died on her youthful pink lips. "Perfect..."

"Vivian, we could never be married." James was sneering now. "For starters, I am already bonded with Joanna and have been for thousands of years. She is not the most forgiving of partners, and I doubt she would take kindly to sharing me with the likes of you. Perhaps she would let me keep you as a sort of pet, but I am not sure I would like that. Pets can be so...messy...and you are best in small doses, my dear."

But Vivian was distracted once more by the changes in her body. Her dress was growing larger, too tight in the waist, and too loose in the chest and hips. It was also getting longer, and her rings were slipping off her fingers. "What is happening?" she asked, panicked.

"I believe you are getting what you've always desired, my dear Vivian. You are getting younger." James was smiling again, but it wasn't a very nice smile, and it didn't do much for his handsome face. "In fact, I think you will continue to get younger and younger until you can't get any more so."

Vivian's bracelet slipped off her arm and crashed to the floor as her wrist and hand shrunk further. "Give me the green solution—we should be able to reverse this," she yelled frantically, tripping on her overlong skirts as she tried to reach the green syringe where James had set it on the counter so he could administer the red solution.

While Vivian was busy disentangling herself from her twisted skirts, James lunged for the syringe, only to watch it disappear under the table clutched in an unfamiliar hand. James grabbed the wrist just as it was disappearing and with surprising strength pulled Mr. Benjamin from his hiding spot.

"Why, Mr. Benjamin. I always warned Vivian that you were not to be trusted, and here I was right all along." James held the struggling scientist firmly with one hand, trying to pry the syringe from his grip with the other.

"Let me have it. We can still save her." Mr. Benjamin was franticly trying to hang on to the syringe despite the pincer hold James had on the pressure points in his wrist. "There is no reason to kill her!"

"Oh," James said, freeing the syringe from Mr. Benjamin's hand at last, "but there is. Vivian has become a liability. She knows way too much about what I have been doing, and she let my do-gooder cousins escape. Now everything that I have come here to do is in jeopardy. All because she couldn't manage to do the simplest of tasks. Truly all she had to do was assign one of her hundreds of servants to watch those children full-time and this would have never happened. But Vivian was too self-absorbed and underestimated them. I really can't let her survive to cause more destruction to my plans."

"She never told anyone what you were doing. She was always very careful to keep your secrets," Mr. Benjamin pleaded. "Please, let her live. I am sure she will never expose you."

"I am not as confident as you that I can trust her. She told you everything, didn't she? Which reminds me—I can't really let you live, either." And he stabbed the green syringe into Mr. Benjamin's arm and depressed the plunger.

James released the stunned scientist, who looked in disbelief at the tiny pinprick on his forearm where the solution had entered his body. "Enjoy your final moments," James said, giving the teenage Vivian and rapidly aging Mr. Benjamin a formal bow, and then he placed the final solution and the watch into his pocket and swept out of the room. He pulled one of the new transport boxes out of his pocket and began manipulating the dials, noticing neither Nickolas cowering behind some boxes in the closet nor the small black shadow that followed him.

⊶☖☗⊷

Charles struggled with the lock picks, his hands shaking just a little. Pixies. He thought they'd gone extinct three thousand years ago in the Faerie Wars. Man, he hated Pixies. He fumbled a few more precious moments, and then he felt the final pin click into place, and the mechanism opened the door. Just as he was prying the door open with one of his daggers, his eye caught a silver glow coming from a window far above. He was just about ready to return his attention to the door after watching the glow fade, but then a second silver glow, smaller than the first, filled the window.

Transit boxes. He quickened his pace and quietly slipped up the stairs. He returned the lock picks to their places in his sleeve and extracted his two longest knives. One glittered in the sunlight pouring through the holes in the weakened floorboards above, throwing faceted sparkles on the stone walls.

⊶☖☗⊷

Deidre and Bard continued to battle the Sprites at the Zen garden bridge. It was taking too long to dispatch each enemy, and as one was defeated, two more were ready to take its place. The muses were being pressed back, and it was only a matter of time before the bridge would no longer be an asset and the remainder of the squad would swarm them.

It would have been different if Bard had had his full attention on the enemy before him, but Deidre could tell that a portion of his brain and all of his heart was up in the tower behind them. Deidre had seen Charles slip through the doorway, and she noticed that he had left it slightly ajar. Perhaps it would be more defendable inside the tower, and that would give Bard a chance to see that Brigitta was safe and then get his whole brain, such as it was, back into the fight. So she touched the broad muse's shoulder and motioned to the tower. That was all the communication that Bard needed to hear, and the two began to back away from the Sprites and toward the tower door.

Brigitta's final scream filled the air, and at the sound Bard whirled and ran full tilt toward the tower. Ramming his ax into its holster, he began to scale the gray stone wall, slamming his fists into the mortar to make hand- and toeholds. He climbed impossibly quickly, higher and higher, leaving Deidre below to handle the remaining Sprites on her own.

⚬彐帋⚬

Charles poked his head into the observatory and slipped unobtrusively into the shadows. The sight that met his eyes was not encouraging. The Pixie had her back to him, but through its bowed legs, Charles could glimpse Sarah and Alec with their hands up glaring at their captor. Brigitta was not in sight, but her two golden daggers glittered on the floor beside the creature's right foot. Knowing Brigitta as he did, the daggers would not be out of her hands if she still was capable of using them.

Well, at least he still had the element of surprise. And with that, he launched himself from his hiding spot and landed like a cat high on the Pixie's back. He plunged his diamond blade between her shoulders, right next to where her wings joined her body.

The furious Pixie dropped Brigitta in a clump on the ground and swung around, trying to find the annoying thing that was poking at her back. Sarah looked up to see Charles clinging to the dagger for dear life as the creature tried to throw him off. Sarah was worried that with the way the Pixie was stomping around, she would step on Brigitta, and Sarah dashed to the muse's side to offer what protection she could.

Brigitta was still conscious, and although she was doubled over in pain, Sarah was confident that she could get the muse to safety. She slipped her arm under Brigitta's shoulders and took much of her weight onto her own slender frame. Suddenly the weight disappeared.

Sarah looked up to see Alec with Brigitta in his arms. He had retrieved his sword, and once again it hung at his hip. Sarah scooped up Brigitta's daggers and helped Alec carry her to the study.

They were just settling her into a chair when Sarah heard a thud coming from the observatory. She dashed to the door in time to see that the Pixie had been successful in dislodging Charles, slamming him against the stone wall in the process. Charles sat sprawled against the wall, dazed and shaking his head, while the Pixie raised her talons to finish him off.

"No!" Sarah yelled as she launched herself across the room and through the Pixie's legs, coming to rest in front of Charles's body and covering his tiny form with her own, daggers raised and arms stiffened waiting for the killing blow.

⋈

Mr. Benjamin watched James leave and ran his hand through his hair. A whole clump of graying locks came away in his hand, and he stared in disbelief as age spots blossomed on the back of his hand like raindrops on a lake. He spun around when he heard a pitiful wail. There, engulfed in her dress, sat a six-year-old Vivian, crying into her plump, dimpled hands. Her auburn hair had escaped its usually neat bun and cascaded in childish curls around her shoulders.

Mr. Benjamin's heart went out to the tiny girl, and he rushed to her side, surprised by how shaky his legs had become and by the sharp pain the exertion caused his lower back. He half crouched, half fell beside the girl and put a comforting arm around her tiny shoulders. "There, there," he said, his reedy voice betraying him. "There, there."

Nickolas watched for a few moments in amazement as the skin on Mr. Benjamin's face seemed to melt like candle wax, forming wrinkles and jowls that sagged on his skull. What hair was left on his head had turned from brown to gray to white in the time it took him to stumble across the room.

"Mr. Benjamin, what can I do to help?" Nickolas ran to the old man's side.

"I fear there is nothing we can do," Mr. Benjamin said faintly, finding it hard to draw a full breath into his weakening lungs.

"Let me go get Brigitta. She can heal people. Maybe she can help you." Nickolas prepared to dash from the room.

"Just a moment—I have something I must tell you."

Nickolas skidded to a halt at the door. "What?"

"The experiment—it is nearly finished. Just follow the notes. I hid the notebook under the sink while Dr. James was talking to Vivian. Under the sink, understand?" Mr. Benjamin was having serious trouble breathing now, and the last of his hair had fallen out.

"Yes, under the sink. Got it. But I have to get Brigitta now. Just hang on, Mr. Benjamin. Just hang on until I get back. Promise?"

And Nickolas dashed out of the laboratory before he could hear Mr. Benjamin's whispered, "Promise." He looked down at the tiny two-year-old girl with the bright-red hair who was silently sobbing in his arms. He pulled her closer to his sunken chest with his thinning arms and gently rocked her back and forth, singing her a nonsense song that his mother used to sing to him when he was very small. The tiny girl wrapped her hand around his finger and looked adoringly into his wrinkled face.

He rocked her as she grew smaller and smaller in his arms, becoming lighter with each passing moment. The red hair had turned very fine and was now just a dusting on her baby head. Tiny Vivian fell asleep in his ever-frailer arms, still grasping his finger in her little hand, each miniature fingernail perfect and shell soft.

Spasms began to shake Mr. Benjamin's body, and he felt his systems failing. His eyes were growing watery and dim, and he was having trouble remembering who he was and what he was doing. The only thing he remembered was the tiny newborn baby in his arms and how much he loved her. He placed a kiss on her sweet-smelling crown, feeling her rapid pulse against his lips. "I love you, Vivian," he whispered, and then he was racked with another tremor. The baby began gasping for breath as if she were a fish taken out of water, and her little face turned blue. But Mr. Benjamin did not notice, for his body lay beside the struggling baby, his eyes closed as if in sleep.

Mr. Benjamin was no more.

CHAPTER 29

BARD BATTLES A PIXIE

❧❦

In which Nickolas sings and Sarah fights

Nickolas arrived in the sitting room just in time to see Sarah rush back into the observatory. He paused only a moment to tell Alec that Mr. Benjamin needed Brigitta before running after his sister. He watched in horror as Sarah slid under the Pixie and raised her arms to ward off the killing blow that was intended for Charles. He had to distract the Pixie, but how?

He searched his pockets and began pulling out all of his paraphernalia: a candle stub, some horseshoe nails, a chocolate chip cookie, a plastic green army man, two marbles, and a ball of twine came out of one pocket. Dr. Montague's journal was in another. But then Nickolas's hand closed on something that would be much more use against the Pixie, and a slow smile crossed his face as he pulled it out.

❧❦

Sarah was braced for the blow, her left arm and dagger protecting her head and her right protecting her torso. Her entire body was sprawled over Charles, who was barely moving after the Pixie had flung him full force against the wall.

She knew that she could not hope to completely stop the Pixie's attack; the beast was just too large and powerful for her to do so. Her only hope was to catch the descending talon on her dagger and deflect it from hitting Charles or herself. She rapidly analyzed the talon's trajectory and adjusted her top dagger as best she could. She didn't have time to do any more, for at that moment the talon hit her blade. The force of it jarred every bone in her body, and it took every bit of concentration that she had to ignore the pain and twist the dagger, adjusting the talon's momentum away from her and Charles. She didn't really have a plan B for what she would do when the Pixie struck again; her only thought had been to protect Charles from the first attack. So she was very lucky that a second attack never came.

❈

"Hey, ugly!" Nickolas yelled at the Pixie, throwing the small vial of mushroom acid he had placed in his pocket before leaving the ranch directly at the Pixie's head.

He missed.

Instead, the bottle smashed against the Pixie's broad back, right over the spot where Charles's diamond dagger had cut into the Pixie's tough hide. The acid sprayed over the spot and burned into the leathery wings. The Pixie gave out a roar of pain and whirled away from Sarah and Charles to face this new threat. Except, unknown to the Pixie, the new threat had just thrown his only weapon.

Nickolas stood there, unarmed and trembling as the Pixie advanced on him. He was trying to remember everything he had ever read about Pixies and was finding that the knowledge his children's books contained were woefully inaccurate in their descriptions. Well, they did have wings, Nickolas thought ruefully.

That might have been Nickolas's last thought before he died, and he closed his eyes so he didn't have to see the final blow. He felt the Pixie's hot breath approaching, and then it just wasn't there.

Nickolas's eyes sprang open in time to see Bard drop from opening the Pixie had ripped in the dome overhead when it had entered with James. Bard's huge arms were wrapped firmly around the Pixie, tackling the monster from above. A random thought that Bard should seriously consider a job as a professional football player ran through Nickolas's head as the muse and beast tumbled to the floor.

The weakened floorboards were no match for the combined weight of the Pixie and Bard, and they gave way with a tremendous crash. The pair smashed through the floor and into the long open air of the tower below. The beast bellowed the whole way down and then grunted as they hit the stone floor.

Nickolas dashed to the huge hole and attempted to peer down into the darkness. But the resulting dust and debris as well as the unlit stone tower made it impossible to see more than a few inches into the chasm. The sounds of snarling and the clanging of an ax on stone came from far below. "Bard, are you OK?" Nickolas yelled.

"Yeah," Bard bellowed back up. *Clang.* "Don't worry, I got this." *Crash.* "Find Brigitta for me." *Crunch.* "OK, Nickolas?" *Growl.* "And check on Sarah and Charles." *Thud.*

"On it!" Nickolas called down and carefully regained his feet.

Through the dissipating dust, Nickolas could just see Sarah leaning over an inert Charles. "Sarah, how can I help?" he called across the gaping hole in the floorboards.

"He's pretty badly wounded," Sarah called back. "I was able to keep the Pixie from killing him, but the talon went through his shoulder. Help me get him to Brigitta."

Nickolas worked his way across the observatory. With all of the debris in the air, it was much harder to avoid the weak spots in the floor, to say nothing of the giant Pixie-shaped hole in the center of the room. But he soon arrived at Sarah's side and saw what she meant. Charles's shoulder was in bad shape. The talon had left a long cut in his biceps, and golden blood was seeping from the wound.

Nickolas removed the lab coat he had donned when working with Mr. Benjamin and grabbed one of Sarah's daggers to cut off both of the sleeves. He folded one of them into a square bandage and used it to close the wound. The second he wrapped around Charles's arm and tied the bandage tightly into place.

"I think we should move him into the lab. Brigitta is there, and she can heal him," Nickolas said. "Help me pick him up."

Nickolas looked expectantly at Sarah, but she was almost as green as Deidre. Nickolas shook his head. "How can you be as tough as you are and turn squeamish at the sight of blood? It's not even red!" Nickolas sighed as he hoisted Charles's torso.

"Just because I think blood and things like that should stay inside the body at all times does not make me squeamish," Sarah glowered at Nickolas, lifting Charles's legs.

"Whatever," Nickolas replied, not really wanting to fight with his sister. "Be careful, there are lots of holes in the floor, and I think Bard weakened the whole structure when he and the Pixie fell through."

"Really, you think?" Sarah shot back. Her brother really had a knack for stating the obvious, and she wasn't really thrilled with him calling her squeamish. After all, she'd just saved Charles's life. She looked at Charles's unmoving form as they carried him across the floor. Well, hopefully she'd saved him.

As they struggled to navigate around the treacherous observatory, they heard more disturbing noises from below. In addition to the clangs and thuds from Bard and the Pixie, they heard Deidre's bellow and the snarls of the remaining Sprites.

"Arrrrrgh!" they heard Deidre yell.

This was followed by Bard's bellowed translation: "Charles, we have company." *Slam!* "Sprites getting past Deidre." *Clang!* "Can you come down and help?"

Sarah looked at the unconscious Charles and then shrugged her shoulders. "Can you handle him alone?" Without waiting for Nickolas's answer, Sarah dropped Charles's legs and, grabbing her daggers from her waist, yelled, "Coming, Bard." And she dashed toward the stone stairwell.

Nickolas gaped after her. Just what did she think she was going to do? He looked down at Charles, then at where his sister had disappeared, and then back to Charles. He sighed. Nickolas decided he would get Charles to Brigitta, get some more acid from the lab, and then try to help Sarah. He sighed heavily and then started dragging Charles across the floor.

Nickolas ran into Alec and Brigitta coming from the laboratory. If truth be told, Brigitta wasn't looking very good herself, and Nickolas was getting concerned about their chances of taking the day. One muse down and another muse hurt left only two muses still fighting, against a Pixie and who knew how many Sprites. Nickolas did not like their odds.

Brigitta quickly looked at Charles's wound and his gray face and instructed Nickolas and Alec to bring him into the laboratory. Alec swept the small muse into his arms and dashed after Brigitta. "Put him on one of the tables," Brigitta instructed as she removed her harp from its case on her back and began to tune it.

Alec turned to the nearest table and started to heave Charles onto it, ignoring the large amount of glassware he was sweeping onto the floor in the process. Nickolas realized that the table Alec had chosen was the one with the second part of the experiment on it. He watched in shock as beaker after beaker teetered off the table and smashed onto the stone floor. His shock turned to horror as he saw the domino effect the glassware was creating, and he could see down the line of destruction that it was only a matter of seconds before the tiny vial of precipitate from the second solution would follow its brother vials and smash on the floor. Nickolas dove to the tiles and slid across the floor, coming to a rest just under the lip of the table beneath the vial. Nickolas reached out his hand just as the vial fell. It touched his fingertips before bouncing off and crashing to the floor. Nickolas had miraculously been able to absorb enough of the vial's momentum that it merely rolled away, unbroken and still stoppered.

With a huge sigh of relief, Nickolas retrieved the vial of precious solution and slipped it into his pocket.

"I need to go and help Sarah," Alec said once Charles was on the table. "Can you spare me, Brigitta?"

"Yes," Brigitta answered. "See if you can get her safely out of the battle. These are not Faeries we are dealing with. Sprites are designed for combat and, unlike Faeries, have actually been trained. She shouldn't be out there."

"I'll do my best, Brigitta," Alec answered, unsheathing his sword.

"She isn't that easy to persuade," Nickolas cautioned.

"I noticed," Alec said grimly, slipping out of the laboratory.

"Should I go too?" Nickolas asked, heading toward the cupboards to find more acid vials to use as projectiles.

"Actually, I need your help," Brigitta said. "I am not very good at healing—not as good as my sisters and certainly not as good as Georgiana. I am very concerned that Charles's injuries are beyond my skill. But I noticed when you were playing my harp at your grandmother's house that you seem to have some talent with muse music. It might have been just a coincidence, but I want to try anyway. It can't hurt, and it might just help."

"Sure," Nickolas said and reached for Brigitta's harp.

She laughed. "I actually need my harp, Nickolas. You can help me best by singing."

"Singing?" Nickolas looked perplexed. "Singing what?"

"Anything," Brigitta said. "I will follow your lead. Just sing what comes to your mind."

Brigitta set her harp on her lap and looked expectantly at Nickolas.

At first Nickolas had no idea what to sing. He wasn't exactly the type to join the school choir or be part of a garage band. In fact, the only place he regularly sang was in the shower. And he only really knew about half the words of the songs that he sang in the shower. The soap had never complained, though. So he pretended he was back home and opened his mouth and sang.

⧉

Sarah rushed down the stairs into the gloom below, daggers drawn. The few torches on the wall were doing their best to illuminate the large chasm, but with the added dust and debris from the crumbling floor above, visibility was nearly down to zero.

What Sarah could make out was Deidre's hulking form directly in front of her on the stairs. Her arms were a dark-green blur as she brought a pike that looked suspiciously identical to those used by the Sprites crashing down over and over on her furry opponent's head. The thing must have had an incredibly thick skull, for one such blow would have toppled a giant of a man with no problem. Deidre jabbed her weapon directly into the Sprite's face, but it merely slipped off the beast's great furry chin and jammed directly into its throat. Whether by luck or intention, the pike had found the Sprite's off switch, for its windpipe was entirely collapsed by the blow and the beast clutched at its throat, desperately trying to get a breath as it fell over the edge of the stone staircase and crashed to the stones below. Sarah could see through the gloom that the Sprite was no longer moving.

Looking back at Deidre, Sarah's heart sank, for two more Sprites had climbed the stairs behind their fallen comrade. Sarah felt completely useless, for she was blocked from descending the stairs to join the fight by Deidre's broad back, and from what she could see, both Deidre and Bard, fighting the giant Pixie below, could use some help. The drop to the floor was too great for Sarah to survive, and even she knew that attempting it would be futile.

She watched as Deidre was slowly being pushed up the stairs by the advancing Sprites, and she did her best to retreat fast enough so as not to get in the muse's way. Best she could tell, there were about a dozen Sprites remaining, to say nothing of the Pixie. As soon as they reached the top of the stairs, the Sprites surrounded Deidre and Sarah. Deidre noticed the girl at this point, and unlike Brigitta, the Amazonian muse didn't try to protect Sarah. She merely grunted and placed her back firmly against Sarah's, trusting that the girl would take care of her half of the Sprites. Sarah held her daggers at the ready as the first monster advanced.

The thing smelled awful, and Sarah forgot her fear of the ugly beast in her stronger desire stop it from breathing its foul breath in her face. Her opponent had lost his sword sometime earlier in the battle and was only armed with its long thick pike. Sarah took a deep breath, and as the Sprite let loose his first blow, Sarah instinctively brought up her daggers and deflected it. Everything that Bard and Brigitta had taught her about using her opponent's momentum against him came flooding back, and by using minimal movements and her daggers to direct, she was able to avoid the flurry of blows the Sprite unleashed on her.

At first the Sprite's yellow eyes widened in surprise, but then the thing became enraged and began to attack furiously. Sarah also remembered Bard's comment about not fighting angry, as an angry fighter made mistakes. So she waited coolheaded for the Sprite to make his, which he did. For in his anger, the Sprite had forgotten to conserve his energy and breath, and he quickly became exhausted. Sarah saw her opening and drove her dagger true. The beast fell in a lifeless heap, and its pike rolled to rest next to Sarah's foot.

In the momentary lull, Sarah returned Brigitta's daggers to her belt and picked up the pike. Having a longer reach would definitely be helpful. Suddenly, another Sprite took the place of its comrade in front of Sarah.

⚔

Bard faced the Pixie on the debris-strewn floor of the tower. Not only were there stones and rotten floorboards to contend with, but also the hulking bodies of the Sprites that Deidra had dispatched before retreating up the stairs.

The Pixie, Bard observed, did not seem to be hindered by the lack of visibility and, being as huge as she was, did not seem to be tripped up by the same obstacles that were hindering him. Bard had never faced a Pixie before except in the battle simulator at school. There he had often fought the Pixie, for it was the only monster that regularly could beat him. His classmates would often line the observation platform and place bets on who would win the match.

Bard was thanking the simulation game makers for doing their research on Pixie fighting tactics, for the beast before him fought very similarly to the beast in the simulation. Except this one had real talons, and her "hits" drew blood, not scores on the LED scoreboard on the arena's wall. But then, Bard thought with a grin, so did his ax.

He decided to use the same tactics he had in simulation and went for the beast's talons. If he could disarm the creature, he had a better chance of getting in for the kill. She was already cradling her left claw to her chest where two of the talons had been severed. But that left her dominant right claw, both her feet, and the talons on her wing joints to contend with.

If only she would just stop talking about Brigitta, he could get on with it. That was something the game makers had neglected to add to the simulation. *That* Pixie was silent, only screeching now and then like a large bird of prey. No mention had been made of their annoying caw-like voices.

The beast taunted him as they circled each other. "That red-haired wife of yours wasn't looking so good after I squeezed her a bit. Her green eyes nearly popped right out of her head. In fact, I wouldn't be surprised if she was dead."

"Brigitta cannot be dead, I would know," Bard retorted and sought the silent bubble that usually enveloped him during fights. He felt that inner peace wrap around him, and the shouts and growls from the battle above faded to nothing. All he saw, all of his concentration, centered on the middle of the Pixie's chest, where she telegraphed her next move—and Bard's ax was there to meet it.

Alec sprinted into the observatory just in time to see Deidre slide a heavy Sprite from her pike into a crumpled mass on the floor. Sarah and the muse had their backs against the curved stone wall of the tower near the stairs, and six dead and six living Sprites surrounded them in a loose half circle.

Deidre was all but a blur as she wacked and hacked at her opponents with her much-nicked borrowed weapon. Sarah had ditched Brigitta's daggers in favor of a discarded pike, which she was using rather well against her huge furry adversaries.

But six against two didn't strike Alec as very fair odds, even if one of the two was a strange green Amazonian woman with twigs and feathers in her hair. Alec hadn't met her before, but he assumed—by the fact she was dressed in a torn black evening gown that complemented the small injured muse's tux—that she was one of the Muses of Music that Sarah had told him about. Perhaps she was even the injured muse's wife. The thought nearly brought Alec to his knees with laughter, as an odder couple could not have been conceived of.

Seeing a Sprite slip though Sarah's defenses and deliver a rather painful whack to her shoulder with the broad side of its pike sobered Alec instantly, and he tightened his grip on his sword and advanced. Without even thinking about it, Alec dashed across the observatory floor, leaping over the giant hole in its center.

Things weren't going so well for Bard. It was one of those fights where he would have lost in the simulator and returned to his rooms to review the tape to see where he went wrong. Unfortunately, in real life, you don't always get to learn from your mistakes, there aren't "do-overs," and you only get one life, no matter how many gold coins you have. So Bard was having to think on his feet.

The Pixie in front of him was just as determined to win as he was. At least he had pressed her enough that she had stopped talking to conserve her breath, but even silenced, she still had more weapons, more appendages, more height, outweighed him by a good ton or two, and had a much longer reach. Even Bard would not have taken a bet on himself at such odds. He had managed to take out a wing and an arm on one side of the beast, but she in turn had given him a head wound, which although not serious, was bleeding rather profusely as head wounds tended to do, and it was interfering with his vision.

To make matters worse, the Pixie was slowly herding him into a corner, and there was little that Bard could do about it. He needed help, like Edmund to put a few arrows into her, or Galahad with his long sword. Even little Charles with his throwing weapons would have helped distract the beast.

"Well, Deidre could help me. She is a better fighter than Charles, anyway," he muttered out loud and then readjusted his stance, wiped some of his golden blood out of his eye, and returned his full attention to the Pixie.

⤙ᕹᕷ⤚

Deidre watched out of the corner of her eye as a tall boy with strange black-and-blond hair killed the Sprite battling Sarah with one thrust of his sword and slipped into their semicircle, taking up

378

the position on Sarah's other side. Deidre nodded her approval, for now there were only four Sprites left. She was just smiling to herself when her keen ears picked up Bard's mutter. For some time she had been monitoring the sounds of battle below and had been concerned that all was not well down there.

She looked at the two children who were determinedly facing the remaining Sprites and made a decision. She hit her opponent on the side of its shaggy head, feinted to the left, and dodged out of the circle to the stairs. The stunned Sprite thought to follow her, but seeing the pile of his comrades felled by the green lady, the Sprite thought he'd have a better chance attacking the children.

⊰🙰⊱

Sarah was startled when the third Sprite suddenly keeled over in front of her, which was probably a good thing, or she might have started attacking Alec as he slipped through the space left by the suddenly missing opponent. His arrival gave her a moment to flex her painful shoulder and readjust her weapons before the fourth Sprite moved into fighting position.

Like Deidre, Sarah also smiled a little when she noticed that only four Sprites remained and that double that number already littered the floor. But that smile didn't last long, for just as suddenly as Alec had appeared, Deidre disappeared, leaving Sarah's left arm unprotected as the two Sprites battling Deidre closed ranks on Sarah.

"Brigitta needs you," Alec said.

"Yeah, I'll just stroll over to her shall I?" Sarah barely caught the Sprite's downward strike on her pike.

"I'll make you a hole, and then I want you to get out of here."

"Why don't you just take one of these three brutes off my plate and help me. Oh, and speaking of holes, be careful of the ones in the floor." Sarah sidestepped a hole and pushed the sword of one of the Sprites away from her with her pike, following up with a blow of her own. These Sprites had horribly thick hides, and most times the pike only seemed to annoy them even when Sarah did manage to make a hit.

"Sarah, I'm serious," Alec said firmly as he pushed his opponent backward into one of the holes in the floor. Taking advantage of its stumble, Alec finished it.

"Nice to meet you, Serious." Sarah blocked the next attack and twisted her pike, sending the Sprite's sword flying.

Alec shook his head; the girl was impossible. He fought on, doing his best to protect Sarah as he battled the Sprites in front of him.

Sarah was tiring—not that she would admit it. It was becoming harder and harder to deflect the blows, and her legs were turning to lead beneath her. Alec, having freshly joined the fray, seemed tireless, and Sarah was determined that if he could do it, she could too. Besides, there were only three left.

⚎

Deidre arrived at the bottom of the stairs to find that the Pixie had cornered Bard against the far wall. She looked at the Pixie's back and saw how one of its wings drooped at an odd angle, and black ichor spattered down its length where two of the talons had been severed. The Pixie also had an odd wound on the center of its back that bubbled and festered. Grabbing two discarded Sprite swords off the floor and setting her pike quietly down on the stairs, Deidre silently approached the Pixie's back.

⚎

The Pixie had gone back to taunting Bard. She had him cornered and wounded, and it was only a matter of time before she would finish him off. "Your little wifey was not much of a fighter. She didn't even touch me with those golden daggers of hers. Did you give them to her? They were quite pretty, if not exactly effective," she said, circling ever closer.

Bard watched intently, waiting for her to get just a little closer. And then, in the distance, between the Pixie's legs, he saw a deep-green foot. A huge smile crossed Bard's face, effectively stopping the Pixie midsentence.

"You are smiling?" she asked, confused.

"Oh yes," Bard said. "I am."

"*Now!*" he yelled, running toward the wall on his right. Hitting it with first one foot and then the other, he launched himself with his battle-ax whirling before him. The Pixie pulled her wing back to swat him out of her way, but then suddenly a blinding pain hit her from behind. The Pixie watched in horror as her wing fluttered uselessly to the ground. She only had a moment of shock, however, for Bard's ax finished the battle with the Pixie once and for all.

The two panting muses paused for a second looking down at the motionless Pixie, and then suddenly something large and furry fell from far above them, heading straight down toward Deidre. With one large hand, Bard swept Deidre out of the way and, grasping his twirling ax, clove the falling Sprite in two.

"Ooops!" came Sarah's voice high above them as her head appeared in one of the holes in the ceiling. "Sorry about that!"

Deidre picked herself out of the rubble and glared at Bard, who grinned back at her. The two began making their way over the mess and up the stairs to find Sarah and Alec covered in sweat and green Sprite ichor, but none the worse beyond a few bumps and bruises.

Sarah was quite concerned about the cut on Bard's head, but he waved it off, and after ripping a swath of fabric from his kilt and binding it around his forehead, he was able to stanch the flow of golden blood. "See," he said happily, "all fixed."

Sarah returned his smile, and then suddenly her face fell. "Charles and Brigitta!" she exclaimed, dropping her pike and grabbing Brigitta's daggers from her waist. She pushed past Alec, running toward the laboratory. But Bard beat her to the door and disappeared into Dr. Montague's rooms.

Sarah rapidly traversed the observatory after him and sprinted to the dressing room. Bard blocked her way where he stood transfixed in the tiny closet before the laboratory door. Sarah shoved at his bulk and was just able to squeeze past him and into the lab. When she saw what had transfixed Bard, she dropped her daggers, her mouth forming a perfect *O*.

⊰⊱

If Nickolas had started timidly, he certainly wasn't timid now. Sarah, Alec, and Bard were gob-smacked watching Nickolas enthusiastically playing air guitar as a smashup of old 1980s hard rock tunes with all the words jumbled together poured from his mouth. He danced around the table where Charles lay, oblivious to the chemistry glassware that he was grinding to sparkly dust beneath his trainers. Brigitta sat serenely on a stool, accompanying Nickolas admirably on her harp. Sarah wondered if Brigitta had ever played hard rock before, although with her wonderful mass of curly red hair, Sarah thought that with the right outfit, Brigitta could have passed for a headbanger with no problem.

Without Charles's glasses, Sarah couldn't see if the pearly mist that had emanated from the muses when they had healed her brother a few weeks ago was swirling around Charles, but she could see the results of Brigitta's healing, as before their eyes, the long slash on Charles's arm ceased bleeding and began to knit together, leaving a long silver scar on his tanned flesh.

Charles's eyes focused, and he sat up groggily. Brigitta stopped playing, and after several moments, Nickolas noticed that no one else was performing and that he had quite the audience. His mouth snapped shut, and he dropped his air guitar, looking sheepishly at his feet.

"Thank you for the serenade, Nickolas," Charles said dryly. "It isn't every day that I get to hear 'Dude Looks Like a Duchess' sung quite so uniquely. Although, I am not a hundred percent sure that those are the words."

Sarah, Bard, Deidre, and Alec nodded mutely in agreement.

CHAPTER 30

PREPARATIONS

In which a mannequin teaches Charles some manners

For a few moments, the quiet was rather unsettling. With the Pixie defeated, the Sprites dead, and Dr. James, Vivian, and Mr. Benjamin all missing, there was a feeling of emptiness that there was nothing left to do. But when you have someone like Brigitta in your group, doing nothing is never really an option.

"OK," she said, strapping her harp back on her back. "Where are we? Bard what is your status?"

"Pixie dead, Sprites smashed...we need to burn them."

"Agreed. Charles?"

"I need to follow James and find out what happened to Vivian and Mr. Benjamin. I also left Fulvio, Zac, and Carole in the passageways and need you to help me heal them."

"Deidre?"

Deidre stoically glared at Brigitta, heavily muscled arms crossed over her chest.

"OK, you can help Bard with the bodies. Nickolas?"

Nickolas raised his eyebrows and pointed to his chest. "Me?"

Brigitta smiled. "Yes, Nickolas, I need an update on the experiments."

"Oh yeah. Mr. Benjamin and I had finished two out of the three steps necessary to make the cure for Simon and the rest. I have the precipitate here." He pulled the vial out of his pocket and showed Brigitta. "Mr. Benjamin told me that he hid Dr. Montague's notebook under the sink and that the third step is outlined in it. Did you find Mr. Benjamin and Great-Aunt Vivian in the lab? Were you able to heal them?"

"They were not here when we arrived," Brigitta said. "Either James took them, or they were able to leave on their own power. There was not a trace of them."

"I don't think they left on their own power. Mr. Benjamin was getting very old, and Great-Aunt Vivian was nearly a baby again." Nickolas shook his head sadly.

"A baby again?" Charles asked. "Explain."

Nickolas described what he had seen. As he was talking, Deidre picked up the empty syringes from the counter and gingerly sniffed the needles. She growled deep in her throat and handed them to Charles.

Charles sniffed them as Deidre had and shrugged. "I can't smell anything wrong with them. What do you smell?"

Deidre said nothing but pointed to a large mound of dust where it lay on the floor.

"Ew," Sarah said, moving away from the pile. Nickolas, of course, knelt to inspect it, but he found it indiscernible from the rest of the debris on the laboratory floor.

Brigitta interrupted with her businesslike voice. "OK, Nickolas, we need you to finish the experiments. Can you do that?"

"I—I hope so." Nickolas didn't sound so sure. He had done lots of experiments back home and was very comfortable around a lab, but making something that people would actually ingest was a far cry from making something meant to blow up in the deserted back pasture. "Is there anyone who can help us?"

Sarah got up from where she was sitting on a stool inspecting one of Dr. Montague's notebooks. "Why don't we ask Fulvio? He knows everyone in the manor and would be able to help us find a trustworthy scientist."

"Good idea, Sarah," Charles said. "Brigitta, why don't you and Sarah come with me and help me to revive Fulvio. Once he is feeling better, we can ask him for recommendations. In the meantime, Nickolas, get started, and we will send you help when we can. But we are wasting time with all this conversation. Let's go."

They all rose to join their prospective teams: Deidre and Bard to clean out the tower and observatory, Nickolas to retrieve Dr. Montague's notebook and start setting up the third experiment, and Charles, Sarah, and Brigitta to go find and help Fulvio.

"Excuse me," Alec said. "How can I help?"

"I think you should stay here with Nickolas and help him set up the next experiment. I don't like the idea of him being alone here with James unaccounted for," Brigitta said, looking thoughtful. "Actually, let me revise that. Alec, could you please help Bard with the bodies, and Deidre, could you please stand guard here with Nickolas?"

"Of course," Alec said, relieved that he would actually be doing something more than watching Nickolas work.

Deidre did not look quite as happy with her assignment, but come to think of it, Sarah had only seen Deidre look truly happy when she got to knock people over the head with a weapon, and even then, her smile was more maniacal than strictly happy.

Sarah watched Deidre's scowl turn deeper when Nickolas complimented her on her sparkly black dress.

⇥⇤

Once they had all split up, Sarah found herself once again in the servants' corridors. They didn't have far to go from the broken door near the observatory before they found Carole huddling over Zac and Fulvio, tucking blankets around their inert forms.

"Thank goodness you came back," she said, giving Sarah a hug and shaking Brigitta's and Charles's hands. "They haven't moved in ever so long. I am quite worried."

Brigitta knelt over the two men and checked the lumps on their heads with her small hand. "I don't think this is too serious. I can heal this myself."

"I cannot tell you how thankful I am to hear that," Charles said solemnly. "I was worried I would have to listen to Nickolas's unique singing again."

Brigitta glared at Charles. "His singing is the only reason you are still alive," she admonished and primed her harp once more.

"That and your quick thinking," Charles said to Sarah. "You are quite good with those daggers, my dear, I will have to tell Ardus to start training you properly."

"Do you think he would?" Sarah asked excitedly. "I mean, when he was here last he only trained Nickolas."

"That is because we had been standing in that statue garden for a hundred years while your society grew up a little. We hadn't realized that you all had evolved to the point where you had figured out that it isn't the way people look on the outside that predetermines what they can be, but rather what is in their hearts and minds. Your brother has the heart and mind of a creator and healer; you have the heart and mind of a leader and a warrior. Now that we know that training you will break no social norms, we shall train you if that is what you desire."

Sarah did not hesitate a moment before agreeing.

"First," Charles continued as Brigitta played her harp, sending its healing properties toward Zac and Fulvio, "you need to have your own weapons. Daggers seem to respond well to you, but you cannot keep borrowing Brigitta's. Bard had those specially made to protect her when he could not, so I am pretty sure she wouldn't part with them, even to protect you."

Charles held out his hand for the emerald-encrusted daggers, and Sarah reluctantly took them from her waist and handed them to him, hilt first. Charles laid them next to Brigitta's harp case and then began searching in his own pockets. "I have two here that will do well for your training. They are strong and functional and easily concealed in your riding boots. Someday we will help you create your own weapons, perfectly suited for your abilities. But until that day, these will do nicely." He pulled from one of his pockets a pair of plain silver daggers. Their blades were straight and a bit thicker than Brigitta's. Their pommels and guards were likewise unadorned.

When she took them in her hands, however, she discovered that they were even better balanced than the ones she had been using, and they fit better into her small hands. The guards were sturdier and angled perfectly for blocking and disarming an opponent. As Charles had said, they also were perfect for concealing in her boots, being just the right height and width to do so.

"Thank you, Charles," she said, putting thought to action by placing one of the sheathed blades in each of her riding boots. "When can I start training?"

"I don't know. Ardus doesn't usually take students as young as you are, so you may have to suffice with me as your teacher for a year or two. But eventually, I want you to train with each of us. Each of the Muses of War have specialized in different forms of fighting, and until you have tried many of them, you won't be able to make an informed decision on the style you like best and have the most aptitude for."

"Will you be training Nickolas and Alec too?" Sarah asked.

"I will not be, but I am sure that Brigitta and her sisters will be taking an interest in Nickolas's singing. I do hope they manage to teach him all the words to the songs, though."

Sarah would have asked more questions, but their attention was turned to Fulvio and Zac, who were sitting up against the wall and sipping water from a flask that Brigitta had produced from her belt.

"Are you OK, Fulvio?" Sarah asked, sitting down next to the chef.

"Never better. Brigitta tells me that you need someone to help Nickolas finish the experiments."

"Yes, do you have anyone in mind?"

"Well, Dr. Trowle is the nearest scientist, but I don't think he is the most trustworthy." Fulvio looked thoughtful. "How about me? There isn't that much difference between baking and chemistry."

"I think that is a great idea. Let's go talk to Nickolas."

Once Zac and Fulvio were back on their feet, the group returned to the observatory.

⊰⊱

Bard and Alec had finished cleaning up all of the bodies by the time they arrived, and they had a huge funeral pyre burning on the breakfast garden lawn. What Great-Aunt Vivian would have thought, Sarah had no idea, but she was pretty sure burning monsters in Great-Aunt Vivian's perfectly manicured gardens was against the rules.

⊰⊱

Twenty minutes later, Fulvio and Nickolas were puttering around the lab assembling the third phase of the experiment. Carole and

Zac were happily washing and drying the mountain of dishes that Mr. Benjamin and Nickolas had left teetering in the sink, and Sarah, Alec, Brigitta, and Bard sat or stood around the corners of the room, watching and trying to make themselves very small so they wouldn't get in the way.

Charles and Deidre had excused themselves to try to find out where James had gone. "I need to get back on his trail," Charles had said to Brigitta. "Call me if you need me, but it looks like you have everything under control here." Brigitta had nodded, and Charles bowed his farewell to Sarah and Brigitta. He hand-clasped Bard, Fulvio, Alec, and Nickolas while Deidre scowled impatiently at the door, waiting for Charles to join her.

"Nickolas, do you think I could have my ring back?" Charles asked, ignoring Deidre's tapping foot. "I have been having a terrible time getting around without it, and I am sure that Brigitta will give you her phone number if you need to reach us in the future.

Nickolas reluctantly removed the ruby ring from his thumb and handed it to Charles. "That ring is really cool. Maybe you could make me one of my own someday?"

Charles laughed. "I would give you one in an instant, my friend, but Ardus and Audiva would most likely not agree. Come to think of it, your parents and grandmother probably wouldn't agree, either. Tell you what—you get all five of them to sign off on it, and I will teach you how to make one."

With that, and another bow to Sarah and Brigitta, Charles and Deidre left the room.

⧈⧉

The two muses didn't go far, for Charles had seen the flashes of silver light coming from Dr. Montague's bedroom. Sure enough, they found the ornate box the Sprite had given Dr. James sitting on the unmade bed. Charles opened it and found the same alterations he had seen in the Paris mansion—alterations that he quickly disabled before pressing the activation button.

Deidre grabbed his shoulder rather painfully as Charles placed his ruby ring against the top of the box. Silver flashed around them, and Charles felt the sensation of transport and the thrill of excitement he always had when on a mission. But he was to be rather disappointed, for when he and Deidre rematerialized, it was in the exact same spot in Dr. Montague's bedroom.

Deidre raised her eyebrow at him, and Charles shrugged. "I have no idea," he answered her unspoken query and opened the transport box once more. The settings were the same as when he opened it the first time, but now he recognized the coordinates. Somehow the device had been reset so that it reinitialized the settings once the box had been used. There was no way they could tell where in the world James had gone from the box. He could be, literally, anywhere.

Charles let out his favorite oath, which made Deidre smile. Perhaps if he took the box to his workroom he might be able to figure it out. So he slipped it into one of his many pockets and returned to Dr. Montague's lab with Deidre behind him.

⇥⇤

Once back in the lab, Charles brought Brigitta and Bard up to date in whispers. A curious and, if truth be told, rather bored Sarah started asking lots of questions about how the boxes worked, and when Alec started adding his own questions, Nickolas found he couldn't hear himself think.

Nickolas turned around and said exasperatedly, "If you aren't going to do any work, would you all please leave the laboratory?

You are making me so nervous I can't think. This is going to take a while, so find something to do. Preferably something that involves bringing me food. I'm starving."

"I think we should go," Sarah said in a stage whisper to the others. "That is about as close to losing his temper as Nickolas gets, so I think it would be a good idea to do what he says." So they all slipped out of the laboratory and into Dr. Montague's sitting room. To Sarah's surprise, Fulvio joined them.

"Nickolas saying that he was hungry gave me an idea," Fulvio said. "I think we should plan a feast to celebrate. There is going to be panicking as word of Lady Vivian's demise spreads among the staff, especially since Louis did not give out the pills this morning. The staff are bound to start asking questions. Most of us can't even remember a time when we didn't live at the manor, and the world out there has changed a great deal while time has stood still here. If we can keep everyone busy until we announce that we have a cure as well as a plan for the future, we can keep the members of the household calm. Carole, Zac, and Nickolas can stay here and work on the experiment while the rest of us can gather everyone together and plan the banquet."

Brigitta grew thoughtful. "Actually, Fulvio that is a fantastic idea. Let me go back and let Nickolas know, and then we can start implementing it. I will leave Deidre here to guard them. She isn't much help planning parties anyway."

Charles snorted. "Well, she and I are the only ones dressed for a formal to-do." He indicated his ichor-covered tuxedo and picked one of the black sequins up off the floor where it had fallen off the torn hem of Deidre's dress.

"Just where did Deidre get that dress? It looks a lot like one I had in my closet in Paris, only it was full-length." Brigitta's brows drew together.

Sarah had a sudden inspiration just exactly where Deidre had gotten the dress, so she hastily turned to Alec and changed the subject. "Speaking of clothes, want to see some of that magic I was telling you about? Come on!" She grabbed his hand and started for the door but then stopped to face Brigitta. "We can go, can't we?"

"Yes, but I would feel better if you kept a muse with you at all times." Brigitta looked around at the remaining adults.

"I will go with them, Brigitta," Charles said. "I am curious to see this 'magic' too."

"Then that is settled. Fulvio, I will accompany you to the kitchens and help where I can. Deidre will stay here and guard Nickolas, and Bard will keep working on cleaning up the Sprites and the Pixie. How will we know when it is time to meet up again?"

"Leave that to me," Fulvio said with a smile. "The house knows how to call everyone to dinner!"

⁍ ⵗ ⵑ⁌

Sarah led Alec and Charles across the breakfast garden, past the huge burning funeral pyre. It looked like Bard might have overdone it a bit as the flames were shooting nearly three stories into the air.

"Charles," Sarah said tentatively.

"Yes, Sarah."

"Do you think we could have a short funeral for Mr. Benjamin before we go? Nickolas is pretty good about hiding his feelings, but I think he is pretty upset. Mr. Benjamin was our friend, even though he was in league with Great-Aunt Vivian. And he gave Nickolas a Bunsen burner when no one else ever did. I think it would be nice."

"I agree, Sarah." Charles looked thoughtful. "I will talk to Brigitta and Fulvio and make sure we arrange it."

"Thanks, Charles."

They crossed the lawn and stopped by the library doors. Sarah was perplexed to find them locked. They had never been locked when they had stayed in the manor. But locked doors were Charles's specialty, and they were soon through it and running up the ladder to her old rooms.

Sarah reached into her pocket and brought out her sapphire key before Charles could bring out his lock picks again.

Inside, her rooms were just as white and flower-filled as when she had last seen them, and they were neatly cleaned and dusted.

Alec and Charles followed Sarah into the dressing room, and she showed them the mannequin. "Watch this," she told them, a mischievous expression replacing the somber one she had worn after her conversation about Mr. Benjamin. Addressing the dress form, she said, "Mannequin, I need a jacket with lots of pockets, please." The most garish jacket appeared instantaneously, covered in patch pockets in every color imaginable. Sarah giggled. "I see you haven't changed a bit. Could we go plainer? And perhaps dark blue?" The mannequin complied, but left an obnoxious orange paisley lining inside the jacket.

Once he had picked his jaw up off the floor, Alec asked, "Can I try?"

"Sure," Sarah said, switching places with him so he stood directly in front of the mannequin.

"What do I say?" Alec asked.

"Just tell her what you want."

"Excuse me, Miss Mannequin." Alec felt foolish talking to the headless dress form. "Could you change the paisleys to, um, stripes?"

Instantly the lining changed to orange, pink, and white striped silk.

While Sarah and Alec took turns asking the mannequin to make wilder and wilder outfits, Charles was inspecting the room, his brow wrinkled. He looked in all the cupboards, checking the walls, sides and tops of the wardrobes, and pressing every few inches on the paneling. He then inspected the mannequin where she was bolted to the floor, and he attempted to lift the wide hoopskirt that Sarah had ordered so he could get at the mannequin's controls.

But just as he had started to lift the skirt, one of the voluminous sleeves of the dress slapped him across the face hard enough to leave a red mark on his skin.

"Didn't anyone ever tell you that it isn't polite to touch a lady's skirt," Sarah said, giggling.

Charles rubbed his jaw and looked thoughtfully at the mannequin. "Sarah," he asked, "are there any other devices like this one at the manor?"

He looked so serious that Sarah and Alec immediately sobered. "Only the food cupboards. Fulvio could tell you all about those. Oh, and there are other mannequins in Nickolas's and Great-Aunt Vivian's rooms."

"Is there one of the food cupboards near here?"

"Yes, downstairs. I'll show you." And the three of them left the mannequin dressed in her pink Marie Antoinette outfit complete with a three-foot powdered wig and headed toward the staircase.

Sarah explained to Charles how the cupboard used to deliver Great-Aunt Vivian's synthetic food directly from the kitchens just a moment after you had ordered it, but that was before the footmen had left the grounds. The muse spent several minutes inspecting the cupboard, but whatever he discovered, he kept it to himself.

"Let's return to the kitchens. I want to talk to Brigitta, and maybe we could be of some help," Charles said. So they left the keeping room, and she led them outside toward the staircase to the kitchens.

⚐⚑

The kitchens were already in full swing preparing for the feast. Brigitta and Fulvio were nowhere to be found, but one of the sous chefs suggested that they look for them in the ballroom, where they were planning on serving dinner. One of the maids led them up a wide staircase and through several corridors until they reached the ballroom. Sure enough, Brigitta and an army of maids were putting together the long dining room table and spreading it with a huge white tablecloth. Fulvio beamed at them from across the room. He still wore his dusty butler's uniform but had grabbed his old chef's hat, which was perched precariously on his head, and his favorite wooden spoon, which he was using to direct the maids like a conductor directs his orchestra.

Sarah loved to watch Fulvio at work, for he seemed so happy and in his element, and it was obvious that his staff loved working with him too. Just what would happen to Fulvio, Carole, and everyone here after they were cured? "Charles, what is going to happen to the manor and its staff? I read in Dr. Montague's will that the manor will revert to the Crown."

Charles looked thoughtful. "I don't think that would be a good idea. James has a lot of things here that really shouldn't fall into the wrong hands, like that mannequin and the gem fountain. I will work with Brigitta and Ardus to come up with a plan. Have no fear, I will make sure that Fulvio and his staff either can

397

remain here or have a place to go." He said this with such conviction and finished his statement with one of those formal muse bows, so Sarah didn't doubt his words. She didn't have any more time to worry about it anyway, for Fulvio put her to work helping a pretty little maid named Jenny set the table.

The topic of conversation turned to clothes as Sarah and Jenny worked. "I will have to make sure I have time to return to my rooms to bathe and change," Sarah was saying. "Fulvio has worked way too hard on this fancy dinner for me to show up in dirty jeans."

"I don't have anything to wear but my uniform," Jenny said, sighing wistfully.

"That's not a problem—I can just make you a dress. Come with me once we are done here, and I will make sure you have something nice to wear. What is your favorite color?"

⁂

The word soon spread that Sarah thought she could make a dress for Jenny to wear, and soon all the maids were crowding around her begging for dresses too. Sarah was a bit worried, for although Jenny was similar in size to Sarah, several of the other maids were much taller and heavier than she was; in fact, unlike the footmen, the maids, chefs, and under butlers were of every height and shape imaginable. But she promised to give it a go.

Sarah began to feel uneasy as she went back to work. She understood why all of the maids and staff were excited about the feast, but she was far more concerned about Simon and getting home to her family than she was about fancy dresses.

When she crossed the room to get more silverware, she stopped by Brigitta.

"This seems to be getting a little out of hand," Sarah confessed. "Shouldn't we be concentrating on getting the cure made more than on parties?"

"If I thought that more people working with Nickolas would make the process go faster, I would agree," Brigitta replied, putting her arm around Sarah. "But unfortunately, it is a job that only one or two people at most can do. And it is also a time-consuming one. Nickolas and Fulvio are both right. Having more people breathing down Nickolas's back will only increase the chance that he will not be successful. And what the staff need most is a distraction to get them through the next few hours. If even one of them realizes that a twelve-year-old boy is at this very moment creating their only hope for life, we would have panic on our hands. Look how quickly word of your making a dress for Jenny spread. Now imagine if it were the news that Carole and Fulvio only had a handful of those pills left. Anything you can do to help keep everyone calm and distracted, allowing Nickolas to do his work, would be a huge help."

"Even if that means making dresses for the maids?" Sarah asked skeptically.

"Especially if that means making dresses for the maids. Just think, most of the people here have never had new clothes. You will be doing them a great service. Sometimes the most important thing that you can do as a leader is to keep calm and keep others around you calm. I am counting on you, even more than I am counting on Nickolas."

"But what about Simon? Shouldn't we at least be getting him some of the pills Carole has to stop the aging effects?" Sarah asked, not looking appeased.

"I talked to Mr. Benjamin about that when we first were setting up the experiments for the lab. While you and Alec were sleeping,

I offered to take some of the pills back to the hospital. He said that the pills would probably not work for Simon as the main ingredient in them was Simon's own essence. Mr. Benjamin and Lady Vivian had developed the pills for the guards while Simon was a prisoner, and at the same time they were working on creating the nutrition shot that they gave Simon to keep him healthy. During their experiments, they found that the processed essence in the blue pills didn't agree with Simon, and they actually made him sicker. So they had to go a different route to make his supplements. I then asked if there were any of those supplements left, and Mr. Benjamin said that unfortunately they were all destroyed in the lab explosion. He thought our best solution to both the staff's and Simon's problems was to concentrate on Dr. Montague's notes. And he begged me to allow Nickolas to stay, as his photographic memory was far faster than copying and searching through the research notebooks."

Sarah looked very serious. "Isn't there anything that I can do? I feel so helpless. I could help Nickolas in the lab."

Brigitta laughed. "I have not noticed that you and Nickolas working together is the best recipe for keeping Nickolas calm and focused. You can help me more here. I will go check on Nickolas now and see if there is anything that he needs. Don't worry, Sarah. We will get Simon the solution the instant it is ready."

Sarah returned reluctantly to her tasks, and for Brigitta's sake, she tried her best to appear excited about the upcoming party.

⊰⊱

After most of the work was done and they were just waiting on the breads to finish baking, Sarah ushered Jenny and a handful of the other maids up to her rooms. She had Jenny stand in front of the mannequin and asked it to make her a beautiful fuchsia ball gown. The mannequin changed her shape to exactly match Jenny, much to Sarah's surprise, and then created a spectacular gown just exactly as Jenny had described.

Sarah sent the maid with the gown to change in her bedroom and had the next maid step up to the mannequin. The mannequin once again changed her form and then created a stunning outfit for the maid. Sarah stood next to the mannequin and helped each woman create her dress, taking a great deal of satisfaction in seeing their astonished and happy faces.

She was sure that by now she had finished dresses for the handful of maids who had accompanied her upstairs, but every time she looked up, the line wound out the door of the dressing room with no end in sight. At one point, a short male chef had reached the front of the line, and Sarah had laughingly sent him off to Nickolas's dressing room to find clothing. He had returned a short time later in a stunning suit and tie to tell her that Alec was over in Nickolas's rooms helping the men the same way she was helping the women. She admired his suit at length and then returned to her mannequin to continue helping the women. Finally, she saw Carole and Brigitta at the end of her line.

"That's everyone," Brigitta said with a smile when they had sent Carole to Sarah's bedroom to change. "Thank you so much for doing this, Sarah."

"You are most welcome! What did you hear from Nickolas?"

"Bard just stopped by and let me know that things are progressing nicely. He had a couple of challenges, but Nickolas thinks he should be done in about an hour."

"And I am done here—well, almost done," Sarah said, looking critically at the muse's dress. "You need something to wear."

"Oh please," Brigitta said with a laugh. "My robes are fine. I wear them all the time."

"Exactly—you wear them all the time. You need something different. Besides, you traveled all over the world, fought Pixies and Sprites, had Charles and Bard bleed all over you, and cooked a feast in them. I think you might want to change." Sarah said this with such a knowing look on her face that Brigitta even looked down to see if her spotless white robes were indeed stained, but of course they weren't.

"You just want to make me a dress, Sarah. It has nothing to do with my current one. OK, do you worst." Brigitta smiled as she positioned herself in front of the mannequin.

"Mannequin, Brigitta likes Grecian flowing things, so can you make her one out of royal-blue silk with lots of tiny pleats and a fine gold-braided trim." Instantly a high-waisted dress fitting Sarah's description and exactly the beautiful red-haired muse's size appeared on the mannequin along with tiny golden dance slippers to match and a pretty little gold fillet for her curly hair. Brigitta put on the dress, hanging her daggers at its waist, and she allowed Sarah to arrange her hair and place the golden fillet on her head.

"You look perfect." Sarah clapped her hands together.

A wry smile crept across Brigitta's face. "Now it is your turn, little one. You really do have monster bits on your outfit. You have been so busy dressing everyone else you have not thought of yourself. Now go jump in the tub, and I will get a dress ready for you." Brigitta practically pushed Sarah out of the room and across the way to the steaming bath waiting for her.

By the time Sarah emerged from the bath, all traces of dirt and ichor were washed from her hair. She found that Brigitta had left, but not before creating a stunning gown for her and leaving it on the mannequin. The dress was seafoam green silk with scrunched silk cap sleeves. It was very simple, with few adornments except for the waist, which was sprinkled with tiny seafoam crystals and even smaller freshwater seed pearls. The back closed up with pretty cream pearl buttons, and a cream-colored silk satin bow tied in the back at the waist. A matching ribbon for her hair was sitting on the dressing table.

She was just slipping on the seafoam green ballet flats when Alec entered the room and collapsed on the poof in front of Sarah's mirror. He was still wearing Mr. Benjamin's oversized clothes and smelled faintly of Sprite guts.

"Aren't you going to change?" Sarah asked, wrinkling her nose.

"I haven't had time—all of those cooks kept wanting to add cufflinks and try out different color combinations. I don't even want to look at clothes again," he complained.

"Don't be silly; come with me." Sarah dragged him back to Nickolas's dressing room and stood him in front of the mannequin.

"Mannequin," she commanded, "I need Alec to look nice at Fulvio's dinner, so can you make him a suit, a shirt, and a tie that will accomplish that? Dark blue would be nice."

And the mannequin complied. Sarah just had time to admire her handiwork when the tinkling of two bells rang overhead and a soft voice said, as if over a very quiet loudspeaker, "Two bells. Please get ready for dinner."

"Oh no. It's time for dinner. Get this on. There's no time for you to have a bath, which is too bad because the baths here are amazing. Hurry!" And with that Sarah ran out of the room and down the hall toward the ballroom.

A somewhat bemused Alec stripped off Mr. Benjamin's billowy clothing and hastened into the mannequin's suit and tie. He was out the door less than five minutes later and headed toward the ballroom.

CHAPTER 31

THE FEAST

+¤+

In which Fulvio cooks Italian

Alec slipped into the ballroom just as three bells were struck. Sarah waved him over to her side of the table and motioned to one of the two empty seats she had been saving. "The other one is for Nickolas if he gets done in time to eat. I wonder what is taking him so long. I really wish he would finish up so we could get that cure back to Simon. Doesn't everyone look nice, though?" she said, looking around the table at all the glittery dresses and smart suits.

"From the way the men were acting in Nickolas's rooms, you would think they hadn't had new clothes in a hundred years," Alec whispered to her.

"Some of them probably haven't. Great-Aunt Vivian was very into telling everyone what to do, so this may have been the first time they got to pick what they wanted in forever. Do you know what Fulvio made for us? I'm starving." Sarah looked at the table settings and was struck how Fulvio had used the same crystal and china that Great-Aunt Vivian had used when she was last in the ballroom, but somehow he managed to make it warm and inviting, not formal and chilly.

Menu

Appetizers:

Capesante Gratin with Besciamelle Sauce
Tiger Prawns in Lime and Coconut Chili Sauce

Main:

Linguini with Clams in White Wine Sauce

Dessert:

Tiramisu

To Digest:

Limoncello

And a special thank-you to Miss Deidre,
who procured all the fresh seafood for me.

There were printed menus on tiny easels around the table, and Sarah asked Alec to hand her one.

> When thinking about this dinner,
> I thought how much you all are my family.
> And my mama, when she cooked for the baronet, she cooked French,
> but when she cooked for the family, she cooked Italian.
> So for you, my family, I cook Italian.
>
> —Fulvio

Sarah looked across the table at Deidre. She still wore the torn evening dress, although it had lost still more sequins and was looking spectacularly tattered. Her hair had come down from its bun, and she had lost one of her chopsticks somewhere. She had also lost several of her twigs and feathers, and both her hair and dress were sopping wet.

"You don't think she bathed in her dress, do you?" Alec asked, following Sarah's gaze.

"No, if I was to hazard a guess, she went diving for seafood in it," Sarah said with a sigh.

Charles appeared at her elbow and sat in the empty chair next to her. "I do believe you are right, Sarah."

Their attention turned to Fulvio and his head staff as they entered carrying huge trays of delectable food. Soon everyone's mouths were too full for any more conversation to take place.

⊰⊱

While Sarah and Alec were getting everything and everyone ready for the feast, Nickolas was working frantically up in Dr. Montague's laboratory. Carole and Zac helped him immensely at first, making sure everything was clean and at his fingertips as he built the final experiment, but then Carole could tell that Zac was making Nickolas nervous by asking tons of questions and touching fragile parts of the experiment. "Why don't Zac and I go help Fulvio in the kitchens," she had said and hustled her son out of the room.

That left Nickolas alone with Deidre. She was actually pretty good company for a busy scientist. She said nothing, made no noise, and asked no annoying questions. But she did have a rather baleful stare at times. So it had been some relief when Fulvio arrived fifteen minutes later with a shopping list and asked Deidre to go get him some things for the dinner. Deidre had looked at the list and grinned rather dangerously before "borrowing" a netting lace shawl from Lady Montague's closet and disappearing.

The third part of the experiment was much simpler than the first two had been, and with the chocolate chip cookies and lemonade Fulvio had left during his visit, the process moved along rapidly and pleasantly.

There were only two major hiccups, which Nickolas was able to solve, albeit one a hair later than he would have wished. And just as the sun was setting over the forest, Nickolas, still humming to himself, had the tiny purple pills drying on butcher's paper on the counter. And it was only shortly after he heard three bells called that he had the dry pills in a brown stoppered bottle, and then he was on his way down to the ballroom for supper.

⊰⧱⊱

A hush fell over the room when Nickolas entered, and every eye was riveted on him. He spun around to see if somehow someone interesting, say Deidre, had entered with him, but there was no one behind him. As he felt the weight of the stares, Nickolas became very self-conscious and hurried across the room to Sarah's side.

"Why are they all staring at me?" he whispered to his sister once he was seated.

"Because you're purple," Sarah whispered back.

"Oh, that. Dr. Montague's solution was having trouble delivering enough chemical to the dying microbios, and Mr. Benjamin recommended that I used the buffering solution from his supplement experiments to fix the problem. It wasn't very successful, and when I first tried it, I turned kind of dark purple as a side effect. You probably don't want to use Dr. Montague's bathroom for a while, either."

Alec snorted but quickly regained his composure while Sarah eyed the vial of purple pills warily. "Are you sure you got it right the second time?" she asked.

"Pretty sure. I tried them on myself, too, and didn't have any side effects, and the solution worked on the sample of my blood I tested it on. Well, I was already purple, so I don't know if I turned *more* purple, but the other side effects didn't happen, so I have a good feeling about this," Nickolas said enthusiastically. Alec dropped all pretense of hiding his laughter, and Sarah and Charles joined in. Even Deidre's lips twitched a little.

"Laugh if you want," Nickolas said, somewhat embarrassed, "but I didn't want to experiment on anyone else before I tried it first." He turned to Charles and said, "Anyway, Brigitta said that you would take one of the pills to Simon right away." Nickolas took a tiny vial that contained only one of the purple pills and handed it to the short muse.

Charles instantly became serious and placed his fist to his chest and bowed to Nickolas before taking the tiny brown bottle and securing it in one of his pockets. "I will be back before you know it and will let you know how your cousin fares." With another bow, the small, dark muse strode purposefully out of the room and toward the gardens.

⊶⊷

Dinner wound down to a close, and Fulvio stood up and tapped his knife lightly on his wine glass for attention. The happy chatter around the table quieted, and Fulvio spoke. "I hope the meal was good, no?" Everyone agreed, and Fulvio continued. "We have much to be thankful for to my friends here." He motioned to Sarah, Nickolas, Alec, and the muses. "For they have helped us once again. As you know, we have been suffering from withdrawal from the synthetic foods, and our brilliant young friend Nickolas, with the help of old Dr. Montague's notes and Mr. Benjamin, has been able to create a cure. It will allow us to return to a normal aging pattern, and although I will miss my youthful glow," he said, patting his round belly, "I actually am looking forward to growing older and wiser.

"Ms. Brigitta has asked that we all stay on here until she figures out what will be happening to the manor. She says that she will either purchase the manor herself or help find Dr. Montague's heir and work with him or her to make sure that we all have a place if we wish it.

"That said, Master Nickolas has the pills for the cure. If you would like to take it, see him and Brigitta. I will make sure that M. Craubateau and anyone else on the grounds who was too ill to come to our dinner gets the antidote.

"Finally, I am passing around to the adults at the table the last bottle of my mother's Limoncello. It is traditional to share after the meal to help digest. For Master Nickolas and his friends, I have concocted a bottle of his favorite lemonade."

Brigitta walked over to Fulvio and whispered something in his ear. Fulvio nodded and then addressed the ballroom once more. "Oh yes, Ms. Brigitta just reminded me of one last thing. You are all invited after dinner to accompany Master Nickolas, Mistress Sarah, and their friends as well as myself to the family cemetery behind the greenhouses. We will be having a small memorial service for Mr. Benjamin there, and you are all invited to attend if you wish. Nickolas's cure would not have been possible without Mr. Benjamin's help and sacrifice. I hope to see you there."

With that, Fulvio walked around the table pouring the drinks out himself and making sure to have a warm word with everyone. He made a show of getting his antidote from Brigitta and Nickolas, taking it calmly. Soon a line formed near Brigitta, and she handed out the antidote to everyone.

"How long did it take for you to turn purple?" Sarah whispered anxiously to Nickolas, watching Fulvio for signs of ill-effect.

"Oh, it was instantaneous," Nickolas said. "If this batch was causing the same problems, everyone would be running for the restrooms by now. They seem OK."

"How will we know if it works?"

"They should be able to tell you now, because the headaches and body pains should disappear just as fast. Fulvio, come here a second." Nickolas waved Fulvio over to the table. "How are you feeling?"

"Never better. Why do you ask, Master Nickolas?" Fulvio said in his usual jovial manner. But then he paused. "No, I really do feel better. I think your cure is working!" And with a huge grin, he swept Nickolas into one of his warm hugs and then clapped him soundly on the back. "Very well done. This is cause for more celebration! More lemonade? More tiramisu?" And he cheerfully filled their goblets and plates.

⚜

Nickolas placed an eggplant flower he had picked in the green-house on the spot where Bard had buried Mr. Benjamin and Great-Aunt Vivian's dust in the family cemetery. The memorial service had been sad for Nickolas. Very few of the staff had come, but the important people were there: Sarah, the muses, Alec, Fulvio, Carole, and Zac of course, and even M. Craubateau had insisted on Bard carrying him to the graveside while a handful of other staff members stood to one side.

Nickolas delivered Mr. Benjamin's eulogy himself. It had been rather short, as Nickolas wasn't very good at making speeches under emotional circumstances, but he had gotten out what he had wanted to say. That Mr. Benjamin had done his best to save them not once, or even twice, but, in his own way, continually since they had arrived at the manor and that he would miss his mentor very much.

No one had said much about Great-Aunt Vivian, so they let Deidre deliver the eulogy for her, which the tall green muse did with her usual verbosity.

⚜

Charles had already contacted Brigitta to let her know that he had successfully delivered the pill to Simon and that he had waited for one of the staff members to go over the boy's vitals and run bloodwork which confirmed that the cure was working the same for Simon as it was for the rest of the Manor's inhabitants. He then requested that Deidre join him to return to their mission of searching for James. And soon the three children and Brigitta and Bard were the only ones left at the manor who didn't live there.

They had already said their good-byes to Fulvio, Carole, and Zac, who the muses had put in charge of the manor. Brigitta had promised to return and help them just as soon as she had checked on Simon and reported in to Audiva.

Sparks had disappeared, and no one had seen her since she had brought the children and Bard to safety the night before, and Sarah had had to tearfully accept that the little dog would not be found before they had to return home. Fulvio had wiped her tears with his apron and promised that he would keep an eye out for Sparks, and Sarah was not to worry.

"Are you ready to go?" Brigitta asked once the service was over and the small party of graveside mourners had broken up.

"Yes," Nickolas said. "But why do we have to take an airplane? We traveled by that box thing just fine on our way here."

"I am still not sure why you could do that," Brigitta said. "It is not designed for anyone but the muses to travel through, and I don't want to put you and Alec in any more danger. I will have an awful lot to explain to your parents and grandma as it is. Plus, I am confident that Alec can't travel that way even if you can."

"Didn't he travel that way when Great-Aunt Vivian captured him from the airport? What Mr. Benjamin described sounded almost exactly like what happened to us on our way here," Nickolas said in a wheedling tone.

Sarah didn't want to sit for sixteen hours on an airplane any more than Nickolas did. "Can't we just give it a try? If it doesn't work, we can get on the airplane like you want us to. We have been away too long as it is."

"Brigitta, let's try. I don't fit in airplane seats," Bard said, adding his pleas to the children's.

Brigitta sighed. "I give up," she said, throwing her hands in the air. "We will try. I will stay back for a second, and anyone who is left here will go on an airplane with me. Deal?"

"Deal!" they all chorused.

They all trooped down to Georgiana's plinth and lined up hand in hand next to Bard. Brigitta adjusted the dials on the box in Georgiana's clearing and pressed the activation button.

Nickolas grasped Bard's free hand, and Sarah held Nickolas's. Alec was next, holding on to Sarah. Bard made a fist and placed his emerald ring on top of the box.

Brigitta watched as Bard disappeared in a silver flash. For a moment, she thought the children would not follow, but the silver glow slowly covered first Nickolas and then Sarah, and they vanished from sight. Alec was engulfed in silver the slowest of all, and it seemed to hover above his skin like a mist rather than permeate his entire body as it did with Bard, Sarah, and Nickolas. Brigitta still wasn't sure it was working on Alec correctly, but then the teenage boy gave her a cheeky wave and winked out. She shook her curls and shrugged, resetting the box. Using her own emerald ring, she left the clearing empty save for Georgiana's box sitting on her plinth and the curious squirrel who immediately reclaimed his stump.

⚜

Sarah stood in her bedroom with her brother and Bard, watching Alec slowly materialize beside her. She wanted to yank him through whatever silver void was keeping him trapped, but she found she was powerless to move her hand from where it was clasped in his. Agonizingly slowly, the glow began to fade, and Alec stood panting next to her, whole once more.

"That hurts," he exclaimed, rubbing his skin.

"Really?" Nickolas asked. "It doesn't hurt for me. It's just really, really cold."

"I feel the cold too," Sarah said. "Bard?"

"Cold? No, no cold. Just a bright light and poof! I arrive," Bard said, looking perplexed.

"Well, it felt like my skin was being torn off," Alec said. "Let's not do that again anytime soon."

Brigitta appeared at that moment with a quizzical look on her pretty face. "I have no idea why you three could do that. And Nickolas, you are no longer purple!"

Sarah stared at her brother, noting that what Brigitta had said was true and he was completely free of purple.

"Aw, that's too bad," Nickolas said, pouting. "I wanted to freak out Grandma Vera."

⚶

They found Grandma Vera in the living room with another surprise, for Mr. McGuire was on the couch, looking hale with a mug of hot chocolate in his hands. Both had looked very worried when they entered the room, but the worry turned to joy as they folded the children into their arms. "Don't you ever do that again," Grandma Vera admonished. "You have taken years off my life, seeing the two of you disappear right before my eyes. What was I to do? Go tell the police that you had vanished, literally?"

"Easy, Mom," Mr. McGuire said as he put a hand on her arm. "The important thing is they are safe."

415

"Yes, and we need to get to the hospital right now to check on Simon. I sent Charles with a cure earlier, and I want to see how it's working," Nickolas said.

"Who is Charles?" Grandma Vera asked, but Mr. McGuire interrupted.

"Well then, let's get in the van." Mr. McGuire made a move to get up, grimacing slightly as he did so.

"Why don't you stay here with Bard, Mr. McGuire, and I will go with Vera and the children," Brigitta said, and Grandma Vera nodded.

"Very sensible plan, my dear. John is not supposed to be on his feet. Mr. Bard, will you please make sure that he doesn't move a muscle while we are away?"

"Yes, I can do that," Bard said, sitting heavily on the nearest chair, nearly flattening it.

As the children, Grandma Vera, and Brigitta headed toward the garage, Sarah overheard Mr. McGuire say to Bard, "Now tell me, who exactly are you, and who are the red-headed woman and the teenager who has a dead skunk on his head?" Sarah wished she could stay and hear Bard's explanation. It could've proven highly entertaining.

⊰⊱

They were ushered into Dr. Lucy's lab almost as soon as they entered the hospital doors. She was hunched over her notes at a large table set up with a complex chemistry apparatus bubbling away.

"Sarah, Nickolas!" She rose from her stool as soon as she saw them. "This is the most fascinating thing. I have almost re-created the solution that stops the aging. Were you able to bring me the mushrooms and the roots?"

"Isn't Simon better?" Nickolas asked, perplexed. "We sent someone with the cure several hours ago."

"Oh, I have been so busy here that I haven't had time to check on him. Let's go now." Dr. Lucy stood up and slipped her lab notebook into a drawer and out of sight.

Sarah was contemplating the experiments set up on the table and didn't notice Dr. Lucy leading Brigitta and Nickolas out of the room.

Something about the way the intern had looked was troubling. She seemed disappointed that Nickolas had finished the cure, and she had rapidly closed her notebook when the children had approached her desk. So when Dr. Lucy, Brigitta, and Nickolas left to check on Simon, Sarah stayed behind. Alec noticed and stayed with her.

"So why are we hanging back?" he asked her.

"Just a hunch. I want to see what Dr. Lucy was working on. She didn't seem to want us to see her notes." Sarah walked over to the table and pulled the notebook out of the drawer.

She carefully looked at what Dr. Lucy had written, and fear clenched her stomach. "She wasn't working on the antidote at all," Sarah said exhaling the breath she had been holding. "She was trying to re-create the antiaging serum that Great-Aunt Vivian was making. She even extracted essence from Simon!"

Sarah showed the notes to Alec. "She was planning on continuing Vivian's research. But how? That information wasn't in Dr. Montague's notes, unless..." Sarah's eyes grew round. "Unless Dr. James gave it to her!"

Alec's mouth thinned to a grim line as he started dismantling Dr. Lucy's experiment. He didn't even discuss it with Sarah; he just began pouring the solutions out in the sink and rinsing out the beakers. It took only a second for Sarah to join him, washing out the equipment and returning it neatly to the cupboards around the room.

By the time Dr. Lucy returned to her lab, the children had left, the notebook had been removed, and the table was spotless. All evidence of the work she had been doing was gone.

⚎

"Where did you two go?" Nickolas asked when he, Brigitta, and Grandma Vera found them in the hospital garage next to the van.

"Brigitta," Sarah said, ignoring her brother. "I need to tell you something about Dr. Lucy." And she told Brigitta everything that she and Alec had observed and what they had done. She finished by handing Brigitta Dr. Lucy's notebook. "We need to get Simon out of here!" she finished.

The whole group returned to the hospital, and as they walked down the corridors toward Simon's rooms, Nickolas pulled Sarah and Alec aside. Quietly, so that Grandma Vera would not overhear, he whispered, "Now when you get to Simon's rooms, don't stare at him."

"Why?" Sarah asked.

"Well, he's changed a lot since he was brought here. He no longer looks like a six-year-old, for one thing. He grew really fast, and now he's more like twenty."

"We were only gone a day!" Sarah exclaimed. "Fourteen years in twenty-four hours? How could that happen? Didn't Dr. Montague take four years to age up?"

"Yeah, but all during that time he was working on a way to slow the aging down. Some of his experiments must have been partially successful. I don't think we can compare Simon

418

to Dr. Montague. Oh, and on Simon, the rapid growth had some bad side effects."

"Like what?" Sarah wondered what Nickolas was having trouble saying.

"Like, well, like he didn't grow evenly. His bones grew too fast for the rest of his body. The doctors aren't sure what the long-term effects are going to be, but his spine is curved and he walks with a limp, and they said something about his brain not growing right, so there's some frontal lobe damage. Something like that—I'll have to look it up when we get home. But the doctors are worried and want him to see lots of specialists."

"Poor Simon." Sarah looked sad. "But we'll get him taken care of, I know we will."

⊰⊱

Simon was sitting up in his bed. The change to him shocked Sarah. Gone was the cherubic blond child with the pinched face, and in his place sat a tall, thin, insolent-looking young man with one shoulder significantly higher than the other. His hair had grown past his shoulders, and it had turned a mousy-brown color. Something about his gaunt face and hooked, long, thin nose looked familiar to Sarah, but she couldn't quite put her finger on why.

"You're looking much better already," Nickolas said brightly. If Simon looked better, Sarah could not imagine how awful he must have looked a few minutes before, but she, Alec, and Nickolas managed to keep up a cheerful banter to cover their awkwardness. Soon Grandma Vera and Brigitta returned to the nurses' desk to arrange for Simon's release.

"How are you doing, Simon?" Sarah asked.

"Better—much better, thank you. The pain is all gone." His voice was flat, and his blue eyes were cool.

"Did anything the doctors do while we were gone help?" Nickolas asked.

"No, I don't remember much except everything hurting and feeling like someone was grabbing the top of my head and my ankles and stretching me out. You certainly took your time about bringing me that cure. I am sure you realized how much pain I was in. Perhaps you just didn't care." Simon looked accusingly at Sarah.

"Simon, of course we care. That's why we went to make the cure in the first place and sent Charles with it the instant it was done. You were the first to get the cure—we even sent it to you before giving it to the people at the manor!" Sarah was shocked by how angry Simon seemed.

"Well, Dr. Lucy didn't care—she just took more essence. She had that same look that Cousin Vivian had when her experiments were going well. You brought me here just to be another lab rat. I thought you wanted to protect me, but obviously I was wrong. Who is he?" he asked, noticing Alec for the first time.

"This is Alec Anderson, Simon. Alec, this is our cousin Simon Montague." Sarah made the introductions, trying to ignore Simon's anger and rudeness. "We found Alec at Great-Aunt Vivian's, so we brought him home."

"You aren't planning on keeping him around, are you?" Simon looked at Alec suspiciously.

Oblivious to Simon's distain, Nickolas jumped in. "Only until we can get him home to his parents and figure out how to explain his disappearance. Brigitta is on it."

Simon shrugged. "Hopefully that will be quick. When do I get to go home?"

"Tonight, I hope," Grandma Vera said from the doorway. "One of the doctors will be in to see if you can be discharged. We want you home as soon as possible, too."

"Did you talk to Dr. Lucy?" Sarah asked.

Brigitta looked serious. "It appears that Dr. Lucy is no longer in the building. Her things are gone from her locker, and she didn't tell anyone she was leaving. Don't worry, Charles will be able to find her for us."

⌐≕⊨⌐

Not long after that, the hospital discharged Simon. The four children, Brigitta, and Grandma Vera returned to the ranch. And once the adults had gotten the two younger children and Simon settled into their rooms for the night, they returned to the living room with Alec.

"Mr. Anderson," Mr. McGuire said warmly. "Mr. Bard here tells me that my aunt was almost as hospitable to you as she was to my own children. He says that you were very helpful and even tried to protect my Sarah on several occasions. I thank you for that."

"My pleasure," Alec said to his shoes.

"Mr. Bard also tells me that you live somewhere around here, but he didn't know where. What are your plans?"

"Well," Alec said, taking a deep breath. "I need to head back to school in the fall, for sure. I will be a junior at Westminster House Prep. But I was supposed to spend the summer traveling the world. My parents made plans for me to spend a week or two with their friends in different countries. But I've somehow lost my luggage and my passport and my itinerary, so I'm kind of at a loss as to what I'm supposed to do next. My parents had other plans this summer. I think they are in Italy, but I couldn't tell you exactly where…" Alec trailed off, opening his hands wide and shrugging his shoulders.

"So if I'm hearing this right, you have no set plans at the moment." Mr. McGuire's eyes twinkled. "So Sarah has brought home another lost puppy. She's good at that. Don't get indignant—I'm teasing my daughter, not you. She has this way of finding people and things who are lost and bringing them home with her. You aren't the first, and I'm confident that you won't be the last. It's a good thing the ranch is very large, and I have need of you anyway."

"You need me?" Alec hadn't felt needed since his sister had passed away. "For what?"

"Well, I hear that you are a fencer and a very good one at that. I'm always looking for new activities for our campers to learn, so how would you like to be our fencing instructor for the summer?"

Alec thought of the empty mansion in Boston that was his other summer choice. "I would be honored, sir."

"Good, my mother will set you up with a room. We will contact your family for permission, and we can get you some clothes and a haircut."

Alec snorted, and at Mr. McGuire's raised eyebrow he added, "You're a lot like your daughter, sir. I think I'm going to like working for you very much."

"I've been told both of those things many times before. Although I prefer to think that my daughter is a lot like me, as I came first."

⧈

Later that night, Alec found himself tucked in a comfortable bed in his own little cabin on the ranch grounds. It had felt good to shower and put on clothes that were made for someone his own size. Mr. Benjamin's clothes had hung off him in folds and had been nearly a foot too short, and the formal suit that Sarah had made him for dinner was rather uncomfortable for everyday wear. But from somewhere, as if by magic, Grandma Vera had managed to find him jeans, a few shirts and even a pair of pajamas that fit him perfectly.

Little did he know that down the shower drain—along with two weeks' worth of dirt and a bit of Sprite ichor—went the last of the microbios that had been sprayed on him in the airport by Dr. James's solution.

Epilogue

In which Mr. McGuire grudgingly accepts his fate

Ardus's Headquarters, Athens, Greece: Consul of Muses of Music and War

"Charles, you called this meeting. How can we help you?" Ardus brought the meeting to order as all of the Muses of Music and the Muses of War took their places around the large stone table.

Charles got to his feet and addressed his brothers and sisters-in-law. "James is causing far more trouble than we initially thought. We observed many troubling things while we were at Vivian Montague's manor. James has given his scientists much of our technology, and not through developing them to invent it themselves, but installed from our factories and created by our scientists.

"In the manor there are replication devices with unlimited access to the solutions needed for them to work. There are also short-range transporters, and in the gardens there is even an off-world portal. I am not sure where the portal leads, but I think it is more likely someplace like Faerie than Muse. He was able to obtain a squad of Sprites and even a Pixie in very short order. And he has set up an alternate transportation network that is off our usual transport grid. He even gave one of his scientists a crate full of atomic blasters when I was at the chateau."

Brigitta interrupted. "He told me that he has been working for some other faction since we were students. It seems that this group has infiltrated the development program and has recruited agents within our own network. Any of the muses on this world could be in league with him. I know for a fact that Karina and possibly Edith are working for him."

"But why? What is his motive?" Ardus asked, looking very concerned.

"Well, he paid for the Pixie in essence." Charles paused for a long time to allow the muses around the table to digest this information. "In human child essence."

There was a collective intake of breath.

"And that is not all," Charles said. "Deidre and I observed some of his other outposts around the world, and he is conducting experiments with the extraction of essence in several other places besides Vivian's manor. Galahad, were you able to free the children at Master Chambre's lab?"

Galahad rose to his feet and placed his right fist to his chest. "I have been working with the local authorities to plan a raid on the site and have been quietly removing the most vulnerable of the children and returning them to their parents with the help of some of the servants in the chateau. We should have his operation completely shut down within the month." Galahad turned to Charles. "You will be happy to hear that I was able to locate Abha and reunite her with her brother. The young man said to give you his undying thanks."

Charles grinned at Galahad. "Well done! I knew you were the one for the job!" And then he added sheepishly to Ardus, "Deidre and I have a list of the other scientists connected to James and what they are working on. I would like to investigate their outposts and observe their experiments once we have found James again."

"Agreed. What of Lady Vivian?" Ardus asked.

"We believe she is dead," Bard interjected.

Audiva looked horrified. "Are you sure?"

"We are not a hundred percent certain, as we did not actually see the bodies, but our best guess is that both she and Mr. Benjamin did not survive. When Nickolas left them to come get me to help, they were clearly dying. By the time I arrived, they were gone." Brigitta spread her long fingers on the table in helplessness.

Charles continued the story. "James killed them using two of the solutions Dr. Montague developed. Nickolas tells me that there was a third solution, and James took it with him. He said that James felt that Vivian was a liability for releasing us; he didn't know why James killed Mr. Benjamin. Perhaps it was because Mr. Benjamin was just at the wrong place at the wrong time and tried to keep him from killing Vivian. Which brings me to Sarah, Nickolas, and Alec."

"Wait a minute, who is Alec?" Audiva's brow was furrowed as she typed notes into her computer.

"Alec Anderson is an American high school student who was captured by Lady Vivian in the Sydney airport as she tried to keep you from escaping with the children. He was extremely helpful in our recent adventures at the manor," Brigitta said.

"And he is pretty handy with a sword, for a human," Charles added. "You might want to take him under your tutelage, Ardus. And speaking of taking people into our care, I think both Sarah and Nickolas should be trained."

"Trained? As in muse trained? But why? They are too young. And they have no strategic role in this." Ardus scowled at Charles.

"Yes, Ardus, as in muse trained. I have suspected for some time that there is more to those children than their shared DNA with Lady Vivian. They are, at the very least, extremely talented in healing and war craft for their age. I sense that in the future they will become adults with whom we should align ourselves. And we may as well start their training now. They know too much about us just to be left to their own devices, even though I think they can be trusted. I would like to train Sarah myself for now. Audiva, can you spare anyone to train Nickolas?"

"Train Nickolas? But..." Audiva looked quizzically from Charles to Brigitta.

"I don't understand everything that I saw yet, but I do agree with Charles. Nickolas has an uncanny natural ability with the powers of music. I have never seen someone like him in all of my alliances with humans. I wish to investigate further, but as I am one of the weakest at manipulating the music, I doubt that I am the best choice to instruct him."

Ardus interrupted. "I don't think there is any valid reason for training the children. James will be far too busy with his scientists and avoiding us to worry about them, and we can keep an eye on them every now and then to make sure that they are safe. I am far more concerned about what James is doing with experimenting and off-worlding essence."

"I agree," Audiva said, looking severely at Charles and Brigitta. "We should have no trouble keeping the children safe without training them. What earthly reason would James have to harm the children?"

Ardus stood and took control of the meeting. "Then it is decided. Charles and Christina, you are assigned to following James and keeping an eye on Sarah and Nickolas. Brigitta and Bard, you are assigned to making sure that the manor is contained. I don't want that technology falling into the wrong hands. I want to lock down that portal and keep James from being able to use it in the future. Let's meet again in six months to revisit this. Any other business?"

As there were no other pressing issues, the meeting adjourned with Ardus and Audiva hastening from the room after one last stern look at Charles.

Charles was furious. Why couldn't those two see the obvious? James was not just going to let the children get on with their lives. Inconsequential or not, to James they symbolized the freeing of the muses and the exposure of his plans. James would not let that go unpunished. Ardus and Audiva were just too good themselves to fully understand how someone like James operated. Charles, fortunately, was just not that good.

Christina only had to look at her husband to know what he was thinking. Long years of being married to the rakish muse had taught her that obeying orders was not his strong suit. Her role as his conscience had begun years ago when they were young children. Christina, almost from the moment they met, had been able to help Charles see reason when the school governors were at a loss as to how to control him.

Christina's nature was one of quiet goodness. Her sisters and friends could always count on her to do what was right and to follow the rules. Her gentle sweetness held Charles in far tighter bonds than any punishments doled out by authority figures could, and she knew that she needed to work quickly to keep Charles from being impetuous. So she crossed the room to his side and stood on tiptoe to kiss his cheek.

As she dropped down to her heels she whispered, "Don't worry, Charles. I will train Nickolas." And with another kiss she was gone, leaving a dumbfounded Charles grinning after her like a lovesick schoolboy.

He was still in the glow of his wife's approval when Deidre stopped in front of him. Charles looked up into her stoic face. It was unreadable as always and could have been carved from green granite. She stared back at him for some time before he cracked his lopsided smile and asked, "How can I help you, Greeny?"

If Christina's endorsement of his plans to train Sarah and Nickolas had taken Charles by surprise, it was nothing compared to the shock Deidre would give him. For it was the first time he had ever, in thousands of years of knowing her, heard her utter more than grunts. He could have fallen over in a slight breeze when she said not one but two words in her gravelly voice: "Train them." before striding purposefully toward the cavern door.

Mrs. Tam's Boarding House, Sydney, Australia: Louis

Louis placed his cardboard suitcase carefully on the bed and opened it. Mrs. Tam had agreed to rent him the room for an unheard of price of a hundred dollars a week. It seemed everything outside of the manor was insanely expensive. The last time Louis had rented rooms, the price had been only five dollars for the whole month. But he had plenty of money, as he had raided Lady Vivian's strongbox before he had left the manor. He had at least enough to hold him over until he found a job.

That might prove a bit more challenging than he had thought, for when he had questioned Mrs. Tam about finding an agency that worked in placing servants she had laughed, saying that the need for servants in Australia was rather low at the moment. She had not elaborated on what she meant, but she found it to be hysterically funny.

But at least for the time being, Louis knew he was fine, for he had the money, a suitcase full of clothing, a room to live in, and the small bottle of pills to keep him alive. Louis carefully removed all of these things from his suitcase and placed them in the drawers of the small dresser included in the room. He would be fine for exactly 937 days because that was the exact number of pills that remained in Fulvio's bottle.

McGuire Ranch, Silver Springs, Colorado: Lord Connelly and Mr. McGuire.

It had been several months since Sarah and Nickolas had returned home from their second visit to Montague Manor. The camps had ended for the summer, and regretfully, Alec had returned to boarding school in Massachusetts. Sarah and Nickolas, not nearly as regretfully, had returned to school in Silver Springs.

Simon had fully recovered from his ordeal in June, save for his curved spine and limp. In spite of having the best psychologists working with him, the McGuires were very concerned about how angry and melancholy Simon had become since returning home from the hospital. In fact, it seemed that every day over the summer, as Alec had become less and less withdrawn, Simon had become more so.

The doctors were stumped; Simon looked to be around twenty years old, but he oscillated between acting like a six-year-old and a fifty-year-old and was prone to periods of irrational temper to the point where the McGuires feared for his and those around him's safety. Even Sarah, who usually could cajole anyone into a good mood, had met her match with Simon.

Mr. McGuire was almost fully recovered from the car crash in May and had taken all of the duties of running the ranch back from Grandma Vera, although his mother stayed on to help with the children and provide a motherly presence for the campers.

Mrs. McGuire had been moved from Denver General to a local nursing home, and they hoped that she could return home to the ranch soon with only some additional nursing care. The doctors were confident that she would have a full recovery, and they repeatedly told Mr. McGuire that it was not that his wife was healing slowly, but that his own recovery had been just short of miraculous.

Sarah and Nickolas were at the kitchen table doing their homework and discussing Sparks's continued absence when the front doorbell rang. Nickolas sprang from his seat and dashed to the door with his sister a half a step behind him. Both children were hoping for a visit from Charles and Christina, or perhaps Brigitta bringing the missing puppy and news from Fulvio as they were all overdue for their weekly visits. So they were somewhat disappointed when they opened the door and found not a muse waiting there, but a tall, thin man in a bowler hat.

"Good evening, children," the man said in a clipped British accent. "I am Lord Connelly of Her Majesty's Service. May I please speak to Sir Montague?"

Simon, who was sitting on the stairs hidden in an alcove, felt his heart leap. Did the man mean him? But the next words out of the man's mouth dispelled that hope. "He must be your father, John McGuire?"

"Sure," Nickolas said. "He's in the living room with Grandma Vera. This way!" And Nickolas led the man to his father, leaving Sarah to close the door.

Lord Connelly was quickly relieved of his coat and hat and given one of the comfortable chairs near the fireplace. Sarah and Nickolas prepared some hot chocolate and cookies in the kitchen with Grandma Vera while Lord Connelly talked to Mr. McGuire.

"Your lawyer, Ms. Telyn, brought to our attention that the first Sir Montague, Baronet of Montague, passed away some time

432

ago. Usually, if a baronet dies without male issue, his title and lands revert to the Crown, unless the queen decides to grant the title to another relative. In your case, Her Majesty desires that you be granted the title of the second Sir Montague, Baronet of Montague, and that your son assume the title of the Honorable Nickolas of Montague, and your daughter the title of the Honorable Sarah of Montague. Your wife is given the styling Lady Montague, and your mother will retain her title of the Honorable Vera McGuire of Montague. Montague Manor in Sydney will be your titled lands, with the line of succession following from you to your son. In addition, the queen has allotted you a stipend to help cover repairs and modernization of the manor. I have all the papers here, and if you would just affix your signature here and here and here, all will be finalized." Lord Connelly handed Mr. McGuire a stack of vellum papers and a pen.

"What if I have no desire to be Sir Montague?" Mr. McGuire asked, holding the pen gingerly as if he expected it to bite him. "I am not exactly the baronet type."

"Your lawyer suggested that you might be difficult, so she asked that I give you this." Lord Connelly handed Mr. McGuire a sealed envelope that had been closed with green wax and impressed with Brigitta's ring. Mr. McGuire broke the seal and read the short note it contained. His demeanor sobered immediately.

"I see. Where do I sign again?" Mr. McGuire quickly signed the papers, and Lord Connelly rose to leave.

"Thank you for your time. Her Majesty will be most pleased that you have entered her service. Whenever you are in London, please let us know, and we will set up an audience for her to meet with you personally."

"I'll do that," Mr. McGuire said, in a voice that betrayed more dread than anticipation.

Once the door had closed behind Lord Connelly, Mr. McGuire called the children into the living room.

"It seems your friend Brigitta has decided that we are going to be responsible for my aunt's manor in Australia, at perhaps even move there, at least part-time," he began.

Sarah and Nickolas didn't know if they were excited or upset by the news. Living at the manor without Great-Aunt Vivian and her guards would actually be pretty awesome, but leaving their horses and family and friends was less so. "What about the camps?" Sarah asked.

"I have no idea. We will have to work all of that out. Brigitta says that she will stop by this weekend and explain everything. This I have to hear." Mr. McGuire seemed absorbed in his thoughts for a moment, but then he shook his head and the usual twinkle entered his eyes. "So Honorable Sarah and Honorable Nickolas, shall the two of you depart for your bathrooms to have your royal baths?"

"Stop it, Dad," Sarah admonished.

"That's *Sir Daddy* to you, Sarah," he said and chased his children up the stairs.

⚜

Simon had retreated to his room and was furiously packing his suitcase. He was the eldest heir, he thought angrily. Why was the title not passed to him? Those meddling muses must be behind this, he decided. It was because of them that he was disfigured and trapped in this infernal mess. If they had never removed him from the manor, he would have never ended up like this. He would fight them. *He* would be Sir Montague, Baronet of Montague. But he needed a plan—a good plan—and some help...

And then he stopped midpacking and thought of who could help him. Who didn't like the muses any more than he did? Who would do anything to get control of Montague Manor out of the hands of the Muses of Music and War? And then a slow smile crossed Simon's face, broadening with each passing thought.

Dr. James would be more than willing to help him. And if he were Sir Montague, Baronet of Montague, then he would control Dr. James as well.

About the Author

N. L. McEvoy lives wherever her husband's job takes her. The concept for this series was started in London as she walked her children down the hill to school and passed a particularly interesting garden surrounded by a high brick wall and accessible only by a blue wooden door partially hidden by vines and locked tight. Her children's curiosity (to say nothing of her own) led her to create the story of Great-Aunt Vivian's magical gardens and the young boy and girl who got to explore behind that blue door.

She is currently living and writing in Orlando, Florida, assisted by her three muses: her handsome husband and two lovely children. Also on team McEvoy are one snoring Newfoundland, whose primary job is to scare off any cats who dare step foot on their property; one enthusiastic British Labrador, whose main job is sleeping on the author's feet as she types; and two introspective tortoises, who really don't do much of anything.

This is her second published book.

Character Index

A Brief Who's Who in *The Muses*

At the Manor:

* Dr. Vivian Montague (Great-Aunt Vivian)—Daughter of Dr. Christopher Montague. First woman to earn her PhD in chemistry from the University of Sydney. Nickolas and Sarah's great-aunt. Owns a huge manor in Sydney, Australia.
* Mr. Basil Benjamin—Scientist who works closely with Great-Aunt Vivian and has for many years. Never graduated from college as Great-Aunt Vivian convinced him to work for her during his final year at school.
* Fulvio de Silvia—Head chef (and later head butler) at Great-Aunt Vivian's manor. Only character who was born at the manor. Has lived there longer than even Great-Aunt Vivian.
* Carole—Head sous chef at the manor. Old friend of Fulvio's. Mother of Zac.
* Zac—Employed at the manor in the kitchens as a dishwasher. Carole's son.

- Petunia—Sarah's lady's maid while she is at the manor.
- Robert—Nickolas's valet while at the manor and one of Vivian's footmen.
- The butler—The nameless butler at the manor and one of Great-Aunt Vivian's most trusted servants.
- Louis—Lady Vivian Montague's secretary.
- M. Craubateau—Stable master at the manor.
- Mr. Fairchild—Chauffeur at the manor.

THE SCIENTISTS:

- Dr. Trowle—Scientist who works with Great-Aunt Vivian. Father of a college age son.
- Dr. Fitzwilliam—Scientist who works loosely with Great-Aunt Vivian. Looking for a cure for a rare form of cancer.
- Dorothy Fitzwilliam—Wife of Dr. Fitzwilliam.
- Dr. Elizabeth (Betty) Candy—One of the scientists in Dr. James's employ. Works with Dr. Ping. Loves food of all types, especially cake.
- Dr. Nikki Ping—One of the scientists in Dr. James's employ. Works with Dr. Candy. Adores nothing more than a well-balanced ledger with lots of black ink.
- Dr. Chambre—One of the scientists in Dr. James's employ. Owns a large Chateau and is thinking about getting his own personal helicopter.

THE MUSES:

- Audiva—Head of the Muses of Music; plays the double flutes.

- Ardus—Head of the Muses of War; uses double swords as his weapon.
- Brigitta—Second of the Muses of Music; plays the harp.
- Bard—Second of the Muses of War; uses a battle-ax as his weapon.
- Christina—Muse of Music; plays the coronet.
- Charles—Muse of War; specializes in espionage and counterespionage. Uses daggers as his weapon of choice.
- Deidre—Muse of Music; uses a danso as her weapon of choice.
- David—Muse of War; uses a pole arm as his weapon.
- Ella—Muse of Music; plays the violin.
- Edmund—Muse of War; uses the bow and arrow as his weapon of choice.
- Francesca—Muse of Music; plays the biwa.
- Ferdinand—Muse of War; uses a Japanese sickle and mace as weapon of choice. Specializes in martial arts.
- Georgiana—Muse of Music; plays the cornet.
- Galahad—Muse of War: uses a long sword as his weapon and is a devote of the art of chivalry.
- James (Dr. James)—Head of the Muses of Science; specializes in biology and botany.
- Karina—Muse of Science.
- Edna—Muse of Education.
- Joanna—Head of the Muses of Mathematics; partner/wife of James.

AT THE RANCH:

- John McGuire—Sarah and Nickolas's father.
- Vera McGuire (Grandma Vera)—Sarah and Nickolas's paternal grandmother.

* Amelia McGuire—Sarah and Nickolas's mother. Currently in hospital recovering from injuries sustained in a car crash.
* Sarah McGuire—Ten-year-old girl from Silver Springs, Colorado; Nickolas's younger sister.
* Nickolas McGuire—Twelve-year-old boy from Silver Springs, Colorado; Sarah's older brother.

AT THE HOSPITAL:

* Ms. Eglantine Grey—Social worker at the hospital. Currently in prison for accepting bribes and endangering children entrusted in her care.
* Dr. Lucy Reynolds—Intern at Denver General Hospital.

OTHER CHARACTERS:

* Simon Montague—Sarah and Nickolas's second cousin once removed.
* Alderic (Alec) Anderson IV—American teenager who dresses goth and gets captured by Great-Aunt Vivian by mistake.
* Delaney Anderson (deceased)—Alec's younger sister.
* Dr. Christopher Montague (deceased)—Sarah and Nickolas's great-grandfather, Grandma Vera and Great-Aunt Vivian's father. Former chemistry professor at the University of Sydney and then Chicago University until his death in the 1940s.

- Victoria Montague (deceased)—Sarah and Nickolas's great-grandmother, Grandma Vera and Great-Aunt Vivian's mother. Died in childbirth in the 1940s.
- Patrick McGuire (deceased)—Sarah and Nickolas's paternal grandfather, Grandma Vera's husband. Died in a car crash when Sarah and Nickolas were very young.
- Mr. and Mrs. Allen (deceased)—Grandma Vera's adoptive parents who ran a small diner in Flat Falls, Michigan.
- Sparks—Grandma Vera's puppy.
- Ten Windsor Grey Horses—Great-Aunt Vivian's horses.
- Blaze—Six-month-old foal, offspring of one of Great-Aunt Vivian's horses.
- Curieux—Stallion and personal horse of M. Craubateau at the ranch. Sire of little Blaze.

THE MUSES:
VENGEANCE OF TIME (BOOK TWO)

--⧈⧉⧈--

When they freed the muses from their great-aunt Vivian's gardens, Sarah and Nickolas McGuire had no idea that they would ever see the muses again, and they certainly never planned to revisit their evil great-aunt.

But things don't always work according to plan. When their cousin Simon comes down with a mysterious illness, they discover that they can only get him well with the help of the muses. Brigitta, Bard, Charles, and Deidre join the children, and they discover that the ingredients that they need can only be found at Montague Manor.

In this race against time, Sarah and Nickolas delve into their family's past, return to Australia, battle Sprites and Pixies, come face-to-face with Great-Aunt Vivian and Dr. James, and learn to play air guitar, all in their quest to save Simon.